Papaya

S.W. Campbell

Published by Shawn Campbell

Papaya

ISBN: 978-1-7332314-1-1

To my parents, for always being loving and supportive, even during my high school years when they probably wanted to break my neck a time or two.

Papaya

Chapter 1

They fucked up the order of the reels. First, third, second. It took the audience a little while to figure it out. There was a sudden change of pace. An unaccounted for shift in the action. A sudden rough transition. Confused people sat in the dark, watching the flickering light from the projector. The realization popped amongst a few scattered individuals. The sparks caught hold and spread. A smartass comment was followed by a second. Voiced complaints went from light to heavy. People began moving towards the exit, demanding an explanation. Someone started yelling for refunds. The pimple faced kid behind the snack counter was overwhelmed. The owner came out of the ticket booth, his voice booming his mantra on endless repeat. No refunds. No refunds. Shouting. A few maintained their posts as the chairs were abandoned. A couple stayed in their chairs near the front, their faces lit by flashes of light on the screen. They were calm. At ease. An island of serenity in the growing storm of chaos. He leaned over and whispered a joke. She laughed. He smiled. It could be the start of the apocalypse and everything would be fine. She kissed him gently on the neck. Someone threw a punch at the owner. The couple started making out, oblivious to the world around them.

The cool breeze swept the memory away. It swayed the palms and fondled the fronds of the banana trees behind the rusted chain link fence at the bottom of the hill. It smelled of the ocean. It felt good. Ted trudged upwards from the mercantile in the evening light with a half gallon bottle of rum in his hand. He was tired. It had been a long day of hiking to farms higher up on the mountain. The light wind crystallized the sweat on his brow and loosened his shirt where it stuck to his back. Ted's eyes stared down at the dirt and gravel of the road, willing his blue denim covered legs to carry his leather booted feet closer to home. With each step droplets of sweat broke loose and ran down his legs, joining their brethren in the fallen socks that bunched about the top of his work boots.

"Theodore my friend. At the rate you're going it will be morning before you get here. Hurry up, my throat is dry."

Charles Xavier Skerritt laughed. Ted looked up at the row of single room houses that was his goal, catching the flash of white teeth in Charles Xavier's dark face. The houses were neatly built with good roofs of sheet metal and solid walls of cinderblocks. There were five of them. White, yellow, red, orange, and purple. They all belonged to the same man, Malik, who owned the mercantile and rented the houses out cheap. All of the houses were identical except in color. Door and window in front. Door and window in back. Blank walls on either side. No reason to need to know what your neighbor was doing. Ted lived in the red one. Charles Xavier lounged in a wooden chair outside of the yellow house next door. Ted took a deep breath, wiped the salt from his brow, and redoubled his efforts. Charles Xavier cheered him on, his long fingered hands lazily beckoning before unconsciously brushing the gray hair at his temples.

Charles Xavier was not a big man, he was lean, his knees and elbows knots of bone. He sat with his chair leaned back against the wall of his house, his feet wrapped around the chair legs. His blue postman shirt hung open and his hands sat clasped in his lap. A half full mailbag sat on the ground next to him. Charles Xavier was not young, but he was not old. He claimed the gray in his hair made his handsome face more distinguished. Every move Charles Xavier made was graceful. Compared to him Ted's movements all felt as ungainly as those of a circus bear forced to walk on its hind legs for a cheering crowd.

Ted flopped down in the offered chair and put the rum bottle on the table between them. He ran his hands through his wavy brownish red hair, thinning already at twenty-two, sat back, and stretched his tired legs out in front of him. Charles Xavier grinned at the younger man, cracked the top off of the rum bottle, and poured two large dollops into the glasses sitting on the small table between them.

"What, no beer my friend? I thought for sure a rich American like you could afford to buy your friend a cold beer."

Ted returned a half smile.

"Not on a Peace Corps salary my friend."

Charles Xavier handed one of the glasses to Ted and lifted his own. He stretched forward and tinked the two drinks together. Both men took a healthy swallow. Charles Xavier's face relaxed with satisfaction. Ted's face contorted into a grimace. The rum was cheap. It tasted like sweetened gasoline. Charles Xavier laughed at Ted's reaction.

"You look tired."

"I am tired."

"Come now, it couldn't have been that hard of a day."

"You try lugging my heavy pack around the mountain all day."

Charles Xavier gave Ted a false look of wounded pride and tapped his mailbag with his foot.

"You think mine is any lighter?"

Charles Xavier laughed again and took another drink of his rum.

"And how were your friends, the farmers, today?"

"Crusty and cranky as ever."

Charles Xavier's eyes narrowed and his lips stretched into a close lipped devilish smile. Ted waited for the next line he knew would come.

"And how about the farmers' wives?"

Ted took another drink.

"The same."

Charles Xavier brayed with laughter. Ted stayed quiet and stared down the hill at the buildings of the town of Titou. The mercantile was at the lowest point in the clearing. Ted had gone down to use the telephone to call home. He had promised his mother that he would do it every week, but in reality it was closer to monthly. His mother had talked about the usual. The squirrels that visited the yard. The family. The neighbors. Everyone was doing fine. How about him? The standard reply. He was fine. How were things? What was it like there? It was nice. Different, but nice. The same closing every time. We're all so proud of you. The conversations with his father were much more succinct. A few short basic questions followed by a quick story about the latest foibles at the potato plant. This week some guy named Juan had wanted to change shifts because both his wife and girlfriend were working the same shift as well. The week before it had been two of the old women in their seventies who checked the potatoes for broken glass claiming that a third was stealing their cigarettes.

Aside from having the only phone in the area, the mercantile also had the only TV. The news had been on when Ted was down calling his parents. He took a sip of rum and tried to change the subject.

"You hear about the tropical storm headed toward Trinidad?"

Charles Xavier didn't take the bait. He jabbed Ted's arm with two fingers. "You need to relax my friend. Maybe reconsider the farmer's wives. Some may not be much to look at, but they know how to help a man relax."

Charles Xavier laughed again. Ted took another drink and looked over at his friend. White teeth and white eyes bright in a black face. For a moment he wondered if it was racist to think such things. Neither Idaho or Montana had been the kind of place where such questions had much of an opportunity to come up.

"I am relaxed."

"You can't lie to me Theodore. Look at you. For god's sake, you're nearly buttoned to the neck."

Ted turned back to the vista of the town and the banana plantation. His hand self-consciously fingered the top button of his shirt. He took another drink of rum. A chicken rounded the corner of the house and pecked the dirt in front of them. Most of the feathers on the chicken's back were gone, pulled off by the rooster in its passion. The breeze felt good. Just a hint of salt from the out of sight ocean. You could see the broad blue waters farther up on the mountain, but in Titou they were still too low. Ted threw back his rum, put the empty glass on the table, and undid the top three buttons of his shirt. Charles Xavier laughed, swallowed the last of his rum, and refilled the glasses.

"See my friend. Doesn't that feel better? If you're going to live on Domenique, you might as well live Domenique."

Ted nodded, but didn't answer. He felt uncomfortable. His fingers played with the loose buttons, wanting to put them back in place. Ted wiped his hands on his jeans and picked back up his refilled glass. He could feel Charles Xavier watching him from the corner of his eye.

"Are you hungry?"

"You don't have to feed me."

"Nonsense. You brought the rum. The least I can do is put some food in your belly."

Charles Xavier cocked his head back towards the open window and gave out a yell.

"Woman. Hey woman. Bring something to eat out for our friend Theodore."

The interior of the house stayed silent. Charles Xavier looked at Ted, then back at the window, and then back at Ted again, his face shifting from smile to worry. Sounds of movement came from within the house. Charles Xavier gave a self-satisfied little grin, took a drink of rum, and sat back in his chair to enjoy the sight of the world below.

Camilla emerged from the cool shadows of the house carrying a tray. Short. Solid, but light. Floating on every step. Younger than the older man, but older than the younger. Charles Xavier clapped his hands and hooted at his wife.

"There you are my sweet one. What have you brought for us?"

Camilla didn't answer. She moved forward on strong legs and deposited the tray on the table between the men. As she bent forward the neckline of her dress hung open. Ted, watching her as she worked, found his gaze slipping into the shadow, past the wonderful contrast of bright green against dark skin. Down into the depths of a hidden world of rounded mounds and dark black nipples. Camilla looked up from her work and her eyes pulled him up from the abyss. Ted's eyes locked onto hers, the flush of his cheeks hidden by his sunburn. Pervert. Immoral. Degenerate. Her eyes said none of these things. They just gazed evenly into his, watching, assessing. Camilla's lips moved upward into a smile.

"Woman, what is this? Just a couple bananas and a single papaya?"

The gaze was broken. Camilla turned towards her husband and shrugged. Ted had never heard her speak in his presence, not once in his six months on the island. Husband and wife stared at each other, fighting a silent battle of wills. Charles Xavier turned away. Camilla shrugged again and headed back into the house. Both men watched the sway of her backside until she was out of sight. Charles Xavier turned towards Ted and laughed. Ted turned back to the vista below.

"My apologies, it appears that this is all the feast that my home can offer."

"It's okay."

Charles Xavier leaned forward, gesturing with his glass, spilling small droplets of rum down his front.

"A guest from America such as yourself deserves to be fed the best of this island. Yam and rice. Fresh fish. Mountain chicken."

"It's really okay."

"Nonsense."

Charles Xavier made as though he was getting up and then flopped back into his chair.

"I guess we'll just have to make do with what we have."

Charles Xavier pulled a pocket knife from his shorts and started slicing the papaya in two. Long clever fingers. Black on top and white on the bottom. Questions of what counted as racism bubbled again to the surface of Ted's mind. Such unbidden thoughts and worries had been plaguing him since he had arrived. Why worry about such things? That's what he kept telling himself. The world was different here. He was the one alone. The clever fingers pulled the two halves apart, revealing the golden flesh within, and shucked out the black seeds. Charles Xavier flicked the seeds onto the ground and took a bite out of one half. He held out the other half to Ted. Ted raised his hands, palms facing outward.

"No please, you have the whole thing."

"Nonsense Theodore. You must have half. Papayas are as sweet as a woman's kiss."

"It's okay. I'll just have a banana."

"I insist. These bananas are not good enough for you. I insist that you share in the bounty of my house."

Charles Xavier stretched forward, pushing the papaya closer to Ted. Ted looked at the open window of the house, then back at Charles Xavier. He took the papaya half. Charles Xavier watched expectantly until Ted took a bite.

"You see Theodore. It's very sweet, isn't it?"

It was. Ted's eyes fell to his hands.

"Yes."

The evening sun sank below the horizon and the first few scattered stars peeked down through its wake. Ted finished his half of papaya, laid the skin on the table, and got up.

"It's getting late. I'm going to head inside."

"Okay my friend. Don't forget your rum. It would be a shame for some delinquent to down it without you."

Ted lifted his glass and drained the last swallow of rum. The world around him felt buoyant and light. He put down the glass, picked up the bottle, and staggered towards his red house next door. Charles Xavier watched Ted as he struggled to mount his porch and open his door. He pulled a small chain off his neck, and fumbled with the two keys on it to get the right one into the lock. The door opened.

"Good night Theodore."

"Good night Charles Xavier."

The inside of the house was dark. Ted felt blindly until his hand came in contact with the string hanging in the middle of the room. A single bulb flared to life, the light blinding at first before fading to more comfortable levels. The house was small, just a single room. The doors sat at the center of their respective walls. The windows were on the opposite sides of their respective doors. Ted put the rum bottle down on the Formica counter to his left, the lime green surface broken only by a small sink and two burner stovetop. The squat fridge at the end of the counter, an old model with a locking handle, belched and coughed to life. The compressor produced a loud hum that permeated the air. Ted locked the door and sat down on one of the two chairs at the small table beneath the front window. The white paint on the table and chairs was chipped and flecking away. Ted slid off his boots and then his clothes, pale and naked for all the world to see. He left his clothes in a pile on the floor. There was no underwear. He hadn't worn underwear since soon after arriving. It was too hot for such things. Too humid.

The toilet was on the same side wall as the table, alone in its corner, separable from the world by a mildew covered curtain. Ted didn't bother to close the curtain when he took a piss. He stared down at the yellow stream and swayed from side to side. He felt drunk. It would probably be best if he got some food in his belly before he went to bed. The toilet flushed with a half-hearted gurgle. Ted stood in the middle of the room, undecided. He looked at his cot setup under the rear window, surrounded by a thin gossamer of mosquito netting hanging from the ceiling. His duffel bag was shoved underneath. His half open silk sleep sack, just a sleeping bag liner with a fancy name, sat on top; the red, white, and blue interior inviting him in with its promises of comfort and concealment. Fuck it. Ted yanked string and extinguished the light. He stumbled through the darkness, careful staggering steps, before finding the soothing confines that he sought. The sweet taste of the papaya was still on his tongue. Fuck it. Fuck all of it. Ted laid in the darkness, staring up at the shadows of the trees and the twinkling swath of the stars. Sleep. Sleep would be good.

Muffled voices emanated from the house next door. A woman's giggle and a man's laugh. Metallic squeaks. Random movements shifting into a steady pace. Heavy breathing. A quiet moan. Sounds growing in volume. A cry in the night, stifled and cut off. A second, this one allowed to go free. Bending over with a smile. The flash of black nipples. Ted stared upward at the stars and pretended not to listen. He tried to think of a world far away. A world of snowstorms, classwork, and flip cup. Another moan. The mind can ignore, but the body listens. Stiffness grew below his waist. Blood flow increased. A tent pole rose in the middle of his sleep sack staring up at him accusingly. Ted rolled onto his side.

The rhythm of the squeaks increased. Faster. Quicker. Harder. A steady guttural chant cheering them on. Sweat covered Ted's body. A burst. A loud cry in the night. Blessed silence. Ted was breathing deeply. The stars winked through the thin glass of the window. He rolled from one side to the other in his sleep sack. It was no good. He couldn't get comfortable. The pumps were primed.

Light skin speckled with freckles. Tan lines. Abrupt sharp borders of light to dark. Hungry lips on his. Pink nipples in his mouth and beneath his fingers. Blonde hair pooling across his lap. A hand on his hip, the nails painted bright pink. Bright blue eyes peering upwards. A woman's husky voice in his ear.

"Do you love me?"

"Yes."

"Tell me that you love me."

"You know I do."

"I want to hear you say it."

"I love you."

Dark brown skin in sharp contrast with his white. Big brown eyes and a laughing smile. Hard black nipples peering from the hidden depths of the open neckline of her dress. Rising feeling. Growing ecstasy. Shame. Shame of thought. Shame of action. Climbing. Climbing to the top. To the peak. All the way. Ted's free hand fumbled around in the duffel bag beneath the cot. He pulled out a pair of boxer shorts. His hips jerked involuntarily. The world spun and came crashing down. The soiled boxers dropped to the concrete floor. Ted laid still and waited for his breathing and heartbeat to slow. Fuck. What the fuck? God damn it. You perv. You dirty little perv. Ted rolled onto his back and stared out the window at the night sky. He closed his eyes and let himself drift off to sleep.

Chapter 2

The small alarm clock jangled, ripping Ted from the seclusion of sleep. His head hurt. For a moment he found himself tangled in the mosquito netting. Panic gave way to a weary groan. Ted's entire body was covered in sweat. It was already warm, it was going to be hot today. The zipper on his sleep sack hissed open. His bare feet touched the ground, one on the concrete floor, the other on the boxers encrusted with his shame. Ted groaned again and kicked the boxers under the cot. He sat for a moment, waiting for all systems to engage. He lumbered over to the toilet for a piss and shit, not bothering to close the curtain. On went a fresh pair of pants. He drank water straight from the tap and popped down a few aspirin. Breakfast was yesterday's rice mixed with some cold chicken and milk from the fridge. He sat at the table and ate slowly. Swallowing was a chore that got easier with every bite.

The outside shower next door kicked on with a sudden burst. Images of rounded curves slipping out of the confines of a green dress filled Ted's mind. The flashing white teeth of a smile. Sparkling eyes with a come hither look. Come on young man. Come on and have a look. Charles Xavier's off key singing floated through the morning air. A warbling tune describing the things he could do with a ten inch cock, scrubbing himself clean to face the morning. The curvaceous image cracked and fell away. Ted looked down at his half eaten bowl of rice and chicken. He was no longer hungry. He put the bowl in the fridge and took another drink of water from the tap. His headache was starting to fade.

What day was it? Thursday, the day Camilla came to clean his house and do his laundry. She didn't charge that much and Ted was glad to let her do it. He had never been much for such domestic chores. He could hear his mother berating him. Sandi hadn't been much of a fan either, though she had failed to mention it until it was far too late for a change to make any difference. Ted didn't know what Camilla thought of it. It had been Charles Xavier who had negotiated the transaction. Thursday. Shit. Ted bent over by his cot and pulled the boxers out from underneath. He held them gingerly by the elastic waistband. There was no mistaking his deed. Ted took the boxers to the sink and washed them as best he could. He wrung them out. They were still damp, but at least the reason would be a mystery. Next to his cot was a pile of dirty laundry. Ted buried the sodden boxers in the middle. It wasn't perfect, but it would have to do, it was time to start the day.

T-shirt, ballcap, socks, and work boots. For a moment Ted looked at the almost empty bottle of sunscreen next to the sink, but he left it where it sat. What was the use? He would sunburn no matter what. Ted went out the rear door of the house, locking it behind him. It was hotter outside. It was going to be an uncomfortable day. To his right was his shower, a simple outdoor affair. A slab of concrete with a six inch high lip. A spout maybe five feet up with a nearby hook for a towel and a soap dish bolted to the wall. A heavy curtain hanging from a circular rod to hide the user from view. On the roof sat a rounded black tank on a small platform. The water was heated by the warmth of the sun. Most people took their showers in the evening. Charles Xavier showered both morning and evening. He claimed the shock of the cold water was exhilarating. Charles Xavier liked to be clean.

"Remember my friend. The two most important things a man can do is stay clean and keep his fingernails well trimmed."

Charles Xavier always made such claims with a hearty laugh.

A little behind the house sat a small windowless shed made of cinderblocks. No fence divided the lot behind the house from its neighbors. The area behind all the houses looked identical, same as the front, except that Ted's was the only one with a shed and without a clothesline or garden. Ted's lot was nothing but hard beaten dirt and scattered patches of grass. The back lots of the neighbors were filled with neat rows of vegetables. Tanias, yams, potatoes, peas, onions, carrots, and garlic. Chickens, skinny little runts compared to their

American cousins, pecked at the ground amongst the rows, minding their own business, hunting for bugs. The shadowed greens of the encroaching forest at the top of the clearing were about twenty feet away.

Two houses down a boy and a girl were playing, kneeling, careful not to get their school clothes dirty. They were poking at something on the ground. Ted couldn't see what it was, but the pair seemed completely enamored by it. Probably a worm, or something like that. The children noticed him watching and looked up, blank stares on their faces. Their mother came out and shooed them back into their purple house. For a moment she eyed Ted, not in a friendly manner, then retreated inside. Mrs. Seraphin. Ted didn't really have much to do with many of the people in the town, none of them seemed very interested in having much to do with him. He knew Mrs. Seraphin because Charles Xavier had pointed her out once, though he had never bothered to make sure they were formally introduced.

"Look at that fine woman Theodore, all alone up here. What kind of fool would leave such sweets just lying about?"

Charles Xavier was right, she was a fine looking woman. Tall and rounded, with long legs and an imperious gaze.

"Where's her husband?"

"Been gone down at the capital three years for work. Used to be at the plantation, but the rum was too much for their taste. Damn shame leaving his woman with two kids back home, but at least the jacket still sends money every month."

Charles Xavier had leaned in close, whispering with a drunken slur in a voice too loud to be confidential.

"He used to put letters in with the cash, flowery poetry that could sweeten even the most sour of drinks. The woman lived for those letters, but her replies must not have been so good. It's been more than a year since it was more than just Lizzies. It's a shame to watch sweet fruit go to rot."

Charles Xavier had given an exaggerated wink.

"Though you can't be too concerned too close to home."

Charles Xavier had laughed uproariously. The whole story had made Ted feel uncomfortable. He really didn't see how it was any of his business.

Ted unlocked the shed with the second of the keys hanging around his neck. It was dark inside, the only light coming from the open door. The air was heavy with synthetic aromas. Rows of chemical jugs lined the shelves inside. Pesticides, herbicides, fungicides, and fertilizers. A large backpack hung from a nail. Several handheld pump sprayers and dry granular spreaders sat on the concrete floor. Ted picked up a thick book with a faded paper cover and brought it out into the light. His fingers ran through the index and then flipped to the correct entry. He made mental note of the chemical name and then placed the book back in the shed. His eyes ran over the rows of jugs, finding what he needed in the shadows near the back. He took the jug, checked to make sure its cap was tight, and then put it in the backpack. Ted put the backpack on his shoulders, lifted a pump sprayer, and went back outside. He was careful to lock the door.

Ted walked between his red house and neighboring orange one. The town of Titou spread its way down the mountainside, about thirty houses placed randomly in the clearing, all sweeping downward towards Malik's mercantile. The banana plantation, perfectly straight lined trees surrounded by a tall chain link fence, butted up against the lower half of the town to the right. People were moving between the buildings on well beaten paths, most headed to work at the plantation, a few older men out to their own fields in cut open spaces nearby in the surrounding forest.

Charles Xavier was standing next to his front door. His blue postman shirt was halfway buttoned, and a straw hat covered his head. His full mailbag hung from his shoulder. Each day Charles Xavier would walk to the post office in the town of Helston, about ten miles away. He would take a long serpentine route, going from community to community, picking up mail from the mailboxes and leaving mail at the mercantiles for the recipients to claim. Helston was only around five hundred people, but it was big compared to the surrounding towns. Once in Helston, Charles Xavier would drop off his gathered mail, refill his bag with incoming mail for people in his territory, relax for a bit, and then start hitching rides back up to Titou, the highest point on his route. Charles Xavier would vary his course each day, his itinerary chosen by his whims and moods. The number of towns visited dependent on his ability to find something of more interest to take up his time. In his territory only Helston and Titou were guaranteed daily mail service, but few ever complained.

Charles Xavier smiled his big smile and slapped Ted on the shoulder.

"Good morning my friend. How did you sleep?"

"Fine."

"I was worried that maybe you had too much to drink."

"No. Just enough."

Charles Xavier laughed his deep laugh.

"Good. I'd hate to have to drink your share. Do you have a busy day?"

Ted put down the hand sprayer and adjusted the straps of his backpack.

"Yeah, I've got to go up to some of the higher farms and spray for bugs."

Charles Xavier made a show of adjusting his mailbag, gritting his teeth with mock difficulty.

"I know what you mean. More and more people are writing letters all the time, and so many bills. It's a wonder anyone can afford to invite a poor postman in for dinner or a drink. I keep telling my boss down in Helston that they need to buy me a motorbike so I can race up and down the roads. The mail would always be on time if I could just get something faster between my legs."

Charles Xavier squatted down with his hands in front of him gripping imaginary handlebars. He twisted the throttle and his mouth spewed the sound of a revving engine. Ted smiled at his friend's antics. Mr. Green came out of his orange house. It was the only house with shutters, whitewashed to contrast with the bright color of the walls. The old man closed the door and lit a cigarette. His hands would not stay still, repeatedly smoothing his shirt. He was wrinkled with just a fringe of white hair around the sides of his bald head. The skin on his arms and neck was loose and a small potbelly pushed against his white button down shirt. The older man was friendly enough, but in a way that made Ted feel that it was because he felt it was something he had to do. Charles Xavier smiled at the older gentleman and raised his voice to be heard.

"Good morning Mr. Green. Does your wife know you're smoking?"

The old man smoothed his shirt again and ignored the question. He stretched his back, popping several vertebrae. When he spoke, his voice was thick with dignity and authority.

"Good morning Mr. Skerritt. Good morning Mr. Nelson."

Ted nodded his acceptance of the greeting. Charles Xavier winked at Ted.

"And how are you doing this morning Mr. Green?"

"Tired, Mr. Skerritt."

"And why is that?"

"I'm afraid I got caught up reading one of my favorites. *The Hobbit*. Have you read it?"

"No. Not much time for such things."

"You should try it. You never know what you're capable of if you never try. I could lend it to you when I'm done."

Charles Xavier laughed.

"I'll be sure to do that."

Mr. Green gave Charles Xavier a long measured look. He raised his white eyebrows and then let them fall back to their original place.

"Though perhaps you would enjoy *Madame Bovary* more. I best be going. It's time to get to work."

"Have a good day Mr. Green."

Mr. Green started shuffling his way down the hill toward a shelter just a little way up from the mercantile. The shelter was already filling with children of all ages. Ted adjusted his backpack. Mr. Green turned back, but didn't stop moving.

"Don't you be bothering my wife Mr. Skerritt."

Charles Xavier laughed again.

"Don't you worry about that Mr. Green. Some fruits are too ripe to pick."

Mr. Green moved on down the hill. Charles Xavier gave Ted a friendly punch on the shoulder.

"That old jacket has been riding my ass since I was in school. He used to slap the back of my head every day to get me to pay attention. He'd slap me twice as hard when I stared at his wife bringing him his dinner. You should have seen the ass on that woman."

Ted gave a half-smile to be polite. Mrs. Green was rarely seen outside the house. She had a bad foot which made it difficult for her to get around. Ted had only seen her once, sitting out in her garden in a chair, her body sloping from her head like a pile of mud. It was hard for him to imagine her as the main player in any school boy's fantasy. Ted took off his ballcap for a moment to wipe the sweat off his brow.

"I better be going. I got a lot of day ahead of me."

"Yes of course. I as well my friend."

Charles Xavier started walking down the hill. He turned his head back as he moved.

"Come by this evening with your rum."

Ted smiled and nodded his assurance.

"Okay."

Charles Xavier whistled as he walked. Ted adjusted his backpack again, turned to the right, and started walking. The gravel road from Helston climbed through Titou, past the plantation and mercantile, and up into the forested mountainside above the town. It was a seven mile hike to the farm he was supposed to visit. The green world swallowed him up. His shirt and pants quickly became soaked with sweat. In amongst the trees there were no cool breezes. The air was stagnant and each step was unnaturally loud. People who lived higher up the mountainside passed him going the other way. Men and women heading to work at the banana plantation. Children on their way to Titou to be taught by Mr. Green. The adults all gave him the dead look, faces devoid of any emotion and eyes boring into him until he passed by. Some of the children stared and giggled at him. A group of boys, somewhere around the age of twelve or so, scooped up small pieces of gravel and threw them at Ted. He scooped up gravel and threw it back. The boys ran down the hill, laughing and yelling, their voices cracking with sudden high pitched notes, stuck somewhere between adulthood and adolescence. Ted felt bad for the boys. When he had been that age his changing voice and inexplicably become stuck at the same tone as his mother's. It had been more than a year before the mistaken identity when he answered the phone shifted from her to his father.

The road narrowed and became a path. The dense foliage closed in. The air gripped him in a hot moist caress. At least the shade blocked out the burning rays of the sun. The trail wound back and forth, climbing higher and higher. In places the trees broke away, revealing terraced clearings where lonely people scratched a living from rocky soil. Free to live in abject poverty, but able to look down their noses at those who worked behind fences to earn a living of relative luxury in comparison.

Ted had met her his sophomore year of college. He was still living in the dorms back then, living under the rules and demands of RAs, tin pot dictators of imaginary kingdoms. He had gone down to throw out the trash. A woman had been in the alley, sorting her recycling into green bins. Blonde hair. Nice figure. She had been sitting on her haunches, facing away. Her shirt had ridden up, revealing a hint of green panties against pale skin. Where Ted grew up they didn't sort the recycling. He had opened the dumpster lid and thrown his trash in. Three bags and a mess of cardboard.

"What the fuck do you think you're doing?"

The woman had risen up, turning to face him.

"You fucking son of a bitch."

Blue eyes. Beautiful blue eyes filled with passion. She had gotten right into his face. A painted fingernail repeatedly jamming its way into his chest. Screaming. The sound echoing off the side of the dorms. A fleck of spit had flung itself out of her mouth and onto his cheek. Self-centered this and environmental responsibility that. What a bitch. What an amazingly beautiful bitch. What else could he have done? He had hung his head and apologized like a child caught with his fingers in the strawberry jam. He had climbed into the dumpster, pulled out the cardboard, and put it in its proper place. What else was an inexperienced virgin to do? Throw out his trash every day after that? Spend hours rehearsing possible future conversations? In the end he had done nothing, too nervous and shy to even make the slightest of attempts.

Chapter 3

The path became rougher and broke out into another clearing. A thin old man sat on a rock next to the path, seeing how far he could spit. His face was covered in dark stubble, and an old loose straw hat sat drooping on his head. The old man saw Ted coming, raised a hand in greeting, and smiled. A third of his teeth were missing and the ones left didn't look good. Ted raised his hand in return and came up next to the old man, breathing heavily.

"Mr. Hewitt?"

"Yep."

The old man's voice was a guttural grunt. Ted paused a moment to catch his breath.

"Your son told me you were having some bug issues in your corn."

"Yep."

The two men watched each other. The old man spit again.

Two days prior Ted had just finished showering when there had been a knock at his door. He had slipped on a pair of pants and answered it. The man waiting had been a younger version, around Ted's age, of the old man in the clearing. The younger version's eyes had kept dropping to Ted's pale, fur covered torso. He smiled in a friendly manner.

"What happened to Ryan?"

"He went back to America."

"Good man that Ryan."

"So I've heard."

It had actually been the first time Ted had ever heard someone compliment his predecessor, though to be fair, the only other opinion he had been directly told up to that point had been from Charles

Xavier. According to his friend, Ryan seemed to have the opinion that he was the king of France or something like that. Such men had a tendency to look down their noses at those they thought beneath them.

"Eugene Hewitt."

"Pardon?"

"That's my name."

"Oh."

"You the new chem man?"

"I'm with the Peace Corps."

"My father's corn has bugs."

"Okay."

"He would like the American to come up and help him out."

"I can help teach him how to take care of it."

"When?"

"Two days. Where's the farm?"

"Up the path and take a right at the third fork. He'll meet you."

"Okay."

Ted had wanted to ask more, maybe what kind of bugs, but Eugene Hewitt had already turned and started away towards the plantation. Ted's assignment on Domenique was to teach the local farmers about the correct application of agricultural chemicals and how the usage of said chemicals could increase their yields and profits. Better crops meant more money, which meant a better life for the farmers. It had made a lot of sense to Ted, except for the fact that he really didn't know the first thing about agricultural chemicals, let alone farming in general. But his predecessor Ryan, a wormy kid from upstate New York, had given him a five day crash course, and then left him on his own to impart the needed knowledge. There was a regional Peace Corps office on St. Lucia, but Mr. Douglas, the Regional Director, didn't really know much about agriculture himself. However, there were plenty of books, and in the end it just came down to reading and following instructions.

Mr. Hewitt scratched a piece of plaque off of one his remaining teeth with his fingernail and spit again. He kept looking up at Ted, waiting. Ted shuffled his feet and bit his lower lip. Somewhere down the mountain a bird warbled. Another higher up answered it. The old man spit again, a gooey stream that hit a rock on the other side of the path. Ted coughed.

"Would you like to show me the corn?"

"Yep."

The old man got up stiffly. His knees were obviously giving him trouble. Ted didn't offer to help. He didn't want to offend the old man. Once erect, Mr. Hewitt moved surprisingly quick. Ted followed him to the next clearing. The farm was not a big one. Crops grew on terraces up and down the mountainside, but were scattered. In many places the terraces were covered by weeds, grass, and the encroaching forest. In other places the terraces were gone, melted back into the hillside by the relentless forces of erosion. Bananas, avocados, and papaya stood out amongst the other crops, towering above the vegetables. The produce would be sold to the local cooperative, run by Malik as all such things in the area were, which in turn would sell whatever the farmers needed back to them. Most of the vegetables would be consumed by Mr. Hewitt and his family.

The corn was clumped together on a terrace about halfway up the clearing. It was still growing, the immature ears just starting to form. Ted bent down and examined the leaves. He didn't see any bugs, but some of the leaves did have holes chewed through them. They were also covered in fuzzy yellow splotches. Ted looked up at the farmer.

"Looks like you have fungus too."

"Rains here. Always fuzz."

"I could've brought some fungicide."

"There's bugs."

Ted looked back at the corn and sat down in the dirt. He unzipped his backpack and pulled out the plastic jug of chemical.

"Do you have any water?"

The farmer nodded, turned, and headed up the hill towards his house, a structure of wood and corrugated metal at the top edge of the clearing. Ted pulled the small instruction booklet from its plastic sheath on the jug and started leafing through it. The old man came back carrying a five gallon bucket full of water with both hands. He plopped the bucket down next to Ted, sloshing some water onto the younger man. The water was cool. Ted thought about dunking his entire head, but instead pointed at the booklet.

"It says here that this pesticide must be applied a minimum of thirty days before harvest."

Mr. Hewitt took the book, held it at arm's length, and squinted at the tiny writing. He handed the book back without a word.

"How long do you think until you harvest the corn?"

Mr. Hewitt rubbed the stubble on his jaw.

"While yet?"

"Thirty days?"

The old man shrugged. Ted bit his lower lip and started reading the booklet again.

"We're supposed to mix it with water at a one to nine ratio. So if the sprayer holds two and a half gallons, how much spray do we need to put in?"

"How many gallons in a liter?"

"The instructions are in gallons."

"I think in liters."

The old man's face was drawn in a hard stubborn line. Ted fought the urge to sigh.

"It doesn't really matter, it's just a ratio."

"I think in liters."

"Around one quarter."

The old man rubbed more plaque from his teeth and spit. Ted pulled a small calculator from his backpack and worked out the numbers. Mr. Hewitt watched over his shoulder. The attention made Ted nervous.

"I got a quarter gallon, is that what you got?"

"I think in liters."

Ted put away the calculator and looked up at Mr. Hewitt.

"It's important to get it right. Too little and it won't do anything and too much is dangerous."

Mr. Hewitt scratched the side of his neck.

"I got about the same."

"Okay."

Ted didn't press the issue. There was a good chance Mr. Hewitt had never had much schooling. Many of the older farmers hadn't, secondary school not having been required when they were children. Ted had thought about making ratio tables, but hadn't gotten around to it yet. Besides, he wasn't sure how he would give them out. Many of the older people were prickly about the status of their education.

Ted popped open the jug of pesticide and poured it into the hand sprayer up to the quarter gallon mark, he then filled the remainder with water. Mr. Hewitt watched the entire procedure, hands hanging down by his sides. Ted pumped up the sprayer and adjusted the nozzle. He thought about trying to explain setting the nozzle to Mr. Hewitt, but decided against it.

"Just set the nozzle to number three."

Number three was good. It was a good mid-range number. Number three was not always right, but it was definitely going to be closer to right more times than not. Ted got up and started showing Mr. Hewitt the proper way to run the spray wand, a steady back and forth motion. He offered the wand to Mr. Hewitt, but the old man raised his hands and shook his head. Ted kept working. Mr. Hewitt watched for about five minutes and then moved a couple of terraces down and started weeding. Ted sighed, but kept working. He couldn't really blame the farmers. They were all most likely capable of handling such a job themselves, but what was the point. For the past ten years a steady stream of young Americans had come to show them how to best apply modern agricultural practices. Each one gladly provided free labor, and if you pretended to be trying to learn, even free chemicals. It was a hard deal to pass up.

When Ted had first arrived he had been full of piss and vinegar to accomplish the task set before him. Ryan had seemed disenchanted, but it didn't mean that Ted couldn't try. He had studied for a month until he felt like some kind of an expert. He had gotten permission from Mr. Green to use the shelter. He had spent a week wandering the mountainside, introducing himself to the farmers and telling them of his upcoming lecture. He had felt like he was going to change the world. Only Charles Xavier and Mr. Green had shown up. Charles Xavier as a friend offering moral support and Mr. Green just to make sure Ted didn't fuck up the shelter.

It didn't really matter. All the farms on the mountainside were the same. Old men, sometimes working with their old wives, puttering across the half ruined terraces, waiting for the next hurricane to wash the last of their livelihood away once and for all. No young men or women worked on the crumbling farms. The children moved downward, working in the banana plantation, or farther on down to the capital, where they could make a better living than breaking themselves against the mountain's rocks. Why would Mr. Hewitt bother to learn about agricultural chemicals? He had lived his whole life in poverty and it wouldn't be long until the clearing lay abandoned anyway. In the meantime, he had a job to do, as did Ted.

Ted emptied his hand sprayer and filled it up again with more pesticide and the last of the water in the bucket, eyeballing the ratio. He was careful to only walk where he hadn't sprayed. After he finished the corn he still had some chemical left in the sprayer, so he sprayed it across the grass on the sides of the terrace to either side of the corn. Ted didn't know if it was okay to do that, but it seemed that the bugs must have come from somewhere, so why not? Ted pictured roving tribes of insects moving across the ground, a gentle mist from the heavens, and then each individual falling to the ground, gasping in horror, not understanding the evil that had come upon them. The old man noticed that Ted had finished. He worked his way back up the terraces. He motioned with his hands. It was around noon.

"Hungry?"

It would be rude to say no.

"Yes, thank you."

Mr. Hewitt motioned for Ted to follow him up to the house. Ted left his things next to the corn and started climbing up the slope. Mr. Hewitt moved with ease. Ted stopped at each terrace to catch his breath. The interior of the house looked about like the outside. The far wall was just the dugout dirt of the mountainside. Inside were two beds, an old fashioned wash basin on a stand, a table and two chairs, and a propane stove. Everything looked old and used except for the propane stove which was vented by a metallic chimney of shiny new metal. The stove was likely an investment by Mr. Hewitt's son. Quicker than wood fire. Ted wondered how long it had been since Mrs. Hewitt had been in the house. Ted didn't ask. She might be dead, but she might have left to go live with another one of her children off the mountain. Such things were common.

Mr. Hewitt handed Ted a bowl of cold corn porridge that tasted bland, no sugar or milk in it, and offered him a plate of bakes, pieces of fried dough. The bakes were hard and stale. For refreshment Mr. Hewitt brought a jug of water out of the cool shadows of a corner. From experience, Ted knew there was a cistern for collecting rainwater somewhere nearby. All of the farms had them. Mr. Hewitt took a drink and passed it to Ted. Ted hesitated and took a drink. He could taste Mr. Hewitt's breath on the rim of the jug. The man hadn't brushed his teeth in some time, maybe ever. The two men ate their meal in silence. A centipede crawled across the blanket on one of the beds. Ted finished and put his bowl down on the table. He nodded at Mr. Hewitt.

"Thank you for lunch."

Mr. Hewitt looked at him with a confused look. Ted silently cursed his American slip. Domenique had not long ago been a British colony. They used the British nomenclature of dinner for lunch and supper for dinner.

"I meant dinner. Thank you for dinner."

The old man nodded, chewing thoughtfully on a bake.

"Well, I better be going."

The old man nodded again. Ted went outside and worked his way back down to the corn. He put the jug of pesticide back in his backpack, shouldered it, and lifted up the empty hand sprayer. He worked his way to the path and looked back. Mr. Hewitt was out amongst his corn, pulling weeds. Ted turned and headed back down towards Titou.

It was hotter back in the shade. The thick branches overhead squeezed the atmosphere into a higher density. It felt more like swimming than walking. When Ted had been a boy in American Falls they had always driven east every August to celebrate his grandfather's birthday in Wyoming. It was always hot, most often over a hundred. The entire family would sit out in the shade of the porch, sipping beer, listening to the old man tell stories and watching the spring loaded arm of the thermometer creep its way higher. Ted's uncles, his mother's brothers, would take bets on how high it would get. Ted's father would always comment on how at least it was a dry heat. Ted had never known how right his father was until he came to Domenique.

Ted mostly stayed in the shade of the porch until his grandfather would gesture at him and tell him to go out and do something so the adults could talk in peace. There wasn't much to do, nothing but sagebrush and sun baked hillsides as far as the eye could see, and nobody to do anything with, none of his maternal uncles had bothered having kids. Regardless, Ted had done as he was told. He'd wander the hillsides, skin burning in the sun, waiting for the yell that would signify it was time for the birthday dinner, called the proper name and served at the proper time. His grandfather's wife, it was his third wife, would make everyone take off their shoes before she'd let them inside the blessed air conditioned interior. They would eat at folding tables set up in the living room, the third wife's Yorkshire Terrier, Buddy, dragging his genitals on the carpet and humping an oversized stuffed tiger. After the meal everyone would be ushered back outside. Ted would sit in the bathroom to lengthen his stay in the AC, reading a dog eared book of Cowpoke cartoons and old copies of the Western Stockman. Through the small high set window he'd be able to hear the murmuring of the adults on the porch. Whenever his name came up he'd sit extra still to hear. The words of his grandfather and uncles were rarely kind...

"Hello jake."

A short man wandered up the path towards Ted, his hand upraised and his eyes merry. Ted instinctively raised his own hand and forced himself to smile back. It never hurt to be friendly.

"Hello."

The short man laughed as he passed Ted on the trail. Ted watched him round a corner and disappear out of sight. The footsteps faded as the man climbed higher up the mountain. Lots of the locals called him jake. It's what they called white people. Sometimes it felt as if the whole country was joking with him in ways he didn't understand. At least it was better than the dead eyed stares.

What was Charles Xavier doing now? Probably enjoying himself, that was for sure. The man seemed to live only for the pleasurable parts of life. Ted could see his friend in his head, walking with a bounce in his step, singing songs that he made up as he went. His hat would be tipped back, and his blue postman's uniform would be halfway unbuttoned. He would come to a house and knock. The door would be opened by a lithe woman with a smile on her lips and a hunger in her eyes. Charles Xavier would ask for a drink of water. A pretext to enter. The first step in a game played many times before. The rules didn't demand such gestures, but the theater was part of his charm. The woman's head would bow down towards her feet, but her eyes would pierce her lashes and stay locked on his. His mailbag would fall from his shoulder. She'd get him a glass of water from the sink. Her husband would be away. The children would be in school. No one but them and the steady drip of the faucet. He would swallow the glass of water in a single gulp, laugh his happy laugh, and take her in his arms. He would raise her chin with his hand and let her drink from his well of unquenchable joy. Every day a different route. Every day a different supporting actress.

The dirt of the path gave way to the gravel of the road beneath Ted's work boots. Had he ever been the source of such joy, or had he been a burden? When did it change? When did Sandi's face turn from beaming to gloomy? When had it become obvious that there was something wrong? When had it become impossible to ignore the signs? How long had she been unhappy before he had even realized? It must have been awhile. The change to him had seemed like a sudden storm with few warnings. A change in the direction of the wind. Distant thunder. How had he been so blind?

"You never take me camping."

"You want to go camping?"

"We talked about this. I'm sick of it. Sick of all your shit."

"You never told me you wanted to go camping."

"There's so much I want to do. You're holding me back."

"I'd be more than happy to go camping."

"This isn't about the fucking camping."

She'd been his first. First girlfriend. First in the physical way. He had never dated in high school, never even shown any real interest in girls, though it had always bubbled unseen beneath the surface. Even his first two years of college had mostly been spent drinking copious amounts of alcohol, or as his father had joked, learning how to socialize. The perceived lack of interest had continued for so long that his mother had finally made the assumption that he was gay. His father had told him about it when he was eighteen. His mother was completely convinced that he must be gay and she was just waiting for the sudden drama of his coming out so she could wrap him in a hug and start proving how supportive she was of her gay son. When he had brought Sandi home for Christmas his mother had hugged her and smiled, but Ted had felt a vague undertone of her disappointment over the loss of a golden opportunity to prove to the world just how progressive she was. The loss of an imaginary world where she proudly introduced her openly gay son, only slightly held onto by the hope that perhaps his apparent straightness was nothing but a phase.

Sandi had shattered his mother's dream and so was never fully accepted into her world. It was no big deal to Sandi. She had little interest in gaining the acceptance of her boyfriend's mother, though she did get along well with his dad. The few times Ted had brought her home were always awkward. His mother would smile and make chit-chat, and then cook elaborate meals as though every visit was a holiday. She'd always ask if Sandi would like to help, and then feign surprise when it was revealed that Sandi's cooking skills started and ended at Top Ramen. It wasn't that Sandi wasn't capable, it was more just a lack of interest. Ted and Sandi would invariably spend the stay watching sports with his dad. Sandi wasn't much of a sports fan either, but it was better than the cheerful condemnation of the kitchen. Ted's dad seemed to enjoy the company, though perhaps he just enjoyed the sudden uptick in the quality of the meals brought by her visit. Ted's dad had never been the type to voice an opinion one way or the other.

Chapter 4

There wasn't a lot of movement in Titou. It was mid-afternoon.
A few women walked the streets or worked in their gardens, but most
hid in the shade of their houses, waiting for the coolness of the evening
to resume the outside chores abandoned as the sun rose towards noon.
Those who were still out and about moved slowly, floating through the
ocean that hung around them. Titou was high enough on the mountain
that at times it got a nice cool breeze. On such days the lazy quality of
the afternoon never took hold. Today was not one of those days. Ted
had never felt the atmosphere so thick. He trudged down the road and
past the identical rows of houses to the familiar crimson shade of his
abode. He unlocked the door and collapsed into the cool embrace of
the shadowed interior. His backpack and hand sprayer fell to the floor.
They yearned to return to the shed, but it could wait.

Ted's stomach gurgled. A rumble that bubbled its way through
all the twists and turns of his gut. He moved over to the toilet, lowered
his pants, and sat down. He didn't bother with the curtain. Next to the
toilet was an old dog-eared paperback copy of *Catch-22*. Ted picked it
up and leafed through it, reading a few passages, trying to find again
the former joy of the irrational, the elation for the absurdity. It was
gone. Perhaps it was a sign of growing up. With each year the magic
faded more and the world became less wondrous, or at least that's the
way it seemed. Why was he here? He was nothing here. Less than
nothing. Ted put the book back down on the floor next to the toilet.
The toilet rocked slightly. One of the bolts was a little loose.

He sat and eyed his surroundings. His place of exile. Things
were cleaner than when he had left. The pile of clothes was gone, the
garbage taken out, the counters and floors scrubbed, and the sleep sack

on the cot completely unzipped to let any smells escape. She had been here. She had been inside. Ted felt naked. Violated. She had been within the protective cover. Could she see? Could she feel how much of a miserable son of a bitch he really was? He didn't want her to see him that way. What the fuck was he doing? She cleaned the house. That's what he paid her to do. He was acting crazy. The strong and silent type. Good humored and carefree. That's what he wanted her to see. Not some sad sack crying on the shitter.

Ted wiped his ass, got up, turned around, and looked down at the contents of the bowl. It was something he always did, he couldn't really say why. Once his father had told him a story about accidentally walking in on Ted's grandfather in the bathroom. The old man had been standing there, his pants still around his ankles, studying the bits of him he had left behind. Ted's father had thought the whole thing rather strange. It had been the only time that Ted had ever felt any kind of connection to his grandfather. He never told anyone about it. It was a secret. Not even Sandi knew that one. It had always been a rule between them. Never shit in front of the other. That was a private thing. Something which required closed doors.

"You know the magic is gone when you've seen your significant other take a crap."

That's what she had always said, always as a half joke. They had kept the rule sacred, but apparently there were other ways as well.

Ted leaned over and flushed the toilet. Now wasn't the time to let his mind go wild. His work day was done early, but he still had things to do. He wanted to take a shower. A lukewarm shower would feel good, but no, first he needed to go down to Malik's. He needed to pick up a few things. Cornmeal, rice, and milk. The staples. Maybe a little bit of chicken. Ted walked over to the fridge and opened it. It was mostly empty. A jar of mustard, a package of lunch meat going green, and a box of baking soda to keep things fresh.

Ted reached in and pulled out the box of baking soda. Inside was crammed his savings. A couple American bills, but mostly East Caribbean dollars. Green fives, blue tens, and red twenties. All graced by the smiling countenance of an idealized and forever young Queen Elizabeth II. The nearest bank was in Helston. Ted pocketed a handful of banknotes, closed the cardboard box, and placed it back in the fridge. Lifting the backpack off of the floor, he pulled out the jug of chemicals, placing it on the counter before shouldering the pack. Bracing himself, Ted opened the front door of his house and pushed his way back out into the soupy heat of mid-afternoon.

Malik's mercantile was by far the biggest building in town, not counting the warehouse in the banana plantation, though in fairness the plantation was not considered part of town. The walls were painted a bright turquoise, brilliant from a distance, but upon closer inspection, revealed to be sloppily splashed across the gray of the cinderblock walls which peeked through everywhere the paint had missed. The roof was corrugated metal, rusted in places, covered by long streaks of canary yellow paint, still holding onto the shoulders of the metal, but washed away from all the grooves.

Next to the uphill side of the building stood three obelisks. Two natural to the left and one artificial to the right. The artificial was a metal tower, forty feet high, topped by a TV antenna. A metal ladder was built into the tower and a long black cable snaked its way around one of the supports, attaching the antenna to the TV inside. When a storm blew the antenna out of alignment, Malik would send one of the younger men scrambling up to adjust it. Malik, his eye on the television, would bark orders from the bar below, relayed by a second man who stood at the door. The man on the tower would be compensated with five beers. The man on the ground with one. When Ted had first arrived Malik had tried to convince him to climb the tower. The bulky proprietor had been convinced that since all Americans had TV, he would better understand the barked instructions. Ted had declined. He had grown up with cable, and besides, heights made him nervous.

The natural were two massive gommier trees growing right next to the building. Both were over ninety feet tall, the trunks at the bottom six feet in diameter. They were covered in vines from the ground to the canopy far above. The trees had been groomed so that the canopy didn't start until at least sixty feet up. Gommier trees had once been used by fisherman to make dugout boats, but these two would likely never meet such a fate. Malik claimed that the original saplings had been a gift of the colonial governor to his great grandfather for saving the governor's life during a hurricane. Charles

Xavier called the story bullshit, first because the trees were too old for that, and second because the whole island of Domenique was covered with gommier trees, so it would have been a pretty shitty gift.

Above the door hung a sign which read, *Titou Mercantile, J. Malik, Proprietor*. Unlike the rest of the building the sign was freshly painted every year. Ted had made the mistake of calling it a store when he first arrived. Having the slab of meat named Malik bellowing in his face had been one of the most frightening moments of his life. In Malik's view a store only had groceries. He was running a mercantile god damn it.

Pushing his way through the double glass doors Ted was assaulted by a blast of cold air, icy fingers flirtatiously playing across his skin. Malik's mercantile was the only place in Titou with air conditioning. The abrupt change made Ted shiver. Malik sat behind a bar that ran along the same wall as the door, smoking a cigarette, and reading from a harlequin romance novel. He was always reading such trash, but no one ever commented on it, at least to his face. Malik was built like a truck. Everything on him was big. Big arms. Big legs. Thick neck. Wide shoulders. He had obviously once been a fit man, people in Titou liked to tell how he had represented Domenique throwing shotput at the Commonwealth Games, but age was catching up. He had developed a gut and had reached the point where his pecs had become man boobs. However, even now as a man in his late fifties he was still an intimidating sight. Next to Malik sat the cash register. A steel monstrosity from another era, bolted down to the top of the bar. Arrayed behind him were the most secure items in the mercantile. Two coolers full of beer and shelves filled with liquor bottles, packs of cigarettes and cigars, lighters, international calling cards, batteries, small radios with built in tape decks, boxes of candy bars, and for some reason known only to Malik, a row of small teddy bears in various colors.

Above the bar was a large portrait of a fat older gentleman in a suit. His head was bald except for a halo of white hair. The man was Malik's father, who had been the first representative for the district after Domenique had been given its independence by the British. Malik's father had been a well-known lover of his country. Malik's mother, again according to Charles Xavier, had been a well known lover of the first president. Above the portrait was tacked the national flag, which Malik's father had helped design. A vertical tri-color of green, yellow, and blue. The green for the land, the yellow for the beach, and the blue for the ocean. Charles Xavier always joked that the yellow actually represented the banana, the island's main export, and source of all wealth for the corrupted men of government. To the side was a second portrait, smaller than the first. An eight by ten of Malik's wife. A small wispy woman of the type often found married to large fit men. The photo was old. Ted didn't know if its appearance held true. He had never seen Malik's wife in the flesh.

Malik looked up as Ted entered. His voice was low and gravelly.

"Be sure you get everything you need. I'm going to be leaving to see my wife tomorrow."

Malik's wife had moved to the capital to allow their children to attend a private secondary school. That had been twelve years ago, and she had never returned to Titou since. The two boys had graduated, and both had taken jobs working on oil platforms off of Trinidad. Mrs. Malik had settled into the cosmopolitan life to which she had become accustomed. Malik made the trip down every two months to visit her. In his absence the mercantile was closed down and locked up tight.

"How long?"

"Five days."

Ted hung his backpack on the row of pegs next to the door. Malik nodded and went back to his book. Ted strode past the bar and into the rows of shelves. He walked as if he was a man with purpose, but purposefully went down the wrong aisle. Malik had no patience for people who browsed, the cool air of the AC was for customers only, not looky loos. A row of circular mirrors sat high on the far wall, allowing Malik to look down all the aisles from his perch next to the cash register. Charles Xavier had taught Ted the trick of always moving. As long as he kept moving from aisle to aisle he was less likely to attract Malik's attention, winning him valuable added minutes in the cold embrace of the mercantile's interior.

Malik's mercantile was the only one for miles and the highest on the mountain. It contained a little bit of everything. Hardware, tools, sundries, household goods, and food. The food ranged from bulk bin items, to milk and juice in coolers, to rows of boxes imported from the US, Brazil, and Venezuela, the origin differentiated by the language on the box. On the far side of the bar from the door was a counter stacked high with catalogs where one could order anything, at a price, not carried on the shelves. Next to the counter, jammed in the corner, was an old pay phone. When he rounded the end of an aisle and passed the phone Ted briefly thought about calling his mother. It would win him all the time he wanted in the chilled Eden, but if he did she might begin expecting him to start calling more. Some things weren't worth the added time in paradise.

He moved his way slowly through the aisles, stopping for a moment to examine a hammer and then again to touch a towel. He looked up at the mirrors high up on the wall. Malik was looking up, watching him. Ted moved towards the grocery side of the mercantile. The reflection of Malik went back to his reading. From the coolers he pulled out a half gallon of milk and a dozen eggs. He made his way to the bulk bins. Id was pouring flour from a big fifty pound bag into one of the bins.

Id was a tall man with big hands and feet. He was around the same age as Ted. His actual name was Avery, but the only one who called him that was Mr. Green, who was his uncle. Malik had graced Id with his nickname when he had started working at the mercantile, because he considered him an idiot. It wasn't entirely fair. Id could carry out any task he was given as long as it was long on labor and short on thinking. Id was most definitely not all there. He largely avoided eye contact and mostly mumbled to himself, unless ordered to speak, in which case he had a surprisingly deep voice. Charles Xavier had once claimed that Id was the way he was because his mother had squeezed when she should have pushed during his birth. Ted had his doubts, but it beat the theory of the older women in Titou, at least according to Charles Xavier, that Id was slow because he was a bastard and that nobody had any clue who his father was. The old ladies thought nothing good ever came from bastards.

Malik used Id as more of a tool than a person. A pack mule, messenger boy, and shelf stocker rolled all into one. Id also worked as a security guard, sleeping every night near the front door on a cot kept in a back room during the day. Many of the people in Titou called him

Malik's dog. The treatment of Id had seemed wrong when Ted had first arrived. The man was obviously developmentally disabled. Ted had voiced his concerns to Charles Xavier, who had responded with his always ready laugh.

"What are you talking about Theodore?"

"It feels like he's being taken advantage of."

"Taken advantage of? He works a job, doesn't he? Half of us would be so lucky to have it so good."

"But…."

"He gets food and shelter."

"What about his family?"

"What family? His mother died of appendicitis, too stubborn to go down the mountain to see a doctor, convinced she was just constipated."

"But Mr. Green."

"What about him?"

"Isn't Mr. Green his uncle?"

"Yes."

"Shouldn't he be taking care of him?"

"Ha. Mr. Green might have the grace to call his nephew by his actual name, but don't be mistaken my friend, Mr. Green only has an interest in those he thinks intelligent. Besides, his nephew is cared for, what more could he do?"

"But what about, you know, a home?"

"He has a home."

"You know what I mean, a place for people like him?"

"What kind of place? One where they'll lock him up, maybe drug him if he gets unruly? This is his home. It's all he's ever known. He's part of the community. Malik may raise his voice, but he never raises his hand, and in many ways the old jacket dotes on him."

"But…."

"Look Theodore. Am I seven feet tall?"

"No."

"Will I ever be seven feet tall?"

"No."

"Then what is the point of me ducking when I go through the doorways. The world is not about ideals, the world is about the best of the available alternatives."

The talk with Charles Xavier had done little to ease Ted's discomfort. Soon after he had tried to broach the subject with Mr. Green. The older man's response had been much more succinct.

"Mind your own damn business."

Ted had quit bringing up Id after that. In the end it had become like many things on the island, something that Ted just had to accept. He might have to accept it, but it didn't mean he had to join it. Ted always made a point of greeting Id every time he saw him.

"Hello Avery."

The gangly man kept pouring flour into the bin, mumbling to himself and staring down at the white powder falls emanating from the bag in his arms. Malik's growling voice echoed down the aisle.

"Say hello Id."

Id stopped pouring and set the flour on the ground. A dusting of powder fell to the floor. Id looked down at his feet, up at Ted briefly, and then back down at the flour.

"Hello."

"How are you today?"

"Good. Good."

Id kept wringing his hands and staring down at the spilt flour. It obviously bothered him, but Malik's command to be social kept him locked to his place on the floor. Id looked uncomfortable, searching his brain for a correct response in a game he didn't understand. Synapses sparked, trying to remember the correct order of operations. Something clicked.

"Do you like Jaws?"

Ted smiled and nodded.

"Yeah, it's a good movie?"

"Yes it is."

With his ordered social obligation fulfilled, Id turned and headed off down the aisle to get the broom and dustbin to clean up the spilled flour, shaking and humming the Jaws theme. Ted filled paper bags with rice and cornmeal and headed towards the front. Along the way he passed a row of boxes of Kraft Macaroni and Cheese. It was expensive, all imported goods were expensive, but he grabbed a box anyway. A box of home would be good.

Ted placed his purchases on the bar next to the cash register. Malik rang them up. Ted's eyes rose from the jangling register to the flickering light of the TV on its stand hanging from the wall. It was an old set with fake wood paneling. An old fashioned remote with only five buttons sat on the bar next to the register. The news was playing. A British woman talking in even tones. In the afternoon it was always on the news. In the morning it was soap operas. It was Malik's TV, so Malik got to decide the programming.

Charles Xavier had told Ted about how once Mr. Green had purchased his own TV. Malik had responded by taking his antenna off its tower, cutting off the signal. The people of Titou had gone to Mr. Green's house and smashed his new television. Soon after, Mr. Green had tried to form a co-op to build its own tower so everyone could have TV, but in a place where half the people didn't even bother to have radios, nothing had ever come of it. The people of Titou just didn't really care. Mr. Green had been forced to accept defeat.

Malik finished ringing up the purchases and slammed his hand on the bar. His voice calm, but direct.

"You wanna watch the TV, you buy a damn beer."

Ted was startled from the spinning storm animation on the screen.

"Did she say something about a hurricane?"

Malik's eyes narrowed, suspicious that the question might be a ruse to gain time in front of his TV or in his AC, but Ted must have looked sufficiently sincere, or at least sufficiently nervous.

"Yeah, they upgraded Anji last night. She's swinging north too."

Ted felt his stomach knot. A sudden lizard brain worry.

"North. You mean up towards here?"

"News says she'll just skim past sometime tomorrow evening. At most we'll just get the edge."

Ted's mouth felt dry.

"Any danger?"

Malik rolled his eyes.

"It's just a category two."

Ted looked down and let his eyes trace across his purchases.

"But..."

Malik looked tired and annoyed.

"Christ, we're up on a fucking mountain."

Ted breathed in and out and did his best to save face.

"We going to get rain then?"

"I'm a purveyor of goods, not a fucking meteorologist."

Ted licked his lips. His eyes darted back up to the TV and then back to the impatient man behind the register. Malik sighed.

"Look jake. She's a small one. Plenty of them blow by every season. We might get some wind and bucketfuls of rain. Nothing to worry about. You got a better chance of being killed by an irate man at a mercantile."

Malik gestured towards the total on the register. Ted glanced back up at the TV. Malik picked up the remote, turned off the TV, and gestured again. Ted pulled the bills out of his pocket and paid. Malik opened the drawer and gave him his change. Ted put his items in his backpack and left the cool refuge of the mercantile.

Chapter 5

The outside world hit him as soon as he stepped out of the doorway. Sweat poured down his brow and his clothes clung to him with the moist embrace of a jilted lover who could not let go. Hurricane. There was going to be a hurricane near the island. A swirling vortex bearing down on the small spot of green in a world of blue. They had warned him that such things could happen. Before leaving the US, they made him sign a mountain of forms, one of which cleared the Peace Corps of any liability for natural disasters. Mr. Douglas had barely touched on the topic during his lectures on St. Lucia.

Ted worked his way up the hill, one heavy booted foot after the other. A nervous vibration was humming in his core, or maybe it was excitement. It was hard to tell. Maybe it would turn? Maybe it would come right at the island? It would be something worth calling home about, that was for sure. How are you Teddy? Doing well, a hurricane hit last week. He could hear his voice in his head, calm and confident. He could hear the worried tones of his mother's reply. Yes, you heard right. A hurricane. No, don't worry, it was only a small one. Ted licked his sun chapped lips. A hurricane was something. A hurricane was something new. The lizard brain was trying to worm its way past the heroic tapestry Ted was weaving. His heart was beating a little faster in his chest. Panic it said. Disaster it claimed. Be afraid. Be very afraid.

Ted took off his cap and wiped his forehead with his forearm. His gaze tracked across the world around him. The people of Titou were still moving at the same sedate pace as they always did. He eyed their faces. Searching. Prying. Those who caught him went stone faced, but others didn't notice. Happiness. Boredom. Cranky. Deep in thought. No sign of worry. No sign of panic. Everyone looked calm and placid. The lizard brain was thrown back. The rent in the fabric of his valiancy was repaired.

Mr. Green sat on his porch in a folding chair, reading a book. He looked up as Ted approached.

"Afternoon, Mr. Nelson."

Ted nodded with his reply.

"Afternoon, Mr. Green."

Mr. Green went back to his book. Ted unlocked his door and opened it. The lizard brain pushed its way back upward. Ted paused and turned back.

"Mr. Green?"

Mr. Green put his book back down, his finger holding his place.

"Yes. Mr. Nelson?"

"Have you heard about the hurricane?"

"I heard something on the radio."

Ted paused, chewing on his bottom lip.

"Any chance it could swing this way?"

Ted felt a cold bead of sweat sweep its way down his back. Mr. Green scratched the side of his neck.

"I wouldn't worry much about it Mr. Nelson. We're fairly high up on the side of the mountain. Even if it did hit us straight on, we'd probably just get a lot of wind and rain."

Ted nodded, doing his best to look nonchalant.

"Have you ever been through any?"

"I've seen three brushes in my life; Boris, Lucy, and Abigail. They chew up the coast, but leave us mostly alone. This one is just going to blow past."

Ted nodded again.

"Okay. Thank you Mr. Green.

Ted turned to go into his house, but Mr. Green's voice froze him at the threshold.

"One thing Mr. Nelson."

"Yeah?"

"I would probably stay out of the forest tomorrow. We'll probably get a lot of wind and rain. I wouldn't want to be out amongst the trees in such weather."

"I'll do that. Thank you Mr. Green."

"Good day, Mr. Nelson."

Ted retreated into his sanctuary and shut the door. It was slightly cooler inside than out. He took the groceries out of his backpack and put them away. He sat in one of the chairs at the small table. The sunlight from the window glinted off the glass of the bottle of rum sitting on the counter next to the jug of pesticide. He got up, tore off the top of the rum bottle, and took a healthy swig. The taste made him gag, but it swept a warmth across his insides, unclenching muscles and calling off any hints of alarm. No worries. Nothing to freak out about. Ted raised the bottle again, hesitated, and lowered it without taking another drink. There was movement out the back window. Ted screwed the cap back on the bottle and stepped out the rear facing door.

Camilla was working along her clothesline, just a wire strung between two poles, taking down Ted's clothes. She was wearing the same green dress from the previous day and a bright red handkerchief covered her head. Her round form bounced with every step. She smiled at Ted as he emerged from the shadow of his house. Ted watched her for a moment, felt guilty, and moved to help. Camilla worked down one side of the line and Ted made his way down the other. The clothespins were a mix of wooden and plastic, the plastic once brightly colored, but long since faded by the sun. Socks, shirts, pants, and towels.

There was only the one pair of boxers. They stood out as a beacon of his shame. Thou shalt not covet thy neighbor's wife. Ted held the boxers in his hand. The stains were gone, removed as though they had never existed. He turned his head. Camilla was watching him, a wide grin splitting her face. Ted felt his face go bright red. She knew. There were few secrets that could be kept from those who cleaned up after you. An unavoidable level of intimacy. She knew, but she couldn't know everything. Could she? She was so quiet. So hard to read. What did she know?

They met in the middle of the line. The clothes in Camilla's arms were neatly folded. The clothes in Ted's arms were a jumbled mess. She smiled at him again.

"Thank you."

She pushed her pile into Ted's arms. He tried to answer, but no sound emerged. He looked into her eyes. They were warm and welcoming, brown pools that sucked him downward into their heavenly depths. His mind scrambled to form a reply, the end result less than satisfactory.

"I'm going to take a shower."

Camilla's mouth split into a smile again.

"Good idea. That's a better place to do it. Less dirty underwear."

Camilla's laugh was long and throaty. Ted tried his best to smile back. He was glad for the redness of his sunburn. Camilla turned and walked back towards her house. Ted retreated back to his. A joke, that was all it was, just a joke. He could see it in her eyes. Her beautiful dark brown mischievous eyes. But what if it was more?

Ted dumped his clothes into the duffel bag, Camilla's folds fading and falling away. The bottle of rum sat on the counter, calling out its promise of relaxing oblivion. A drunken man sitting alone, screaming obscenities at an empty apartment. Ted ignored the rum. He took off his boots and slipped out of his dirty clothes. He wrapped himself in a freshly cleaned towel. His mind drifted for a moment. Her hands had been on the towel just minutes ago. Ted sucked in a breath, the terry cloth did nothing to hide his rising arousal. Ted cracked open his back door and peered out. Nothing. Nobody within the sliver of view. He opened the door wider and stuck out his head, arching his neck back and forth. Nobody was there. A mixture of relief and disappointment. Part of him had hoped that she had taken his statement as an invitation. Stupid. He was just being stupid.

Ted crept outside. One small step, two, and then rushed to the safety of the encircling shower curtain, stepping carefully to make sure he didn't trip on the six inch lip of the concrete shower basin. He pulled the curtain closed, out of sight, out of mind, and hung his towel on its hook. He turned the valve on the shower head, releasing lukewarm water to flow down his body to the drain at his feet. The gurgling of the water was loud. Noisy enough to mask the sounds of the outside world. He was alone. Isolated. As detached as an astronaut floating in a tin can high above the Earth. Camilla was right. It was a better place to do it.

Ted let himself get swept away into his fantasy. Exploring hands working their way across his skin. A body pressed tight against his. One moment light, the next dark. Images whipped through his head. A collage of naked forms, faces stretched in beautiful agony. Frantic jerking movements. The flip of a switch. Electrical commands switching from the higher brain to the lower one. A surge. A pop. An involuntary moan. The dribble of unborn children down the plastic of the curtain. Giggling. High pitched. A failed stifling. Ted's brain re-engaged, forcing him back into reality. Ted whipped his head out of the confines of his secluded world.

The two Seraphin children were crouched by the corner of his house, nearly close enough to touch. The boy and the girl, hands over their mouths, were desperately trying to keep their laughter contained.

"Little bastards."

The sight of Ted's florid face made the two Seraphins jump. Their eyes grew wide and they fell backwards in a pile. The white demon was on the loose. They scrambled to regain their feet. Ted's hand wrapped itself around the soap in its dish. His arm whipped around, but the shot went wide, the light blue projectile skidding across the ground to come to rest amongst Mr. Green's tomatoes. The Seraphin kids ran to the safety of their own back lot, squealing and laughing. Ted pulled his head back behind the security of the curtain. Fuck. He shouldn't have done that. How was he supposed to take a shower without his damn soap? Stupid.

The remains of his enjoyment stared at him from the shower curtain. Ted filled his mouth with water and spit at the offending remains. Down the curtain it skidded, swirling around his feet before disappearing down the drain. Ted rubbed his body with water the best he could. The drizzle went from lukewarm to cold. The tank on the roof had a float in it like a toilet. When it got too empty it would automatically refill. The shower never ran out of water, but it needed time in the sun to be warm. Ted turned off the valve and dried himself with his towel. The terry cloth felt rough against his sunburnt skin. It was his only towel. He had brought two, but one had disappeared within a month of his arrival. Charles Xavier had just shrugged his shoulders at the news.

"Things happen."

Ted wrapped the towel around his middle and pulled the shower curtain aside. The two Seraphin kids sat on their haunches by their back door. They started giggling as soon as they saw him. Ted ignored them. He moved across the dirt and grass and bent over to dig the bar of soap out from underneath Mr. Green's tomatoes. The of the two, the girl, rose up and took a couple of steps forward. She looked behind herself at her brother, then back at Ted, and took a few deep breaths. Her voice was shrill.

"You shouldn't back your fist every day. You'll go blind."

The girl retreated, nearly bent double with elation for her joke. The boy rolled on his back, wracked by convulsions of hilarity. Ted raised his index and middle finger in a V, the knuckles pointed out. The gesture made the kids laugh even harder. Ted retreated. The kids watched his every move, impish grins on their faces, waiting to see if he would do anything else entertaining. Ted brushed the dirt off his soap as best he could and put it back in its dish. He refused to look at his tormentors, knowing he'd been beaten. He pulled open his back door and abandoned the fight for another day.

Ted rubbed the dirt off of his feet with the palm of his hand and hung his towel on the back of one of the chairs to let it dry. He put on a pair of basketball shorts and a fresh t-shirt. He was tired. The kitchen sink was dripping. Plop…...plop…...plop. The sound was soothing. Electrical storms swarming between neurons fell quiet. The world shrank down to a single motion and a single sound. Plop…..plop…...plop. It was a nice place. No needs. No worries. No concerns. Just a steady never ending rhythmic beat. Breathe in with every plop, let out at every in between, a steady beat from a natural metronome. A drop hung, breaking the cadence, and then fell. No more followed. A heavy pounding on his front door broke the silence. How long had he been sitting there? The room was darker. It was getting late. The hammer of a fist sounded again on his door. Ted raised his weary bulk and answered it. Charles Xavier pushed his way in, smiling and exuberant.

"There you are Theodore. I've been waiting on that rum. What's been keeping you my friend?"

Ted gestured aimlessly at the air around him.

"Just taking a shower."

"Good idea. The ladies love a clean man, but only if he has a dirty mind."

Charles Xavier laughed. His eyes fell on the bottle of rum on the counter next to the jug of chemical. He winked and pointed at his goal.

"You best be careful storing those together. A man with a mighty thirst might make a mistake."

"Shit, I meant to put it away."

Charles Xavier laughed again.

"Tomorrow Theodore. Tomorrow my friend."

Charles Xavier picked up the bottle, and cradling it like a baby, sat down at the table. He cooed and pretended to tickle the bottom of the bottle's imaginary chin. For a moment he was lost in his own little world and his Cheshire features fell into a frown. Ted closed the door and stood staring at his friend, daydreaming of the peacefulness of the falling water drops. Charles Xavier looked up at Ted and his smile returned. He gestured with his hand towards the cupboards.

"Are you just going to sit there all night catching flies Theodore. How about some glasses?"

Ted walked over to the cupboard. He opened it and pulled out two glasses, cleaned immaculately by Camilla's beautiful hands.

"Do you want ice?"

"Ice. Ice the man says. It's as though I'm drinking rum with the queen herself. Yes my good man. Let's have some ice."

Ted opened the fridge and then the ice box within. The ice tray had five cubes left in it. He put two cubes in one glass and three cubes in the other, leaving the empty tray on the counter. He turned and placed the glasses on the table, the glass with three cubes in front of his guest. Charles Xavier smacked his hand on the table.

"An insult. An insult is it?"

Charles Xavier's face was twisted in mock indignation. His long finger pointed at the glass. Ted stared at it, trying to understand what was wrong. Charles Xavier jabbed at the glass' rim.

"Do you think I don't know what you're up to? Do you think I don't have a brain?"

Ted paused, unsure. The face looked less mocking then it had a moment before. He couldn't tell if the other man was being serious.

Flashes of green dress mingled with the sudden ferocious swing of a fist. Charles Xavier's face was frozen with contempt.

"Do you think I don't know your game? Did you think I wouldn't realize what you're up to with the ice?"

"The ice?"

"Yes, damn you, the ice. I get three cubes. You get two. You get a whole cube more rum than me."

Charles Xavier's eyes bulged from his face, his mouth locked in a frown. The corners of his mouth began to flutter. His eyes bulged further and with a sudden explosion of hysterics he fell back. His hand slapped the table, jingling the ice in the glasses. He erupted like a volcano, his words squeezed between joyous fits.

"Almost got you. You should've seen your face."

Ted laughed too, embarrassed, but wanting to join in the fun. He moved back to the counter, filled the ice tray, and put it in the ice box. Charles Xavier switched the glasses, removed the bottle's plastic cap, and filled both to the brim.

"Would you mind getting the light Theodore? I'm starting to blend in with my surroundings."

Ted did as he was asked. The shadows fell back to their hiding spaces. Ted sat down at the table. Charles Xavier took a long drink and sighed with pleasure. He rubbed the cold glass across his forehead. Ted took a few sips. Next door he could hear Camilla humming one of her songs, upbeat and alive, cooking her husband's supper. Charles Xavier was rambling, but Ted wasn't listening. All Ted heard was the humming in the other house. A happy tune with just the hint of sadness. Charles Xavier reached over and tapped him on the arm.

"Are you listening Theodore?"

Ted jumped and looked over.

"Yeah. Yeah. Sorry."

"Are you feeling okay?"

Charles Xavier's eyes were filled with worry and concern.

"Yeah. I guess. Just been feeling down lately. You know, the job and all. This place. Nothing is what I expected."

Charles Xavier leaned back in his chair, glanced out the darkened window and back, and gave the world a brave smile.

"I know my friend. We all feel that sometimes. Sometimes our lives don't turn out the way we think they will. Sometimes you just have to decide to be happy, and do the best with what you have."

Charles Xavier took a long drink of rum. The muscles in his throat slipped up and down. A flash of color on the dark skin. A bite mark on his neck. Charles Xavier lowered his glass and stared out the window.

"Life is funny. Life is always funny. You just have to figure out what the joke is."

"Yeah. I guess so."

Ted took a big swallow of rum. The sickly sweet taste pooled on his tongue and leaked down his throat. How could he? How could such a man go hunting when his freezer was full of the finest cuts? Bastard. His friend. A bastard. Camilla deserved better. What place was it of his to judge? Who was to say that it wasn't Camilla's mark upon her husband's neck. Charles Xavier stared out the window, taking occasional drinks from his glass. His world was far away. Ted stared out the window too, looking at nothing, seeing everything. Sandi's blue eyes. Camilla's deep brown, almost black. Charles Xavier's full of concern for the plight of a man to whom he owed nothing.

"Did you hear about the hurricane?"

Charles Xavier gave a half smile, but didn't look away from the window.

"Still talking about storms are we?"

The humming next door stopped. Charles Xavier's glass hit the table with a loud clunk.

"I better get going. Camilla has probably finished supper."

Ted nodded. He drained his own glass. Charles Xavier rose.

"Would you care to join us?"

Ted stared at the ice floating in his glass.

"No. I'm not that hungry."

Charles Xavier nodded and headed for the door. His hand gripped the door knob. Ted put his own glass down with an audible thunk.

"You have a bite mark on your neck."

Silence filled the house. Charles Xavier paused, rubbed his hand on his neck, and turned back. There was something in his eye, something dangerous, but it disappeared in a moment, replaced by a coy glint and a cocky grin.

"You wouldn't believe how excited some people are to get their mail."

Charles Xavier turned and walked out the door, humming, picking up the song where Camilla had left off.

Chapter 6

The light coming from the front and back windows was muted. The sky was gray and overcast. Dark clouds groaning in growing discomfort as they marched across the sky. Ted lay in his sleep sack, tucked away from the outside world in his blue, white, and red refuge. There was no reason to get up. Mr. Green had said to stay out of the forest. There'd be rain and wind by the evening or late afternoon. It didn't matter. There was nothing that couldn't be put off until later. Nothing ever had to be done right away.

Ted's head hurt. The rum bottle sat next to the toilet, half empty. It glistened in the muzzled morning light, the gleam refracted, bent, and scattered across the wall. Next door the sound of lovemaking began. Rising and falling in volume, floating like stinging wasps through the air. They hadn't even bothered to eat breakfast. Good god, how many biscuits could the man butter in twenty-four hours?

Ted yearned for the release of the golden medication. The gentle numbness of a quiet mind, synapses falling silent until nothing else mattered beyond the world confined and compressed to a single moment. No past. No future. Just now. Deja vu. An apartment filled with dust. A man lying on the couch, staring at a silent television. His mother walks in. She fusses. She frets. She pulls the curtains open, letting in the hated sunlight. The chipper morning with chirping birds and whistling mailmen. His mother sits on a chair facing him, her wedding ring catching the light, spraying refractions across the floor. She frowns in that disappointed way that only mothers can do. Words. A flood of words, trying to batter their way through the swaddling fog of chemical inertia, trying to re-establish a sense of shame in oneself.

It was strange how a mind wanders when one lets it. Random images ricocheted across the confines of his head. Ted usually tried his best to avoid letting his thoughts traipse about as they so chose. The ambling drift of his reflections too often led to places that he'd rather not relive. Memories once good, now bad. Words never said. Words he wished he had never said. A never ending litany of imaginary one sided arguments and a pointless infinite evaluation of scenes to try and figure out what had gone wrong. Nothing good could come of it. It was a trap in which he had too often found himself shoving his own leg between the sharp steely jaws. It was okay to let his mind roam as it would, but only if it stayed within the confines of its fenced in pasture. As long as it didn't conjure memories of blonde hair and blue eyes. A small ass in tight high cut shorts. A turn of the head. A finger pushing a lock of hair back behind an ear. Narrowing eyes and a soft smile on her lips.

"I want you. I want you right now. Fuck me. Fuck me right now."

God damn it. Retreat. Pull back. No use. Slippery slope. Easy to enter. Hard to exit. Someone knocked on the front door. Thank god. Thank fucking god. The knock was repeated, too hard to be meek, but too soft to be authoritative. The rap of fist on wood dug its fingers to the center of Ted's tender skull.

"I'm coming. I'm coming."

Ted slid out of his sleep sack and pulled on his shorts and t-shirt from the night before, reclaiming them from the floor where he had left them. The concrete was warm beneath his feet. Ted tromped over, rubbing gunk from his eyes, and opened the door. Eugene Hewitt stood on the other side, his face serene, his hands drumming the sides of his legs.

"Good morning."

Ted squinted against the muted light of the outside world. The sky was gray. A steady wind pushed its way through the trees. Ted let his gaze come to rest on his visitor.

"Good morning."

Eugene quit his drumming.

"I was on my way to work, but my father wanted me to stop by and thank you for your help yesterday."

"No problem."

Eugene nodded his head in response. His eyes flicked to behind Ted, back to Ted, behind Ted again, and then back again. A man trying to get a glimpse into the hidden habitat of an American. The ocular intrusion made Ted feel annoyed. He wasn't sure what to do. He wanted to close the door and climb back into his sleep sack, but the curious man was not moving from his doorstep. Eugene's hands started drumming the side of his leg again.

"He also wanted me to ask if you could come up again soon. He says he has some kind of fungus."

Ted let out an audible puff of air from his nostrils. He gestured with his chin towards the gray clouds above.

"No work today. Not until the hurricane blows past."

Eugene nodded his head in understanding.

"Of course. Of course. Lucky you. No worries. Just when you get a chance."

Ted tried to detect any signs of hostility in his visitor's tone, but there was nothing but cheerful friendliness.

"Yeah, sure. Sometime next week."

"Sounds good. I'll let him know."

Ted chewed on his upper lip. Eugene's eyes flicked behind Ted again.

"So where you from man?"

"Excuse me?"

"Where in the States you from?"

For a moment Ted hesitated to answer, doing his best to process the sudden personal question.

"Idaho."

"Close to Miami?"

Ted did his best not to roll his eyes.

"No."

"Ryan was from some place called Buffalo. You know, like the animal. Up by New York City. Anywhere near there?"

"No. Up in the Northwest, up by Canada."

Eugene raised and lowered his eyebrows and gave a half smile. Ted's stomach shifted and he could feel bile at the back of his throat.

The change from vertical to horizontal wasn't doing him well. The world was getting washed out. He wanted to lay back down.

"Well, if there's not anything else, I have things I need to get done today."

Eugene smiled.

"Of course. Of course. Me too. Got to get to work. Not all of us are so lucky. Thank you again."

"Goodbye."

Eugene turned and walked away. Ted closed the door and laid back down on top of his sleep sack. The world's spin slowed back down to a more manageable level. He found himself wishing that he had talked to Eugene more. Eugene didn't seem to be a bad sort, just curious. It had been awhile since he had managed a real conversation past Charles Xavier. Ah well, another day. Ted closed his eyes and let himself drift downward back into the Land of Nod.

Nothingness. Floating in a void. Bobbing along amongst the cosmos. A sound. A ripple across the starscape. The sound again. Ted opened his eyes. How long had he been asleep? Ted sat up on his cot and rubbed the crust from his eyes. Knuckles smacked against the wood of the door. Quick. Furtive. Agitated. Ted rose and opened the front door. Mr. Green was standing on the porch, looking annoyed. His eyes swept up and down Ted. Mr. Green's mouth tightened. Ted let out a yawn, covering it with a hand.

"Yes?"

"It took you a bit to answer."

"I was sleeping."

"Half the morning away?"

Ted raised his eyebrows, but said nothing. The old busybody son of a bitch. What business was it of his if Ted slept in late? Christ, Mr. Green had been the one that had suggested not going up into the forest. What was he supposed to do? Mr. Green waited for a response. When none was forthcoming he let out a sigh and smacked his lips.

"I'm just going around door to door to let everyone know that I heard on the radio that Anji has shifted course."

The wind tugged insistently at the hair on Ted's legs.

"Who?"

"The hurricane."

"Changed course you said?"

"Yes."

"Towards what?"

Mr. Green gave Ted a look that heavily suggested his opinion of Ted's intelligence.

"Domenique."

The feeling sparked in Ted's gut again. Half nerves and half thrill. He looked at the gray clouds overhead. An image of his solitary figure flashed forth in his mind, laughing in the face of the wind and rain, arm protectively holding Sandi, her face blanched with fear. Ted knew it was a silly thought. A ridiculous one, no matter how good it felt. Niggling worms of doubt burrowed their way through. The pace of his heart increased just a little more.

"Do I need to do anything?"

"Say a couple prayers for those down on the coast would be good. She's been lifted to a Category 3."

A Category 3. The fantasies of a weeping Sandi in his arms redoubled, but so did the tunneling worms.

"What about up here?"

"We'll be fine. Maybe a few mudslides. Little wind damage and maybe a few trees coming down. We might lose power for a few days. Elevation has its advantages."

Ted nodded with pretend understanding. The Ted in his mind had been through many such things before.

"Okay. Thanks for letting me know."

Mr. Green nodded his head.

"I better get moving to the other houses. They expect her to make landfall late this evening. Goodbye, Mr. Nelson."

"Goodbye, Mr. Green."

The old man turned and walked away, his step bouncy and his back straight. A man with a self-assigned important job to do. Other people moved about the town. No one seemed rushed. No one seemed worried. The world was moving forward just as it always had. Ted closed the door. Nothing to do, but he might as well get started with the day.

Breakfast, or was it lunch? Brunch was a nice compromise. Brunch was composed of grilled eggs and Spam chased by a big glass of water. Brunch was followed by donning jeans, a fresh t-shirt, and work boots. Next came tidying up the house. Dirty clothes were put in a pile. The rum bottle was put on the sink, but not until after a small drink. There was a hurricane on the way after all. Crusted vomit was chipped from the rim of the toilet. Ted's small world was put back to as it belonged. The chemical jug still sat on the counter. Ted picked it up and headed out the backdoor. He left it unlocked behind him.

Ted was thankful for the clouds. He wouldn't burn with them above. The dirt and grass were all a darker shade, less vibrant. The world was full of sounds that he did not want to face. Children laughing. A steady wind through fronds and leaves. Muffled voices and bursts of static from Mr. Green's radio floating through his open window. Ted kept his head down, staring at the ground. He moved at a rapid pace to the shed, unlocked it, put the jug inside, and locked the door again. Adolescent screams rent the air. Without command Ted's eyes jerked away from the optical safety of the dirt below his feet. It was the Seraphin children. The girl was on top of the boy, shoving his face into the ground. One of the boy's arms was stretched behind his back, his hand firmly clasped around a knot of his sister's hair. Mrs. Seraphin barged out of her back door and started yelling, making sharp cutting gestures with her arm. She grabbed both children by an ear and hop marched them back into the house, yelling threats of what would happen when their father returned home. It would be quite a wait. According to Charles Xavier, Mr. Seraphin only climbed the mountain at most once or twice a year. If half of Mrs. Seraphin's threats were true, the man likely spent the entirety of his visit disciplining his children.

The seal was broken. The world around him was real, flashed into existence by an involuntary movement. He allowed his gaze to track its way across his surroundings. Empty lots and expectant gardens. The plants raising themselves up from the dry earth, waiting for water. A chicken was pecking halfheartedly near Mr. Green's tomatoes. Camilla came out her back door, wearing a red dress and a yellow handkerchief around her head. She smiled and waved at Ted. He smiled and waved back. Camilla moved over to her garden and got down on her hands and knees to weed. Ted hesitated for a moment, then walked over to help. Camilla looked up at his approaching form, nodded her thanks and smiled again, bathing Ted for a moment in her brilliance before getting back to work.

It was nice working next to Camilla, never having to say a word. Never feeling an awkward silence. The woman exuded a sea of tranquility which rippled around her with every movement. No judgments. No demands. On his knees, in the dirt, working near her, the world fell away. Camilla hummed as she labored. Ted tried to guess the songs, but almost all were unidentifiable, though he thought he recognized some that sounded like reggae. Many seemed to be just random notes clinging to each other as they escaped the confines of her head.

He watched her from the corner of his eye as she worked the row next to his. He watched her hands. Her small stubby fingers wrapped themselves around a weed, entwining the base where the green gave way to the rich redness of the soil. A quick jerk rippled its way up the muscles of her arm. The white roots sprung forth out into the sunshine. The threat removed, she shuffled forward towards the next. Ted's admiring gaze flowed across her hands from her wrist to the tip of each finger. Her fingernails were cracked and jagged, chewed down to the nubs. Her hands were covered in scars, calluses, and broken patches where blisters had come and gone. Her hands were not appendages, but finely crafted tools, forged to carry out delicate work and apply brute force when needed. Occasionally, the weed would snap off at its base. Her fingers would plunge down into the dirt, a constant motion worrying away at the resistance of the ground, exposing the root desperately clinging to life.

Her face was covered in sweat, but she never brushed it aside. It overwhelmed the defenses of the handkerchief on her head, flowing downward to drip off the tip of her blunted nose, a perfectly shaped drop which glinted in the sunlight as it fell before being swallowed up by the thirsty land. Her eyes kept to her work, only lifting to watch a passing bird trilling its happiness at being alive or to check on Ted's progress, smiling as he fell behind. Each yank of her arm shook her entire body, jiggling her unbound breasts beneath the protective red cover of her dress. Ted felt like a pervert for watching such a movement with such rapt attention, but he couldn't look away. A queen. No, a goddess. Camilla was not attractive. Sandi had been attractive. Camilla was beautiful.

Ted's wandering eye was costing him in efficiency. Camilla steadily pulled ahead. Ted tried to concentrate on his work, but was distracted by the roundness of her ass sticking up into the air. Ted tried not to think about it. About her bent over the table in his house. About the feeling of her hard nipples between his fingers as he pushed himself in. Weeds. He was pulling weeds. He was being a good neighbor. He was doing a good deed. Camilla stood up on her knees and stretched, arching her back, holding her arms above her head. Ted felt himself stiffen. Weeds. Weeds. Just concentrate on the weeds. He worked with renewed vigor, pulling back even with her. Hands. If he must look at something look at her hands. They were safe. Her beautiful hands. Wrapped around his…..god damn it. The pair reached the end of their respective rows, shifted over, and started again.

Ted kept his head down and his hands moving. Sandi. Sandi had always wanted a garden. You couldn't have a garden in an apartment. Nothing was ever good enough for her. He was never good enough for her.

"What if we put a planter box out on the patio?"

"The lease says we can't have planter boxes."

"So?"

"The lease says…."

"Fuck the lease. Who's really going to care?"

"It's what we agreed to when we signed."

"Jesus, Ted."

"What?"

"Why don't you just start goose stepping."

"Excuse me."

"You heard me."

"I don't see what the big deal is."

"You wouldn't."

"What's that supposed to mean?"

"Christ Ted, do I have to explain everything to you?"

"Why don't we just get some herbs to grow on the windowsill."

"I don't want fucking herbs on the windowsill. I want vegetables on the patio."

"Well, then you should've put your damn name on the lease."

Yelling. Lots of yelling. What had it all been about? What had been the point? Just fucking planter boxes. Just another small thing to throw on top of the pile. Had that been it? The fights? Could that really be it? Sure, they fought, but who didn't? Maybe if he had just let her have the damn planter boxes. Maybe that would have fixed everything. No. Probably not. There was something else there. Something she wouldn't say. A constant storm. A never ending maelstrom of feelings and emotions sweeping across his life with sudden rattling gusts which brought his psyche to its knees. Why wouldn't she say it? Why did it have to be a secret? What could he do if she never spoke up?

Into the next row. A steady shift from guilty lust to the constricting confines of his own inadequate memories. The dark gray clouds continued to fill the sky. Ted could see them thickening until they blotted out the sky. No, they were just clouds. Same as they had been when he had first woken that morning. Nowhere was safe. The only sure thing was to put all his concentration on the work at hand. See a weed. Grab the weed. Pull out the weed. Repeat. See a weed. Grab the weed. Pull out the weed. Repeat. Machines don't have thoughts. Machines don't have feelings. Machines never go out looking for a place to heal. A place to magically fix everything wrong inside. Idiot. He was a fucking idiot.

All the weeds were gone. The two were on their hands and knees at the end of the last two rows. Camilla's hand came down on top of Ted's and gave it a gentle squeeze. It lingered. He looked up. She was smiling. Camilla rose and stretched her back. Her skirt was stained a reddish brown from where it had been pressed between her knees and the ground. Ted felt his blood surge again to lower regions. He stood up next to her, the knees of his pants the same shade of brownish red, and rubbed his hands together to remove the dirt. They stood there together, the silence suddenly awkward. He looked at her, and her she shyly looked away. A sudden girl in a woman's body. Ted kept rubbing his hands together, unsure what to do, not knowing what to say.

"I'm thirsty. I think I'll go down to the mercantile and get a beer."

Ted moved away before Camilla could answer, fleeing between the houses of red and yellow.

Chapter 7

The mercantile was closed, the doors locked. Ted felt stupid for walking down. He had known it would be closed. Idiot. Fucking god damn idiot. For a second, he saw two deep brown eyes looking up into his. There was a nervous smile across her lips. A quiet gaze upward through eyelashes. The gentle clasp of a hand, staying in place a little longer than it should. He could feel the pressure of that hand squeezing his entire body from the inside out. Idiot. Fucking idiot. The face vanished, replaced by the smiling visage of Charles Xavier, his long fingers holding out the golden fruit.

"Take it my friend. Taste it. So sweet. You'll see. So sweet."

Ted slammed his open palm against the metal of the door. It echoed dully within the hidden confines of the mercantile. Ted waited, listening, his ear close to the blockaded portal. Nothing. No sound. Just the creak of the gommier trees swaying in the wind. Back and forth. Low groan then high creak. Back and forth. Wait. Was that a sound? It sounded like slow and steady breathing, the respirations of a man trying to remain as quiet as possible. The inhales and exhales of a man trying to listen as keenly as he could. Ted held his breath and knocked lightly on the door. The breathing stopped.

"Avery, is that you? Id? It's me. Ted. I just want a beer."

Nothing. Silence, just the wind. The breathing started once again. Id was always left behind. The guard dog. Why take a guard dog away from what it was supposed to be guarding? Ted could imagine the tall man with the nervous gestures leaning up against the other side of the door, doing his best not to move a single part of his body. Listening. His ears filled with the sound of his own pumping heart. Waiting. Sweating. Arms wrapped around himself. Hands kneading his biceps. Eyes round with fear and worry. What the hell

was Ted doing? Scaring the shit out of a mentally handicapped man.
Making demands that no one in Titou ever would. The mercantile was
closed. That was that. He'd been given warning. He had no excuse.
Idiot. Just a fucking idiot. Ted leaned in close and whispered into the
crack of the door.

"I'm sorry Avery. I'm sorry. I hope you have a good day."

Ted backed away from the door. He walked around the side and
put his back against the smooth bark of one of the gommier trees. The
whole world seemed to rock in a steady rhythm. How windy was it
where the trees touched the sky? Ted let himself fall until he was
sitting down. His hand traced across the dirt, picked up several rocks,
and threw them towards the road. The feeling of a hand on his. Rough
and calloused. Familiar, but different. Sandi's hands had been soft
and smooth. Ted doubted she had ever done a bit of hard work in her
life. She had always floated, a phantasm able to connect and
disconnect with the world around her at will. Brown eyes. Open
wide. Taking it all in. The eyes are the windows to the soul. Blue
eyes. The shutters closed. It was nothing, just a friendly gesture.
Different things meant different things to different people. He was
being foolish. You couldn't read another's mind. Wasn't that the
lesson he had learned before? Look at the world as it is, not as you
would want it to be.

The world was slowly draining of all its color. It was noticeable,
even in the short time since he had left the shelter of his house. Men
and women were walking up the road. Workers from the banana
plantation. It was unusual. It was still too early. The day wasn't
done. The shift wasn't over. The men and women moved in knots and
alone, silent and brooding, chatting and laughing, smiling, nodding,
and frowning. All of it was cut by an underlying current of animalistic
attention. Be ready. Be prepared. Something is out of the ordinary.
Something is going to happen. Some of the men glanced at him as
they passed. Quick. Furtive. A few openly stared, their faces blank as
always. Ted got up and walked to the edge of the road. The men and
women were pouring out of the plantation gate. A solid dark mass
breaking apart, up the road through Titou, down the road towards
Helston, splitting off on paths to villages and houses hidden away in
the forest. The crowd was charged with electricity. Ted could feel the

static moving between his skin and his clothing, raising the hair on his body.

A knot of men around his own age stood just a bit up the road from the plantation gate, passing two large beer bottles around their circle. One Ted recognized from around town, a familiar face on a stranger. The rest were sons of farmers, men of the mountainside above Titou. Ted knew them from the paths they took to familiar terrace filled clearings that looked all the same. Amongst them was Eugene Hewitt. He was laughing and smiling as he spoke, gesturing aggressively with his hands, spilling precious dollops of beer on the ground to the admonishment of his fellows. Eugene passed the beer and looked over, his eyes catching hold of Ted. He smiled. A wide grin punctured by a few missing teeth. Eugene raised his arm and waved. Ted fought back the unconscious need to look behind him to verify he was the intended recipient. He bent his face into a halfhearted approximation of a smile to hide the worries, and raised his own in return. Eugene motioned for Ted to join them. The other men kept their faces blank except for two. The man from town raised his eyebrows and a short wiry man with bulging eyes frowned. Bug Eyes hissed at Eugene, his voice just loud enough to overcome the wind.

"You stakki Eugene? Not the fucking jake."

Eugene ignored the other man. His smile stayed wide, drawing Ted further in. When Ted reached them he grabbed Ted's hand and gave it a good hard shake.

"The man from Udaho. How you doing?"

Ted tried kept a friendly smile on his face, but he couldn't help but notice that he wasn't exactly welcome. Bug Eyes was openly scowling, his unnaturally broad shoulders for his frame visibly clenching. The man from town and another, both wearing khaki shirts, avoided looking him in the eye. The final man, a pudgy figure in a Buffalo Bills shirt kept laughing into his hand. Ted could feel the sweat beneath his arms. His inner thigh itched, too close to his balls for him to scratch.

"It's actually Idaho."

Eugene took one of the beer bottles and took a drink.

"I know you are, but it's okay, a man has to make a living."

Eugene laughed and slapped Ted on the back. Buffalo Bill laughed with him, though still into his hand. The man from town and his fellow khaki wearer grinned at the ground. Bug Eyes kept scowling. Ted managed a nervous chuckle. He took a quick breath and let it out, focusing on Eugene as the friendliest of the group.

"Getting off work early?"

Eugene spread his hand towards the dark clouds in the sky.

"Hurricane man. The bosses in all their wisdom are letting us go home before the hurricane."

Buffalo Bill took his hand away from his mouth. His face turned serious.

"I heard it's going to be a cat three. Got the bosses all kinds of nervous. They took the trucks down."

Bug Eyes scowled and spit.

"Bunch of fuckery. The bunch of jackets just wanted to get home to Helston early to make sure no grindsman is getting their ladies. The big jakes ain't going to like it."

Buffalo Bill grinned.

"Nothing but batty washing sketels in Helston."

Bug Eyes rolled his eyes.

"How the fuck would you know?"

The man from town cut in. He was taller than the others, almost the same height as Ted, but skinny to the point of gauntness with long arms and legs.

"I heard it may be a cat four or more."

Bug Eyes drank from one of the bottles and spit again.

"Where the hell you hearing such fuckery Eliud?"

"From Crispin. He heard it from his sister in the office."

"Crispin is a stakki and his bleachface sketel sister gives all the bosses cocky kisses."

Buffalo Bill cut in.

"It's hard to know the weather when you always got your eyes on your work."

Bug Eyes and Eugene chuckled, but Eliud pressed on.

"Maybe that's when she heard it?"

Buffalo Bill let loose with a derisive snort.

"Oh yeah, I'm always talking about the weather when I have a mouth on my buddy."

The whole circle laughed, even Eliud, though his was more controlled than the rest. Ted laughed too, though mostly just to fit in. He was having trouble following the conversation. Most people he dealt with were always careful to avoid using slang in front of him. They always spoke precisely and slowly, as though he was some kind of an idiot. Eugene took a drink from one of the bottles and gestured with it.

"If it's a cat four, going to be bad news down low."

Eugene passed the beer bottle to Ted. Bug Eyes gave him a dirty look. Ted thought about wiping the mouth of the bottle, thought better of it, and took a drink. Buffalo Bill looked thoughtfully down the road.

"Really tear shit up down there if it's that bad."

Bug Eyes sneered.

"Fuck those lows. Fuck them right in the ass."

The circle fell quiet. Ted tried to hand the bottle to Eliud, but he wouldn't take it. Ted passed it back to Eugene who took a drink and tried to pass it to the still silent man in the khaki. The man stared at it a bit, looked at Ted, chewed his lower lip, and raised his hands, signaling he didn't need it. Eugene shrugged and finished the beer. A gust of wind bent the two gommier trees by the mercantile. Two men slid the plantation gate shut. They locked it with a click and then started walking down the road towards Helston. Distant thunder rolled across the heavens. A few fat drops fell from the sky. Eugene threw his beer bottle into the bushes.

"Looks like it's about time to get going."

The man in the Buffalo Bill's shirt looked up at the sky.

"Probably be a bit yet."

Eliud finished the last of the other beer.

"Supposed to be sometime tonight."

"More cocky kiss rumors?"

"No. Mr.Green."

Bug Eyes rolled his oversized peepers.

"That old jacket, marching around like he's Queen Lizzie's corgi."

Buffalo Bill and the silent man chuckled. Eugene turned to go. "I need to help the old man get the farm ready."

The other men nodded. Eliud broke away towards town, and as a mass the others began moving up the road. Only Eugene bothered to wave goodbye. Ted watched them move up the hillside until they became lost in the thickness of the forest. A large raindrop hit his nose. There was no reason to stand about. Best to head back towards home.

It was there again, that strange fearful thrill of anticipation. A little boy waiting in line for his first rollercoaster ride. The people of Titou didn't seem panicked. They didn't seem worried. They moved at the same slow steady pace that they always worked at, moving things into their houses or standing in groups to gossip with neighbors. None looked concerned. Every now and again one would look upwards at the thick gray clouds in the sky, but that was all.

Mr. Green was sitting on his porch, gently twisting the dial of his radio from point to point. Nothing but static came from the speaker. Sometimes soft. Sometimes loud. Occasionally popping in rhythm with a distant roll of thunder. Ted stood there for a moment, waiting to see if Mr. Green would look at him, but he didn't. All of his attention was focused on the radio.

Ted unlocked his door and walked into his house. He shut the door behind him. It was dark inside though it was no later than mid-afternoon. The rum bottle still sat on the counter. Ted picked it up, held it for a moment, and put it back down. He opened the fridge and looked in. He closed it again. He walked over, pulled the mosquito netting aside, and sat down on the edge of his cot. His sleep sack was half open, the patriotic color combination of the interior out for all the world to see. It had been a gift from his mother. Anxious eyes over a loving smile. Ted grabbed the top of the sack and pulled it closed. He drummed his hands on his knees. He looked around his house. It didn't take long. The shed. Had he remembered to lock the shed? Ted got up, unlocked his back door, and went outside.

Camilla was sitting against her house, her back against the wall just below the back window. She had a chicken in her lap, one of the runty island chickens that ran wild through the village, their eggs the property of any who could find the birds' hidden caches. She was stroking the chicken in the same way that Ted would've stroked a cat, from the red of its crop to the tips of its black tail feathers. The chicken was clucking to itself contentedly. Camilla raised her head. She raised her hand. Ted waved back, an unconscious jerk of the arm, a puppet controlled by strings of his parent's years of lessons on the importance of returning signs of greetings. Camilla gestured for him to come over. Ted did as he was bid. The frightened thrill growing in his chest with every step. She patted the ground next to her. Ted sat, and leaned back against the yellow wall of the house. They sat there, just the sound of the chicken. When she spoke, her voice was honey.

"How was the beer?"

Ted stared at the chicken in her arms.

"The mercantile was closed."

Camilla nodded, showing no signs of judgments of Ted's error.

"If you wanted a beer all you had to do was ask. Charles Xavier has some in the fridge."

Ted moved his gaze to his booted feet. There was a lump in his throat. He licked his dry lips and swallowed it back down.

"It wouldn't seem right to take his beer."

Camilla chuckled softly to herself.

"It won't hurt him to share."

The gray clouds moved by overhead, thicker and blacker than they had been earlier. Ted dried his hands on his jeans. Thoughts rose unbidden, speculations that he banished before they could take root and grow. Gestured up above them.

"I heard it might be cat four."

Camilla didn't raise her eyes, preferring to keep them to the chicken.

"What's going to happen will happen. It's a little late to start worrying about it now."

The silence descended again. Thunder sounded in the distance. The creeping fingers took hold, green shoots pushed upward into the light. An image formed in his mind. A storm wracked mountainside. Two figures in the rain. Ted holding her close, murmuring comforting words, their lips moving together.

Ted shifted back to the exterior world. He stared down at the chicken in Camilla's arms. He watched her hands smooth the feathers.

He reached out a hand. The sharp beak shot forward, pecking him on the hand, forcing him quickly back. Camilla laughed and winked. One hand clasped the chicken on the back, and the other waggled a finger in front of its face, similar to a mother lecturing a naughty child. With a sudden movement she flipped the chicken onto its back and held it there, gently stroking its sternum with the spread of her thumb and index finger. The chicken struggled at first, but then its head fell back and it went still. The chicken looked dead.

Camilla wiggled its curled up legs and giggled like a little girl. She raised her eyes to Ted, gazing through hooded lashes, and smiled coyly. Ted felt his lips move upwards in response. Camilla reached over and placed her hand on top of his, rubbing her thumb across the sore spot where the chicken had pecked him. Ted felt the surge of blood through his body, his entire being growing stiff and unwieldy. She didn't move her hands. Doubts rose and fell in never ending waves. Two figures moved closer together. Charles Xavier was holding out the half of papaya, smiling and gesturing for him to take it. The taste sweet, oh so sweet. No, it was nothing but fantasy, but still her hand lingered.

Mr. Green's door opened. Ted jerked his hand out from underneath Camilla's. The old man glanced over, paused for a moment, and then moved to close the shutters on his house, grumbling as he did. Ted rose and mumbled a goodbye. He walked with unsteady steps back towards his own house. At the door he paused and looked back. Camilla was still sitting on the ground, her eyes following him, her mouth set in a straight line. He turned back to find Mr. Green watching him with narrowed eyes.

"Anji's whipping herself up into a frenzy, Mr. Nelson."

Ted stood there, unsure what to say. There was a hard and growing knot in his gut. His head was spinning, though he told himself it was just because he had gotten up too fast.

"Any advice for how to get ready Mr. Green?"

Mr. Green's field of view traced its way over Ted and then his house.

"Get H.G. Wells to let you borrow his time machine and go back a month to get better prepared."

The rock in Ted's stomach plummeted into his intestines. Mr. Green grunted, turned, and walked back into his house. Ted looked back over at Camilla. She wasn't paying him any mind. In her lap, her hand was gently supporting the lolling head of the hypnotized chicken, her fingers unconsciously and lovingly stroking the helpless form in her arms.

Ted went into his house and shut the door. He felt the sharp taste of panic in the back of his throat. He forced it back down. He couldn't seem to get himself to focus. He could hear the wind moving through the trees outside. The rum bottle sat on the counter, but he refused to walk over to it. Instead he walked over to his cot and sat down. He studied the world around him, unsure of what to do. Time passed. How much time had passed? He was unsure. The whole world felt unsure, a strange place bathed in gray twilight. He felt tired. His mind exhausted. He slumped over and laid down. He shivered a little. He unzipped his sleep sack and pulled it partly over himself. His eyelids dipped, sprung open, and dipped again. The world disappeared, replaced by an unknowing bliss.

Chapter 8

Yellowstone. Geysers. Wildlife. A line of cars moved in a row down a strip of blacktop lit by flickering sunlight forcing its way through the trees. Independent entities joined by timing. A tribe built by a thousand choices leading to one single moment. She sat on the seat next to him. A supple finger, with its nail painted bright pink, pushed a lock of blonde hair that had escaped her ponytail back behind an ear. The further of her two tanned legs was propped up on the dash. One of his hands rested on the steering wheel, the other on her closer leg, his fingers softly stroking her inner thigh. The car came to a clearing.

His foot moved to the brake, easing the car to a halt. The line of cars behind slowed and stopped as well. Tourists piled out, cameras at the ready, hands shading eyes which probe the scenery for the fantastic beasts that are not there. They must be there. Why else would the car ahead of them stop? His foot moved back to the gas pedal. The car started moving forward. Disappointed tourists returned to their cars, though a few of the more stubborn continued to scour the tree line, refusing to give up hope. He laughed. She rolled her eyes and turned away. He could see the hint of a smile at the corner of her mouth. He gave her inner thigh a little squeeze. She turned back and kissed him on the neck. She started at the neckline of his shirt and moved her way up to his ear. Her voice was a husky whisper.

"You are such an asshole."

He smiled.

"I know."

Her hand moved onto his lap and squeezed him through his jeans. He breathed in deep and let it out, inhaling the scent of her shampoo. The first of the cars left behind caught up. She pulled back to her side

of the car. His fingers worked their way up to the hem of her shorts.
She pushed his hand back down. Her smile is coy. Her eyes hungry.

"Soon."

Someone was knocking at the door. Not just one knock, but a
thousand. A never ending litany of staccato taps, rising and dropping
in force with the heavy breathing of the outside world, separating and
melting together with random rhythm. It wasn't just the door. The
multitude crowding around the house was knocking on the windows
and on the walls, even on the tin of the roof. Thousands of irate
woodpeckers, desperately trying to break their way in, their frantic
efforts played over an underlying gurgling and an unending static,
ranging from the terrifying moan of the banshee to the roar of a 747
taking off right over one's head. Mother nature was angry. Her fury
had been unleashed.

Ted sat bolt upright on his cot, tangling himself in the mosquito
netting. He wrestled with it, ripping the entangling gossamer from the
hooks that held it to the ceiling, madly pulling the snaring spider web
from his skin. The wind roared and the roof of the house shook. The
front and back doors wobbled in their frames. The bitch was trying to
work her way in. She was trying to get a finger into a crack, gain
some leverage, tear the house to shreds. Everything was dark. The
world was gloom and shadow. Ted pulled the loose sleep sack more
tightly around himself. His heart was beating like mad. The wind rose
with sudden ferocity. The whole house seemed to shake. Ted rose to
his feet, his sleep sack still wrapped around him, and moved to the
front window. A world of fog and mist. Ted wiped the window clear
with his arm, the moisture clammy against his skin, revealing a never
ending opaque wall of water continuously supplied by rapidly falling
rampant drops the size of his thumb. The lights of Titou rippled
through the liquid wall.

Ted was sweating. His shirt and pants were soaked. He could
feel the cold drops snaking their way down beneath his clothes,
hugging his body to avoid the halting folds of fabric. Icy highways
down his spine and inner thighs. Trapped. Besieged by the awesome
forces of nature. The ominous growl of the inhale. The awesome roar
of exhale. Growing with every round. A rising tide of Gaia's hate for
those who dared to soil her kingdom. All sinners collapse to your

knees, for the end of the world has come, and you have been found wanting. The monster screamed and the whole house shook again. The roof rose up and slammed back down with a metallic snap. Water dripped to the floor below. Ted's world creaked, but would not give in. The house of cinderblocks was built like a bunker. It was built to keep the beast at bay. Loud cracks sounded in the distance, the colossus snapping trees like matchsticks between its claws.

Ted leaned closer to the window, trying to discern shapes through the watery film. Greenery and branches rode the maelstrom. Sheets of tin and pieces of wood from less well built sanctuaries violently floated upon the stratospheric sea. The dark shape of a house collapsed beneath the onslaught. A figure ran through the night, seeking shelter. The bellow rose to a fever pitch. The figure was lifted into the air and thrown twenty feet into the underbrush. In a single blink the world disappeared. The lights of Titou cut to black. The sound of breaking glass. Ted jerked himself back from the window. Fool. Fucking idiot. What was he doing? What was he thinking? Ted cowered in the center of the house, unsure what to do, using every bit of his will to fight back against the growing panic. It wasn't supposed to be this terrifying. No one had seemed worried.

The wind backed up and threw itself forward with the power of a battering ram. The front door flew open, unleashing a wall of pixelated water which soaked Ted's sleep sack. The door hit the table with an intense thunderclap. Alone. Completely alone. Madness. The world was descending into a chaotic hell. Lucifer had broken his restraints. He had to get out. He had to escape. Ted tried to close the door, but the wind ripped it from his fingers and it swung back into the table with a bang. It was inside the house. An arch of dark moisture covered the concrete floor, spreading its way further in. Rapid heart. Eyes unable to focus. Panic. The back window shattered, covering his cot with splintered diamonds, a branch sticking halfway through. He had to get out. He had to get fucking out. People. He needed other people, other souls to anchor him with reality.

The wind roared again and fell back. The sleep sack fell to the floor in a sodden heap. Ted found himself outside, wet as a drowned rat, the moisture hiding his snot and tears, small particles whipping him into submission. He hugged the wall of his broken fortress, moving towards the corner, each step as quick as he could make it, trying to cover the distance before a demonic hand swept him away. A torrent of water raced between the houses, collected into an artificial canyon. Ted stepped into the water. It was knee deep. The strength of the flow swept his feet out from under him and filled his boots with mud. Ted's fingers scrabbled for purchase and caught the post supporting the porch of the yellow house next door. His mouth and eyes filled with water and mud. He pulled with all his strength, dragging himself from the current, extracting himself onto the porch. The wind howled and fell back. Ted rose and raced across the porch. He pulled open the door, entered, and slammed it closed before the maelstrom could rip it from his fingers.

The house was dark. The furniture was in disarray. Table, chairs, an old style ornate dresser, and a big queen sized bed, covered by a mosquito net hanging from above. Ted's hair was plastered to his head. His sodden clothes hung from his frame. His chest rose and fell with rapid shallow breaths. Water fell from his body onto the concrete floor. Muddy footprints trailed his route from madness. With the door closed the bellow of the beast seemed muted. Camilla stood next to the kitchen counter, a carving knife in hand, her eyes narrowed, her body tense and ready to spring. Charles Xavier was nowhere to be seen. Her eyes widened when she recognized her intruder. The knife dropped into the sink. She took a step forward. Ted fell into her arms. Hugging her tight. Soaking her dress. His body convulsed with sobs. Camilla held him, rocking him, whispering unheard comforts into his ear.

Ted collapsed and she went down with him. She drew back and shook him. Her hand flashed and slapped him across the face. She began shaking him again, her mouth moving in silent admonitions, her lips repeatedly forming the same word again and again. Stupid. Stupid. Stupid. She pulled him close again, his head resting on her bosom, drinking in her warmth and comfort. She held him for a moment, protecting him as a mother does a son, until the snap of a falling tree spurred her back into action. She stood and yelled something at him, but he couldn't hear over the cries of the demons outside. She yelled again, her face filled with impatience and frustration. Ted felt the distance growing and wished she would take him in her arms again. Camilla huffed and proceeded to try and drag her refrigerator towards the back door. Ted watched her in confusion. The woman rocked the fridge from side to side. Ted rose to his feet to help.

The fridge was heavy. Together they walked it across the house and pushed it firmly against the back door. Camilla motioned at Ted and moved to the big bed covered in thin blankets. She ripped the mosquito netting down, tossed the blankets to the floor, and started scooting the bed towards the back door. Ted did his best to help. After the bed they moved the dresser, then the table, then the chairs. All of it pushed and thrown onto the growing barricade. When nothing remained, she pulled Ted to the center of the floor, pushed him down, followed, and wrapped them in the blankets. It was hot underneath. Ted tried to pull them off, but Camilla slapped him again, not hard, just enough to get his attention. She motioned for him to stay put. The house vibrated with the power of the storm. An electrical current running through their bodies.

The wind screamed with the energy of countless tormented souls in the bowels of hell. The pair sat in darkness. Two children, scared of the dark, believing themselves safe in their enveloping sanctuary of cotton. The doors shook. The windows rattled. Ted's breathing was deep and rapid. He was drowning. He couldn't get enough air. His whole body was shaking, every single one of his hairs pulling away from his body. Camilla's hand moved over and covered his. An electric shock flashed in the darkness. Her breathing was slow and easy. In. Out. In. Out. A metronome running counter to the rapid beat of his heart and the outside world. She wasn't scared. She wasn't worried. She was just waiting. Waiting for the storm to end. Ted's body quit shaking. His breathing slowed until it matched hers, forming a pocket of tranquility in a world of chaos.

The beast outside shrieked its fury at being ignored. Its barbed fist flung a branch with all its might. The front window shattered. Glass sprayed across the room, covering the floor and the two recumbent figures beneath their protective layers. Ted's entire body jumped. Camilla's hand tightened around his, pulling him back from the edge. His breathing slowed again, his heartbeat moderating itself to the tempo of her pulse. Where was Charles Xavier? How could he leave Camilla alone? Helston. He must not have returned from his route. The crazy bastard. Ted hoped he was okay. What if he had gotten caught out in the open? What if he was pinned somewhere underneath a tree? Dying. Alone. Ted tried not to picture it. Trapped. Unmoving. Camilla's hand squeezed his again. Her hand was rough and calloused, the palms dry. His own were soaked with sweat.

The behemoth lifted its bulk further up the mountain, trying to bring its full weight to bear down on the insignificant island, to crush the impediment, to grind it back down into the sea. A rumbling sound moved its way into existence, rising from a feeling to the range of human hearing. It grew in volume, intruding upon the noise of the howling wind and lashing rain. The ground began to shake, the last sturdy portion of the world giving in to the madness of Anji's fury. It was coming. It was coming down the mountain. Charging horseman bearing down with their spears levelled for the killing thrust. Closer. Rapidly closer. All other sounds fell away. The titan in the heavens became secondary to the one assaulting its way along the ground. It was nearly on top of the house.

Ted screamed and tried to leap away. Camilla tackled him, wrapping him firmly with her arms and legs. Their bodies lay half out of the blankets, sharp edged glittering diamonds scattered all around them. He could feel her hot breath on the back of his neck, smelling of cinnamon. Tears ran down his cheeks. He was desperate to escape, desperate to be held, praying for it all to end. A thunderclap sounded, loud enough to make his ears ring. The house shook as though it had been built on a foundation of Jello. The back window shattered. An errant piece of glass sliced its way across Ted's arm, leaving a shallow gash that quickly filled with blood. The bottom half of the back wall seemed to move forward half an inch. The bolt of the back door snapped and the door came part way open, pushing back the barricade of everything Camilla and Charles Xavier owned. A slurry of mud and water flowed in, grew tired, and went still. The rumble of the terror moved on down the mountain, expending its terrible energy, fading into nothing.

The tones of the wind and rain rose back to prominence, but seemed less than what they had once been. People were yelling outside. Sudden rising peaks that fell back beneath the storm. The man and the woman lay on the debris covered floor, careful not to move lest they cut themselves on unseen jagged edges. The man lay with his arms up over his head, dripping blood from his wound, hiding himself from the outside world. The woman was tight to his back, her face pressed up against the hair on the back of his head. They lay there, waiting, breathing as one, two hearts beating together, working in tandem. He screamed and cried and she pretended not to notice. She was strong, so he didn't need to be. A muddy rivulet of water flowed past them, making its way from the back door and pooling near the front. They lay there, waiting, time meaningless.

The long limb of the monster raked its talons across the island, but the winds were moving it more distant. Each blow was less than the one before. The hateful roar dissolved into a plaintive cry of pain. The rain went from a barrage to a thorough pelting to a gentle massage upon the wounded earth. The dark clouds lightened and broke apart, allowing morning sun to poke its way through. Neither of the castaways in the red house noticed the end of the assault. They both laid in slumber, exhausted from the battle.

Chapter 9

A bird landed on the rear empty window frame and sang a cheerful tune. Ted opened his eyes and gazed out at a world transformed. Glass glinted across the floor. A tiny stream of water, a Nile for ants, worked its way across the concrete. Sunshine flowed in, raw and unfiltered. He lifted himself up on one arm. Broken shards fell from the blanket to the ground. His movement woke the woman beside him. She sat up and surveyed with the eyes of a newborn, her lips compressed. They stood as one, the blanket sloughing off their forms, unleashing a wave of glass which shattered on the concrete. Ted turned in a slow circle. Four walls and a roof. The basic structure was still intact. Camilla examined the cut on his arm. There was dry blood around it, but it had already scabbed over. Finding nothing but a superficial wound, she bent to examine several small cuts on her legs. The two of them were dirty and beaten, but still alive.

A pair of sneakers sat by the front door. Ted stepped with impunity, the thick rubber soles of his work boots grinding the glass beneath them. He brought the sneakers back to Camilla. They were too large. They belonged to Charles Xavier. Camilla hardly ever wore shoes, just a nice pair of flats for formal events or the occasional trip to Helston. She pulled on the sneakers, one hand on Ted's shoulder for balance, and pulled the laces as tight as she could. She ventured forth carefully to the sink and tried the tap. Nothing. Ted pulled the concealing curtain away from the toilet. The bowl was empty. He jiggled the handle. Nothing. Camilla moved to the front door and flicked the light switch next to it. Ted's house only had a string. It was a strange thought to pop up at such a time. The click of the mechanism was uncharacteristically loud, but the solitary bulb stayed dark.

The bird let out another burst of song and then winged away into an overcast sky. Ted walked over to the window. High overhead the clouds were still moving at a rapid pace, but down below the air was still. Things were not as they once were. Where once had been a garden there was now red mud piled up to just below the window sill. The wall of greenery had been pushed back another ten feet or more. Resilient giants still stood, holding back their fallen comrades, but the underbrush had been completely swept away, with only hints of fading life scattered and half buried in the mud. The slope was an open red wound which gaped wider as Ted's eyes tracked from left to right, rivulets of blood seeping through cuts and channels. The last remains of a wall of water, still desperately seeking the lowest point. The devastation crawled up the mountainside, broken survivors growing thicker the higher he looked. The world shifting from red to green. Trees had been snapped off at different heights, broken bones thrust through rent flesh. The signs of life were strewn across the landscape. Steam rose from puddles and oversaturated soil. There was nothing in view that had not been scarred by the horrors of the night before.

Ted turned away, back to the interior world. Camilla had gotten out her broom and was sweeping the broken glass into a pile. Her head was down, her movements calm and measured. The glass scraped across the floor with each pull of the broom. Ted started laughing. He couldn't stop himself. A loud burst of half madness and half relief that lifted itself upwards from his center and bent him over, his hands on his knees. A wild eyed ejaculation of survival. Camilla looked at him, worry in her eyes giving way to her own insanity, a charming glint and a smile which creased her features. She motioned with the broom at the ground.

"We have to start somewhere."

Ted laughed again and Camilla laughed with him. Two crazed souls washed up on an unknown beach. Unsure, but alive. Camilla went back to her sweeping. Ted tried to help by using his boot to kick the glass around him into a pile, but to little effect. The shards just broke into smaller pieces. He stopped and gazed downward at his failure.

"Should've put some tape on the windows."

Camilla didn't look up to answer.

"Too late for that."

Ted bit his lip. He walked across the broken glass and gazed out the front window where tiny jagged chunks sat like rodent teeth in the frame. Titou was in ruin. A shattered place half hidden by rising mists. The world below was a red one, the gardens and grasses of the clearing, lacking the protection of the trees, battered down to nothing by the fierceness of the rain and wind. Debris both manmade and natural filled the world. Branches, palms, broken boards, tin roofing and siding. The houses made of cinderblocks still stood, bunkers amongst the destruction, though some were missing portions of their roofs. The same could not be said of the houses of wood and tin, little better than shacks. A few still stood, but most were in some state of collapse. One leaned severely toward the downhill side. Others were little better than piles of wreckage. A few of the power poles were broken, but most still stood, the lines between them sagging or in places lying upon the ground.

Ghosts moved amongst the ruins, cloaked in silence as they wandered, dirty shapes which stood about or drifted as they would. They stood with blank eyes, some digging through the ruins of what had once been homes, others sitting and waiting for the world to make sense once again. There were signs of injury here and there. A wrapped head, a bandage, and even one older man with an arm in a sling made from the ripped remains of a flowered sheet. Their silence was unnerving. Nobody called out. Nobody screamed. At most there might have been mumbling by a few in tight knit groups, but little of it carried its way upward. They were dead to the world, roused only by the occasional stronger gust of wind which raised their weary heads in sudden animalistic panic, before fading back to nothing. They were specters of a world now past. Memories of a place that had once been. They shambled across the landscape, the walking dead.

Ted let his gaze track across what had once been the town. To the right the gravel road still stood out, a gray line cutting through the red. The gate and chain link fence of the banana plantation still stood defiant, though a large palm tree had fallen across a section, ripping a hole in the barrier. The interior of the fence had proven less sturdy. Where once banana trees had stood in straight rows marching out of sight around the hillside, now half their number were slaughtered.

Mangled remains lay in the dirt. Others still stood, though all signs of life had been stripped from the trunks. To the left was the scar of the landslide. The onslaught of water had made its way throughout the town, but only to the left had the earth fully given way, a wall of mud rushing downward. It was lucky. The slide had almost completely missed the town, only a few houses on the edge partially buried. It had swept along the edge, more liquid than solid, before swinging back in toward the natural bowl of the landscape, inward toward the mercantile.

The bastion of Malik's power had been hit hard. His pride, the two mighty gommier trees, had fallen, smashing their way through the metal roof and stout cinderblock walls. The mudslide had hit full force, flowing into the breach and turning the ruin into a quagmire, the interior and exterior worlds mixed into a morass of waste and loss. The remains of the roof stretched upward from the ground toward the far corner where the walls remained solid. The tall metal tower still stood, the antenna gone, likely blown away, but the structure itself still jutting into the sky like a defiant middle finger.

The scrape of the broom pushing glass ceased. Ted turned and looked over his shoulder. Camilla was staring at nothing, listening. Ted took a step toward her.

"What is it?"

Camilla motioned for him to be quiet. Ted looked back towards the outside world. Camilla leaned her broom against the wall, yanked open the front door, and marched outside. Ted waited for a moment, unsure, and then followed her, careful to close the door behind them. Camilla moved rapidly up the road leading further up the mountain, careful to avoid the deep water filled ruts, her oversized shoes squelching with every step. Ted did his best to keep up, slipping in the mud, going down on one knee, his legs and hands taking on an earthy reddish hue. Camilla pulled herself over fallen trees with ease. Ted rolled in the muck like a pig, his body growing stiffer with each tumble. Amongst the trees the steam thickened, a choking sauna with no exit. Camilla's rapidly moving form kept disappearing from view.

Ted fell again, sitting in the mud, staying down this time to catch his breath. He could hear her footsteps splashing as they receded. Someone yelled in the distance. A weak plaintive cry of a wounded animal, communicating its pain and suffering without words. For a moment Ted thought it was nothing but the wind, but the sound rose again, this time breaking down into haggard sobs which were unmistakable. Ted forced himself up and started climbing again. He did his best to run up the hill, stilted leaps throwing himself forward. The road narrowed into the path. Camilla squatted in the mud next to a fallen gommier tree, her fingers scraping mud off of an object in her lap. It was a man. A filthy wretched man beneath the weight of the trunk, with only his head and one arm still free. It was Eugene Hewitt. The young man's eyes were red rimmed and scared, his breathing quick and ragged. His face was covered in blood, a mixture of dull dark red slowly crusting over and bright new crimson. Ted stood over them, his mouth agape. Camilla's hands were bloody too. Ted kneeled down beside her. She looked at Ted, her features set tight, every movement under her direct control.

"Go get help."

Ted nodded, but didn't move. Camilla grabbed his wrist, her thumb pushing into his palm. The blood on her hands smeared onto him. He couldn't stop staring at it. The stickiness of it made him feel ill.

"Go get help."

She flung him away with both her arm and voice. Ted rose and bolted back down the road as fast as his feet could take him, half running, half sliding. In Titou people stood in sullen groups, family and friends, some talking amongst themselves, others staring at nothing. Their guard was down and all of their emotions were seeping through. How could this have happened? They said it wasn't going to be this big. They'd promised we were going to be all right. What are we supposed to do now? We've lost everything. Their eyes followed him as he moved down the hill. Empty eyes watching. Ted stopped. Mumbling. Incoherent words. Fucking jake. What's he so upset about? They said it was only going to be a small one. It wasn't supposed to be this bad. They lied to us. They wanted this to happen. Not one face looked friendly. A few seemed openly hostile. Ted felt strangely guilty as though he had been the one to incorrectly guess the storm's strength.

Mr. Green was sitting on the edge of his porch. His clothes were clean, but he was bleeding from several small cuts on his arms. Ted turned and jogged over to him. The old man was staring at his feet, not moving.

"Mr. Green?"

Ted tapped him on the shoulder. No response.

"Mr. Green, I need help. Eugene Hewitt is trapped under a tree where the road turns into the path. I think he's dying."

Mr. Green looked up at Ted. His eyes were bright red in a puffy face. The two men stared at each other. Mr. Green went back to looking at his hands, studying every crease and line. Tears fell down Ted's cheeks. He reached down, grabbed Mr. Green by the arm, and wrenched the old man to his feet. Dead weight. Mr. Green would not stand. The moment Ted let go he fell back down into a sitting position on the ground. A formless lump. Ted turned back towards the people of Titou. They stood watching, waiting, their eyes fixed on the inert form.

"God damn you! He's hurt! He needs help!"

Ted's scream echoed in the silence. He looked back up the mountainside. Camilla was carefully picking her way back down the road. Ted ran to meet her. The people returned to their own little worlds, trapped by their inability to accept the change around them. The bottom half of Camilla's dress was covered in mud. She was pulling herself across the last tree when Ted reached her.

"Eugene?"

Camilla shook her head. Ted's legs went out from under him. He sat in the mud, his back against the tree trunk. Camilla continued down and joined a circle of people. She spoke to them calmly, gesturing back up the road. A group of four men broke off and started up, one pausing long enough to go into a house and grab a sheet. They passed by Ted, climbing over the tree. One of them was one of the plantation workers from the previous day, the one called Eliud. They looked at Ted out of the corner of their eyes. Ted rose and tried to follow, but Camilla took him by the hand and led him back to her house. Ted could feel the stickiness of the drying blood on her hands. Mr. Green had disappeared, gone back inside his own house. Camilla sat Ted on her porch, he let her to do it without a word. She went back inside to finish her sweeping. Knots of people were coming back alive. Groups glanced upwards at him and whispered quietly amongst themselves. Ted stared at the ground to avoid their eyes.

Ted's hand and wrist had blood on them. Eugene's blood. The foreign feel of it made him sick to his stomach. Eugene's bloody face floated in front of his, the mouth open, desperately sucking in air, the eyes unnaturally wide and filled with fear. Ted rose and walked over to the nearest puddle. He scrubbed off the blood in the muddy water. He sat back down. He could feel them watching him. They were moving amongst their own houses, doing what they could, but all watched him, judging him.

Ted got up and went to his own house. The door wouldn't open. He looked in through the broken window. The mudslide had pushed its way through the backdoor and filled the inside. A pile of mud sloping its way upward from the front to the back. Ted climbed down off the porch and found a rock on the ground. It fit comfortably in his palm. He got back up on the porch and used the rock to clear the jagged pieces of glass still in the window frame. He carefully put down the rock and stuck his head in. His table and chairs were pushed tight against the near wall. His cot and sleep sack were down near the cupboards, half buried. He pulled his head back out. He stood on his porch for a moment, unsure what to do. Camilla came outside, looked around, and walked over to him. She led him by the hand back to her own house and had him help her move her furniture back to its correct place. She even plugged back in the refrigerator despite the fact there was no electricity.

Ted could take commands, but had no initiative. Without orders he stood stationary, his brain lacking the spark to create thought. He started shaking. Sweat pooled on his brow and his breathing became deep and ragged. The walls closed in. A tightening embrace that brought both terror and comfort. Camilla took him by the hand gently. Her hands were clean. When had she cleaned her hands? She led him back out to the porch and sat him down. She went inside and brought him back a beer before disappearing into her house once again. Ted took a drink of the beer, an automatic motion. It was warm. His breathing slowed. He sat, watching the world below, but feeling nothing.

The people of Titou were split. Some remained mostly unmoving, still half in their old reality. Others were picking their way through the remains of their belongings, digging through the remains of what had once been their homes and stacked what they found on pieces of corrugated metal siding. The children were the first to fully shake off the effects of Anji. Some of the older ones continued to help their parents, but he younger ones began to run around, splashing in puddles, wrestling in the muck, laughing and screeching. Their mothers, needing time to think, ignored them as best they could, only managing the occasional cuff to get them back in line.

Ted finished his beer and put the bottle down by his feet. He studied his hands, eyes probing every nook and cranny. There were still hints of blood here and there, or maybe it was just mud. Eugene's face floated in front of his. Twisted in pain. Begging for help. Ted got up and washed his hands in the muddy water of the puddle again. Camilla brought him out a banana and something in a bowl with a spoon in it. Ted ate it, not really knowing what it was. He put the banana peel in the bowl and carried it back into the house. Camilla was at the counter, cutting thin chunks off a raw chicken, putting the chunks in a jar. The glass was all swept into the corner by the table, a crystalline pile sparking in the muted light of the indoors. All of the cupboards were open. Ted placed the bowl in the sink and watched Camilla work. Her eyes came up and met his, but her hands never stopped moving.

"Lemon juice. It cooks the meat."

Ted stood in silence, his breathing loud in his ears. Camilla went to the refrigerator, grabbed another warm beer, popped off the top on the edge of the counter, gave it to Ted, and pushed him back outside. Ted took back up his station, sitting on the porch. Scattered fat raindrops fell from above. Skittish people cast worried glances upward. Ted sipped his beer. Two men were trying to start a fire, but everything was too wet. Some people ate meals that required no preparation. Some of the more industrious were using pieces of tin to create lean-tos against the still standing houses. Ted finished the beer and set the empty bottle down next to the other one. He wished he could have another one, but didn't want to ask. He started to study his hands again, but quickly forced himself to look away. People began to emerge from the forest. Small groups here and there, mostly older people, almost no children. Ted recognized them. Men and women from the nearby farms, carrying small bundles in their arms. The newcomers either joined an existing group, or sat apart by themselves.

Ted got up and walked back over to his house. He picked up the rock and used it to smash out the wood of the window frame. He put the rock carefully down again and crawled in through the hole. His eyes searched the darkened interior, searching for something, but unsure or at least unwilling to know what. The rum bottle was sitting on its side in the sink, miraculously unbroken. Ted took the bottle and climbed back through the window. He sat on his porch, unscrewed the cap, and starting sipping the sickly sweet liquor. The bloody face faded from view. The harsh corners of the world were smoothed.

They started coming up one by one. Nervous. Furtive. Determined. They were not coming up to see him. First came Mrs. Seraphin, a cut on one cheek, the roll of her hips still noticeable even in her agitated and nervous movements. She came up, cleaned her hands on her dress, and knocked on Mr. Green's door.

"Mr. Green? Mr. Green, are you okay?"

Her voice was hoarse. Silence. She waited a moment. Knocked again. Waited. Silence. She turned and went back to her own house. Others followed after. Every single one was the same. A knock. A request, some firm, others almost begging. Silence. Mr. Green could be dead for all the sound that came out of his house. Mr. Green's shutters were closed tight, allowing in no prying eyes. Ted watched the hope drain from the eyes of each supplicant, replaced by uncertainty. None of them looked at him as he worked his way into the comforting numbness of inebriation.

The world around him was no longer real. It had been this way before. During the day he would go through the motions, stocking shelves at the grocery store, banned from the registers due to, as the manager called it, his declining people skills. In the evening he'd return home, turning on the television though it was unneeded, at least creating the illusion that he wasn't staring at nothing while he drank, waiting for someone to come though he knew nobody would. The people he had known had been more her friends than his. Without her they had increasingly found little reason to come around.

The day marched its way towards evening. A group of men came down the road, double the number they were going up, carrying something wrapped tightly in a muddy sheet. Amongst their number was Mr. Hewitt, hobbling on a sprained ankle. People rushed to meet them, taking the weight off their shoulders. Camilla came out of her house and hustled over to help. Ted took another drink and did his best to study the worn leather of his work boots. Tears rolled down his cheeks. The face smiled grotesquely. The crowd carried the body into one of the intact houses below. Many went in and the rest milled about outside.

The tired sun, hidden in the overcast sky, began to sink below the ground. A single figure worked its way up the road from the direction of Helston, picking its way over fallen trees and through patches of thick mud. The figure looked tired, but still had a bounce in its step. It stopped for a moment to look at the commotion at the house where they had taken Eugene's body, but didn't join. It kept walking higher up towards Ted. The figure was strangely clean. Charles Xavier sat down on the porch next him, his face glistening as though freshly washed, and smiled.

"Theodore my friend. You look none the worse for wear. Where's Camilla?"

Ted gestured down the hill with the bottle, his voice slurred.

"Eugene's dead."

Charles Xavier's smile fell. His eyes tracked across the mob. People crying. People talking. People milling about. He reached over and took the rum bottle. He drained the last dregs and let the bottle drop with a splat to the ground.

"Well, that's a damn shame."

Ted let his eyes rest for a moment on the people below, but not long. The face of Charles Xavier was a safer place to look.

"Where you been?"

"Helston. Took the whole fucking day to get up here. The road is completely washed out. Had to bushwhack."

"So how long until help arrives?"

"Helston looks worse than this. I really thought old Greenie would have the place whipped into shape by now."

Ted didn't say anything. His eyes had fallen back to the mourners. No relief. What was he doing? Camilla had spent the whole day working. What had he done? Sat around and got drunk. Tears ran down his cheeks.

"I feel terrible."

"What for?"

"I've pretty much just been getting drunk all day."

Charles Xavier nodded with a sympathetic air.

"That'll happen."

"No, I didn't do anything to help."

Charles Xavier picked up the empty rum bottle and rolled it in his hands. His thumb brushed red mud off of the label.

"Did you know this island was originally French?"

"What?"

"It got ceded to the British after some war."

Ted looked at the other man's profile. Charles Xavier's face was completely serious, his eyes locked on the rum bottle label.

"Just imagine, we were so close to all speaking French instead of English."

Ted shook his head to try and clear it.

"What the fuck are you talking about?"

Charles Xavier's face broke into a wide grin.

"Well, it's just my opinion, but I think French sounds a hell of a lot sexier than English, but I guess I'm a bit of a fool always thinking of the possibilities of the past."

The crowd below was breaking up. Dark figures in the twilight. Several were making their way up the hill. One broke into a run. Charles Xavier stood up, took several steps, and stretched his arms out wide.

"There you are woman. I've been waiting for you to notice."

Camilla threw herself into Charles Xavier's arms, tears flowing, kissing his lips, his cheeks, his neck, anything she could reach. Charles Xavier was laughing.

"Calm down now woman. You should know better than to think that even a woman named Anji would keep me from you."

Ted's world was wavering. He scooted himself back and pressed himself against the wall of his house. Camilla and Charles Xavier, tight in each other's arms, walked into their neighboring home. Across the town the people of Titou were bedding down for the night. Some in the ruins of their or their neighbor's homes, and some out in the open, lying on palms or anything else they could find to keep them out of the mud. Blankets were freely shared and those with little huddled close with those who had been spared. Ted sat and watched. He listened to the sounds of Camilla's and Charles Xavier's love making, followed by rapid whispers too low to hear. It sounded like Camilla was doing most of the talking, silent to all but her chosen paramour. The clouds above parted and the stars shined down. Ted slowly drifted off to sleep, repeating a mantra in his mind. Tomorrow. Tomorrow I will do better.

Chapter 10

It was the middle of the night. Ted's head was a prison for vile demons trying to club their way free. The world was black, the stars hidden by the return of overcast skies. He was lying on his back, the rough wood of the porch hard beneath him. A weight lay across his body. A blanket, warm and comforting. One arm was free, cold in the night air. Part of the weight on his chest shifted. Four points of pressure, pushing down and letting up in cycle. Alive. Ted screamed and with his free arm flung the blanket from his body. The weight on his chest lifted, flew through the air, and landed with a thump and an angry squeak. Rats. Loathsome rats. Gnawing. Nibbling. Chewing. Cold claws. Naked tails. Climbing. Seeking. Ted shuddered. The thought made him feel nauseous, or perhaps it was the sudden ninety degree shift in posture. How many of the vile creatures were out there? They had to be out there. The first envoys of the hordes of chaos. The world was spinning. He had to lay back down. Bile rose to the back of his throat. Ted pulled the blanket over his body and head, tucking the edges, forming a cotton cocoon. Fucking rats. How could a man sleep surrounded by god damn rats?

He must have been able to. The hum of many voices filled the air, talking quietly amongst themselves as they moved closer. Awake. Ted was thirsty. He opened his eyes, squeezed them back shut to block out the brightness of the morning, rubbed the grit from the corners, and opened them once again. A crowd of people had gathered. Tired. Despondent. Scared. A decision made, they started working their way up towards the row of houses at the top of the town.

Ted tensed. Him. They were coming for him. The jake. The selfish bastard who had responded to tragedy by getting drunk. They were a dirty ragged group, only about half wore shoes. Eliud and the short man with the bug eyes were in the front. The empty rum bottle lay in the mud, its surface dazzled by the sun. Ted sat up, scooting himself back towards the far corner of his porch. The mob halted, murmuring to itself. Several hands pushed Eliud forward. The man's eyes were unnaturally wide in his head. He took a few breaths, looked back at the waiting mass, turned forward, stepped up, and knocked on Mr. Green's door. The sound reverberated. Nothing happened. The throng commenced to murmuring again, and then fell silent. Eliud knocked on the door again. His voice was strained.

"Mr. Green, could you please come out? We need to talk to you."

The crowd waited with baited breath. Someone kicked a rock which rolled ten feet back down the hillside. Eliud looked lost, more scared boy than man in his mid twenties. The murmuring started again. A flock without its shepherd. What the fuck are we supposed to do now? Maybe we should go to Helston? Shut up, I know what we need to do. Fuck off. Where is the bastard? God damn it. Helston, we ought to walk down to Helston. Eliud knocked on the door again, his voice, almost pleading.

"Mr. Green?"

"What's with all of you harassing our good friend Mr. Green?"

The voice was loud. The murmuring stopped. Charles Xavier was standing on his porch, leaning against the post, his shirt hanging open. Camilla stood in the doorway behind him. Bug Eyes took a step forward and gestured with his hands.

"We're thinking of going down to Helston."

Sounds of assent and derision answered the proclamation. Charles Xavier's eyebrows climbed higher on his head.

"What for?"

Bug Eyes spread his arms wide to encompass the ruins around them. Charles Xavier craned his neck to look down the hill, taking it all in as though noticing the destruction of Titou for the first time.

"And you think Helston will be better?"

Bug Eyes shrugged his shoulders. Charles Xavier waited, letting the silence build before he spoke.

"I was down in Helston. Things there are just as bad as here, maybe worse. I can't imagine it getting much better the further down you go."

Bug Eyes spat on the ground. He opened his mouth, but Charles Xavier beat him to the punch.

"Lot of people here probably couldn't make the trip. Kids. Old ones. What are they supposed to do if you go to Helston?"

Eliud stepped down off of Mr. Green's porch.

"So what are we supposed to do then?"

Charles Xavier smiled.

"Get to work."

The crowd buzzed. Bug Eyes spit again.

"Have you seen this fucking place?"

Camilla came up behind Charles Xavier and gave his shoulder a squeeze. She got up on her tiptoes and whispered in his ear. Charles Xavier clasped her hand on his shoulder with his own.

"We have some dead that need burying. We best get to it."

The crowd nodded and murmured their approval. Bug Eyes scowled, turned, and stalked back down the hill, every muscle in his unnaturally broad shoulders clenched. Charles Xavier watched him go then turned his attention back to the crowd. He clapped his hands and rubbed them together in an exaggerated gesture.

"Well, let's get to work."

The crowd didn't move. Charles Xavier and Camilla moved down the hill towards the mercantile. The crowd followed, Ted rose and trailed along behind.

The building was a wreck. Only the downhill and road facing walls still partially stood, the ruins of the roof sweeping down sharply to where the trees had fallen across the rest. The remains were a chaotic frozen maelstrom of scattered cinderblocks, tin, broken branches, and mud. Charles Xavier walked around the ruin, surveying every nook and cranny carefully while the people waited. Between the roadside wall and the sloping roof was a hollow. Charles Xavier bent down and stuck his head in. He pulled himself inside, disappearing from view for a moment before reappearing. He rose and stretched his back.

"We'll need flashlights. Anybody got any flashlights?"

Children were sent running back towards their houses. Charles Xavier eyed the people in front of him, sizing them up.

"Eliud. Crispin. Just the men for the job."

Eliud stepped forward. The children came running back with the flashlights. Charles Xavier handed one to Eliud. Crispin held back. He was a small man, bird like in stature, his movements nervous. Charles Xavier gestured at him with one of the flashlights.

"C'mon now Crispin, your brain not sparking?"

"Why do I have to go in there? I don't want to go in there."

Ted pushed his way through the crowd and stepped forward. He raised his hand.

"I'll go in."

Ted could feel the eyes on him, watching. Charles Xavier smiled warmly at him.

"Sorry my giant friend. You're a little too big for this ride."

Charles Xavier gestured with the flashlight towards Crispin once again. A woman next to him with mocha skin and matching delicate features pushed him forward. Crispin walked up to Charles Xavier with the face of the condemned. Ted gestured at the hole.

"I want to help."

Charles Xavier clapped him on the shoulder.

"Then wait here."

The three men got on hands and knees and crawled into the hollow. Ted crouched and watched them go. There wasn't much to see in the muted light that quickly fell to blackness. The entryway by the door was still intact, but filled with mud, the space just big enough for man to turn around. Ted could make out the edge of the bar. The roof had collapsed on top of it, forming a tunnel. The three men worked their way behind it and disappeared. Ted pulled his head out of the hole, stood, and stretched his back. The crowd was murmuring to itself. Several rats scurried out of the hole. Ted crushed one with his heavy work boot and kicked it away from himself. The Seraphin boy scurried forward and cautiously approached the broken body. He gave it a kick with his bare foot. His mother strode forward, grabbed him by the arm, and pulled him back, giving the back of his head a thwack for good measure. The minutes ticked by. Some of the people stared up at Ted, but they looked away when he glanced down at them. Ted felt useless just standing around. His head hurt. The sun was too bright. The whole world was steaming.

Another group of rats scurried out, working their way along the ruins to holes too small for interlopers to enter. Eliud pushed two shovels out of the hole. He was covered in dirt. Ted went to his knees and pulled the shovels out of the burrow.

"How bad is it?"

"Fucking tighter than a virgin poom-poom."

Some of the more sensitive members of the crowd murmured quietly over the choice of language. Eliud turned and disappeared back behind the bar. Ted leaned the two shovels against one of the fallen gommier trees. Charles Xavier was the next to appear, pushing a hoe and a shovel in front of him. Ted pulled the implements from the hole.

"How's it look?"

Charles Xavier brushed dirt off of the top of his head.

"You can work your way all the way to the back behind the bar. There's a nice little pocket where the tools are. Some of the shelves are even still standing."

"What about food?"

"Couldn't get over there. Too much piled on top. No space. The rats are having a feast. Must be over a thousand in there. Crisp got himself a little kiss from one."

Charles Xavier laughed. Ted looked back across the crowd and then over their heads to the row of five houses at the top of the town.

"Any sign of Id?"

Charles Xavier spit to one side. He twisted his head to look back into the darkness behind him, paused, turned back, and shook his head.

"I can't imagine anyway him being happy."

Charles Xavier turned and crawled back in.

Crispin was the next to round the corner of the bar. He had two hoes in front of him. His breathing was heavy. His right ear was bleeding. As he neared the light several rats made a break for freedom, skittering across his hands and legs. Crispin's eyes went wide in his head, exposing white all the way around. He let out a half stifled scream and threw the hoes out of the hole. His hands scrambled for purchase as he desperately clawed his way free from the confines. Ted grabbed one of the flailing arms and gave it a jerk. Crispin rolled in the mud. Several people laughed. Crispin lay on his side, shaking and hyperventilating. His sister rushed forward and sat by him, dabbing his bloody ear with her skirt. A voice yelled above the crowd.

"You going to try for another kiss Crispin?"

Crispin violently shook his head back and forth. Parts of the crowd laughed again. The man in the Buffalo Bill's shirt came forward. He got down onto his hands and knees and went in, his girth making it a tight fit.

The three men in the hole made several trips back and forth. From the darkness they brought shovels, hoes, machetes, hatchets, buckets, various hand tools, and even a few boxes of nails, out into the sunshine. The implements were pushed into Ted's waiting hands, who in turn put them against the trunk of the fallen gommier. The last loads were several sticky cases of glass bottled Coca-Cola which had been found underneath the bar. Some were broken, but most were intact. The Cokes were passed out amongst the people of Titou, the tops carefully banged off against cinderblocks. The pop was warm, but tasted good. Ted hadn't realized how thirsty he was. He had seen a few people earlier drink from some of the muddy puddles, but had refrained from doing so himself. Buffalo Bill and Eliud came out of the hole, refusing Ted's offered helping hand. The two men were filthy. Charles Xavier was the last to exit, a bottle of kerosene clutched tightly to his side. Charles Xavier took Ted's offered hand with a smile.

The people of Titou drank their Cokes in the sunshine. The empty bottles were thrown on top of the rubble of the mercantile. Camilla moved amongst them, handing out buckets, hatchets, and machetes to the men and some of the younger women. Charles Xavier climbed on top of the gommier trunk and yelled for silence.

"We need water. Eliud, you lead up to the reservoir and see how things look."

Eliud nodded and started climbing the hill, the newly created bucket brigade following after. The reservoir was about a mile above Titou in the forest. Given the state of things it wouldn't be an easy task. Ted moved to follow them, but Charles Xavier jumped down from the gommier, grabbed two shovels, and cut him off.

"Not so fast Theodore. I need your help."

Ted didn't argue. He took the offered shovel, shouldered it, and followed. Camilla took charge of those who remained. Older men, women, and the children she could corral. Camilla set them to gathering anything dry that would burn. Charles Xavier led Ted across an area of flattened mudslide and found a piece of still solid ground near the tree line. With a grunt he broke the ground with his shovel and started to dig. Ted joined him.

"What are we digging?"

Charles Xavier didn't look up or stop working.

"A grave."

The people gathered what dry wood there was not far from the mercantile. There wasn't much. Everything was still thoroughly soaked. Ted could see them as he worked, watching for brief moments when he added red dirt to the growing pile. Finding nothing else, the wood gatherers shifted their efforts to boards from fallen houses, tar paper, and a few pieces of furniture mostly volunteered by their owners. Ted noted people carting the chairs from his house, but said nothing. No one had asked him, but the furniture wasn't actually his. It belonged to Malik. Mr. Hewitt expertly hewed the wood with a hatchet, breaking it down into kindling. When the pile was big enough, Camilla poured on some of the kerosene and lit it with a match. The fire flared, died, and flared again with the gentle breaths of Mrs. Seraphin.

With the fire lit, the women began gathering what food they had that needed to be cooked before it spoiled. Chicken was skewered and placed over the flames. Random tidbits were combined in pots and placed into the burning coals. The children were sent scurrying into the forest. Charles Xavier yelled at a group running by.

"What you little monkeys doing?"

A girl with a missing tooth yelled back, her voice lisping through the hole.

"Any fruit we can find. Nothing rotten except papaya. Camilla said bring back all the papaya."

The girl was gone. Anji had scattered the fruit from the trees, but some of it might still be good. Camilla herself was never still. While the people worked around her she moved from house to house.

Assessing the damage, poking her nose into the cupboards, taking note of everything.

The ground was a water filled sponge. Each shovelful of red dirt was heavier than the last. Water flowed in crimson rivulets from the growing pile of soil. Ted's shoulders ached. The wood of the shovel handle rubbed a blister into his palm. Ted broke it with his teeth, ripping the skin away. He did his best not to think about what they were doing. Not to think about the bloody face. His movements were automatic, an excavator in an ever growing cavity. It seemed strange to be digging where they were. Titou had a graveyard, though it was a mile and a half away through the forest. He almost asked why they weren't burying Eugene there, but he caught himself before the words spilled out. The path would be just as bad as all the rest. There were more important things to do than clear it. The bloody face gave him a congratulatory grin. Ted did his best to think about something else.

He was back in Bozeman, driving with Sandi in the passenger seat. She was laughing at something he said. He couldn't remember what. A station wagon with wood paneling pulled alongside. The man in the driver seat had his window down and was screaming at Ted, angry as hell. The man threw a fountain cup of soda. It crashed against Sandi's window, cascading brown sticky liquid across the glass. The station wagon sped up and then slowed down, coming alongside again. The man was hanging half out of his car, shaking his fist, his wife trying to drag him back in, the kids in the backseat crying. The man spit. A large gob of half chewed candy hit the side of Ted's car. Ted looked at Sandi, perplexed at the antics.

"What the hell is his problem?"

Sandi was shielding her face from the outside world with her hand.

"Jesus Ted. You need to learn to pay attention."

Ted was sweating heavily. Charles Xavier had hung his shirt from the branch of a fallen tree. What the fuck was he doing? Why was he thinking of that kind of crap? Here he was, right in the middle of disaster area, and he was thinking about his ex-girlfriend. Delving back up the questions never answered. What the hell was wrong with him? Was he really that self-centered? The people of Titou had lost their town. Eugene had lost his life. No one had any idea when help was going to come. Stupid. He was fucking stupid.

Charles Xavier tapped him lightly on the arm with the handle of his shovel.

"That's enough now. It's deep enough."

The hole was about six feet deep, up over Charles Xavier's head. Both men threw their shovels up. Ted boosted Charles Xavier, who in turn gave Ted a helping hand as he scrambled his way out. Both men sat in the mud, their legs hanging over the edge, breathing deep, resting. Charles Xavier picked up a few pebbles and tossed them into the hole, targeting a spot smoothed by a shovel strike low on the far end. When his hand emptied, Charles Xavier searched about for more to throw. Ted helped him look.

A man was standing about ten feet away. Watching. Silent. Ted almost didn't recognize him. It was Mr. Green. His clothes were strangely clean compared to the rest of the people of Titou. Nearly immaculate except for the cuffs of his pants and his bare feet. His body didn't match his garments. Hollow cheeks. Red rimmed bloodshot eyes sunk deep into his skull. Gray hair frizzed out from the sides of his head. Back bent. Shoulders slumped. Ted felt like he should raise his hand in greeting, but didn't dare. Mr. Green was staring at the freshly dug hole. With a slow and slight flick of his wrist, he motioned for Charles Xavier to come over. Charles Xavier rose up and did as he was bid. The two men whispered for a short time. Charles Xavier's hand came up and rested itself on Mr. Green's shoulder. Mr. Green turned and walked away, back up towards his house. Charles Xavier walked back to Ted, his face set in stone. He picked up his shovel.

"We're going to need another hole."

Chapter 11

Eliud and the group sent up to the reservoir came back by mid-afternoon. Ted was in his house, digging out mud. He had crawled in the window and managed to get enough out to open and close the front door. His cot was a mangled mess pressed against the cupboards, its thin metal bars bent and the springs askew or hanging loose, broken by the mud which had torn with its insidious filthy fingers into what had once been his sanctuary. Ted had thought about abandoning it, but with a little bending here and there it proved to still be serviceable. The sleep sack had been half buried nearby. It sat on the porch, its white, blue, and red interior exposed, drying in the sun. His duffel bag of clothes hadn't turned up yet, still somewhere beneath the invading soil. With each shovel load of dirt, thrown out of the shattered frame of the front window, he moved back in time, restoring the world to its former order.

Charles Xavier was sitting on his porch, helping Camilla go through a pile of papaya that the town's children had gathered from the forest floor. Each was cut open, the black seeds scraped into a bowl between the pair, and the orange fruit sorted into edible and rotten. Their lips sucked juices from sticky fingers. Eliud's brigade filed past Ted's window, water sloshing from buckets filled as close to the brim as possible. They were sweaty, scraped, and cut, but miraculously clean compared to their fellows. A small well earned benefit from their hours of hard labor and toil. Eliud came to Charles Xavier's porch alone, while the water bearers waited a short distance away. Ted kept working, pretending not to listen.

"Where do you want us to put the water?"

"Down by the fire is fine. Let everyone know it's all we'll have until tomorrow. We'll send a group up for more in the morning."

Ted strained his ears, waiting for more amidst the sound of the couple. Charles Xavier's voice again broke the silence.

"How was the path?"

"Pure fuckery. Took us most of the time just to clear it enough to get through."

"And the reservoir?"

"Gone."

The sound of slicing and scraping fell silent.

"Gone?"

"Yeah, one whole side of the dike gave way. Waters still flowing in, but almost none is staying."

The Titou water supply came from several streams that flowed down the side of the mountain and were collected in a small reservoir built by the British when Domenique had still been part of their global empire. It was nothing much, with a levee of packed dirt, and occasionally treated with chlorine stored in a nearby shed. Ted had come upon it once during his first month, when the paths around the town had still been a mystery. There had been a dead bird floating in the water. At the time, Ted would have rather the source of his drinking water remained a mystery.

The world remained quiet. Ted wondered if they were picturing the same thing he was. A wall of water and mud coming down the mountainside. Charles Xavier broke the silence.

"Water still look good?"

"The reservoir looks pretty nasty, but we filled our buckets up one of the streams a bit. Nice little waterfall."

Silence again. The work on the papaya restarted, joined by Eliud's feet shuffling in place.

"What are we going to do when the dry season hits?"

Charles Xavier laughed.

"Don't you have enough to worry about today?"

Eliud moved off down the hill. Ted got back to his digging.

It was late afternoon when they buried Eugene Hewitt and Mrs. Green. Mr. Green didn't attend the funeral. Charles Xavier and Buffalo Bill went into Mr. Green's house and came back out with the body wrapped in a white sheet. Mr. Green watched them work their way down the hill and then closed the door behind them. Ted was standing next to Camilla.

"Isn't he coming down?"

Camilla held her face still and started down the hill.

"He's probably had plenty of time to say goodbye."

Mrs. Green had died of a heart attack, frightened to death when the mudslide hit. Eliud and Bug Eyes carried the body of Eugene wrapped tightly in its own sheet. Bug Eyes had disappeared for most of the day. No one had bothered to ask where he had been.

The bodies were laid in their holes. Someone had pounded crude lashed together crosses in the ground next to each one. There was no one to do the ceremony. The nearest preacher was in Helston. He came up on Sundays to say mass in the same shelter where Mr. Green taught school. A few of the more devout older women led the rest in singing a few hymns. A few of the men joined in, but most stayed silent. They stared with sullen tired eyes at the twin wounds in the scarred visage of the town. Mr. Hewitt stood next to his son's grave with his battered straw hat in his hand, his face betraying no emotion. Ted tried to stay near the back, out of the way, but Charles Xavier and Camilla drug him forward to stand next to them. The people on the other side of the graves glanced at him, then let themselves fall back into the acts of mourning. Singing with eyes closed, staring at the bodies in their holes, or looking upward at the gray clouds skidding across a blue sky. None of the glances were anything approaching friendly. They were the glances one gave when someone brought an uninvited guest to a party.

Many of the mourners began to cry. Women openly sobbed. Men stared at nothing as tears rolled down their cheeks. Ted had only ever been to one other funeral. His grandmother had died three years previous. It had been the same as now. Standing, numb, feeling nothing. Ted had never really known his grandmother, his father's mother. The woman, though she lived in Boise, had never really ever been around. Her passing left not a single mark upon his psyche. Ted had mostly been surprised at the number of people who had shown up. The church was full to bursting. It seemed strange for so many people to feel a connection to someone who couldn't even take the time to visit her own grandchildren. When he came back all of his classmates had signed a card. It seemed strange. Half didn't know him very well, and it was guaranteed that none had ever met his grandmother.

Ted's mother had cried incessantly throughout the service. She had clung alternately to her husband and son, soaking the front of their suit jackets with her tears. Ted couldn't remember whether or not his father cried, though when it came time to file past the open casket, his father had leaned over and kissed the cheek of the preserved remains. Ted had stared down at the corpse, trying to conjure up some type of emotion, until his mother poked him in the back to get him moving. All Ted could think of was the time his grandfather had sicced the Yorkie on him for wearing shoes in the house. It was a strange thought to have, given it had nothing to do with his grandmother, but it was all he could think of all the same. After the graveside, Ted's father had sat by the lowered coffin for two hours while Ted and his mother waited in the car.

Ted wondered if his mother was crying now. He had called just a couple of days before. They wouldn't be expecting another for at least a week. Even then it would be less worry and more agitation at his failure to keep a promise. Did his parents know about Anji? Had it been big enough to appear in the nightly news? Hard to say. Probably at most a quick blurb, something easily missed. Were they going about their ordinary lives, unaware of the dangers their only child had faced? Ted could see his mother sitting on the edge of her bed, clutching the picture she liked of age nine Ted when he played Little League, body shaking, salty droplets falling on the glass. Her bent form kissing his preserved cheek as he lay unmoving in his box. Were they making calls at that very moment? Trying to track him down? Trying to find out if he was okay? What was it like outside of Titou? Charles Xavier had said Helston was just as bad or worse, but what about the capital? What about the surrounding islands? Was the Peace Corps looking for him? What about his mother? What if she didn't even know?

Ted stood and stared down at the grave. The bloody face scowled at him. Eugene Hewitt had been kind to him. An oddity where so many treated him at best as a strange curiosity. A pale cousin come to stay for awhile before drifting on. A friendly gesture, that was all it was. A man, who aside from Charles Xavier, was different from all the rest. It was sad to see him go. The thought twanged some inner tendril. Ted's eyes filled with tears. He wiped them away, hoping nobody could see, but they kept flowing. It had felt nice to feel less alone.

The singing stopped. The people fell silent. Mr. Hewitt put a shovel load of dirt on his son. Charles Xavier put one on Mrs. Green for Mr. Green. The people began to move away. Eliud and Buffalo Bill began to fill in the holes. Mr. Hewitt didn't move. He watched the red dirt cover the white sheet. A few came forward and patted him on the back and then moved on. Ted waited until most were gone, and then walked over to give his condolences.

"I'm sorry for your loss Mr. Hewitt."

The old man grunted, but didn't look up.

"He was a good man."

Mr. Hewitt's face rose like a shot. He was a head shorter than Ted. His tongue moved across what teeth he had underneath his upper lip. The punch was so quick that Ted didn't have time to react. The fist connected with his jaw and he fell sprawling into the mud. Mr. Hewitt looked down on him and then turned back to his son's grave.

"You didn't know my son jake."

Charles Xavier helped Ted regain his feet. He pulled Ted away, whispering something that Ted didn't hear. Mr. Hewitt kept his place, not moving until the holes were completely filled. Charles Xavier took Ted to the water buckets and had him wash out his mouth. There was blood in his spit. When he looked up, his friend was waiting patiently.

"What about Id?"

Charles Xavier looked puzzled.

"What about him?"

"He's dead too."

Charles Xavier shrugged.

"You can't bury what you don't have. His turn will come."

Ted rose to his feet.

"What now?"

"What do you mean?"

"What happens now?"

"We celebrate."

"What?"

"Normally the dead get nine nights, but these poor jackets only get one. We can at least make it the best one possible."

Ted quit asking questions, he let himself be led back up the hill.

The sun sank into evening. The fire was built up, hot enough to burn even the wettest wood. Smoke rose in a column, whipped this way and that by the wind. The people of Titou gorged themselves on anything that would spoil. Cooked meat. Warm milk. Rotting fruit. The people began to sing. Shadowed forms rose up and danced around the fire. Ted watched from his porch. Camilla brought him up a plate of food and a glass of warm milk and he consumed it without question even though the chewing made his jaw hurt. The food was all spiced heavily and he was glad to have the milk, even if it tasted a little sour. Camilla sat next to him and they watched the people dance and eat. Charles Xavier was whipping himself into a frenzy, throwing his body around with spasmodic jerks which matched only the rhythms in his head. Ted raised a hand and rubbed the side of his face where Mr. Hewitt's bony fist had connected. Questions percolated in his mind, but none of them were the one that emerged into the world.

"It's strange."

Camilla looked at Ted quizzically, her face flickering in the distant fire light. Ted gestured with his hand towards the gyrating forms.

"It's just strange, you know. Yesterday. Everything. Now they're dancing. Yesterday I saw a man die, today I saw two people buried, and now this."

Camilla's voice was puzzled.

"What are they supposed to do?"

"I don't know. We buried two people today. How can they dance?"

"Eugene and Mrs. Green are not the ones who will suffer."

The pair sat and stared at the flickering light and its cavorting figures. Camilla hummed quietly to herself. Her hand came down on his and gave it a squeeze. She rose.

"You should come join."

Ted shook his head. The movement brought a fresh wave of pain to his jaw. Camilla started down the hill to join her fellow mourners.

Ted watched her go. She joined the circle. Her hips began to sway, a boat rocking on the sea, merging with the beat of the others. Her shadow disappeared behind the flames and consolidated with the surrounding forms. None of it made any sense. Sandi probably would have joined them. She had loved to dance and none of the world's troubles had ever stuck to her. The pang of guilt again. A sour taste in the back of his mouth. A selfish thought in a world of shit, watching the inhabitants dance amongst the ruins. Ted turned away from the spectacle. The light danced off the fronts of the houses and glinted off the eyes of one other watcher, staring out from the dark interior. Perhaps it was just a trick of the light. For a moment there, then gone.

One of the shadowy figures below detached itself and moved up the hill. For a moment Ted hoped it was Camilla, coming back to provide comfort, but the shape was wrong. Charles Xavier smiled as he approached. His legs were wobbly, his breathing hard, and his shirtless body slick with sweat. He flopped himself down onto the porch, slapping Ted on the knee, a boneless sack of energy and goodwill.

"Theodore my friend, what are you doing up here all stroppy in the shadows?"

"Wasn't in much of a mood for dancing."

Charles Xavier laughed.

"Your jaw can't be that sore. It was a good right, but he's getting pretty old."

Ted didn't feel much like laughing. He stared down at the fire. For a moment he thought he caught sight of Camilla again, but then she was gone. Charles Xavier's face turned serious.

"I just wanted to come up to tell you, we're making sure everyone has good shelter."

Finally, something that made sense.

"Of course. There's still a lot of mud in mine, but how many do you want to put in?"

"Only one."

"I could fit more."

"No need my friend, just one."

Ted was quiet. The unfriendly faces sat just behind his eyes.

"Who?"

"Mr. Hewitt."

Silence.

"Mr. Hewitt? But...."

Charles Xavier's look forced Ted back into silence. The other man breathed in deep and let it out, his eyes watching the figures below.

"He's the only one who would stay with you."

"What?"

The two men sat, watching for the form of the same woman. Charles Xavier gave Ted's knee a friendly shake and stood.

"Men can be emotional at such times. It will be all right."

Charles Xavier turned to go down the hill. The words spilled forth from the deep recesses of Ted's mind, pulled forth by his utter exhaustion.

"Why do they hate me?"

Charles Xavier turned back and forced a smile.

"They don't hate you. They just dislike you."

"Why do they dislike me?"

Charles Xavier took in a breath and let it out.

"You should come down."

"Why do they dislike me?"

Charles Xavier stood in the darkness. For the first time since Ted had known him he seemed unsure of what to say. Ted sighed and looked down at his feet. When he looked back up Charles Xavier was gone, merged back with the movements below. Ted went inside his house, taking the sleep sack with him. He set the cot up where he had cleared next to the fridge, put his clothes on the counter, his boots by the door, and climbed into his sleep sack. The people of Titou sang. Ted wondered if Sandi would come to his funeral if he died.

Chapter 12

It was pitch black when Mr. Hewitt came into the house. The scrape of the door awakened Ted. The sounds of revelry were gone. No singing. No beats pounded out on buckets and anything else at hand. The shadowy figure limped inside, a tired stuttered step. For a moment childhood nightmares rose their ugly heads from the depths of buried memories. Monsters under the bed, beasts which inhabit closets, and things that go bump in the night. A small flashlight flicked on. It ran across the mud filled interior of the house. It came to rest on Ted's prone form, a larvae encased in the safety of his sleep sack. Ted's eyes were gummed up with sleep. His mind was muddled. His mouth could utter only a coherent mumble at best.

"Mr. Hewitt?"

The dark form limped forward. Ted's heart kicked into overdrive. He struggled to pull himself from his sleep sack, once a sanctum, now a straitjacket. Two wiry but surprisingly strong arms shot out. The flashlight beam skittered along the wall. The cot tipped, dumping Ted and his sleep sack to the muddy floor.

"What the......?"

The cot was set back up. The shadow laid down. The flashlight flicked off. Ted dared not move lest he reawaken the mysterious wrath of his new roommate. The old man's breath became slow and even. His body stank of smoke. Air wheezed through his nose, whistling its way past the confines of his sinuses. Ted escaped from his sleep sack as silently as he could, naked in the darkness, each scrape making him wince and pause. Free. Ted sat and thought about his situation. There was little he could do. He might as well try to get some sleep. Ted pulled himself up onto the mud, found a relatively flat spot near the broken back window, got back into his sleep sack, and let sleep take him once again.

It was still dark when it began to rain. A torrent of tings on the metal roof. Starting slow, but gaining pace. A steady drumming that drowned out the slumbering wheezes of Mr. Hewitt. Ted awakened with a start. Hurricane. Another hurricane. No. Just the rain. Nothing to worry about. Ted drifted back to sleep. The water gathered into puddles and flowed downward through the freshly laid mud, cutting rivulets, mirroring streams and rivers in all but scale. Water came down the side of the mountain, not a flood as with the hurricane, but a steady flow which found its way to the lowest points. The water flowed in through the broken windows, and made its way to the floor where it gathered, hemmed in by the tight seal of the front door. Several fingers of moisture found their way to Ted, caressing the sleeping sack, slowly working their way through the insulating layer.

Dawn. The first hints of morning. The cold shock of wetness on his back brought Ted back to the world again. The fingers were gathering and growing thicker. His brain only half functioning, Ted struggled from his sleep sack and retreated from the growing onslaught. There was already two inches of water down by the front door. Mr. Hewitt slept safe and sound on the cot. Ted scrambled to the table in the corner, it's legs still half buried in mud. Ted climbed on top of the table, pulling his sleep sack up with him. His boots were still on the floor next to the door where he had left them. Ted hopped into the water, grabbed his boots, put them on the counter, and returned to his dry island. He unzipped the sleep sack all the way and wrapped himself in it, careful to avoid the wet spots as much as possible. He lay in the fetal position on the rough table top, waiting miserably for his return to the sweet release of sleep.

It didn't come. He just lay there, staring at the water trickling in, slowly carving itself a deeper channel on its journey to the growing reservoir by the door, his body chained to the real world, but his mind still free to wander. Three days. Did his parents know yet? Did anybody know? Did anybody care? Ted hoped his parents didn't know. There was nothing they could do. Ignorance was bliss. If his mother knew nothing than it would be impossible for her to worry. He was trapped. No, it wasn't true. He could walk to Helston. Charles Xavier had made it, so why not him? But what then? Head down to the coast? Things weren't likely to get any better. It was best to just stick it out. Besides, there was plenty to do in Titou. The people of Titou needed him. It was best if he stayed.

Ted's stomach hurt. Not a strong pain, just a dull ache on the edge of consciousness. Did Sandi know about the hurricane? Was she worried about him? Ted could see her fretting the way she sometimes did. It was strangely comforting to imagine her filled with anxiety over his possible demise. It was hard to imagine her still worrying about him, but it was his imagination, so he let her evolve past the likely reality. She sat in some apartment in Portland. One much like the one they had lived in together in Bozeman. She was crying. That guy John came over to comfort her, but she pushed him away. It was a nice thought, but an ugly one. A fantasy in which he dare not dwell.

The rain stopped. Mr. Hewitt farted, rolled over, and rose into a sitting position on the cot. His feet splashed in the pool of water on the floor. The old man's eyes were bloodshot. His skin hung loosely from his skull. He splashed his bare feet in the puddle, watching the ripples move their way across the surface. He groaned. The water was halfway up his calves. Without a word he rose and forced open the door, breaking the seal. The water flowed out. Mr. Hewitt left the door open and walked outside. Ted stayed on the table. The pressure in his gut built higher, going from a dull ache to a sharp pain. There wasn't much time. He threw on his pants, pulled on his shirt, and forced his unlaced boots onto his feet, and ran behind the house and into the forest. His choice of final location was decided by the sudden insistence of his bowels. Everything was loose. Panic set in. Questions whether or not it would ever end. The ripped off sleeve of his t-shirt made for acceptable toilet paper. After the deed was done he ripped off the other for the sake of symmetry and put the cloth in his pocket for later use.

Everyone in Titou was sick. Figures moved along the ragged tree line, desperately searching for some shred of modesty before giving into the insistent demands of bellies overfilled with half rotten food. Ted watched, first as he got water from the buckets, and then from his porch. The people of Titou battled with their gastrointestinal demons.

After conquering her own, Camilla moved from person to person, feeding them spoonfuls of papaya seeds from the bowl she and Charles Xavier had prepared the day before. She gave Ted two spoonfuls, and when he started to question the treatment, quickly cut him off.

"Kills worms."

Camilla moved on, all business. Ted watched her go. Charles Xavier gathered several of the younger men and together they returned to the mercantile to renew their foraging in the ruins. Ted went down to join them, but it was obvious that nobody wanted him around, so after a bit he walked back up the hill. Hearing a scraping sound behind his house, Ted walked around back and found Mr. Hewitt digging. At first Ted couldn't tell what the old man was doing. He was digging a trench behind the five houses, about a foot deep and a foot wide. It angled downward as it moved to the right. The answer came to Ted in a sudden flash. He rushed back down the hill toward the mercantile.

The foragers were already having success. New items were already stacked up outside the hole. More shovels, a length of rope, a couple large tarps, and an assortment of other tools. Ted took one of the shovels and ran back up the hill. He started digging alongside Mr. Hewitt. The old man looked up, watched Ted for a moment, and then got back to work. The two worked in silence, Mr. Hewitt only gesturing once when Ted put the dug out dirt above the trench rather than below it. Ted corrected his mistake. When Mr. Hewitt seemed satisfied that Ted knew what he was doing, he moved down to the houses and began scraping dirt out from beneath the rear window, leveling the surface and creating a lip between the level of the mud and edge of the window frames.

The world below was a bustle of activity. People carrying buckets to get more water. People cleaning out houses as best they could. People on roofs hammering tin back in place. People using whatever they had at hand to improve and build more lean-tos. The children moved through it all, taskless, playing games in the rubble of the mercantile. Their parents didn't seem to mind as long as they stayed out of the way. Camilla led the search for dry wood with which to restart the fire extinguished by the previous night's rain. The houses were gone through again. Ted watched them roll the table out of his house and break it into kindling. As she helped with the table, Camilla noted Ted watching and flashed him a smile. Ted felt his guts twist and he doubled his efforts, but soon after was forced to run into the tree line for a repeat of the morning's stomach issue. No one in Titou was spared, and there was a constant frantic movement as people suddenly stopped what they were doing and rushed to the forest's edge with an awkward half-stepped gait. Many didn't make it and Ted quickly learned to keep his eyes locked on his work.

The power lines caused the only other disruption that morning. The black vines drooped between the poles and lay across the ground. Though the lack of light made it obvious that they were dead, people still were careful to avoid them, stepping near them only when they had to. They were in the way, blocking free movement through the town. Titou was divided between those who wished to leave them in place and those who wished to get them out of the way. Charles Xavier ended the issue with a swing of a machete where the wires began their march down to Helston. The broken end was wrapped around the pole. The other fallen wires soon after met a similar fate.

Mr. Hewitt and Ted remained above it all, digging their trench. Mr. Green's house was silent. The shutters were still closed. Ted thought he saw Mr. Green peeking out through the slats, but it might've just been sunlight glinting off the still intact glass beneath. It was strange to look across the backside of the houses where once there had been chickens pecking amongst the gardens. Now there was just mud, the metal poles of the clotheslines half buried. The useless showerheads sitting lower on the walls. Only the top half of the chemical shed behind Ted's house was still in view. Something crashed inside Mr. Green's house, a sound like a breaking plate. Ted thought about going around the front and knocking on the door, but decided against it. If Mr. Green wished to be a hermit, it didn't seem his place to ask questions. Another crash was followed by quiet chuckles which broke into muffled laughs. Ted was glad when they moved on behind the next house.

When Ted and Mr. Hewitt started digging behind the Seraphin house, the Seraphin girl ran around the corner, screaming and throwing rocks at Ted. Several hit him, one a solid strike to his back as he retreated. Mr. Hewitt laughed uproariously. Hearing the commotion, Mrs. Seraphin came up from the cooking fire. After taking it all in, she grabbed the girl by the arm and gave her a couple hard thwacks with the back of her hand. The girl ran away, crying. Ted emerged from his hiding place around the corner of Mr. Green's house.

"Thank you."

Mrs. Seraphin stalked off down the hill without a word, but a short time later she returned with two glasses of water. She smiled at Mr. Hewitt, even reached out and gave his arm a reassuring squeeze, but only stared at Ted with hard eyes. Ted thought about trying to say thank you again, but the woman was gone before he could even try. The two men got back to work.

By dinner time the ditch stretched all the way behind the five houses. The women at the fire yelled for the others to join them and the people of Titou lined up to get their food served with an odd assortment of plates and silverware, scavenged from the various households. Ted wasn't the last to reach the line, but people cut in front of him until he was at the end. He kept his mouth shut and let them, their blank faces filling him with apprehension. Dinner was a communal affair, everyone pitching in what they could, knowing that Camilla had already taken note of everything they had. Rice mixed with the varied contents of several cans, meat from the night before boiled until chewy and textureless, and a multitude of bananas borrowed by the children from the trees still standing behind the plantation fence. Charles Xavier made space between him and Eliud for Ted to sit, and though Eliud looked less than pleased, he still scooted over. Ted was grateful. Charles Xavier was his usual smiling self.

"Theodore, good work with the trench behind the house. I thought the bed was going to float away last night."

Ted stared down at his food to hide a partial smile. When his face was back under control, he looked up into the other man's gaze.

"It was Mr. Hewitt's idea. I just helped."

"That old man is a clever jacket. I knew putting you two together would work out."

Ted peeled his banana with difficulty. It was a little less ripe than he liked them, but it certainly was not the time to complain. He distracted himself from the taste by asking a question.

"Did you manage to get anything else out of Malik's?"

"Bits and that."

"Any food."

"No. Nothing but tree, wreck, and mud on that side. Take us a bit to even make a dent with the tools we have, and even if we did, wouldn't be anything by the time we got to it. Damn place is thick with squeakers. Not much more where we can get it on the good side either. We're going to try taking apart one or two of the wheelbarrows so we can get them out."

After dinner Camilla gave everyone another spoonful of papaya seeds. The children were sent into the forest to search for more. The plates and silverware were scrubbed so not a fleck of food remained on them. Mr. Hewitt headed back up the hill towards Ted's house. Ted moved to follow, but Charles Xavier blocked his way.

"Come my friend. I've got a job for you."

Ted followed Charles Xavier to the far side of the mercantile. There, hidden from the bulk of the town, someone had roped off an area between the still intact wall and the trees. The two men stood and stared at the roped off area, Ted trying to puzzle it out and Charles Xavier grinning.

"Okay, I give up, what is it?"

"A place to shit."

Charles Xavier proudly showed off the creation. People would be required to do their business in the roped off section. That way they wouldn't be defecating willy nilly across the town. A bucket full of water and several bars of soap sat near the cinderblock wall. Ted wasn't sure what to say, but a complement seemed appropriate.

"It's a good idea."

"It was Camilla's. That woman is full of them."

"So what's this have to do with me?"

"It's your job to clean it."

"My job?"

"Yes. You need to bury the what you get left several times a day and make sure the washing water stays clean. Be sure to carry up a drinking water bucket with you when you go. No reason to waste a hand and no time to back your fist."

"It's my job?"

"Yes."

Ted felt hurt. He had thought Charles Xavier was his friend, but now here the man was giving him the worst possible job.

"This is what you want me to do?"

Charles Xavier's face turned serious.

"It's a shitty job Theodore, but someone has to do it."

Charles Xavier managed to keep a straight face for about ten seconds before erupting into laughter. For a moment, Ted grabbed onto the glimmer of hope that his friend was joking, but it quickly became apparent that the only source of mirth was the pun. Charles Xavier's face became serious again. He gave Ted a friendly slap on the back, turned, and walked around the corner. Ted sat down along the wall. Buffalo Bill came around the corner to use the facilities. He gave Ted a dirty look. Blonde hair and a bloody face flashed through Ted's mind. He sighed, got up, and started digging a large hole between the ropes.

The evening meal was the same as the midday one. Camilla scooped the food onto the plates herself, carefully measuring each share. Everyone cut in front of Ted. Charles Xavier made a space for him, but Ted chose to eat off by himself, leaning against the trunk of one of the fallen gommier trees now encased within Malik's mercantile.

The sun was setting. Movements slowed. The last few dishes were being cleaned and people were beginning to move toward their own domiciles. A distant whooping whooshing filled the air. A chopping sound that grew louder as it came. People's heads rose, bloodhounds trying to catch a distant scent. Ted, at the wash bucket cleaning his plate, raised his head with the rest, the pounding of his heart increasing with the volume of the disturbance. He knew the sound. They all knew the sound. Voices began to yammer, working to climb above each other and the approaching salvation. Tones of excitement, joy, and relief. They weren't alone. They hadn't been forgotten. Fears left unsaid, suddenly pouring forth now that they were being dispelled.

The helicopter came into view. A growing black speck on the horizon. It was an old Huey, surplus from a bygone day. It dropped in low over the tops of the trees, whipping the greenery with its powerful downdraft. With a swing of its rudder it was over Titou, gliding slowly overhead. Dark faces peered down from an open hatch. People cheered and hugged one another. Eyes filled with tears. Hands stretched upwards, apostles reaching for a descending angel. The Huey hung there for just a moment, gliding by, before reorienting itself and with a sudden roar shooting off towards the plantation. Joy turned to puzzlement, bitterness, agitation, and befuddlement. People didn't seem to be able to understand. Some still held their hands in the air. The helicopter disappeared, dropping down out of sight beyond the curve of the slope.

Bug Eyes' voice cut through the chaos.

"Fucking bird landed at the plantation buildings."

The proclamation drew out derision and confusion. An old man next to Ted mumbled something about fucking jakes. The last fingers of sunlight were retreating behind the mountainside. A sick feeling was growing in the pit of Ted's stomach. More people were mumbling about jakes. Bug Eyes was reveling in his sudden authority.

"Someone ought to check it out."

People yelled affirmation, snorted derision, or remained silent. The old man next to Ted mumbled something about jakes again. Ted could feel a cold sweat across his body. He slowly began to move his way out of the crowd. Charles Xavier's face broke above the rest.

"What you going to do, go stumbling around in the dark?"

The more skeptical nodded their heads in agreement, as did a few of the quiet. Bug Eyes spread his hands, taking in the crowd.

"They're in the plantation. We ought to know what they're doing."

The supporters yelled their assent. Mostly younger men and women, though Ted noticed that Eliud was among the quiet. Charles Xavier moved closer toward Bug Eyes.

"It can wait until morning. A mere bit of child's curiosity is a stupid reason to go stumbling through the dark."

Bug Eyes closed the last few steps. The two men were standing toe to toe. Bug Eyes' face was filled with contempt. His voice was measured, but menacing.

"You really think you're something, don't you postman?"

Charles Xavier stared the other man down. People held their breath. Almost everyone was watching. The world jittered with violent vibrations. Waiting with cold anticipation. An evil grin began to break its way across Charles Xavier's face. His face leaned in toward his opponent. Ted knew what was coming next. He silently begged Charles Xavier to keep his mouth shut. The other man's eyes narrowed in anticipation. His hands closed into fists. Bug Eyes knew what was coming too.

"Your mother really thought….."

The chopping racket of the rotor returned to life with sudden ferocity. People turned toward the hiding turn of hill. The helicopter rose back into sight, an ungainly bird hanging magically in the air. It rotated, shifted, and started moving off, gaining speed as it went. The people of Titou watched until it was gone. Bug Eyes spit in the dirt at Charles Xavier's feet. Charles Xavier laughed in return. The crowd began to break apart, their disappointment audible even among those who did not speak. Ted went over by the exposed roots of the fallen gommier trees and stayed out of the way. Camilla took Charles Xavier by the arm and led him upward toward their home. Ted waited, watching the dying embers of the fire, until the world and his heart grew still. He began making his own way up the hill, the moon brightening the darkness with shadows.

By the time Ted got back to his house Mr. Hewitt was already snoring on the cot. Where the table had once stood someone had used a shovel to clear a spot big enough to lay Ted's sleep sack. Ted looked at the old man sleeping on the cot. The old man farted. Ted pulled off his boots and took off his shirt, but he left his pants on when he crawled into his sack. It seemed awkward to sleep as he was used to doing with Mr. Hewitt there.

Ted woke in the middle of the night, his guts twisting. He struggled out of his sleep sack and rushed out the front door. In the moonlight he could see Mrs. Seraphin sitting on her porch, staring down the road towards Helston. She didn't even glance over. There was no time to get to the far side of the mercantile. Ted, doubled over in pain, went between the houses. The tree line. He had to get to the tree line. Ted slipped in the mud and went down next to his house's rear window. No time. Ted jerked down his pants and let nature take over, praying that the sounds would not awaken the sleeping Mr. Hewitt. It felt horrible. A bursting scouring of the gut that seemed as though it might never end, scraping him clean of energy, leaving him a broken husk laying in the mud. Ted laid there for a moment next to his shame, his pants still around his ankles. He rose to a seated position and looked down at it. There was more papaya seed than shit. Ted wiped his ass with the shirt sleeve from his pocket. He dug a shallow hole and used dirt to push it in, burying it as best he could. Exhausted, he rose and half walked half crawled back around to the front. The door hinge squeaked when he opened it. Mr. Hewitt's eyes glinted in the moonlight. The prone old man was grinning devilishly up at him, a low dry chuckle in his throat. Ted ignored his roommate. He crawled back into his sleep sack and went to sleep.

Chapter 13

The shots rang out in the late morning.

It rained again that day. A steady unending deluge which refused to slacken, blanketing Titou in a world of gray and twilight. The ditch dug the day before did its work. Viscous muddy water flowed down the mountainside, but none reached the houses in the row. Miniature streams were brought into alignment by the bypass, frolicking, concentrating, then dispersing, spreading out and gone, the problem of those further down the mountain. Puddles grew into ponds. The fire sizzled and died early in the assault. People sat in their homes and on their porches, watching through tired sunken eyes as the soil saturated water flowed past like blood from cut veins. No one smiled. No one laughed. The weather was a grim reminder of all that had transpired.

The rain didn't stop Charles Xavier. Fueled by the warmth of Camilla's kiss as he stepped off his porch, he marched through the rain, a man on a mission, banging on doors and cajoling his friends and neighbors to get off their asses and to get to work. They were people of the Caribbean. A little rain was nothing new. There was so much work still to do. The people of Titou sat in their houses and stared at nothing, the excitement of the evening before forgotten. Many could not be risen. Many refused to acknowledge the call. The breaking of the dam was sudden. Pushed by Charles Xavier's insistence and a growing guilt for allowing the doldrums to take them, first one and then more heeded the call. Eliud was the first. He was not the last. They came out and stood, their clothes slowly gripping their bodies tighter. Sodden and slumped. Stubborn beasts who would rather remain indoors. Charles Xavier set them to work, refilling empty water buckets and tying tarps onto leaky roofs. Above the top row of houses he had men work on Mr. Hewitt's ditch, increasing its width and depth.

Titou was trapped under the unending assault of the aquatic siege. Ted heard the call and rose to meet the day. Mr. Hewitt stayed on the cot, his hat over his face, pretending to be asleep. There was a crust of dirt on Ted's clothes. His pants, shirt, and socks all smelled terrible. Ted shook his shirt before he put it on, releasing a wave of dust into the air and cracking the grimy stiffness. The moment he stepped outside he was soaked. Filthy trails worked their way down his arms and fell from the cuffs of his pants. Ted cleaned the so-called bathroom, shoveling melting piles into the deep pit he had dug. The pit was half full of water. Some sank and some floated. If the pit had been dry he would have thrown a thin layer of dirt in on top, but given the circumstances such an attempt seemed pointless. The dirty water for washing was dumped at the edge of the forest and a new one retrieved from the source up by the broken reservoir. The path was slick. Ted fell several times. With his assigned task done, Ted joined the unlucky few volunteers still outside digging. No one said a word. They made space for Ted, working with eyes down, obeying Charles Xavier's gestured orders, bending the flow to his will.

Five smaller channels they dug across the town, running at a slight angle to the perpendicular, shunting the water to the side before it could gain enough power to start sweeping more of the world down the mountainside. The shifted flow moved alongside the low earthen dam of the landslide, pooling at the bottom near the mercantile, threatening to form an unnatural body of water that would flood across the flats. The workers rushed down as the lake grew and made itself apparent. With shovels they attacked the landslide, cutting through a wide channel to allow exit to the forest beyond.

People watched the work through broken window frames and lace curtains of water dripping off of rooftops, averting their gazes whenever noticed. Eyes rolled across the soggy landscape, down the mountain toward the battered fence of the plantation. Watching. Wondering. Waiting for something to happen. Silence. Just the raindrops throwing themselves against the earth, the scrape of shovels, and the breathing of the workers. Children grew restless, tiny bodies buzzing with pent up energy. Parents did their best to check the boundless vitality within the confines of four walls, but such exuberance could not be contained. The life filled miniature versions exhausted the resolve of their adult cellmates and made their escapes into the saturated outside world. They bounded into the puddles and newly dug ditches and ran amongst the trees, screaming in high pitched voices in their exuberance of being alive. Ted watched the Seraphin boy lead another over the plantation fence where it had been crushed by the large fallen palm tree, undoubtedly to gather bananas and the praise such actions had garnered before. Bug Eyes jostled Ted with the handle of his shovel. Ted gave the man a dirty look.

"Watch where you're shoveling."

Bug Eyes glared back.

"Quit crowding me jake."

The work continued. A race against time necessitated by their own meddling. Frantic beings splattered with mud until they looked to be the ill begotten children of what they fought. A shovel struck the winning blow and the water began to flow out in a sudden torrent. The lake began to drain. The worker cheered as their leader, the muddiest of all, extolled them to widen the gap.

The first echoing blast sounded like thunder, bouncing off the mountainside. By the second Ted knew what it actually was. People came out of their houses, standing on porches and in doorways, heads raised, eyes roving across the countryside for the source. The sound of the second shot hung in the air and faded into the pitter patter of the rain. People looked at each other, unsure, even Charles Xavier. Above, Camilla was out on her porch, her face made of stone. A morbid silence hung over the town.

"Aurelius! Rosi!"

The children's names exploded from a mother's lips, triggering the brains of every other mother in town. More names bellowed forth, a fretful lowing, demanding and on the edge of panic, calling the brood home. Eyes darted back and forth, desperately looking. Tiny forms broke from the cover of the forest and ran up to the porches, obeying the unquestionable tone of the commands.

A third shot rang out, separate from the other two. People flinched. Not all of the children were accounted for. Two mothers started screaming, one of them Mrs. Seraphin. Eyes roved across the edge of the forest, desperately searching. Crispin was the first to see them. He pointed and shouted.

"There! Over there!"

The two boys were running at full tilt, their mouths open, gulping air, their eyes twice their normal size, their bodies coated in mud. The people of Titou moved en masse to the plantation fence. The boys reached the rusty chain link where it still stood tall and panicked, moving back and forth, unsure where to go. People shook the fence, shouting and pointing directions. The small chests were heaving, desperately sucking air. The eyes were wild in their sockets.

Charles Xavier shouted to be heard above the rest.

"This way! This way!"

He ran down the fence towards the breach and the boys followed. They reached the fallen palm and climbed across into waiting hands which yanked them safely to the correct side. The two boys collapsed crying into their mothers' arms. The mothers cried too, alternating between hugging and smacking their sons. Charles Xavier talked quietly to the boys. One was beyond communicating, but the Seraphin boy pointed back into the plantation. The questions and replies drifted through the crowd, propelled from voice to voice, facts losing clarity, but emotion heightening with every exchange.

A man. There was a man in the plantation. With a gun. He shouted. He had a gun. A rifle. He shot at the boys. At the boys? Maybe up in the air. He chased them. He chased them through the trees. The boys fell down. The boys got up. The man shot again. At them this time? Maybe. They were panicking. Panicking bad. Who knows. Bastards. I can't believe the bastards. Fucking jakes. Money. We're starving and they send guns. Fuckers. Fucking jakes. For what? For fucking bananas. Bastards. The boys all right? Yeah, just scared. Warning shots. Worked there twenty years. How many of us work there? A lot, that's how many. Fucking jakes.

Charles Xavier stood up on the trunk of the fallen tree and shouted to be heard. Eliud and Crispin yelled as well, demanding people be quiet. The tumultuous volume subsided.

"Everyone please. Please go back up to your homes."

The proclamation was met with disdain. People yelled over one another, each wanting to be heard. The crowd was shushed again.

"There's nothing we can do all standing here. We'll find out what's going on, I promise, but first the rest of you need to go back to your homes. Get back to work."

The crowd began to shout again, but Eliud, Buffalo Bill, and Crispin began to herd them up the hillside. Bug Eyes stood defiant for a moment. Buffalo Bill put a hand on his arm. He jerked away and stalked back up toward Titou. Charles Xavier motioned for Eliud to join him. Camilla came up and whispered in his ear then moved away. Charles Xavier motioned for Ted as well. As Ted approached he could hear Eliud whispering to Charles Xavier, a hiss that was louder than necessary.

"Why bring the jake?"

Charles Xavier whispered back his response.

"I doubt they'll shoot at a white guy."

Eliud nodded. He flicked his chin upwards at Ted in greeting, a slight smile on his lips. Charles Xavier smiled big.

"Theodore my friend. Are you up for a little walk about?"

Ted wasn't. He was unsure. Something was wrong. Something that ripped deep inside of himself. The tearing of an understanding. He was afraid. He didn't want to cross the fence. He bit the insides of his cheeks and looked at his feet, searching for some way to save himself.

"Why would somebody have guns?"

Eliud's hand clenched into a fist. His voice was harsh and filled with disdain.

"Fucking jakes, that's why."

Charles Xavier's tone was more kind.

"That's what we have to find out."

Ted felt uncomfortable in the rain. His clothes clung to him in an unfriendly embrace.

"What if we get shot at?"

Charles Xavier laughed and clapped Ted on the shoulder.

"Then we'll count the number of holes in our bodies. As long as there's no more than the original nine we should be fine."

Eliud spit on the ground and glared at Ted.

"For you that's ten."

Charles Xavier boomed out a mighty chuckle and Eliud snickered at his own joke. Ted felt his face burn red. He choked down a need to meet Eliud's disdain with a physical rebuttal. Eliud and Charles Xavier got their mirth out of their systems. Eliud pointed back towards the mercantile.

"Should we grab machetes?"

Charles Xavier shook his head.

"We might need them."

Charles Xavier laughed.

"What do you think you're going to do with it?"

Eliud took in a breath, let it out, and nodded his reluctant agreeance. They all stood shivering in the rain. Charles Xavier clapped Ted on the shoulder.

"Are you ready my friend?"

Ted looked at the two men, down at his feet, swallowed a lump in his throat, and then nodded. He could feel the people of Titou watching from above.

"Sure. Yeah, sure."

"Okay then, let's go."

Ted's heart was hammering heavy in his chest. The three men, moving together, climbed over the tree breaching the fence, and entered the plantation.

The banana trees grew in rows with fronds at head level. The three men moved at a crouch, eyes peering between the green and brown trunks, feet padding softly through the mud and rain beaten grass. Charles Xavier was in front, Ted in the middle, and Eliud brought up the rear. Ted was careful where he placed his feet. He tried to walk on his toes as his uncles had showed him the one time he had been taken deer hunting as a teenager. They had called him The Elephant before half the day was done. Then fucking worthless clodhopper when their patience grew too thin for jokes. Each step sounded like thunder in his ears. He could feel Eliud giving the back of his head dirty looks. The symmetry of the rows was broken by fallen trees, snapped at varying levels and ripped from the ground roots and all. Banana leaves lay in the dirt, drying in the sun amongst yellowing fruit, some already turned the brown of decay. Eliud spit and cursed in a whisper.

"Bastards. Half of this is rotting anyways."

Charles Xavier motioned for silence. Eliud didn't notice, his eyes still roving the trees.

"Many of these still up need to be harvested soon. Fucking waste."

The stare of Charles Xavier's brown eyes was enough to silence the whisper. The three men crouched down in the grass, their eyes strained to see through the broken rows, striving to discern something from the repetitive pattern of nothing. Ted breathed. Each exhale whooshed out like a wind tunnel. His palms were sweating. His hand closed into a fist and only loosened with a conscious thought. The rain beat an off rhythm on the leaves over their heads. A slowly rolling snare drum masking the world around them. Droplets pooled and flowed down green banks to magnificent waterfalls which poured from the ends of the broad leaves overhead. After a bit Charles Xavier motioned, they stood again, and moved on. Ted was unsure what they were looking for, but he knew he didn't want to find it.

Movement in the trees ahead. A splash of crimson. Charles Xavier dived behind a fallen tree. Eliud and Ted quickly followed. A man was moving toward them down a row two over from their own. He was short and skinny, almost to the point of looking unhealthy. He wore cutoff jean shorts and a red shirt, bright against his dark skin. He carried an M-16 by its handle. His movements were lazy and casual. A man taking a pleasant stroll. Ted held his breath. His whole body tensed, ready to run at a moment's notice. The man stopped ten feet away, taking shelter against a banana tree. His eyes roved slowly across his surroundings. He looked up at the sky, wiped water out of his eyes, and spit. Charles Xavier moved his finger carefully to his lips, signaling for Ted and Eliud to remain quiet.

The man took out a plastic bag and pulled out a pack of cigarettes and a lighter. The man smoked and listened. Charles Xavier and Ted remained perfectly still. Eliud unconsciously moved his hand. A twig broke. The man with the gun sprang up, the M-16 to his shoulder, the cigarette tightly clamped between his teeth. The man took a step forward. The barrel of the gun tracked across the fallen tree, moved on, came back, and moved on again. The man took another step closer. Ted braced himself, panic rising. His entire body began to shake.

"Wilky, vous ici?"

The man turned away. A second man was coming down the row. This one in a dirty striped polo, his M-16 cradled in his arm. The first man lowered his gun and raised his hand to wave.

"Par ici."

The second man walked up. The first one offered the cigarette which the second happily took for a few puffs before passing it back.

"Voir beaucoup?"

"Seulement des bananes."

The second man laughed.

"Qu'est-ce, pas plus d'enfants a tirer sur?"

"Tais-toi."

The second man laughed again. The first man smoked his cigarette and glowered.

"J'ai tiré en l'air."

"Frantz veut que nous verifions sur l'ouest. Jude va regarder le village. Il est moins declencheur heureux."

"Tais-toi."

"Allons-y."

The second man started to move away. The first flicked away his cigarette and followed.

"Je desteste la pluie."

"Vous ne serez pas fondre."

The two men moved on out of sight. The men laying behind the fallen tree stayed still until they were sure the two men were gone. Ted looked to his right and to his left. Charles Xavier's face was serious. Eliud's eyes were wide in his round head. His voice was a harsh whisper.

"Martinique?"

Charles Xavier shrugged.

"Maybe Guadeloupe."

"Haiti? Lots of poor people in Haiti."

"Lots of poor people everywhere. Haiti seems pretty far to get them here so quick."

"Probably Haiti. Lot of poor people in Haiti."

"Fuckers."

The word came out like a spit curse. Ted was confused.

"What are they doing here?"

Eliud's face was tightened into a sneer.

"Jakes."

Charles Xavier looked tired.

"Lots of money to make a plantation. Lots of fancy nice equipment."

Eliud sniffed back a load of snot.

"Kids were just grabbing bananas."

Charles Xavier shrugged again.

"Lot of dumb in desperate. French was never the brightest language."

Both of Eliud's hands were curled into fists. Charles Xavier reached over Ted and gripped his upper arm.

"Nothing much we can do about it. Come on, let's go."

The three men rose into a crouch and started working their way back to the fence. Eliud spit and looked crossly up at the sky.

"I hate the rain."

Charles Xavier leaned over and picked up a fallen bunch of bananas, ripening but not yet rotten.

"So do lots of folks."

In Titou the people gathered around as the three men climbed back across the fallen tree. Camilla rushed forward and hugged Charles Xavier and then Ted. It surprised him, but it felt good to be held tight in her welcoming embrace. He held on for a moment, wishing it to never end. Charles Xavier explained the situation, ending with a declaration.

"Stay out of the plantation. They're dangerous men. No telling what they might do."

The crowd growled and raised its hackles. They mumbled and they fumed, but there was nothing they could do. Ted felt some eyes fall on him again. He thought of hunting with his uncles again. The sight of a deer with its head up, its ear twisting this way and that. He uneasily worked his way up the fence, moving away from the center of attention. Bug Eyes was yelling to be heard above the mass.

"It's all right fucked up. Jackets with guns. Shit getting worse every day. We just sit playing in the mud. We're all stakki for staying here."

Charles Xavier didn't raise his voice. The crowd hushed to hear his reply.

"Help will come when it comes. There's still a lot to do in the meanwhile."

Bug Eyes waved his arms at the world around them.

"You stakki man. We need to get out of here. We need to head down to Helston."

Charles Xavier stared at his rival. His voice was hard.

"Just say fuck off to those who can't make it then?"

"I...."

Charles Xavier cut him off.

"Nobody is making you stay."

The world was silent. Everyone was watching Bug Eyes, waiting. He looked at the people around him. Eliud took a step up behind Charles Xavier. The last one he looked at was Camilla. She stared at him, her face blank. Bug Eyes raised his large shoulders and let them fall. He stalked away.

Dinner was a variety of things shared from cans, served cold because no one could get the fire relit with all the rain. Ted shared a can of beans with Charles Xavier and Camilla on their porch. Afterward he wandered down to use the facilities, such as they were. As he walked he looked back. Camilla and Charles Xavier were talking quietly, Camilla doing the lion's share, and Charles Xavier nodding his head. Both of their faces looked worried. The conversation ended and Camilla began marching down the hill. Ted turned his attention back to his own business.

About an hour after the midday meal, Bug Eyes and a small group of eight younger men and women left. Buffalo Bill and Crispin's sister were with them. They marched down the rutted gravel road with bags and bundles in their arms. Charles Xavier watched them go and then set the people of Titou to working on a new project. The shelter where Mr. Green had taught school was partially buried under a foot of mud. A deep ditch was dug around the upper three sides to keep water from flowing in. Eliud was lifted to the roof where he knocked a medium sized hole in the tin on the ridge with a hammer. Tarps were lashed to the sides, more furniture was sacrificed, and soon a cheerful fire was burning, safe from the elements. The rain stopped soon after they got the fire lit. Charles Xavier set people to gathering wood to be set to dry by the fire. Ted went off and cleaned the informal bathroom behind the mercantile.

Supper that night was just plain rice with some beans mixed in and the bananas brought back from the final trip into the plantation. Camilla watched every scoop of rice with a careful eye, making sure every portion was equal. Ted stood in line with the rest and let people cut him as they always did. Not everyone did it this time. Three old women and an old man lined up behind him without complaint.

Parents kept their children close, keeping them from wandering far into the twilight. Charles Xavier cleared a space for Ted next to him. Ted gladly took it. Ted ate in silence. Charles Xavier talked enthusiastically about the work of the day. Pointing out the various features and those responsible.

"Camilla thought to use the shelter, but it was Eliud who did the rest. He's a bright boy that one. Even the jakes in the plantation knew that well enough."

It was when the sun was setting that Buffalo Bill came back into Titou. His jersey was muddy and torn. His features were tired and sheepish. Charles Xavier waved at him as he nervously approached.

"What you doing back?"

Buffalo Bill looked at his feet.

"The road was pretty bad, we had to go up into the forest but half the paths were gone. Roosevelt got us pretty lost. Got into a bit of a scuffle."

Charles Xavier nodded. He rose, picked up a banana, walked over, and held it out. Eliud rose with him, standing a few feet back. Buffalo Bill stood looking at it for a moment, not daring to meet Charles Xavier's eye. Finally he reached out and took it. Without looking at anyone he started shuffling up the hill, disappearing to be by himself. Charles Xavier turned to Eliud and spoke louder than needed.

"I bet the only reason he came back was because he realized Trisha wasn't going to give him a cocky kiss."

Eliud laughed so hard he nearly choked.

The people of Titou drifted back to their houses. Ted trudged up the hill with Camilla by his side. She smiled at him and hugged him tight before they went their separate ways. Ted didn't want to let go, but in the end he had to. In the house, Mr. Hewitt sat on the cot, picking his nose and flicking the boogers into a corner. About half the mud inside had been cleared away. Ted wondered what the old man was doing with all the dirt. Ted's duffel bag sat on the floor, filled with mud and wrinkled clothing still half folded. Mr. Hewitt snorted and spit a loogie into the corner, kicked the duffel bag with his foot, and looked up at Ted.

"You need to change your clothes. You stink."

Chapter 14

The morning of the fifth day after Anji's fit was a clear one. The clouds parted and the sun shined through, filling the world with mist which floated lightly along the muddy ground. The air was dank and filled with the smells of rot. This was the world into which Mr. Green at last emerged.

When Ted woke that morning he rifled through his duffel bag and found the least dirty of the clothes inside, put them on, and went out onto his porch to escape the laughter of Mr. Hewitt. The old man apparently found the sight of Ted's naked white body to be one of the most hilarious things he had ever seen. Ted stared down at the world below, his focus on the plantation. Charles Xavier emerged from his own house, stretching his back and popping his vertebrae in series. He yawned and smiled at the bright world and his neighbor.

"Theodore my friend, how did you sleep last night?"

Ted scratched the thickening stubble on his face.

"Good enough I guess. You?"

"Well enough I suppose. The man next door was snoring so loud it was hard to get to sleep."

Ted tried a half smile.

"Must have been Mr. Hewitt."

Charles Xavier snorted and gave a hearty laugh. He twisted back and forth at the waist, breaking free the last of his slumber stiffness.

"Big plans for the morning?"

Ted shrugged.

"Just the usual shit."

Charles Xavier laughed again.

"Well, when you get done come find me, we'll be getting the mud out of our new ditches and any help would be welcome."

Ted nodded.

"Will do."

Charles Xavier gave a sharp salute with two fingers and moved down the hill to start rousing his work force. Ted watched him go, his eyes falling on the plantation once again. None of it made any sense. The leaves of the surviving trees in the plantation almost seemed to float in the air. Bananas were cheap. Sixty cents a pound back home. It just didn't make any sense. Ted sighed, shook his head, and headed down toward the mercantile. It wasn't until he was halfway down that he noticed Mr. Green.

The stooped form stood alone at the bottom of the hill next to the scars in the earth where they had buried Mrs. Green and Eugene Hewitt. It took a moment for Ted to recognize the figure as Mr. Green. He stood, quiet, staring, doing nothing. Ted watched him for a moment, running a hand through his greasy hair. For a moment he thought about walking over, but it was an idea he quickly quashed. In a case such as this it seemed obvious that it was best to mind one's own business. The people of Titou obviously felt the same. They rose and went about their tasks, pretending not to see the ghost in their midst. Mr. Green for his part ignored the world around him. The only thing that existed was the grave before him. Nobody in Titou was willing to break his solitude. People worked, ignoring the emerged hermit, watching him only from the corner of their eyes.

When Ted finished with his usual chore he went over to where Charles Xavier was supervising a group of men re-clearing the channel through the mudslide. There weren't enough shovels to go around. Several of them were on their knees, using their hands. Ted joined their number. A few of the men moved away from him, but most ignored him, keeping to the task at hand. The men threw the mud in wheelbarrows, which others took to the tree line where they spread it as evenly as they could in order to avoid impeding the flow of water.

Ted stayed quiet, listening. If he looked at anyone their faces would go blank. If he showed signs of listening people would stop talking. But as long as he kept his head down and kept working, people seemed to forget that he was there, no different than the family dog or a child, not expected to understand. It was strange. They joked and jostled, told stories from months or years ago, and discussed the task at hand. The two most immediate issues seemed almost to be taboo. They didn't talk of Mr. Green or the events of the day before, though from their glances both at the lone figure and the rusted fence Ted could tell that thoughts of both filled their minds. When they did speak of the plantation, it was of the mundane.

Going to screw up the harvest cycle that's for sure. Guessing Anji already did that pretty well. Going to take months to replant. Yeah, and nine months from there till back at full production. Might affect the price. Look at Keynes over here, master of the banana market. The number six conveyor still needs greasing. It'll keep. Lots of good bananas still over there. Doubt they'll last.

None of the conversations lasted long. The flow shifted or the words broke down to silence. The world filled just with the sounds of the work. Ted thought about saying something. He thought about asking, but he didn't. He did his work in silence.

At mid-morning Mr. Green left the graves and walked over to the buckets of clean water. The pace of activity slowed as attention was diverted from the tasks at hand. Mrs. Seraphin had just put down a bucket she had carried in on top of her head. She backed away as he approached, refusing to risk missing anything by turning around. Mr. Green stooped with cupped hands and took a drink. He let the water fall through his fingers. His eyes watched the dappled reflection of the sunlight on the wavering surface. His shrunken frame reared back with great effort, stretching tight muscles, before falling back. The haggard old man looked about, taking the world into his tired view. No one dared to meet his eye. Satisfied with the response, Mr. Green began walking towards the men.

Mr. Green's face gave nothing away as he approached. The men stopped their work. They watched the scene unfold. Mr. Green walked up to Buffalo Bill who was holding a shovel still half stuck in the ground. Mr. Green calmly reached forward and took it from the other man's hands. Buffalo Bill didn't move a muscle. Mr. Green turned and walked away with his prize. With the air of a man strolling to the market, he strode over to the ruins of the mercantile, bent down, and climbed into the blackness of the hole.

Nobody was sure what to do. People stopped working, their curiosity focused on where the old man had disappeared. Quiet conversations spread from mouth to mouth. Charles Xavier made his way over to the hole, and with all eyes on him, crouched down and climbed in. Silence. The wind worked its fingers through the ragged trees. Loud yelling. The sharp metallic clang of a shovel hitting something solid. Charles Xavier emerged from the hole as fast as he could. Camilla went to her husband. He was leaning against the fallen gommier, his face angry, his body shaking. They spoke in hushed tones so no one else could hear. She put a hand to the side of his face. He shook his head no. Camilla walked over to the hole, crouched down, and crawled halfway in. People waited with bated breath. Camilla crawled all the way inside. Nobody moved. Charles Xavier spread his gaze across them. Everyone pretended to go back to work, but nothing was getting done. After a few minutes Camilla re-emerged and walked back to Charles Xavier. Ted started walking towards the mercantile, pretending to be going back to the bathroom area, but it was only an excuse to be close enough to listen.

"So what did he say?"

"He says it's his nephew."

"Id? Id's dead."

"He says Avery's his nephew, and it's his responsibility to make sure he's properly buried."

"Stakki old jacket. Doesn't he know the whole thing's liable to collapse if he digs around too much?"

Camilla's voice was calm.

"I'm sure he knows."

Charles Xavier sucked in a breath and let it out. Without another word he turned and stalked off to get people back to work. Camilla did the same. For the rest of the morning people found reason to be near the hole that led into the remains of the mercantile. The last holdouts who had been refusing to use the staked out area for their shits gave in, their disdain for organized authority overcome by the convenient proximity and the perfect excuse for nosiness. Ted himself took full advantage of the opportunities provided by his given job. He put his ear against the rough stone of the cinderblock wall, trying to discern any sounds from those of the outside world. He thought he heard the scraping of a shovel and the grunting of exertion, but he was unsure from which side of the wall they came.

By dinner the private conversation between Charles Xavier and Camilla had spread to every ear. Ted sat quietly by himself, listening to the conversations around him. All the talk was of Mr. Green. The general consensus seemed to be that he had gone mad, though a few suggested a theory that he was actually searching for some secret money hoard of Malik's. Crispin was the biggest proponent of this idea, but most knocked it down as ridiculous. Mr. Green would never steal, and besides, Malik was known to use the bank in Helston. Ted's ear tuned it all out, fishing for any word of the true elephant in the room.

Mrs. Seraphin was talking quietly to another woman.

"God, I'm sick of rice."

"You could always eat bananas."

"Some joke."

"Fifteen years my husband's worked there."

"What you expect?"

"They shoot at kids, they shoot at anybody."

"Fucking jakes."

Mrs. Seraphin looked over at Ted when she said it. She noticed him listening. She gave him a vile look that turned Ted's stomach sour and changed the subject to Mr. Green.

Charles Xavier sat quietly amongst the chatter, obviously deep in thought. His forehead was creased by deep lines and the bridge of his nose was pinched. Camilla glided by him holding a plate full of food and a glass of water. She carried them to the hole in the mercantile. She crawled in part way and returned empty handed. Camilla moved between the eating people. She stood over her husband. He looked up at her with searching eyes. She smiled down at him, put his face between her hands, leaned down, and softly kissed his forehead. Charles Xavier smiled, a weak smile that didn't reach his eyes, but a smile nonetheless. Camilla moved on.

Ted got up, washed his plate, and wandered off to be somewhere else. He was tired of the voices around him. He walked across the gravel road to the rusted fence. It was tall, at least nine feet, with loosely hung barbed wire across the top, jutting outward. He put his fingers through the gaps, gripping the metal tightly, peering at the world beyond. His eyes searched for any signs of the strangers with their guns. The plantation was silent. It didn't make any sense. Why send armed men? Why bring them from someplace else? They were just bananas. What were things like farther down the mountain? Why weren't people angrier? The best they seemed to have was a castrated ill will. Maybe they were actually angry, just hiding it. Why? None of it made any fucking sense.

"Theodore."

Ted jumped a little and turned. It was Camilla. She had moved quietly on her bare feet. How long had she been there? She gestured toward the fence.

"I hope you weren't thinking anything chupid."

Ted let go of the fence and shook his head no.

"Good, come help me with a job."

Ted nodded and followed her up the hill to the clothesline behind her house.

The clothesline behind Camilla's house was still standing, though the metal poles were half buried and the wires were sagging badly. Ted helped her untie the wires, pull them tight, and retie them once again. Camilla seemed pleased at the work.

"Good enough to keep a shirt off the ground."

Camilla walked over to the back of her house and slumped against the wall where the shower had once been. The circular rod was still there, but the curtain was gone. Ted walked over and slumped down next to her, the now pointless shower head jutting between them. Next door they could hear Mr. Hewitt digging. All day he had been working to dig the mud out of Ted's house, placing what he had removed on an old sheet which he dragged to dump on the other side of the gravel road.

Camilla and Ted watched a bird flit along the tree line. Camilla smiled. Ted licked his lips.

"Do you think any of the chickens will come back."

"They'll know when it's time. They prefer the grass."

They lapsed back into silence. Camilla leaned back against the wall, her eyes closed, her breathing steady. Ted watched the rise and fall of her breast with every breath. He studied the contours of her face. He watched the tightness around her eyes and mouth fade as she fell into an alternative existence where Anji had never happened and

Titou was still whole. Ted found himself silently hoping he was in that reality. A smiling figure next door. A man clasping his arms around her. Ted shook his head, scattering the thoughts about him. She was beautiful. A rock in a frothy sea. A foundation on which was built the shining light which called them all to safety. She was beautiful. He wanted to reach out and touch her. He was drawn to her. A moth to a flame. He couldn't be having such thoughts. He shook his head to scatter them once again.

"Why aren't people angrier?"

Camilla's eyes fluttered open. The creases returned to her forehead.

"Why aren't who angrier?"

"Everyone, about the plantation."

Camilla gave a smirk and closed her eyes again. It was nice in the sunlight, a warm blanket without any weight.

"Do you really think this is the first time something like this has happened?"

Ted was unsure how to answer. Camilla waited and then filled the void.

"They do the same thing every time there's a strike. I don't know why this would be any different."

"They bring in men with guns?"

"When I was a little girl there was a big strike. We heard about it even high up on the mountain. They shot someone that time, though it was accidental. They were just firing their guns into the air to scare people. Still, dead is dead."

They shot a few people that time, though it was just from bullets fired in the air coming back down. Only one died."

Camilla opened her eyes and looked over. Ted was staring at her, the gears in his brain grinding as they shifted without a clutch.

"How could they get away with something like that?"

"Everything has value Theodore, even us. They gave enough money to the dead man's family that they never had to worry again, and the wounded were taken care of as well. As for the rest, a good bump in wages helped everyone forget. Of course they brought in more machines then. Titou used to be bigger."

Ted's head was whirling. He saw fat old men high up safe in towers of ivory and gold, smoking cigars and charting profit figures on graphs, slapping each other on the back and chortling with manic glee.

"Why would anyone work for somebody like that?"

Camilla had closed her eyes again.

"Fifteen Lizzies a day. Twice as much as what most farmers make."

Ted put his hands in his face and pulled them to the back of his neck.

"It just doesn't make any sense."

Camilla smirked.

"What makes sense depends a lot on where you are."

The two lapsed back into silence. After a bit Camilla opened her eyes, stretched her arms, and stood.

"Best be getting back to work. Still things to do today. Thank you for the help."

Ted nodded. Camilla walked around the corner and disappeared. Ted rose and looked at the torn edge of the forest. The bird was still flitting from tree to tree, oblivious to the wider world. Ted started walking back down the hill, off to clean the afternoon offerings in his kingdom of gong.

Chapter 15

Supper was rice with a limited mixture of a few canned vegetables. Helpings were smaller than the day before. Fewer people cut Ted in line. One of the old ladies even gave him a friendly smile. Some people grumbled over the portion sizes, but nobody verbalized beyond the person next to them. The glances continued to give away what most were thinking. The hole into the depths of the mercantile, the chain link fence around the plantation, and a new one, the gravel road leading down to Helston. Whether for escape or salvation, Ted wasn't sure, but he wondered about it. Mr. Green didn't come out of his hole. Camilla took him his supper, bringing back his dinner dishes to wash. He didn't emerge either when the evening turned to nightfall. He had once again disappeared from the wider world, a name without a form. One of the bolder women asked about whether or not some people ought to be moved into his house, but her house was still standing, and nobody else seemed inclined, so the matter was dropped. It was never said, but Ted could feel it. Somehow it felt disrespectful.

When Ted returned to his house he found it more than half cleared of mud, the industrious Mr. Hewitt snoring softly on the cot. Ted, careful not to disturb him, changed into a pair of athletic shorts and climbed into his sleep sack on the hard concrete floor. The night was hot so Ted left his sleep sack unzipped halfway open, sweating, listening to the sounds of lovemaking next door, and wondering if he would ever fall asleep until he finally did.

Darkness was all around him. Loathsome clawed feet skittered their way across his arm, dragging a furred body and naked whip like tail. Ted rose with a guttural scream, swinging his arm violently. The repugnant form flew away from him through the air, landing with a thump on the prone form on the cot. Mr. Hewitt, already groggily awakening from Ted's scream, suddenly found himself with a new bedmate. He jerked and kicked out with a grunt of shock and disgust. The rat disappeared in the darkness. Mr. Hewitt rose, his hand scrambling along the counter.

"Where is it? Where is it?"

Ted pulled himself out of his sleep sack and found his feet. Mr. Hewitt found his flashlight and clicked it on, blinding Ted in the process. The beam of incandescence swung wildly across the interior of the house. The rat ran through the beam and disappeared again, too quick for the old man to follow. The rat ran near Ted's bare feet. He yelled and jumped up onto the counter. Mr. Hewitt bellowed instructions as he raced for the shovel still stuck in the mud near the back door.

"Block the door. Block the windows. Don't let the dirty jacket escape."

Ted was more than willing to let the rat escape the house, but Mr. Hewitt was less forgiving. He veered the flashlight this way and that, spotted the fugitive, and swung the shovel. Sparks flew when it hit the concrete. The rat disappeared, still unscathed. The light caught it again. It skittered along the wall, behind the fridge. Mr. Hewitt rushed forward, barking orders.

"Help me move it. Quick now."

Ted didn't want to get down.

"Unclench your batty hole jake."

Ted jumped down off the counter. He grabbed the side of the fridge and helped drag it out of the way. The rat cowered in the corner, unsure where to go, an escaped convict illuminated by a spotlight. Mr. Hewitt didn't hesitate. Down came the shovel. The rat squealed in terror and then it was done. Mr. Hewitt scooped up the limp form and threw it outside. The old man leaned the shovel against the wall, flipped off the flashlight, and returned to snoring on the cot. Ted climbed into his sleep sack, but he couldn't sleep. The thought of rats filled his head. Dozens of rats. Legions of rats. All crawling across his body, nibbling and clawing. Ted rose inside his sleep sack and put his back against the wall. The first signs of morning were starting to push their way through the window frame. Ted rubbed his arm where the rat had run across it, trying to brush away the sickening feeling in the pit of his stomach. Part of him felt bad for the rat. In its last moments, it had just looked scared and confused, wanting out, just uncertain on where to go.

Ted and Mr. Hewitt were not the only ones to face such an assault. The rats emerged from the ruins of the mercantile in force. Charles Xavier would later claim at dinner that they had been coerced into evicting the ruins of the mercantile by the presence of Mr. Green and his probing shovel, a conjecture that would earn him a sharp rebuke and a hard smack from Camilla to reiterate her order that Mr. Green be left alone. Whatever the reason, the brown flea ridden forms emerged from their hiding places, hunting for whatever nourishment they could find.

Screams punctuated the emerging morning as the invaders were discovered throughout Titou. Of everyone, Crispin had it the worst. Numerous rats, three according to witnesses, ten or more according to Crispin, crawled across his blankets. Crispin, a deep sleeper, didn't awaken until a pair of sharp incisors bit into his left ear. The screams echoed off the mountainside. The slight figure exploded from the doorway of the house he had shared with his sister, his hands desperately scraping imaginary vermin from his body. His eyes were wide and rolling wildly in their sockets, tears streaming down his cheeks, his mouth open in an unending hyperventilating scream. Crispin didn't stop freaking out until Buffalo Bill unceremoniously punched him in the chest, knocking him to the ground. Crispin sat in the mud, his body shaking, for close to half an hour, left alone to regain his composure.

Afterward the morning progressed much as all the previous. Work still had to be done. Ted couldn't help but notice that not all of the assigned tasks were the most productive. Many seemed to be more aimed at just keeping people busy. Buffalo Bill was put in charge of a group which began to clear the path toward the cemetery. Eliud and another group were set to attacking fallen trees along the forest edge with hatchets, the broken wood stacked for later burning. Women were sent ranging into the forest, looking again for any fruit that might have been missed in earlier foraging expeditions. The rest stuck to the important jobs of carrying water and cooking. While the old women fussed around the fire, getting in each other's way, the old men helped as they could, though increasingly they broke off to lounge in the sun, most at least having the good manners to look guilty about it.

Charles Xavier pulled aside all but the youngest children and set them to killing rats. He armed them with rocks and hoes, the edge of which Eliud sharpened between two stones. Thus armed he sent them out on their mission of rodent eradication. The miniature army was Charles Xavier's creation, but it was Camilla's watchful eye that kept them in line. Any that became too unruly or too wild with their swings were removed from the ranks. One of the first to be removed was Mrs. Seraphin's daughter, who made a mighty stroke with a hoe that caught a large rat right between the eyes, but nearly took off Crispin's foot. The poor man, not yet recovered from the trial of the early morning, found himself nearly constantly surrounded by a horde of armed children all convinced that he was some type of rodent magnet, a fact that was continually proven true by their repeated appearance within his presence. Finally, unable to handle the dual horrors of rodent infestation and their assigned eradicators, he retreated into his house and refused to come back out for the rest of the day. Charles Xavier tried to reason with him, but after finding Crispin shaking uncontrollably with his feet planted by his ass on the seat of his one remaining chair, he decided that it was a lost cause and gave up. Slowly the horde was whittled down to the best, but the numbers were so few that Charles Xavier sent some of the younger men to help.

Ted started the morning in his usual manner, gathering and burying shit. To help the day go faster he chose to fill in his current hole and dig another. After that he returned to his house to try and help Mr. Hewitt in his efforts. The old man was sweating profusely, his shirt open, exposing a body of nothing but wire and bone. It took a moment for Ted to realize that the shirt Mr. Hewitt was wearing was his own. The tails hung almost to Mr. Hewitt's knees. Ted decided it was best not to say anything. He tried to dig alongside the old man, but Mr. Hewitt was less than welcoming, though he never said a word or made any noise of protest. However, after accidentally getting jabbed in the ribs for the third time by a shovel handle, Ted got the idea and went out to find something else to do. First he joined Buffalo Bill and the men clearing the path toward the cemetery, but there were too few machetes and other tools to go around. Ted went through a couple rotations, but found himself mostly standing around. Eventually Charles Xavier found him there, and seeing men doing nothing, gathered them up, Ted included, and sent them to help Eliud.

Eliud's group had a similar problem. There were only so many hatchets to go around, but at least there was wood to carry down to the fire, though the pace had to be kept slow in order not to outpace the ability of the hatchets and those swinging them. Ted tried to take a turn chopping, but no one seemed interested in giving up one to a jake, though they gladly traded amongst themselves. After awhile Charles Xavier found too many men sitting around again, Ted again amongst them. This time he set them to killing rats. It was much easier for Ted to claim a hoe from a child than a grown man, though the child was still not pleased by the demand. However, it might have been wiser to leave the implement in the more proficient hands. He was not the quickest man, lumbering behind the scurrying menace, his tongue lolling, his aim decidedly less than accurate.

Dinner proved to be a poor affair, rice with the last of the canned vegetables. People grumbled, but again said little beyond those right next to them. The eyes again shifted throughout the meal, jumping from the road to Helston to the plantation fence. Mr. Hewitt came down for dinner with his new shirt still unbuttoned. He took his plate and wandered down to his son's grave where he sat and ate by himself. When he finished he didn't return, apparently preferring the company he had. Charles Xavier, careful not to intrude, personally carried the old farmer's dirty plate and fork back up to be washed. Ted, feeling the need to try and comfort the old man, wisely ignored the sensation and climbed the hill to his house. All of the mud was gone from the interior.

He examined the change with wonder. Bits of dirt were still here and there, and mud stains still climbed the wall, but otherwise all evidence of the slide within the house was gone. Ted was further surprised when he opened his back door. A set of rough stairs had been cut into the dried mud. Turning his head to the left and right showed that the same had been done for all the houses in the row. Ted closed the back door, walked to the center of the room, and slowly turned in a circle. It was then that Camilla found him.

"He does good work."

Ted nodded.

"Doing anything?"

Ted shook his head.

"No."

Camilla motioned for Ted to follow.

"Get a shovel and follow me."

Ted did as he was bid, grabbing Mr. Hewitt's abandoned implement. She led him down the hill to a pile of dead rats on a sheet. There must have been close to a hundred of them, all victims of the culling. As each was killed the children brought it to Camilla, who with grace and words of thanks had taken it and added it to the growing pile. Camilla took two corners of the sheet and motioned for Ted to do the same. Blood dripped out of the stained bottom of the impromptu bag as it rose. Ted tried to hold the mass as far from himself as possible, but the weight proved impossible with the shovel in one hand. He was forced to hike it over his shoulder, causing the mass to bang against his leg. Ted retched but swallowed it back down. Camilla was holding the bundle in the same manner with the same results, though likely with some difficulty due to the differences in their heights. She made no sign of complaint. They walked into the forest, and after a quarter mile Camilla halted and pointed with her free hand at the ground.

"Dig there."

Ted dug a shallow hole and Camilla watched. When she judged it big enough she stopped him with a gentle hand on his and then threw the bag into the hole. Ted filled it back in. As they walked back towards Titou he looked down on her and asked the question in his head.

"Why didn't we just bury them with the shit?"

Camilla didn't take her eyes off the world in front of her.

"They're full of disease, but people get hungry."

The thought of eating one of the dead rats made Ted's stomach turn. Like many things, it didn't make any sense to him, but he decided against asking anymore questions. Supper was much the same as dinner, only just rice and a few beans without any vegetables. The people of Titou ate in sullen silence, this time not bothering to hide the bitter glances they shot toward the chain link fence. The old woman smiled at him again in line, and fewer faces went blank when he looked at them, but Ted still did his best to stay out of everyone's way. Most people went back to their houses before it was even dark.

Mr. Hewitt didn't eat supper with them. He didn't come up to the house either. He remained next to this son's grave. Ted looked at the empty cot as he prepared for bed, his stomach growling softly, then laid down on the floor in his sleep sack. Mr. Hewitt still hadn't come in by the time he fell asleep.

The next morning the house reeked of rotten lunch meat. Ted was still alone. The terrible stench had been unleashed by the now open refrigerator door. The lunch meat was green and covered in fuzz. The only other thing in the fridge was a box of baking soda, sitting on its side, a pile of white powder on the bottom shelf. The money was missing. Ted slammed the fridge closed and ripped open his front door. The muddy landscape was covered in a morning mist. Nobody stirred. Mr. Hewitt was gone.

Chapter 16

Charles Xavier couldn't stop laughing. Ted was ranting and raving, charging this way and that in the tight confines of Charles Xavier's and Camilla's home. The room was bigger than it had once been. The table and chairs were gone, as were the cupboard doors. Camilla was sitting on a blanket covered mattress on the floor next to piles of clothes. She watched the spectacle in silence. Outside people went about their business, pretending not to notice, but many finding reasons to remain close enough to broaden their minds with the most creative of American curses. With no Mr. Hewitt magically appearing from the floorboards, Ted's anger swerved to the next closest target.

"What in the hell are you laughing about?"

Charles Xavier could hardly get his response intelligibly through his guffaws.

"What were you going to spend it on?"

Ted's blood burst into a violent boil. His voice boomed off the tin metal roof.

"That's not the point."

Camilla spoke, her voice a quiet pool of calm, demanding all to listen.

"Did you think he was working for free? It wasn't his house that he cleaned. Payment for a service is not stealing."

Ted stood, breathing hard, his mind, scrambled by rage, unable to keep up. Charles Xavier was doing his best to stifle his chuckles. Camilla stared at him with an unbreaking gaze. Finding none of the sympathy required, Ted turned, left the house, and stalked down the hillside to do his morning work. His stomach was twisted with hunger, and his throat hurt from all his yelling. The people of Titou quickly returned to the tasks they were supposed to be doing, keeping their eyes to themselves, laughing behind their hands and turned backs.

Ted grabbed a shovel and started digging a new hole to bury shit in. It wasn't needed, he had just dug one the day before, but he did it anyway. He attacked the ground with a ferocity that soon left him winded with his back against the ruins of the mercantile. He could hear scraping sounds on the other side of the wall. Mr. Green digging away. Ted let his breathing slow. Id was dead. Eugene Hewitt was dead. They were right. He was being stupid. It was only money. Just pieces of paper. His house was clean, and at least now he would be able to reclaim his cot. That had to be worth something.

Dinner was only rice. Ted ate his portion alone by the mercantile, embarrassed, avoiding eye contact as much as possible. For their part the people of Titou ignored him, even Camilla and Charles Xavier. After dinner it began to rain, and the people of Titou hid themselves in their houses except for a few, led by Eliud, who labored to keep at least an ember of the fire going. The world turned gray, all the colors washed out. It was depressing to watch the work of the morning slowly melt beneath the probing fingers of the downpour.

Ted lay on his reclaimed cot and watched the rain drip on the empty window pane at the back of the house. The cot smelled like Mr. Hewitt, who aside from getting caught in the occasional precipitation, might have never bathed a day in his life. He was trying to read his copy of *Catch-22*, which he had found in his unearthed bag. Some of the pages were yellowed with moisture, but still legible, but the rapid tap of the drops on the tin roof was distracting. Ted heard the back door of Charles Xavier's house open followed by the squelching sound of bare feet in mud. Ted knew it was Camilla. She was humming as she worked, hanging dirty clothes on the clothesline to take advantage of the rain.

Ted watched her through the empty window frame. She was wearing a yellow dress that was quickly soaked by the downpour. It clung to her as though a lover, caressing every part of her, running its moistened fingers down her body. Her hands were deft and sure, no mistakes and no false moves. She turned and he quickly went back to his reading, refusing to look up in fear that she might know what he had seen. He laid back and stared upward at the wooden rafters and tin roof above.

The university's women's center had been putting on sexual harassment seminars. Everyone in the dorm had been required to attend. They crowded into the rec room, a mixture of sexual knowledge ranging from experts to no-nothings with Ted far down on the latter end. It was a man who did the training, a mostly bald man in his mid-forties who had the strange need to do air quotes whenever he said the word "sex". The man had brought with him a volunteer, a college aged woman which he referred to as a young lady. The woman hardly said a word throughout the presentation. Her entire purpose seemed to be so that the man could throw examples of inappropriate things to say at her.

"Let's say we were at a party, just hanging out with the bros, and I nudge you and say, hey, look at that babe over there with the nice boobs. What would you do?"

Silence. The man waited through a ten count than forged on with lecture, each example getting lewder and more graphic. Ted didn't listen. He couldn't take his eyes off the woman who was taking the theoretical harassment with an air of boredom. It was the same woman who had berated him about recycling a month before. Every described situation, met without response, filled Ted's head increasingly with thoughts that could in no way be construed as appropriate given the subject matter being discussed. When the man's spiel came to an end, and people rose to leave, Ted stayed, his legs crossed awkwardly. The woman, much to his horror, had walked up to him and kicked his foot with hers.

"I've met you before, haven't I?"

Ted had forced the words from his lips, trying and failing to sound nonchalant.

"Yeah, about a month ago. You yelled at me about the recycling."

The girl smiled. It was a coy smile. She had very white teeth.

"Sorry about that. Sometimes I can get a little intense. My names Sandi."

She stuck out a hand. Ted awkwardly took it while remaining seated.

"Ted."

"You enjoy the lecture?"

Ted gave his best approximation of on open and honest smile.

"Yeah."

Sandi gestured towards her partner who was talking to a knot of people.

"I swear to god I hear worse shit out of that pervy bastard's mouth than anyone else's."

Ted nodded, molding his face to exude a sympathetic air, unsure what to say.

"You want to get out of here Ted?"

"Excuse me?"

"Do you want to go someplace with me and hang out? I feel like I owe you after being such a bitch to you."

Ted tightened his crossed legs, willing things to make their way back down.

"Right now?"

Sandi locked her eyes onto Ted's. They were a beautiful blue.

"You know, nobody is going to say anything."

Ted could feel the color rising on his neck and cheeks.

"What?"

Her eyes dropped down his body and raised up again, a small smile on her lips.

"Nobody is going to say anything to you. So if you don't care, it doesn't matter."

Sandi offered her hand. Ted took it, uncrossed his legs, and followed her from the room. Within a week he had kissed her at a house party.

Supper was just rice again. The rain continued throughout the night. It was still raining the next morning. Charles Xavier walked through the town, knocking on doors and lean-to roofs, cajoling the occupants to come out and work. People grumbled and groaned, but many heeded the call, Ted amongst them. By afternoon the would be workforce disbanded. The necessities had been taken care of, and nothing else seemed as important as escaping from the rain.

Ted sat on his porch, watching the world below. Eliud and Charles Xavier were minding the fire, while Camilla prepared the rice for supper. Months ago he had sat on the porch next door with Charles Xavier on a day similar to the one before him now. Camilla had been cooking in the house, and the two men had been passing back and forth the rum bottle. Charles Xavier's voice had been a low drone rising slightly above the static of the pelting drops.

"I was raised in Titou, but she came from the highest farm on the mountain. A place where the clouds sit just a few feet above the ground and the soil is more rock than dirt. She never came down when she was younger, it wasn't until her mother died that her father began bringing her down to Titou when he came to buy supplies. She was beautiful. A mountain bird come to visit from up on high. I knew from the moment I saw her I had to have her. I climbed the mountain to talk to her, but her old man chased me off with a machete. I came back anyways, visiting in the evening for the short time between him sending her to cook supper and him quitting for the day. It wasn't enough. I had to see her more. I started leaving my route half undone so I could sneak up and watch her work. When my bag became too heavy I started dumping the letters on the ground, scattering them across the mountain. But her father was a stubborn jacket. He didn't want me to be near her."

Ted had taken a drink of rum and let it pool on his tongue. His voice had been slurred when he asked the question.

"So how did you two end up getting married?"

Charles Xavier's face had broken into a wide grin.

"Everyone was tired of not getting their mail."

Charles Xavier had burst out laughing. Behind him Camilla had been standing in the doorway, smiling and rolling her eyes.

It was still raining the next day. The people of Titou faded into specters. Only a small handful came out to help when Charles Xavier wandered the town, beating a stick against a bucket, Ted and Eliud amongst them. They gathered what wood they could, refilled the water buckets, and cleaned the bathroom. In the afternoon Charles Xavier tried to get them to help him keep the ditches clean, but in this effort he was abandoned. It was a cold rain, and no one felt as strong as they once had.

Ted returned to his own house where he worked scraping the remaining caked dirt off of every surface with a spoon. The walls, the

fridge, the counter, and the toilet. He missed Mr. Hewitt. The two had
never really spoken beyond a few grunts, but it seemed lonely without
the old man there. By mid-afternoon the project was abandoned,
replaced by Ted laying on his cot and letting his mind wander as it
would.

Why him? It was the question that all men asked themselves, or
so at least he believed. Why of all the men in the world would she
pick him? It had been her that had suggested the hike to Palisades
Falls, only two miles both ways. On the way back he had reached out
and grabbed her hand. She drug him off the trail, into the forest. They
had started kissing. At first lightly, then frantically. It had all
happened so quickly. His pants came down. Her mouth had found the
part of him that wanted her most. People had been still hiking by on
the trail, partially hidden by trees and foliage. One had turned his head
at just the right time. His eyes had met Ted's. They stared at each
other until the man turned bright red and turned away. That's when he
came. Ted had never felt so powerful. So in control. When they had
gotten back to the car he had driven them onto a lonely gravel road and
there lost his virginity, a giant amongst men.

The rain refused to let up. People came down and lined up for
their shrinking ration of rice. They stood in a sodden line, silent in
their anguish. Fewer eyes looked longingly toward the road. More
were bitter, flashing toward the plantation fence. Only Mr. Green
wasn't present and accounted for when it came to meals. He stayed in
his warren, still digging and having his food brought to him by
Camilla. If he had any complaints about the growing situation, none
were communicated via Camilla's defiant features. She faced the
world without blinking, challenging any to question or subvert things
as they were. None did.

People stopped emerging in the morning when Charles Xavier
beat his bucket. Titou became devoid of movement other than the
muddy water flowing down the hillside and Camilla and Charles
Xavier cooking the rice over the fire. The only times other people
emerged was to form the line for their diminishing sustenance and to
relieve themselves of what waste they still produced.

The hollow in Ted's stomach was a constant background pain. At
first he felt guilty when he refused to rise when Charles Xavier beat his

bucket, but in the end such guilt fell away to moral bargaining. Everyone else had quit too, even Eliud. It was okay if he gave up. It was okay to remain indoors.

The seasonings ran out, the magic powders that made the rice at least have flavor. Grumbles in the line turned into shouts and pushing. Accusations were thrown of possible hoarding. Greedy haves who were hiding their last luxuries from the have nots. The sparks petered out before they fully caught, withered by Camilla's hard eyes and the unending showers from above. People ate their rice and returned to their houses. Saddened visages peered out of windows at a dissolving world, trapped by the shackles falling from the sky. Some of the younger may have talked of escape, but it was too late, and they knew it. The world was consuming them, and they lacked the energy to fight.

Charles Xavier seemed to gain the strength of ten men. He worked all day in the rain, helping Camilla keep the fire going and clearing the ditches whenever he had time. It was a losing battle, a failing one man effort to keep the world from being swept away. Mud filled the ditches and water overflowed their banks, flooding downward across the town. For many, the few things that had still been dry became wet, drowning out the last flickers of hope. Charles Xavier didn't stop. He flung himself at it, desperate to save what could still be saved.

At dinner there were bananas with the rice. Nobody said where they came from, but it seemed to raise people back up at least slightly, a strange move from despondent to dejected. Eyes filled with thanks for the unforeseen addition that all were glad to see even if they knew it was still not enough. That evening Ted heard Charles Xavier yelling next door. A terrible scream filled with anger and fear. It was followed by sounds of love making so raw and filled with emotion that Ted clamped his hands over his ears and cried, praying that it would end.

They had been dating a year when she had suggested going to an all you can eat Indian place for lunch. By that evening she was blowing out both ends. She was stubborn. She had always been stubborn. It wasn't until she had broken out with a fever, so weak that she could barely stand, that she had finally given in to his demands to the hospital. When the nurse had taken her into the examination room he had joined her despite her protests. While waiting for the doctor her bowels had proved too impatient. He had taken paper towels and cleaned her as though she was his child, telling her everything was going to be all right as she cried and curled herself into a ball in an attempt to disappear from the world. It had been while digging through a closet to steal a set of scrubs for her to wear home that he had realized that even then he still found her beautiful. It had been at that moment that he knew he was in love.

For nine days it rained. On the last day Charles Xavier didn't beat on his bucket. The door of his house remained closed. The fire was allowed to die. The last of the rice was gone.

Chapter 17

The tide had been rising slowly, moving its way upward inch by inch, straining the moorings of self-control until at last they finally snapped. Such things may seem to happen suddenly, but the signs are always there for those who know how to look. When does fear turn into contempt? What winds blow sparks into the flames of action?

The morning sky was clear and bright, with just a few cheerful fluffy white clouds strolling across the blue expanse. People rose to this new world, squinting sadly with nocturnal eyes at the ruins of all they had tried to save. The world was a place of mud, footsteps sinking down up to knees in some places. They moved in a daze, unsure of themselves, but somehow feeling lighter, freed from the weight of the heavens' bounty. In small knots they worked their way down to the extinguished fire, half dragging and half carrying their offspring. There was nothing there. Just assorted pots and pans lying in cold ashes. No happily flickering flames and no sustenance, just a few scraped clean cans and the remnants of rice bags giving evidence of what once had been.

"Mummy, I'm hungry."

The tiny voice pierces the air. It's joined by more, small copies produced by plaintive figures with big eyes begging upward for the protection that's always there. The rumble of stomachs grow deafening in the crowd.

"Mummy, I want some food."

There is no fear as great as the fear of such failures. There is nothing in the world that can tame such a beast when it's unleashed. The women snapped first, as always is the way when it comes to their brood. It began with the younger ones, clutching their young protectively to them, providing what comfort their warm bodies could still bring. Next came the older women, their children now grown and gone, but still holders of primal memories, needs that are impossible to ignore. A virulent vibration filled the air. An animalistic insistence that something had to be done. At last it spread to the men, dull witted in such manners, but no less terrible when roused. Once the self-proclaimed protectors from the times when lonely tribes moved across the land. A role they fall back into with the trepidation and violent joy of purpose. The tribe was in trouble. They knew what to do. The men beat their chests and made declarations. Those too old raised their voices and joined the whipping words of the women, lashing the beasts into a growing frenzy.

Ted woke with his body covered in a cold sweat. He rose shaking from his cot, his heart fluttering madly, unsure why he must feel so afraid. He girded himself for battle. Pants, shirt, and heavy work boots. The sounds of many distant voices filled the air. He walked over to the front window, a hand tightening around his throat. The atmosphere was thick with disheartening malice. He looked over the precipice into the tempest. His stomach filled to the brim with dread. He could feel their eyes bounding up the hill in pairs of ones and twos. Quick glances that broke away. He wiped his sweaty hands on his pants. His lily white hands. The logical brain was yelling at him to stay calm, but the lizard brain screamed for him to run. He stayed at the window, unsure what to do. He could feel it. The growing need to lash out. The sudden answer to his doubts and questions. Time. It was always just a matter of time. Ted's hands refused to stop trembling. He looked at them, more afraid than he had ever been.

Words flowed between knots of people. Frustrated, angry, and frightened words which coalesced with the voices of others, pulling the knots tighter together, forming them into a crowd. The words flowed in a circle, growing each time someone opened their mouths, parroting what had just been said, boosting the malignant energy of those around them. A perpetual motion machine of building hate. The words were unfocused at first, stabbing wildly into the darkness, but everyone knew. Dark looks flashed from bitter eyes, growing into steady stares. Some found their way up the hillside, but most were leveled with malevolent focus on the chain link fence. One by one the people of

Titou were swept away, broken free of their sullen moorings, energized by a feeling of righteous need and purpose. The flames fanned themselves into an inferno.

The murmur grew to a roar. Ted's entire body began to shake. He could see Eliud's tall thin frame amongst them, trying to be a calm center in the growing storm, but his movements were shifting rapidly toward panic, and he kept looking upward at Charles Xavier's closed door. The rest were no help. Buffalo Bill was throwing his arms in grand gestures as he screamed, a dog finally off his leash, relishing the chance of being beyond the reach of his master's hand. Mrs. Seraphin held court near the center, her frightened children gripping her skirt, tears pouring out of her eyes as she yelled to be heard above the crowd. Crispin, in a blind panic, grabbed whomever he could, screaming into their faces before being pushed away to find a new victim. Even Mr. Green emerged from his hole, leaning on his shovel in a watchful silence next to the ruins of the mercantile.

The door to Charles Xavier's house opened. He and Camilla emerged. Charles Xavier, no smile on his lips, his official blue postman's shirt fully buttoned, stood for a moment and surveyed the mob. Camilla whispered something into his ear. Charles Xavier was sweating heavily. Camilla whispered in his ear again. He swallowed, straightened his back, and stepped off his porch, his long strides carrying him down the hill. Camilla remained on the porch, her face made of stone. Ted opened his own door and came out onto his porch.

Eliud rushed up to meet Charles Xavier. He was yelling to be heard, his arms moving frantically as he spoke. Charles Xavier moved to the edge of the crowd, Eliud trailing after. He yelled to be heard above the din, but his voice was swallowed by the multitude of competitors. Charles Xavier and Eliud stood there for a moment, neither seeming sure what to do, then they waded in. It was pandemonium. The people of Titou crowded around the two men, screaming at them and at each other. Charles Xavier yelled something, slamming the back of his hand into his open palm. Dozens of voices yelled back. What little sense of order Charles Xavier had brought with him collapsed.

Camilla bit her lip as her husband screamed for calm. Mrs. Seraphin screamed in Eliud's face. Charles Xavier grabbed Eliud's arm to try and yell something in his ear, but the other man, ripped his arm away, shouting back. Eliud was lost, and with him went any chance of controlling the mob. They began to move as one down the hill toward where the tree had fallen across the banana plantation fence, dragging Charles Xavier along with them. Camilla jumped down from her porch, took a few steps forward, but then stopped. People fell and rose, covered with red mud. Some grabbed shovels and the sharpened hoes used to kill the rats, and a few even rushed back to their houses to grab machetes. Crispin and Buffalo Bill emerged at the front, making their way forward with resolute steps. Both men were smiling, their faces beaming manic glee. Eliud remained near the back, his head hanging, tears streaming from his eyes. Ted watched, unsure whether to curse or cheer.

The mob reached the fence line. Buffalo Bill began to mount the fallen trunk of the tree, the wild eyed crowd screamed profanities and encouragement. Crispin moved to climb up behind him. A bullet ripped its way upward through the air, its sudden echo silencing the world. The suddenly subdued members of the mob all took an involuntary step back. Buffalo Bill jumped back to the ground and retreated to the safety of numbers. Eight men emerged from the shadowed straight rows of the banana trees. Eight dirty unwashed men with hard faces and M-16's levelled at the people on the other side of the rusty chain links. They moved forward, the barrels of their guns slowly and methodically moving back and forth. One of the men pulled himself up onto the fallen tree and shouted, the words lost into an unintelligible jumble by the time they climbed the hill. The crowd began to murmur. The man yelled again, gesturing with his gun to emphasize his point. The crowd fell silent.

Charles Xavier pushed his way forward, taking a step beyond the edge of the crowd. Camilla let out a choked cry. Charles Xavier shouted something back, his arm stretching behind him in an arc encompassing those behind him. The man with the gun yelled. Charles Xavier took another step forward. The M-16's stopped their tracking motions. All eight leveled themselves at a single point. The man on the tree yelled again. Charles Xavier shouted back and took another three steps forward. Tears flowed down Camilla's face. Ted stopped breathing. The lanky figure of his friend stood alone. The man on the tree was reared back, a snake ready to strike, his focus snapping back and forth between Charles Xavier and the crowd. The seven men behind the fence twitched nervously. Charles Xavier spoke again. With his arms by his sides he took another three steps forward. His eyes stared upward into the eyes of the man on the tree. The shaking barrel of the M-16 was only a foot from his face.

Camilla screamed and ran down the hill. The two men stood, the center of the world. With a slow motion Charles Xavier brushed the barrel of the M-16 aside and climbed up onto the tree. The leader of the gunmen took a step back and poked the barrel towards Charles Xavier's chest. Charles Xavier grabbed the barrel and jerked it aside. The leader stumbled and lost his footing, falling into the grass. Charles Xavier stared down at him. The crowd moved forward. They began to crawl across the breach. The leader rose. The men with the guns were falling back, unsure what to do. The leader yelled at them. They ignored him. He yelled again. They retreated, falling back into the depths of the plantation. The leader followed, looking back once before disappearing.

Charles Xavier jumped down on the plantation side. Pandemonium broke out. Cheering people pushed their way across into the plantation and began stuffing themselves with bananas. People swarmed Charles Xavier, laughing and crying at the same time. Men and women hugging him, shaking his hands, slapping his back, and kissing his cheeks. An excited Mrs. Seraphin kissed him right on the mouth until she was pushed away by Camilla, who slapped him hard across the face and then threw her arms around him, kissing any part of him that came close. Charles Xavier's legs collapsed and he fell into the mud, pulling Camilla down with him.

The people of Titou gorged themselves, eating bunches at a time. The people filled their empty bellies until they could hold no more, vomited, waited for their stomachs to settle, and started eating again. They fell into what grass still remained, collapsing into a stupor of satiation and victory.

Ted didn't join them. He walked down the hill toward the ruins of the mercantile. Mr. Green was still standing there next to his hole, watching. For a moment their eyes met, and then the old man broke away, climbing back to continue his search. Ted cleaned the bathroom. The first time it had been cleaned in days, much of the waste nearly melted entirely away into the soil. When he finished, he climbed the slope again and began to shovel mud out of the ditch above the row of houses. It was there that Eliud found him. The other man brought with him two bunches of bananas. He was still vibrating with excitement, but he seemed almost shy as he approached, holding out one of the bunches.

"Camilla told me to bring you these."

Ted stopped shoveling and took them, nodding with acceptance.

"Thank you."

Eliud stood there for a moment, and then the dam broke. He started babbling like an over stimulated child.

"You should've seen it. He walked right up to them. The jacket kept yelling for him to step back and he just kept moving forward. I thought he'd gone stakki. He just kept repeating the same thing over and over. These people need to eat. You'll have to shoot all of us. I've never seen anything like it."

Ted stood, bananas in one hand and shovel in the other. The two men stood staring at each other. One unsure what to say and the other boiling over to say it all again. Eliud's need for action proved to be the end of it.

"Well, I've got to take these others to Mr. Green."

Eliud retreated down the hill, anxious to rejoin the revelry. Ted got back to work. By midday the people of Titou were stuffed and overwhelmed. They fell on both sides of the fence, many lying out in the warmth of the sunshine, basking in the bounties of the world. Ted grew hungry once again. He made his way down the hill and climbed over the fence. Charles Xavier was lounging with his back leaned against a banana tree, watching the world with half closed eyes, his face split by a smile showing all of his teeth. Camilla was dozing with her head against his chest. Charles Xavier waved Ted over to join him. Ted did as he was bid, careful not to step on anybody. He sat down in the grass next to his friend, shaking his head ruefully.

"You crazy son of a bitch."

Charles Xavier sounded half drunk when he answered.

"It was strange my friend, so strange. I've never felt so scared, but at the same time I didn't even feel like I was really there."

Ted stared down at the grass and broke several blades off with his fingers.

"You could've been shot."

Charles Xavier giggled to himself.

"Don't ask me how, but I knew they wouldn't do it. I just knew."

Ted didn't answer. Charles Xavier murmured to himself as he fell back into sleep.

"Just a hell of a thing Theodore, just a hell of a thing. I'm invincible."

Chapter 18

The sound of birds calling out their songs in the afternoon heat was drowned out by the deep guttural rumble of a diesel engine. The people of Titou awakened from their slumber and with groggy eyes gathered on the road to watch a yellow D-8 Cat slowly cut its way through the fallen debris. The tracked monstrosity clanked its way to the ruins of the mercantile and came to a halt. Behind it came an all wheel drive truck, Malik behind the wheel and Id riding shotgun.

The engines of the D-8 and the truck came to a rumbling halt. The people of Titou stood in silence, watching with mud covered faces. The man in the open cab of the D-8 put a leg up and lit a cigarette. Malik, already smoking a cigar, opened his door and stood on the truck step, surveying the scene before him. His eyes went first to the fallen trees and ruined mercantile, his face saying nothing, then up the hill to the row of five houses at the top. The big man spit out of the side of his mouth and hopped down to the ground. Id followed suit, mumbling to himself. The slamming of the two doors was unnaturally loud. Malik put his hands on his hips and spit again.

"I have food."

Charles Xavier stepped forward. Malik was nearly twice the bulk. They eyed each other up and down.

"What took you?"

"Things are a fucking mess. They get worse the farther down you go."

Charles Xavier grunted his understanding. Malik flicked his cigar butt into the mud.

"I have got rice, flour, canned vegetables, Spam, some canned fruit."

"How much?"

"Some. Not as much as I wanted, but some."

Charles Xavier nodded, a hint of a smile on his face.

"Any rum?"

A slow smile spread across Malik's lips. A low chuckle emanated from his throat.

"Yeah. I brought a couple cases."

Charles Xavier laughed and slapped the big man on the shoulder.

"Well, all right then."

The citizenry moved forward on the truck as one to examine what had been brought, Camilla and several of the other more prominent women pushing their way to the front to take inventory. The men surged around Malik. Laughing. Shaking his hand. The big man took it all with the reserve of a person uncomfortable with attention not under his control. The children climbed on the truck like monkeys, desperate to be involved in the action.

"Avery?"

Mr. Green was standing next to the hole, covered in dirt, his clothes ripped and his body bruised. With a shaking hand he tried to flatten the wispy white hair frizzed out on either side of his head.

"Avery!"

Mr. Green threw down his shovel and ran forward, pushing his way through the crowd. Id was happily bobbing his head with the excitement of the crowd, oblivious to the onrushing form. He gave out a squeal of fright when the old man's skinny arms were suddenly forced around him. For a moment he struggled before giving in, his entire body going stiff. Mr. Green was babbling like a child, tears pouring down his cheeks, his head only reaching to the top of the slow man's chest.

"Avery, Avery, Avery, you're alive, you're alive."

Id's frightened unsure eyes were locked onto Malik. Malik didn't look pleased, but he nodded and raised his voice to be heard above the noise of the crowd.

"It's all right Id. It's all right."

Camilla and another woman were up in the back of the truck, Camilla taking note of and the other shouting down each new discovery. People began to holler and push. Disagreements broke out over what to do with the food. Where to put it? It couldn't just be left on the ground, too many rats for that, it had to be stored somewhere. Whose house? No, not her house. You can't trust her. Two women began to scream at each other. Eliud tried to push his way between them. Charles Xavier climbed up onto the back of the truck and yelled to be heard.

"Everyone, everyone, listen to me."

The crowd fell silent.

"This is a great gift. Let's not spoil it by fighting. It will be fine on the truck for now. Tomorrow we'll figure out what to do, but tonight, tonight we celebrate."

The crowd cheered. Malik climbed back into the cab, pushing the children who had filled it out of the way, and returned with a large bag filled with notes and letters written by loved ones and given to Malik to carry back up to Titou. Malik shouted names above the clamoring of the crowd and one by one the people came forward, smiles on their faces, to claim their share of evidence of the continued existence of the outside world.

Ted waited with all the rest, but wasn't sure why. He knew there most likely wouldn't be any letters for him. There were no stamps. Half the letters didn't have envelopes. It wasn't the mail, just scribbled notes pushed into the hands of a man working his way up the mountain. How long had it been now? Over two weeks. His parents had to know by now. Malik had said it just got worse the farther down you went. Surely something that big had wormed its way into the news in Idaho. Even if it hadn't, how long would it take his mother to search out news on Domenique once he didn't call? They had to be worried. He could see his father comforting his crying mother, muttering platitudes that the boy had to be all right. Ted felt guilty. How long had it been since he had thought about his parents? It was a strange guilt, an unfair guilt, but it was there all the same. Ted knew better, but he stood and waited anyways, watching the crowd disperse to reconnect and rejoice in the existence of loved ones in private.

The last of the names were called. There were still notes in the bag. With a few of the names no one had come forward to claim them. The cowards. The runners. A few disappointed people remained. They gave Malik the chance to call more names, and when he didn't, moved off dejectedly. Ted knew it was foolish, but he had to ask. If he asked he had done his part. If he asked he didn't have to feel guilty for not worrying about his mother as much as she worried about him. Ted took a step forward, a request to look again forming on his lips, but Mrs. Seraphin beat him to it. The woman's handsome face was twisted with foreboding. Ted took a couple steps back to a respectful distance, but he watched from the corner of his eye. Mrs. Seraphin said something quietly and gestured at the bag. Malik didn't look back through the remaining notes. He breathed in slow and deep, and let it out. He put a beefy hand on Mrs. Seraphin's shoulder, leaned in close. It was impossible for his deep voice to be quiet.

"He was working clearing rubble. I asked him. He said to tell you that he was dead."

Tears wet the woman's cheeks. She jerked away from the big man. He tried to put his hand back, but she pushed it away, turned, and wandered back up the hill toward her house. Ted could hear her muttering as she moved by.

"Fuck him."

Ted waited a moment for the world to settle, and then moved forward with trepidation. Malik, his shoulders sagging, his eyes watching Mrs. Seraphin go, was lighting another cigar.

"What do you need?"

Ted looked at Malik's feet, licked his lips, and looked up.

"I know it's unlikely, but was there anything for me?"

Malik sighed, clenched one fist, and let it go.

"It's probably going to be awhile before we get much mail from the outside."

Ted nodded, knowing the question had been stupid from the start, but still fighting a feeling of disappointment. Malik blew smoke through his nose.

"If you write a letter I'll try to get it mailed when I go back down. I'm sure they'll have something set up."

"Thank you."

The big man nodded. Ted held out his hand to shake. Malik, after a pause, took it, and shook it lightly like one would do with a child. The audience was done. Malik turned and walked over to the D-8 to talk to the driver.

Preparations began for the celebration. The women, under the watchful eye of Camilla, relit the communal fire and took food from the back of the truck. The children were hustled away to play whatever games they chose, and Mr. Green, finally separating himself from Id, returned to his house with a jubilant step. The men gathered about the truck with glasses and sipped on rum provided by Malik, talking of all that had happened and coaxing the story from Malik's formidable visage. Even Ted was allowed to take part, on Charles Xavier's insistence, though he stood more outside the circle than in it. Beyond Ted were the children, close enough to listen, but far enough out to avoid attention.

Malik had left the capital with six cases of rum, but had lost all but two in making it back to Titou. The rum had been the hardest item to secure, but proved to be better than money the higher up the mountain he traveled. The capital was in ruins. Probably half the buildings had been knocked flat by Anji's rage. Malik had been there when it had hit. He had seen with his own eyes the waves of the ocean washing through the streets, carrying the boats from the harbor to the outskirts. He had watched as roofs were snatched from the tops of buildings and the occupants were sucked into the heavens. He had witnessed the debris flying through the air like a swarm of hornets, battering the city into dust. People had hidden in their basements, but when the water came they were forced to escape into a world where death came from every direction.

It had been twelve hours before the first helicopter had arrived, and two days before the first relief ship. Chaos. Hoarding. Armed soldiers and police in the streets. Men and women marked by red crosses had arrived. Volunteers carrying clipboards and bringing with them crates full of supplies emblazoned with American flags. People were quickly organized and put to work. The start of the process to move the city back up the hierarchy of needs. Food, water, shelter, healthcare. Thirty percent of the population of Domenique lived in the capital city. Twenty-three thousand endangered souls. Sixty percent lived near the west coast, right in Anji's path. Who had time to care about a hundred far up in the interior?

From the first day after the hurricane, Malik had been trying to make his way back to Titou. His house in the capital had been destroyed, but he and his wife had been taken in by a close friend of hers, a member of the House of Assembly. Malik had winced for a moment when he said it, a momentary squint that went away before it had even begun. On the fourth day Malik had been arrested for trying to bribe a police officer in order to sequester supplies. He spent several days in prison before the charms of his wife could convince her Assemblyman to secure his release. However, when it came to securing supplies and materials for Titou, the Assemblyman had been less impressed with Malik's wife than he was with Malik's money. Even when it seemed to be the end of times, the gears of pure capitalism ground on.

On the ninth day Malik had left the capital with his truck full of supplies with an old D-8 cat in the lead. It had been slow going. From the start the roads were in poor shape, blocked by fallen trees and mudslides. After three days he had reached Helston, but lacked enough fuel to push onward. The town was half abandoned when Malik arrived, though many of the buildings were still in good condition. Malik gave half of his supplies to the people still there, and then drove the truck back to the capital to get more diesel. It had taken a bit of time to secure, but his wife's Assemblyman had happily taken more of his money. Malik had driven back to Helston on the fifteenth day, delayed by mudslides and a group of policemen at a roadblock on the edge of the city who had joyfully traded four cases of rum in return for not asking any questions about where Malik had gotten the truck and supplies. On the morning of the sixteenth day, he had set out from Helston.

Eliud took the lead in telling what had happened in Titou, with others adding comments as they felt needed. Charles Xavier remained silent, sipping at his rum, those around him looking on with pride. Even Malik's features failed to hide the fact that he was evidently impressed. Never once was Camilla mentioned. Ted turned and walked away.

Chapter 19

The celebration began when the sun kissed the mountainside. People gathered about the fire, plates in hand, and ate their fill. The supper consisted of rice, vegetables, and Spam in a broth thickened by flour, plus bananas for anyone who could stomach a second round. Charles Xavier was served first and Malik second. Ted stayed near the back of the line and let anyone who wanted to pass him by. Only Eliud didn't take him up on it, the young man instead insisting that Ted go first. The ground was still muddy. People brought out blankets to sit on and even a few chairs that had miraculously survived. Two of the chairs were given to Charles Xavier and Malik. Many of the men, Ted included, carried over cinderblocks from the remains of the mercantile. Malik watched them, but said nothing. The only one who didn't join them was the D-8 driver, who not wanting to associate with hicks, politely took his helping and returned to his machine.

Crispin and Buffalo Bill carried the two cases of rum from the truck and began putting healthy pours in everybody's glasses. Charles Xavier stood on his chair and people hissed for silence. He raised his rum up into the air and everybody followed suit.

"To Titou."

The crowd responded as one.

"To Titou."

The glasses were tipped back, Charles Xavier and most of the younger men draining all of the golden liquid, others just taking a healthy sip. Ted took no more than a mouthful. Bright smiles spread across every face. The empty glasses were refilled. Eliud rose to his feet.

"To Charles Xavier."

"To Charles Xavier."

Again the glasses tipped back, again the ones who needed it were refilled, Ted amongst them this time. Charles Xavier rose again.

"To Malik."

"To Malik."

Someone shouted an addendum from the crowd.

"May his prices always be this cheap."

People laughed and even Malik gave a hint of a smile. Ted drained his glass with all the rest. The burning sweetness of the rum kissed his lips, poured down his throat, and lifted him from the ground. None of it felt real. A strange dreamscape interwoven with a sudden madness. They were alive. Things at last were going to be all right. Camilla sat on a blanket at the foot of her husband's throne, sipping at her rum and smiling at the world around her. Ted came unsteadily to his feet, his glass held high, his voice rising above the laughter and the murmured jokes.

"To Camilla."

Silence. Everyone stared up at Ted, their faces filled with surprise at the sound of his voice. Ted licked his lips, uncomfortable. Charles Xavier stood again.

"To Camilla."

The crowd raised their glasses.

"To Camilla."

Ted drank, his face bright red, Camilla watching him over her glass. People talked and the voices combined into a growing chatter. None of the glasses were allowed to stay empty. Someone began to sing and more voices rose to join them. Two of the water buckets were dumped and flipped so they could be used as drums. Men and women began to dance, swaying in the intermingled last hints of sunlight and the glow of the flickering flames. Ted tried to stay to the side with those who preferred to watch, but Charles Xavier pulled him into the rhythmic crowd where he shuffled awkwardly, eliciting loud guffaws and polite giggles from the gyrating forms around him.

The people of Titou twirled around Ted. Charles Xavier howling at the moon. Eliud with a bottle in each hand. Crispin and Buffalo Bill drunkenly stumbling through their steps. Camilla shaking her hips, coming close, almost close enough to touch, then moving away. Mrs. Seraphin took two younger men by hand and danced with both, her eyes wild and bright, her body wantonly shimmying like a snake. She took a drink from each of Eliud's bottles, screamed upward at the stars, and then dragged the reluctant D-8 driver into the crowd, plying him with rum until his prejudices fell away and he danced with all the rest.

Camilla came close again, her skin glowing with perspiration. Ted could feel the heat coming off of her. They locked eyes and she smiled and spun away. Charles Xavier grabbed Ted's hands and the two spun, clearing a space around them until without warning Charles Xavier let go, sending them both sprawling backwards into the mud. Ted felt the air leave his lungs with a loud whump. Charles Xavier's loud laugh rattled above the music. Several hands helped Ted back to his feet. Charles Xavier was already standing, Eliud pouring rum down his throat, the excess running down his chin. Charles Xavier howled again and grabbed the nearest woman, lifting her off her feet, spinning her through the air.

Ted felt dizzy and a little sick. He was covered with sweat and mud. He pushed his way out of the circle and worked his way down the hill toward the tree line, leaving the cacophony of the celebration behind. It was cooler away from the fire. A soft breeze kissed the leaves in the trees. The graves of Mrs. Green and Eugene Hewitt reared up out of the darkness. Ted stopped a respectful distance away. Eugene's bloody face clawed its way forward.

"It's strange isn't it?"

Ted jumped and jerked his head around. Mr. Green had appeared silently from the darkness. The dirt had been scrubbed from his body. He wore clean clothes and his hair was neatly combed. Ted said nothing, but his face must have shown his confusion. Mr. Green gestured back toward the fire.

"Strange how the world works. What it takes for us to show what we can truly be. How losing ourselves can teach us so much about who we truly are."

Mr. Green walked forward and stood next to Ted. He looked down at the graves and let out a sigh.

"She was a good wife. I wish I had told her more how important she was to me when she was alive. She was a better person than me. She always wanted me to have Avery live with us instead of down in the mercantile. I don't know. Maybe I was just stubborn."

Mr. Green stood quietly, his hands clasped in front of him. Ted felt unsure what to say.

"Eugene was kind to me once. It meant a lot to me."

The shadow that was Mr. Green nodded its head.

"He was a good boy. Always stayed and helped clean up when he was in school."

Silence once again. Eugene's bloody face stared at Ted through the darkness. He looked back at the firelight.

"Are you going back to the fire?"

The shadow shook its head and swayed. Mr. Green was a little drunk.

"No, I think I'll stay here for awhile. Ask my wife for some advice. Maybe this time I'll actually listen."

Ted nodded, stood for a moment, and turned away to make his way back toward the fire. The only light was the nearly full moon and the flames glinting across the empty rum bottles littering the ground. The crowd was less, many had gone to bed. Others lay strewn where they had dropped, their bodies bent in strange positions, snoring peacefully amongst the chaos of those who still danced. A chair, whole and unbroken, burned on the fire. The beat of the drumming and singing had slowed. Mrs. Seraphin, her eyes closed, danced in the center, the D-8 driver pressed up against her back, Eliud clasped against her front. One of her hands was up behind her shoulder, gently caressing the side of the D-8 driver's face. Her eyes opened, cold feline eyes, and searched across the crowd, hungry. Malik was still sitting in his chair, watching the world with an impassive air. Charles Xavier was crouched next to him. The two men were talking, Malik sedate, Charles Xavier's gestures broad and on the edge of control. Charles Xavier looked at Mrs. Seraphin and her dance partners, took a drink of rum from his glass, and smiled, his lips slowly peeling back from his teeth. His laughter carried out across the night. Camilla glided out of the dance floor and over to Ted.

"I need your help."

"What is it?"

Camilla motioned for Ted to follow. She led him around the outside of the circle, careful to step over a sleeping Crispin. The two Seraphin children lay huddled together, sleeping on a half sodden muddy blanket.

"We need to put the little ones to bed. Their momma won't quit dancing."

Ted looked back into the center, following the gaze of all eyes still alert and part of the present world. Her body moved as though it had no bones. The D-8 driver's hands worked their way across her thighs.

"C'mon now, we can't let them sleep in the dirt."

Camilla lifted the boy into Ted's arms. The mass grunted in his sleep, but made no other sound. Camilla picked up the girl and started walking up the hill. Ted followed. It was darker away from the fire, but his eyes adjusted. Each step squelched and he was careful not to step in any of the half full ditches. His socks were wet. He wondered how long it had been since he had noticed. Camilla cradled her cargo as though she was an overgrown babe. Ted carried his like a bag of grain, unsure of exactly what the appropriate way was. When they arrived at the house Camilla had Ted wait outside. She carried the girl in, returned, then took the boy from his arms. When she came out the second time she pulled the door closed behind her.

"Thank you."

Ted nodded, his eyes tracking back down toward the fire. Camilla's view followed his.

"Don't judge her too harshly. We all have our times."

Ted nodded again. He felt dizzy. Camilla stepped forward, kissed him gently on the cheek, and moved away.

"You coming back to the fire?"

Ted felt ready to drop. His head was swimming.

"No, I think I'll just call it a night."

Camilla nodded and headed down the hill. Ted watched her go and then walked over to his house. He stood on the porch for a moment, scrutinizing the world below. Another chair had been thrown onto the fire, reigniting the vigor of the singers and drummers. Mrs. Seraphin still danced in the center, only one man with her now, a shirtless shadow against the dirt stained yellow of her dress, the hem pulled up above her knees by furtive hands. Ted went into his house and shut the door. It was hot inside. The sounds of the celebration carried through the walls and broken windows. He undressed and climbed into his sleep sack, leaving it half unzipped. He stared upward at the ceiling, waiting for sleep to come.

Sandi twirled around him on the dance floor, her blonde hair whipping behind her like the tail of a comet. He brought her in close, his hand on her lower back pressing her up against him, and kissed her lightly on the mouth. Her blue eyes sparkled as she pressed every inch of her body against his. He could feel himself stiffen with anticipation.

"Spin me."

With a twist of his wrist he whipped her away from his body, rolling her down his arm. She spun as she moved on an outward arc, stretching away with only the clasp of a hand connecting them. He jerked his wrist to pull her back, but somebody came between them, pulling her away, breaking the last network of their fingers. Charles Xavier swept her across the dance floor, his head kicked back, his laughter filled with joy at being alive. Sandi was laughing too. Ted tried to follow, but couldn't. His feet were stuck to the ground. Charles Xavier and Sandi spun around each other, orbiting Ted like he was the sun, diving in and pulling out, but always just out of reach.

The front door of Ted's house opened and closed. The world was filled with silence. The sounds of the celebration were absent. Ted sat up on his cot, the springs squeaking. A familiar shadowy form was outlined in the dim light of the moon from the window. A shape recognized from furtive desperate dreams. The shadow pulled its dress up over its head and let it fall to the ground. It stepped forward.

"What...?"

A finger pressed against his lips, silencing his words. The shadow opened his sleep sack and a calloused hand reached downward where the blood had already began to flow. He could hear her breathing, rapid and shallow. His own breathing was the same. Ample thighs pressed down on either side and she hissed softly as she put him inside. She rode him to the rhythm of his beating heart. Faster and faster. He tried to rise up, but a strong arm pushed him back down. Flesh on flesh. Heavy breathing. The squeak of the cot springs. Uncontrollable sounds emanating from deep within him, growing until he screamed with the peaking of his ecstasy. Ted melted into his sleep sack, unable to move, his body and mind weak in the aftermath. Camilla climbed off of him, pulled her dress back over her head, and walked back out into the night.

Chapter 20

Ted woke with a bad headache and a fuzzy mind. His body was drenched with sweat, the air already hot and humid. A bird sat on the back window frame, proudly tweeting a couple notes above a miniature grove of green shoots topped by the start of newly emerging leaves. The bird took flight off into the distance. Ted climbed out of his sleep sack and pulled on his clothes. In the town below he could hear singing. Not the frenzied singing of the night before, but the calm jovial singing of happy labor. Despite the rigors of the previous night's festivities, the people of Titou were already hard at work.

Ted stood on his porch and looked down upon the town. It was an anthill of activity. People finishing their breakfast next to the fire, people carrying buckets full of water from the reservoir, people cleaning the diversion ditches full of mud, and children chasing rats, real and imagined, with sharpened hoes. The only one not moving was the D-8 driver, who leaned against his machine, smoking a cigarette. Malik stood next to his truck, checking off items on a clipboard as people carried boxes, bags, cartons, and cans into one of the still better standing houses near the fire. The former occupants, carrying what meager belongings they had left, were dispersed amongst their neighbors.

Ted's eyes tracked across the scene, searching. She wasn't by the fire. She wasn't amongst the ditch diggers. Perhaps she was in the house turned warehouse, taking note of everything brought in. Charles Xavier was amongst the men digging out the ditches. He looked up and saw Ted up on the hill. He smiled and raised his hand in greeting. Ted forced a smile and waved back, guilt playing its way across his conscious. Charles Xavier got back to work. Ted stepped off the porch to join them.

Breakfast was bulgur porridge with canned fruit mixed in. It was the first time Ted could remember eating canned fruit since arriving on Domenique. Ted did his usual duties behind the remains of Malik's mercantile, re-digging the hole to bury the scat, gathering and disposing what had already been left in the designated area, and retrieving a bucket of water from above the reservoir for washing. Behind the ruins of the mercantile he felt relaxed. Safe from prying eyes. Alone to think about the events of the night before. He wanted to ask Camilla about it, but didn't know what to say. What did it mean, what should he do, and most importantly, would it happen again? The thought of her on top of him filled him with a barely contained lust. A sharp counterpoint to his nausea, the product of a gut full of guilt and cheap rum. Maybe it was nothing. Maybe just a drunken dream. No, it had been real. A fantasy brought to life. He just wished he could talk to Camilla.

Dinner was the same as breakfast, though nobody went without their fill, which in itself was a pleasant change in pace. Ted looked for Camilla by the cookfire, but she wasn't there. The cooking was being overseen by the lithe form of Mrs. Seraphin who eyed the world with a fierce determination, a tiger broken free from its chains, challenging any to question the stretching out of her limbs. She made jokes and laughed with the abandon of someone who had not done so in some time, and openly flirted, both verbally and physically, with every man who was not Ted. All Ted got was an expressionless face and a helping of food, though the eyes at least weren't cold.

Charles Xavier insisted that Ted sit next to him. Ted did as he was bid, his joints and movements stiff. Ted ate in silence and listened to Charles Xavier rib Eliud for the quality of his dancing.

"I thought your feet were nailed to the ground the way you moved. Even my friend Theodore here, little better than a shaved bear shuffling about on his hind legs, at least knows to keep his paws moving."

Eliud laughed and poked the other man with his elbow.

"Better than you my friend. I thought you had gone stakki the way you were throwing yourself about. It must have been why your wife was dancing with me. She was afraid of losing an eye."

"My wife is a charitable woman."

Both men whooped and roared and an involuntary smile played its way across Ted's lips, followed by the question ricocheting its way through his brain.

"Where is Camilla?"

Charles Xavier shrugged his shoulders as nonchalantly as he was able.

"I haven't seen her all morning."

Ted wanted to ask more, but Charles Xavier's attention had already shifted to the cook fire where Mrs. Seraphin was swatting her son's ass with a wooden spoon, punishment for some unknown transgression. The boy was howling and the woman was releasing an unending chain of curses which threw themselves from her mouth in rhythm with the whacks of the wooden spoon. Half of the town was doing their best to find something else to look at, and the other half was laughing uproariously as the boy squirmed. Unable to take anymore, the boy threw all of his weight forward, dragging both he and his mother to the ground. Mrs. Seraphin rose to her hands and knees, but the boy was already running out of reach. His sister took after him, slapping him about the head and shoulders as they ran. Charles Xavier was almost choking he was laughing so hard. Eliud was one of the ones not laughing.

"She shouldn't beat the boy like that."

Charles Xavier elbowed him sharply.

"You're just jealous because you wish you were on the receiving end."

Eliud fidgeted and looked away. Charles Xavier's mirth redoubled. He poked Ted with his elbow.

"Nothing like a woman to scramble a sensible man, ain't that right Theodore."

Ted felt his guts twist. Mrs. Seraphin got up, brushed off her skirt, and stalked after her brood, every muscle in her face and arms tightened with tension. Eliud got up and went back to work. Everyone else soon followed.

The afternoon was much like the morning. People mostly kept their heads down and worked. Ted kept his on a swivel, his eyes hunting for Camilla, but couldn't find her anywhere. Charles Xavier seemed unconcerned. He worked alongside Eliud, throwing a shovel load of mud onto the younger man from time to time and dodging the mud thrown in return. Ted mostly worked in areas by himself. Out of sight and out of mind, he could concentrate on replaying the events of the night before over and over in his head, a voyeur to his own actions. He ached to feel it all again.

The D-8 left soon after dinner. The growling of the beast was heard for some time after it disappeared from view, working its way back down the mountain. Malik made plans to leave as soon as the truck was fully unloaded. He would return to the capital and then come back in about a week with more supplies. It was around mid-afternoon when he was ready. The people of Titou gathered around to watch him go, crying out reminders for him to let various relatives know that they were still alive. Ted was behind the mercantile, dreaming his dreams and cleaning up the shit once again. The commotion by the truck gave way to yelling. A solitary voice above them all.

"You're not taking him! He's staying here!"

Ted rushed around the ruins. Amongst the mass of people, Malik and Mr. Green stood facing each other. Malik looked bored and a little disgusted. Mr. Green looked pissed, his body shaking as he screamed. Id stood between them, slightly to the side, his big body shivering, his eyes wide with fear. Malik was easily twice the size of the diminutive Mr. Green. Malik said something too quiet for Ted to hear. Mr. Green screamed back, repeating his declaration. Malik moved forward to take Id by the arm. Mr. Green screamed again and rushed forward. A skinny arm shot out, catching Malik a solid blow to the side of the nose, unleashing a trickle of blood. A big fist shot back and then Mr. Green was on the ground, the bigger man on top of him. It was almost ridiculous. Two old men rolling in the dirt. Somebody yelled, a high pitched woman's voice. Several men moved forward to break them apart, but Id beat them to it. Id, screaming incomprehensibly, grabbed Malik by his shoulders and threw him to the ground. Then he was on top of him, swinging wildly, his words echoing clearly from the mountainside.

"Don't fight! Don't fight! Don't fight! Don't fight!"

It took four men to drag Id off. He took a few last wild swings and then collapsed to the ground, crying like a small child. Mr. Green, his lip split and one eye blackened, crawled over to comfort him. Malik stood up and spit a mouthful of blood into the dirt. He took a white handkerchief from his pocket and wiped the blood from his nose. He said something that Ted couldn't hear, and then climbed into the truck, cranked the engine, and headed back down the mountain. People milled about for a bit, quietly talking, and then got back to work. Ted followed suit. It was only when the last sounds of the truck disappeared that he remembered he was supposed to give Malik a letter for his parents. He cursed to himself, but otherwise was unaffected. Any feelings of guilt were buried by his more immediate questions and musings.

Camilla had still not returned by evening. Ted didn't go down to the fire for supper. Charles Xavier brought him up a bowl of bulgur and a banana.

"I thought you might be hungry."

Ted nodded his thanks. He wished Charles Xavier would leave, but the other man sat on the edge of Ted's porch so Ted felt obligated to join him. The two men watched the world below in silence. A day of working alone had done little to sort out Ted's mind. Where was Camilla? Did Charles Xavier know what had happened? Was he angry? He didn't seem angry. Maybe he didn't know. Ted's throat was tight. It was hard to swallow. He felt guilty. He felt angry at himself for feeling guilty. Angry at Charles Xavier. He felt guilty for feeling angry. Camilla was Charles Xavier's wife, but given how he was, what right did he have to judge what Ted and Camilla had done? Who had the right to hold others to a standard they couldn't hold themselves to? It felt awkward sitting in silence. Ted eating. Charles Xavier watching the people of Titou finish out their day. Charles Xavier was peaceful, almost serene. There was no evidence of a storm like the one working its way through Ted. Not knowing what else to do, Ted was the first to open his mouth.

"What happened down there with Malik?"

Charles Xavier let out a little sigh.

"Just a little disagreement on whether Id should stay or go."

"I can't believe Mr. Green took a swing at him. Malik's got to be twice his size."

"I think Mr. Green might be a little scattered. Big things like death can do that sometimes."

The two men lapsed back into silence. Ted finished his supper and placed the plate down on the porch. He licked his lips. Part of him was screaming to confess, but he shoved it back down deep.

"I'm worried about Camilla. I haven't seen her all day."

Charles Xavier gave Ted a long appraising look, his eyes searching Ted's face for a bit before turning back to the outside world. Ted shoved the thoughts of confession down deeper.

"Sometimes when you bring a mountain bird down to lower altitudes, they need to go back up to where the air is a little more thin. It's not the first time. She'll be back when she's ready."

The sunset was quite beautiful. The two men sat and watched it slip below the horizon, the only sound the occasional twitter of a bird in the forest. The muddy streets and paths of Titou became empty and quiet. When the last rays disappeared, Charles Xavier got up without a word and went into his house. Ted sat and waited for a bit and then went to bed himself. His sleep sack was cozy and the springs on the cot creaked beneath him.

In the middle of the night he woke to the sound of Charles Xavier and Camilla making love next door. Ted's hands clenched tightly into fists. His jaw hurt. Images flashed through his mind. Charles Xavier throwing himself into her with wild abandon. Camilla on top of Ted. Sandi in the same position. Sandi sucking some guy named John's dick. The look on her face when she came to the apartment to get the last of her stuff. The man named John waiting in a car to take her off to Portland for what she called a fresh start. Tears in his eyes. Camilla silently putting back on her dress and walking out the door. Ted tried to cover his ears, but it didn't work. It was too hot in his sleep sack. Sweat covered his body. His stomach was roiling. He felt like he was going to be sick. Ted pulled himself from the sleep sack, not bothering to unzip it the entire way, oozing his way out. He rushed out to the porch wearing nothing, holding himself up against one of the posts.

The moon was out. The wind frolicked its way peacefully through the branches of the trees. Ted fell to his hands and knees and puked up the bulgur and banana Charles Xavier had brought him. He spit the last of the bile from his mouth and rolled into a sitting position.

The sounds of passion continued unabated. What the fuck was wrong with him? The world around him was nothing but shadows. A stifled cough sounded to his left. Ted turned his head. Two houses down. Mrs. Seraphin stood on her porch, a shadow in the night, staring downwards towards the road. Her shadowy form moved stiffly, every movement sudden and quick. Haggard breathing. The sounds of lovemaking reached a crescendo and then fell silent. Murmuring in the darkness. The form of Mrs. Seraphin wiped both eyes with the back of her dark hand and the shadow disappeared back inside. Ted sat on his porch and cried, and when all the tears were gone, went back inside and went to bed.

She came for him the next afternoon. He did his best to avoid her, but she hunted him out.

"Could you help me with some laundry?"

Ted didn't really want to, too many questions were boiling their way through his head. Too many accusations. Camilla seemed not to notice the turmoil that she caused.

"We could wash yours as well."

No. What was the other night about? What was she doing? What was going on?

"Okay."

She turned and started walking and he followed, a wayward puppy climbing up the hill. They washed the clothes in buckets behind her house, twisting out the water and dirt, hanging the clothes on the line to dry. He refused to meet her eye. At most he looked at her hands. Her beautiful hands that had taken him and…….god damn it. Ted focused on the work, filling his senses with nothing but washing of the clothes until suddenly there was nothing left to focus on. He stared at his own hands. He heard her laugh.

"You could use a good scrubbing yourself."

He looked up at her. She was smiling coyly at him. Doubts and questions, all silence by a sudden primal understanding. She went to her house and came back with a bucket of clean water and a soft sponge. They went into his house. For a moment the logical parts of his brain pushed their way to the forefront again, but they were quickly silenced. She pulled off his shirt and unhooked his jeans. She pushed him onto the useless toilet and took off his boots and pants. Words rose from his throat again and again, but each time were killed before they could be emitted, silenced before they broke the soap bubble of the dream. He was naked before her. She took a sponge from the bucket and scrubbed him from head to toe. He felt like years since the last time he had experienced a true scrubbing, not just splashing some water on himself to take off the worst of the caked on dirt. She scrubbed one place longer than the rest. She didn't use the sponge. He was scared. He could hear people working farther down the hillside. She helped him relax with her touch. They made love. She left. He stayed, feeling dirty, but euphoric.

Chapter 21

It was a week before Malik returned. For the people of Titou, it was all together not that unpleasant. It continued to rain intermittently, but the first signs of new growth were beginning to appear. Patches of green amongst the red of the mud. People with full bellies looked out at the ruined world with a new gleam in their eyes. The hunger was gone, replaced by a need to make the world right again. Perhaps some would've preferred to rest after their long ordeal, but Charles Xavier kept at them. There was too much to do to start doing nothing. Water still needed to be packed and the ditches still needed to be cleared.

Early one morning he set a group, Ted amongst them, to chopping away with hatchets at the tree across the plantation fence. It was a large formidable palm. They worked in teams, one resting while the other chopped. Ted was paired with Crispin, whose long time working in the plantation office showed in the clumsiness of his efforts. Ted did little better, until Eliud kindly showed the two of them how to improve their swings. Afterwards Ted's efforts became much more effective, though Crispin's remained mediocre at best. Crispin could at best go for fifteen minutes at a time. Ted pushed himself over half an hour. Crispin complained. Ted said nothing. The other men noticed. Ted caught Buffalo Bill rolling his eyes whenever the other man complained.

"Why are we fucking with this? It's the fucking plantation's problem, not ours."

Charles Xavier handed his hatchet to Eliud and laughed at the other man's whines.

"Listen to my friend Crispin. He worked in an office yet he knows nothing about keeping books."

Crispin gave Charles Xavier the evil eye and spit in the mud. Charles Xavier's smile faded and his features turned serious.

"We did what we did because we had to, but we aren't thieves. We don't need anymore, so we'll not take. The least we can do is put back up the jakes' fence."

Buffalo Bill chimed in from the other side, his voice thick with sarcasm.

"Can't we just ask our jake whether or not it's all right to eat his bananas?"

The men laughed and Buffalo Bill gestured towards Ted.

"What about it jake? Can we enjoy the harvest of our labors?"

Charles Xavier sprouted a grin that would put a Cheshire cat to shame.

"You dunce bat, that's the wrong jake."

"My mistake. They all look alike. Bright red."

Ted didn't know how to feel. It seemed like gentle ribbing, but all the attention made him uncomfortable. Eliud filled the silence between chops.

"Charles Xavier is just nervous that if Camilla has an endless supply of bananas she won't need his anymore."

The men broke out laughing, Ted along with all the rest. Charles Xavier parried back.

"At least mine doesn't get left out until it's brown and mushy."

The steady beat of the hatchets halted as the men guffawed. The words came out of Ted's mouth before he realized he was thinking out loud.

"Charles Xavier's just upset because the plantation is full of Cavendish while all he has is an Orito."

The group went silent. Ted was surrounded by a sea of white eyes and tight mouths. He licked his lips nervously. Charles Xavier's face twitched and then burst like a firework of amusement.

"That's okay, everyone knows Oritos have the sweeter taste."

The men laughed in a rolling wave, their faces split with uncontrollable mirth. Charles Xavier wrapped Ted in a bear hug and tried to lift him off his feet. Several of the other men patted him on the back and murmured words of encouragement.

"We thought you had him jake. We thought someone finally had him."

The chopping began anew. The men started singing and Ted sang along, though he really didn't know the words. The tree was in enough pieces to be lifted not long after dinner. The crushed chain link of the fence was raised back up, straightened as much as possible, and secured to its poles with pieces of heavy duty wire that somebody had dug out of the remains of the mercantile. As the others filed away, Ted looked through the newly repaired fence at the lines of banana trees. His eyes probed between the rows, but there was nothing there. It was another world, now once again completely separate. Ted turned and walked away.

That night people laughed and joked at supper. There was even a little dancing, though nothing like the night of the celebration. People were happy and it was hard not to feel the growing beat of their ecstasy.

The next day Charles Xavier set them to dismantling the debris that had once been Malik's mercantile. More tools were pulled out of the tunnel, and they started on the far side, sorting wood, tin, and cinderblocks into separate piles. Malik was a tightfisted son of a bitch, but he had come through when he was needed and the favor had to be repaid. Others were set to cutting wood for the fire, and clearing the path to the cemetery and to the world farther up the mountain.

After dinner Eliud tapped him on the arm, a quick furtive movement meant to keep contact to a minimum.

"Hey jake, help me refill some buckets."

Ted nodded his head.

"Okay."

With two buckets each they climbed the mountainside behind Titou. Mr. Green was sitting on his porch with Id, trying to teach him the alphabet. Id mostly stared off down the hill. Mrs. Seraphin was behind her house, washing clothes. Eliud's head turned to watch her as they moved past. It took awhile to reach their destination. The trees closed in around them. Both were soon covered in sweat.

What had once been the reservoir was now at best a swamp of mud and shallow water. Mosquitoes buzzed en masse, a flickering carpet upon the water's surface. Around two hundred feet above the reservoir was the small waterfall, maybe seven feet high. A perfect place to fill their buckets. Eliud stood in the cool water, holding the buckets in place while Ted handed him the empty and took the full. When the last bucket was filled Eliud held his head under the falls, shaking it with the enthusiasm of a dog. Ted cupped some water in his hands and splashed it on his face, letting the excess drip down to wet his shirt. He ran his hands through his beard and lengthening hair. He tried to think of something to say. The decrepit shape of his grandfather filled his mind.

"Hot today, isn't it?"

Ted's grandfather had always said to talk about the weather. Everyone could talk about the weather. Eliud's long legs were knees deep in the water, his face content.

"Better here than down in Helston. At least we get a breeze now and again."

Ted nodded as though he understood. For a moment the men with guns flashed through his head, then Camilla, then Sandi, then his mother, then the guns again.

"If it's better here why do all the plantation bosses live in Helston?"

"More people means more stuff. More people like them too. All they got up here is Malik, and he's not really the friendliest soul on the island."

Ted nodded again. Eliud sighed and climbed out of the water.

"Ten miles closer too if shit goes bad. People on Domenique, they like the coast. The world is down there."

Ted didn't really know how to answer. An image of Camilla filled his mind again. Her hands around him. He watched her every chance he got. He hadn't had a chance to really speak to her since the last time, nothing beyond pleasantries, but whenever she caught him looking she would give him a little smile, a secret smile. It set his blood on fire, but Charles Xavier was always somewhere near. Ted would lay in his cost each night, praying that he wouldn't have to hear Charles Xavier and Camilla make love. His prayers had been answered. The work of the day dulled all of Charles Xavier's wants and needs.

Eliud grabbed two of the buckets and gestured with his chin.

"C'mon jake. Still things to be done."

Halfway back down there was a rustling in the thick greenery.
The two men paused. Eliud put his buckets down and took a step
forward, half crouched and waiting. Ted saw a flash of orange
feathers to his right. A pale arm swung and a bucket flew through the
air. Water splashed, grass and branches crunched, and the chicken
gave out a loud squawk as forty pounds of water and blue plastic came
down on top of it. Ted walked off the trail to retrieve the bucket, Eliud
scrambling after.

"Is it dead?"

Ted gingerly picked up the chicken by its feet. The head hung
loose, the neck nothing but jelly. It made his skin crawl to be holding
it, but Eliud was laughing and slapping him on the back.

"I've been trying to catch that jacket for over a week. Kept
hearing him move around every time I came up here. That was one
hell of a throw."

Ted held out the chicken for Eliud to take, but Eliud held up his
hands.

"You killed it. It's yours to have. Lucky jake. Everyone would
kill for some fresh meat."

They didn't bother to refill the bucket. Ted carried it in one hand
with the full bucket, and carried the dead chicken with the other.
 When they got back to Titou the two Seraphin kids were rough
housing behind their house, covered in dirt from head to toe. The two
children didn't notice the mud they splattered on their mother's drying
clothes. Mrs. Seraphin was sitting on the porch in the front of her
house, watching the people below working on the mercantile. Eliud
eyed her as they moved past. Ted put down his bucket and
approached. Mrs. Seraphin didn't look up until he was close.

"What do you want jake?"

Her voice was a dull knife cutting the air. Ted held out the
chicken.

"Eliud killed this chicken today on the path, he wanted you and
your kids to have it."

Mrs. Seraphin looked up at Ted, studying his face. She leaned
over and looked at Eliud, still standing a ways back behind, gawky and
nervous. She looked at Ted again and took the chicken. It was a

skinny thing. More feather and bone than meat. Mr. Green was watching from his porch. Mrs. Seraphin's forehead wrinkled.

"Eliud killed this chicken?"

Ted nodded.

"Yes ma'am."

Mrs. Seraphin rose to her feet. Her eyes locked onto the man behind Ted. Eliud turned and fled down the hill, sloshing water as he went. Ted returned to his own buckets and followed. That evening at supper Mrs. Seraphin brought a cooked chicken leg to Eliud. She sat next to him for a bit and the two talked, too quiet for Ted to hear from where he sat a little distance away. When Mrs. Seraphin got up and left, Eliud followed her with his eyes, the traces of a smile on his lips. He glanced at Ted, but Ted only saw it from the corner of his eye, he was already moving up the hill to his own house to sleep.

Charles Xavier was sitting on his porch. His body was slumped and his eyes vacantly stared at nothing. The moment he saw Ted his back straightened and a wide smile split his lips.

"Theodore my friend. How are you this evening?"

"Doing well, and you?"

For a moment Charles Xavier was quiet, his brain slowly grinding its way forward.

"Fine as a woman's kiss."

Charles Xavier laughed, but it lacked some of its normal jovialness. He patted the porch next to him. Ted hesitated, but sat down. Neither man spoke. They sat quietly, watching the fading twilight. Charles Xavier took in a deep breath and let it out.

"Almost like it was before, just missing the rum."

Ted smiled in the growing darkness.

"To be honest, I'm not really missing the rum."

Charles Xavier smiled as well.

"Yes, there are definitely things in life much sweeter. It's probably best not to have any, still so much to get done."

The two men fell quiet again. Charles Xavier's head began to slump. Soft snores growled through his nose. Ted rose and walked toward his own house. Mr. Green was sitting on the porch next door. He looked over the sleeping man in front of the red house.

"Mr. Skerritt seems pretty sleepy."

Ted nodded.

"Yeah, pretty worn out I guess."

Mr. Green smiled sagely.

"A lot of eyes can wear you down to a nub."

Ted didn't know how to answer so he went inside. He climbed into his sleep sack and reveled in the silence, dark shadowy hands groping their way across his body.

Camilla found him on the fifth day after Malik's departure.

"I need your help with that clothesline again. It's beginning to sag."

He followed upward toward the row of houses. They walked between the yellow house and the red. She grabbed his hand and drug him into his house. His heart did its best to hammer its way out of his chest. Endorphins bogged down his system and made it impossible to string together coherent thoughts. She didn't bother to take off her dress. She just hiked it up around her thighs and pulled Ted down on top of her. It made Ted nervous, the sounds of people working and singing drifting through the broken windows, but it also lit a charge within him which he had never felt before, exciting him until he was more beast than man, ravishing Camilla until she was forced to bite down on a wadded hem of her dress so as not to attract any attention. She whispered in his ear. Urging him on, boosting him higher with the urgency of her demands.

"Camilla. Camilla. Where are you woman?"

Charles Xavier's voice was working its way up the hill. Camilla pushed Ted off of her, stood, straightened her dress, and made her escape out the back door of Ted's house. Ted sat on his cot in a confused daze, his pants still around his ankles, his lust out in the open for all to see. Charles Xavier's head appeared in the broken window frame. The other man glanced in as he passed by, drew up short, looked again, and let out a laugh.

"Jesus, Theodore. We all have needs, but try to have some class. What if poor Mrs. Seraphin walked by while you were cranking your pump? Now hurry up and finish, there's still a lot of work to get done today."

Charles Xavier laughed again and then moved on to his own house where he greeted his wife with a loud hello and the smack of a kiss on the lips. Ted was too ashamed to finish himself off, so he spent the rest of the day moving carefully, a pain in his crotch like a hand tightly squeezing his testicles. Ted didn't sit with Charles Xavier on the porch that night. He made excuses that he was tired and went straight to bed.

When Malik returned, his truck was not only loaded with food, but also lumber and other building materials. Charles Xavier and Camilla supervised the unloading, making sure the lumber was stacked underneath a tarp so it would stay as dry as possible. When Id saw Malik he charged down the hill to show him how he now knew the first eight letters of the alphabet, though he could only recite six in the correct order. Malik patted Id on the shoulder and then sent him back to Mr. Green.

Malik also brought paper, pencils, and envelopes. People clamored around him for the chance to send more notes and actual letters back down the mountain, Ted amongst them, anxious to assuage the guilt he felt he should have. With the necessary materials in hand, he retreated back to his house to write.

The counter was the only good writing surface left. Ted bent over it, pencil at ready, trying to think what to write. What could he say about what was going on? How could he describe what had happened? Images of Camilla filled his mind. He forced them back, replacing them with his mother's tear filled eyes. People had always said he had his mother's eyes. Maybe they thought he was dead? Maybe they had already had a funeral, burying an empty box in the ground. The thought made Ted laugh to himself, but he banished it away as well. He was being silly. Stupid even. His mother wasn't that type of person. She was probably calling the Peace Corps every day demanding answers, alternating between cursing and guilt inducing pleading, making her way up the chain of command. She'd talk to the president if she had to. He was, after all, her only son, risking his life to volunteer for his country. In truth, Ted wouldn't have been surprised to see her walking up the road from Helston. He would've been horrified, but not surprised. No, that wasn't right either. He couldn't discount the passive influence of his father. Ted's father was the type to let those who were supposed to be doing something do their jobs. He was able to wait. He'd let the Peace

Corps make sure Ted was okay. But where was the Peace Corps?
Why hadn't anyone come looking for him? What was going on in the
wider world?

Ted took in a breath and let it out. He had no excuse. It wouldn't
be right to send nothing. He had to write something.

Mom and Dad,

*I'm writing to let you know that I am all right. Anji, the
hurricane, hit Titou quite badly. All communications were knocked
out and the road was only recently reopened. This has been my first
chance to get word back out to the wider world. The town is in poor
shape, though it sounds as though not as poor as down on the coast,
but I am healthy and helping to do what I can here. Please do not
worry. I will write more as soon as I get the chance, but for now,
know that I am okay.*

Love,
Ted

It seemed incomplete. It didn't tell the whole story. Ted knew
what his mother would likely want him to do. She would want him to
catch a ride with Malik back down the mountain. She'd tell him to get
his ass back home where he'd be safe. That was a relative term. It
wasn't like Ted was in any danger where he was. God only knew how
bad things were in the capital where the brunt of the storm had hit.
No, better to stay in Titou. Better the known than the unknown. He
was helping here. It was better if he stayed put. Besides, it would be
easier for the Peace Corps to find him if he stayed. It was all a bunch
of bullshit. Ted knew it was, but what was he supposed to do? He
sure as hell couldn't put in the letter that he was staying because he
was involved in an affair. Ted knew what his mother would think of
that. Her opinions on such things were no secret. She had no patience
for homewreckers. He wasn't so sure about his father, outside of the
day to day at the potato plant the man didn't speak much, especially on
a personal level. God only knew what went through is head.

Ted sealed the letter in the envelope and wrote his parents'
address on the front. For a moment he thought about writing a letter to

Mr. Douglas too. Ted didn't give it much thought. Fuck it. It had been weeks since the hurricane and still nobody had shown up to check on him. If they wanted to know he was alive, they could wait. What did they expect him to do? Go down to the capital? Start making a big huff because he was an American? Jesus, the whole island was devastated. Lots of people were hurt. Plenty were worried about their loved ones. What made him so special? Why should he get special treatment? It wasn't right. It wasn't fair. No, Ted would stay put. It might be months until things got sorted out, but it would be best if he stayed where he was. His parents would know he was okay. That was the important part.

The next morning Ted took his letter to the truck and handed it to Malik, who added it to a growing bunch in an old plastic shopping bag. Ted didn't have any stamps, or even any money to pay for them. Most of the letters didn't. Malik never said a word about it. He took the letters and left later that morning, the big tires of the truck squelching their way through the mud, churning up the recently risen young grass.

Chapter 22

The people of Titou fell upon the building materials with a gusto. The first thing they built, much to Ted's relief, was a twin set of outhouses. Eliud had clever hands. Under the supervision of Charles Xavier he completed the construction. It took less than a day. Lots of hands meant less work. The next morning they dug the holes. The outhouses were built on skids so that they could be easily moved once a hole was filled. Ted didn't think that was the best idea. He voiced his concerns about long-term durability to Charles Xavier, but the other man just laughed and clapped him on the shoulder.

"Do you think it's always going to be this way?"

Camilla was given the honor of the inaugural use. She was paraded down from her house, precariously balanced on the shoulders of Eliud and Charles Xavier, the two men singing barely intelligible songs peppered with scatological references at the top of their lungs. Firmly ensconced on her throne, everyone fell back to a respectful distance to let Camilla bless the commode. She exited five minutes later to the roar of lusty cheers, her embarrassed eyes staring sheepishly at the ground until Charles Xavier ran forward and raised her arm in triumph. She smiled, but made her escape as soon as she was able, hiding around the bend of the mercantile. Ted followed to make sure she was all right. She was leaning against the wall, breathing in and out with slow measured breaths.

"You okay?"

She nodded.

"Just a lot of people. I'll be fine."

Ted smiled.

"Lot of pressure I guess."

Camilla began to laugh. A heavy chuckle for her size. It was infectious.

"I couldn't even go."

"What?"

"It was even the seat from my own toilet, but I still couldn't go. I waited to come out. I didn't want to disappoint everybody."

She gave them a whole minute of laughing together. A wonderful minute that felt like forever but seemed to end too soon. She straightened and wiped her eyes. She kissed him on the cheek then was gone.

Few people had the same issues as Camilla. Most of the rest of the day was wasted with people using the new luxury. Buffalo Bill used it eight times, often exiting just to rejoin the snaking line again. He was given, as Charles Xavier put it, a great deal of shit about it at the evening meal. Ted allowed himself to laugh with all the rest.

Supper was a simple affair, what it lacked in variety it made up for with sustenance. Ted waited as he always did for the food line to form and then moved toward the end. The group of older women there moved aside and gestured for him to go ahead of them. Ted shook his head, and moved to go behind them, but again they gestured. Finally one old woman with a kind wrinkled face spoke up.

"You work. You eat first."

Ted didn't know what to do. He looked up the line, to the front where Camilla was serving. She was too busy to notice. His eyes felt wet. He smiled, nodded his thanks, and got in line in front of them. Ted got his food and a warm smile from Camilla. He took both and sat slightly by himself, but still within the spread out confines of the greater group. He ate in silence, watching the world around him. Charles Xavier was listening to Eliud while the younger man drew diagrams on the ground in the dirt. Buffalo Bill was telling Crispin and a group a joke. Old men were talking about when they could go back up to their farms. It hit him suddenly. There were almost no blank faces. The people of Titou were alive around him, not necessarily going out of their way to talk to him, but not hiding themselves from him either. Even Mrs. Seraphin, eating with a group of women near the fire, at most gave him a scowl when his view roved past. Ted could feel the tears coming, but he forcefully choked them back. It would be a hell of thing to start crying in front of everybody. He looked at Camilla again. She smiled at him, their secret smile, and went back to eating.

After supper Charles Xavier stood on top of a pile of cinderblocks and waved his arms for silence.

"Tomorrow my friends, tomorrow we'll start fixing homes."

Some people cheered, others murmured. Aside from the few homes made of cinderblocks, most of the houses were in some state of disrepair. Some only had minor damage, maybe a missing door or a few pieces of tin from the roof. Others were missing entire roofs or were half collapsed. Some were completely thrown down, their inhabitants sharing space with other families or cowering under lean-tos. The wood from these fallen homes had long since been burned in the communal fire.

Debates began to break out. Whose house would get repaired first? What kinds of repairs would be prioritized? What about the people in the lean-tos? For a moment, Charles Xavier seemed to wilt, slumping like a turned off robot. The smile never left his face, but his eyes lost focus. Then he was up again, waving his arms to get people quiet again.

"We'll build new houses first. Nobody should have to sleep on the ground."

The announcement elicited cheers from many, and even clapping from those who didn't fully agree. Crispin's voice rose over the falling tumult.

"What about roofing?"

Charles Xavier gestured toward the fallen mercantile.

"Doesn't look like we have any kind of a shortage."

Ted glanced at Malik, but the big man gave no evidence of what he thought of that idea. Crispin wasn't done.

"How will we decide who gets to move in first?"

Eliud, standing behind and a little to the side of Charles Xavier, shot Crispin a dirty look. Charles Xavier looked tired again, but he forced himself onward, his new found power endlessly cracking its whip.

"We'll do like the children. We'll draw straws if it comes down to that."

The people were satisfied. The crowd began to break up for the night. Charles Xavier climbed off of the cinderblocks and began pulling himself up the hill. Camilla remained behind, her and Eliud having a quiet conversation. Ted felt a surge of jealousy, but quickly quashed it. He was being silly, but he still remained close, unlacing and retying his boots. Eliud was leaning in toward Camilla, their faces almost touching.

"Can you talk to him about these houses?"

"What about them?"

"We could build better ones."

"Better ones mean we build fewer. Lots of people need homes."

"If we had mortar and rebar we could build proper houses."

"We have what we have, maybe it's all Malik could get."

"More like all Malik wanted to bring. If we're going to build new houses, they might as well be better than the old ones."

"I'll have Charles Xavier talk to him next time he's here. Maybe next load he can bring up what you want, but for now, we have to do the best we can with what we have."

The two divided, Camilla heading up the slope and Eliud walking down toward the ruins of the mercantile. Ted finished tying his laces and headed for home. Both Charles Xavier and Camilla were inside by the time he arrived. He took off his clothes and climbed into his sleep sack. The white, red, and blue interior was fading, nowhere near as bright as it once had been. It was another night of blessed silence.

The next day the construction began. It rained, but nobody cared. The house would be a simple affair. Four posts driven into the ground to form the frame, walls of overlapping boards, dirt floors, no windows, one doorway. There were too many people wanting to help, so Charles Xavier set many to other tasks. Some were instructed to continue scavenging the mercantile, separating what could be re-used from the rubble. Others were allowed to take small amounts of wood to affect some repairs on their own domiciles. The remainder were set to the never ending busy work of clearing the ditches, though with the reappearance of the greenery it was becoming less of a necessity.

The grass grew quickly. The once dark red scar of the mudslide was covered by a verdant layer only worn away where people shuffled back and forth between the houses. Young roots stretched their way down into the soil, gripping tightly, holding it in place, and slowing the ever downward movement of the mountainside. Water droplets from the never ending rains glittered like diamonds on the green blades when the sun managed to force its way through. Outside the rear window of Ted's house grew a miniature grove of lengthening green stalks, topped by bunches of leaves which swayed in the breeze and let out popping sounds as the droplets fell on them. Each leaf was a flattened hand with five knobbly fingers, and a number of these brushed their way across the empty window frame, a couple even daring to venture inside. They were comforting to Ted. The signs of a rebuilding world. He moved his cot to the corner by the back window so that they would be the last thing he saw at night and the first thing he saw in the morning.

Even as the world grew fat, Charles Xavier seemed to waste away. The evening after the building of the first house began, Ted climbed the hill to find him slumped over on his porch, sleeping deeply. During the day he was surrounded, inundated by unending questions. His opinions and authority needed for every decision. Charles Xavier still laughed loudly and often, but in Ted's ears it sounded hollow. It had a strange echo to it as though it was emanating from a growing emptiness inside. Charles Xavier never wanted to talk on his porch anymore. When he wasn't working he was hidden away from the world in his house.

It didn't matter to Ted. Camilla was the one he watched. At night he could feel her imagined hands running across his body. Insistent. Daring. No nonsense. Hands that knew what they wanted. During the day he watched her. He gazed at her as she sauntered across the new green world, her hips rolling enticingly with every step. Sometimes she would catch him watching, and though she moved away, it was with a sly upturn playing across her lips and her eyes coyly half closed. In those moments, Ted felt himself overcome with lusts to the point of bursting, but such times were few and far between.

Charles Xavier was almost always near his wife. All the eyes of the Titou were upon him, but his never left Camilla. Ted watched his rival jealously as Camilla walked beside her husband, whispering in his ear as the questions were flung at him with wild abandon. When Charles Xavier wasn't with Camilla he was with Ted. He'd walk over with a smile and greet Ted with a joke and a hearty slap on the back. It was inevitably followed by finding the two of them something to do. Sometimes they'd go fetch water together. Sometimes they'd dig at the ditch above the row of houses. It almost felt as though Charles Xavier was seeking him out purposefully. Charles Xavier was constantly looking over his shoulder as they worked, and at times he'd have them stop and change jobs for no obvious reason. It made Ted nervous. It made him afraid of what Charles Xavier might know, but whatever he knew, he kept it to himself.

The first house was finished after four days. The lucky winners with the short straw abandoned their lean-to and moved in with the few possessions they still had. It wasn't an impressive house, more of a shack, but it was better than a lean-to. The completion put the people of Titou in a celebratory mood, but Charles Xavier declared that it was too early in the day to quit. There were still many who needed better shelter from the rain, sun, and wind. When he finally released the people from his iron grip that evening, four poles for a second home had already been set in the ground. The people celebrated that night with a feast and dancing, though all of it was subdued, lacking the needed energy provided by rum and desperate hope. They were over the top of the hump, climbers on the descent, weary from their journey. Ted stayed by the fire and let Eliud and a few of the other younger men bait him into jokes, most of them at his expense, but his hopes were dashed by the presence of Charles Xavier, who danced only with his wife, and took her up to their home before the sun had even set. He was up early the next day, rousing his workforce. There was still much to be done.

It was the middle of the next day when the man from the government arrived. He was a short thickset man with a thin moustache across his upper lip. He came in a Suzuki pickup with Domenique's green, blue, and yellow flag emblazoned on the side, driven by an unsmiling man in an official looking olive uniform, covered in mud up to the knees, his eyes hidden behind a pair of aviators. Ted was sitting above all on his porch, wearing a button down shirt hanging open. He had taken to eating his dinners alone in order to give himself a period of privacy to crank away his unquenchable thirst brought on by the rolling hips and feverish memories.

The government man climbed up on the hood of his vehicle and the people of Titou gathered round. Ted didn't go down to join them. The government man spoke loudly to be heard above the crowd, but his voice was extinguished by the rain before it had even the remotest chance of reaching Ted. When the government man finished he climbed down. The crowd broke up into familial units. A few individuals broke away and went over to the government man, talked with him a bit, and then returned. There was an excitement in the air, a droning that was less sound and more vibration. The government man went over and talked to Charles Xavier for a time. He gestured back the way he had come. Charles Xavier listened and nodded before walking over to Camilla to discuss things with her. Camilla nodded her head, but looked less than happy. Her husband broke away and started up the hill.

Charles Xavier wasn't smiling. He came up the slope with the slow steps of a deposed king leaving his throne room for the last time. He paid no mind to Ted's curious glances, but went into his house in silence, coming out a few minutes later wearing the blue shirt of his profession with shoes on his feet. Ted stood and intercepted him before he made his way back down.

"What's going on?"

Charles Xavier looked half dead on his feet, but his eyes were the bright eyes of an exhausted fanatic.

"They're hiring people to fix the roads and clear the paths in the district."

"Are you going to take them up on it?"

"No. I have to go with him to Helston. They want to get the mail going again."

Ted's heart exploded in his chest. Charles Xavier looked down at his feet, and with a smile whispered almost too quietly to hear.

"Not rain, nor storm, or hellfire."

Ted wasn't really listening. His head was full of images of entwined limbs and frantic movements.

"When will you be coming back?"

"Tomorrow I imagine."

Ted felt a surge of glee, though was careful not to let any sign show on his face. His mother had always told him that he had a very expressive face. Charles Xavier took a breath in, let it out, and made his way down the hill to squeeze into the waiting Suzuki. The government man made him sit in the middle. The engine roared to life. The Suzuki turned around, crushing greenery as it went, and carried the three occupants back down the mountain.

The people of Titou didn't work anymore that day. They gathered in tight knots, conversing excitedly. It was all anyone could talk about. It pervaded the atmosphere all afternoon and was the only topic discussed at supper. Ted didn't notice. All of his attention was on Camilla. She said nothing to him. She didn't say anything to anybody. She sat alone, lost deep in thought, and left supper as early as she could without being rude. Ted stayed a little longer, listening to Mr. Green continuing his lessons with Id. Lessons that sounded much the same as they had a week ago. When it grew dark he climbed the slope to his house and waited in a nervous sweat for his goddess to come over. She didn't. The night crawled on. The rain softly tapped on the roof, finding places here and there to leak into the interior. He paced back and forth, his stomach twisted into unreleasable knots. He imagined going over, knocking on her door, entering the house and her. He didn't. He took off his clothes and laid down on his cot. He fell asleep confused and hurt, wondering if he had done something wrong.

The government man and his Suzuki returned in the morning. Charles Xavier wasn't with them. The government man brought a clipboard and a big pile of forms for people to fill out. Ted stood apart and watched. Nearly everyone in town got in line to sign the forms. The majority of the few who didn't were farmers from higher up the mountain. Skinny gnarled old men who almost all disappeared by the end of the day, back up the slopes to check on their farms. Neither Mr. Green or Camilla signed up either, both never leaving their houses. Nor did Eliud sign. He stood by himself with his arms crossed by the poles which marked the start of the second new house. His eyes tracked across the line, falling again and again on the lithe form of Mrs. Seraphin. Ted walked over and stood by him, and after waiting a moment to make sure that it was okay, opened his mouth to speak.

"Seems like everyone's signing up."

Eliud grunted his response.

"Good money."

"Are all of these people really going to work?"

Eliud spit on the ground.

"No, but it's better to sign up and not show. If you never sign up, you never get to work."

Ted nodded and watched the line snake forward. People surrounded the pickup, using it for a hard surface to write. The driver sat behind the wheel, his face unreadable behind his aviators. Eliud spit again. Ted worked up the balls to ask what was on his mind.

"Aren't you going to sign up?"

Eliud looked at him, then down at the ground, then back at the line, buying himself time to decide whether or not to answer.

"Somebody has to stay around here. Still lots to get done."

"But the money?"

"I'll be fine."

Eliud's tone conveyed that he had little interest in carrying on the conversation. Ted didn't say anything else, but he didn't move either. Neither did Eliud.

The line reached its end after a few hours. Only the children under fifteen and the obviously infirm were not allowed to sign. The government man got on top of his Suzuki again, and this time aided by the power of a bullhorn, yelled instructions. Ted didn't really listen. It wasn't important for him. Work would start the next day. He bellowed out five locations for people to meet to work. Tools would be waiting for them when they arrived. As far as Ted could discern, the government man made no attempt to split the people into groups. He turned to ask Eliud about it, but the other man seemed to sense what the question would be, and answered before it could leave Ted's lips.

"They'll go where they want anyways. If all the tools are taken, they'll send them on to the next."

Ted nodded. It didn't seem his place to question. The government man put away his bullhorn and climbed down. The Suzuki headed back down the mountain. People broke into groups, debating on which location was the best or discussing who would actually go. Eliud knocked on one of the poles of the house still under construction with his fist and let out a sigh.

"Not going to get much done today either I guess. Come help me get some water."

In the middle of the afternoon there was a guttural roar like a chainsaw. It started down the road, but quickly cut the distance, shooting from the tree line and spraying dirt as it came. It was a motorbike, a little 1980's Honda with scratched paint and a big dent in the gas tank. Two extra fuel jugs were strapped to its sides. Charles Xavier sat upon his steed with a straight back and a grin bigger than his face. He performed two laps around the town, children screaming and trying to run alongside. Some people cheered and clapped their hands. When he brought the engine to a stuttering halt people crammed around him, brushing their hands on the motorbike with reverence and shouting out a thousand questions. Where did he get it? Who gave it to him? How was Helston? Why did they give it to him? Had he seen so and so's cousin? Charles Xavier didn't answer. He just yelled out above the crowd.

"Camilla woman. Where are you?"

Joyous hands pushed her forward. She stood, giving the metal beast between her husband's legs a wary eye.

"C'mon woman. Get on."

Camilla shook her head, but neither Charles Xavier or the town would take no for an answer. As Charles Xavier yelled encouragement the people of Titou dragged Camilla over to the bike and set her down behind her husband. He kick started the motor and resumed his circuits of the town. They zipped between the buildings, her with her face buried in his shoulder, loudly declaring her dislike, him laughing like a madman. After three full circuits he gave in, depositing her where they had started. Camilla got off shaking, people laughing and clapping her on the back. An old man climbed on next, and after him a gang of three children. Everyone wanted a ride, and Charles Xavier did his best to make sure everyone had a chance. Mrs. Seraphin took her turn, her skirt billowing behind her, revealing her long legs. She clutched a blank faced Charles Xavier tightly, screaming like a banshee, her eyes filled with a wild light. Eliud refused a turn, as did Ted. One who didn't refuse was Id. Normally not one for loud noises, he came bounding down from Mr. Green's house and in his way made his wants known. They put him on the back, but the ride was a short one. It was impossible for Id to stay still and the motorbike toppled over several times before he was satisfied enough to rejoin his uncle.

The fun was only halted by the setting sun and the draining of one of the jugs of fuel. As supper was served, Charles Xavier pushed his prize up next to his house where he sat in the growing twilight, polishing it with an old wet shirt, his entire body fidgeting with his pride and glee. People continually came up to see it, their voices filled with envy and congratulations. The only other man who had ever owned a vehicle in town was Malik. The banana plantation also had its own fleet of vehicles, but they of course didn't count. Finally, as darkness began to take hold, Camilla shooed them all away. It was night. Time to sleep. The people moved back to their own houses and shelters, dejected, but elated at the same time. It was official now. Charles Xavier was somebody. Ted waited for the last of the admirers to leave and then came over and stood by the edge of the porch. Charles Xavier was staring at the motorbike in the moonlight. Ted cleared his throat.

"It's a nice bike."

"It's a beautiful bike."

Ted kicked one foot with the other, not really sure what else to say. He could hear Camilla getting ready for bed inside the house. She was humming. Ted imagined her naked form. He glanced at the broken window in hopes of catching sight, but old sheets had been hung, blocking the view. Charles Xavier's mind was obviously elsewhere.

"They used to have four carriers in Helston. Now there's only one. Me. The other three, poof, disappeared. No idea. They need me to cover more ground."

Ted licked his lips.

"So you're going to be away longer then."

Charles Xavier nodded.

"It's going to be hard going until they get all the roads and paths cleared. Probably be gone days at a time."

Ted didn't answer. He was eying the stained flowered sheet in the window frame again. Charles Xavier chuckled to himself.

"Going to have to avail myself to the kindness of strangers to find places to sleep. Shouldn't be too hard. Lots of people been probably missing my mail deliveries."

Charles Xavier looked up at Ted, his smile a white flash in the darkness. Ted licked his lips again.

"I can imagine it will be hard being away."

Charles Xavier gave an exaggerated wink.

"A real hardship assignment."

Charles Xavier laughed and Ted let out a chuckle alongside. They fell silent. Ted stared up at the moon, but Charles Xavier only had eyes for the motorbike. Ted cleared his throat.

"Well, I guess I better be going to bed. Good night."

"Good night Theodore."

Ted started to walk toward his house, but he turned at the sound of Charles Xavier's voice.

"Theodore?"

"Yeah."

"You're my friend, correct?"

Ted nervously rubbed his palms against his jeans.

"Of course."

The shadowy form of Charles Xavier nodded.

"Good. Good. Can I ask you a favor?"

"Anything."

"Can you watch out for Camilla for me when I'm gone?"

Ted's entire body stiffened. His face flushed, unseen in the darkness.

"Of course I will. It will be a pleasure."

Chapter 23

Malik showed back up two days later. This time he didn't give anything away for free, but set up a wall tent next to his ruined mercantile and started selling. Rumors spread that it had been Malik who had convinced the man from the government to come to Titou to offer the jobs. Malik was many things, but he was a businessman first and foremost. He spent most of his time in his tent amongst his wares. Mostly canned goods, toilet paper, cheap rum, and small one burner propane stoves. He slept in a cot in the corner and paid children with bottles of Coca-Cola to watch things when he had to do nature's business. Ted never bought anything, he didn't have any money, but when he walked by he could see Malik inside, leaning back in a metal chair, reading an old dog-eared harlequin romance with the practiced eye of a connoisseur. People claimed that he had a gun, but if he did, Ted never saw it.

The return of commerce spelled the end of the communal way of life which had followed the hurricane. The government paid in cash after the first two weeks of work. Brightly colored bills graced by the smiling face of Queen Lizzie, trading hands and all ending up in Malik's pocket. The most popular item was the propane stoves. No more would people be committed to the communal fire. No more would their diets depend on the demands of the masses. The ants all turned to grasshoppers. Individual wants trumped group needs. The embers were left cold and abandoned. The old folks still sat around the deserted fire pit at times during the day, telling their stories and gauging the weather, but this was no different than how they had lived prior to Anji's wrath.

In this segmenting of the community, the caring of Ted fell to Camilla and Charles Xavier. The latter, when he was there, would laugh and clap Ted on the back whenever he shared a meal.

"What's mine is yours my friend."

Ted believed him, but noted that Camilla was keeping careful track of all he ate and everything she did for him. Patiently waiting for the day capitalism caught up with Ted as well.

With so many people gone during the day, Titou seemed empty, at least until the evening, when those working for the government would return, refilling the town with a bustling life. Sometimes, if it rained too hard, they'd return early. Other times, if the weather stayed good, they didn't return until after dark. Ted enjoyed the evenings, sitting on his porch, looking down at the world below. He missed the days of the communal fire. The feeling of everyone moving together with purpose. It almost entirely faded away, gone as though it had never been. Sometimes Ted walked along the plantation fence, gazing in and wondering about the men within. It felt as though he was the only one who even remembered they existed. Nobody spoke of them, at least not where he could hear. If they were still there then they were hidden, out of sight at the central buildings over the rounded slope of the hill.

The second most popular item that Malik sold from his tent were vegetable seeds. Tanias, yams, potatoes, onions, peas, carrots, and garlic. All that had once been could be again. Many of the women had gone to work, 'chasing the easy money,' as Eliud put it. The women who remained broke the ground behind their houses and laid the start of a new beginning. Their voices filled the day with happy melodies, songs that couldn't be drowned out by even the most torrential of rains. Their hands were stained red by the earth and they watched with joyful suspense for the seeds to germinate, rising phoenixes which would herald the return to normalcy.

Ted helped Camilla re-establish her garden on the pretext of paying her back for her kindness. They broke the ground with hoes, chopping through the immature grass growing in the dirt of the slide, replacing it with different life, chosen to meet the needs of a higher power. The pair worked in silence, just as it had been in the beginning. Camilla humming tunes to herself, Ted following her every movement from the corner of his eye, yearning to feel a touch. It was worse than before. His needs had grown greater since slaking his thirst at her well. Camilla acted as though she didn't notice, though Ted thought such a thing likely impossible.

Charles Xavier had departed, returned, and departed. Nobody was really sure when he would return again. When he came back the first time, the sound of him and Camilla making love had nearly driven Ted into madness. He couldn't take it. She had barely spoken to him during Charles Xavier's first absence. Unable to handle the evidence of the couple's continued love, Ted had fled into the darkness, down through the town where everyone slept but Malik, reading a book by flashlight, watching Ted pass with a disinterested eye. Ted had stumbled blindly on, unsure of where he was until he fell across Eugene Hewitt's grave, cutting his head in his tumble. The shock had knocked him back into reality, and after sitting awhile, he had made his way back home, thanking god upon arrival that the noises had ceased.

When evening fell, Camilla and Ted left the newly planted garden. They washed together in a bucket of water, Ted's entire being vibrating with each accidental touch of their skin. She sat him on the porch and went inside to prepare supper, a can of chicken soup. They ate in silence, her slightly slurping every spoonful. The sun slid out of sight. Ted was a pile of explosives next to a book of matches. His being was slipping away, drowning in the chaos of his needs. When she reached for his bowl to take it back into the house he grabbed her wrist, not hard, but gently. It was automatic. She looked up at him questioningly, her face somber and calm. Desperation. An act of desperation. The words escaped his lips, inner thoughts expelled into the outer world.

"I want to fuck you."

Ted felt stupid the moment he said it. He felt embarrassed. Ashamed. He wished he could suck the words back in. Camilla only stared. Her free hand put her bowl back on the porch. She began to laugh. Her quiet throaty laugh. She rose and pulled him up with her.

"Then do it."

Early morning twilight made its way in through the broken windows. Ted watched it from the bed, the shape beneath the covers next to him breathing peacefully. The bed smelled of Camilla and Charles Xavier. A combination of sweat, cinnamon, and rum. He wondered if his scent would be intermingled with their's. Would Charles Xavier be able to smell him? The mattress and box spring were on the ground. Everything that could be had been carted to the communal fire. No bed frame. No table. No chairs. The cupboards had been smashed and taken, all but the portion holding up the sink. Pots, pans, clothing, and other belongings sat in orderly piles across the floor. Standing guard were the unusable refrigerator and toilet, their surfaces polished to a high sheen. Camilla mumbled in her sleep and Ted followed her down into the unconscious depths.

When he woke again it was full morning. Camilla was gone. It felt wrong to be there at such an hour. It felt wrong for anyone else to know. Ted got dressed and opened the back door of the house. He kept low, peering over the parapet of the eroding stairs cut by Mr. Hewitt. The Seraphin children were playing with a soccer ball behind their mother's house. Ted waited until their backs were turned and made a run across the space towards his red home. It had rained during the night. The steps cut by Mr. Hewitt at his house had worn away completely, leaving nothing but a ramp. Ted went down hard, sliding down against the back door of his house with a curse. The two Seraphin children ran over to see what had happened. The boy laughed at the site of Ted sprawled in the mud, but the girl only stared. Ted glared at the children sullenly, too dazed to do much but lay in the mud. The two children got bored with the antics of the stupid jake and walked away.

The next evening Ted returned to Camilla, and the evening after that as well. During the day he worked with Eliud, packing water, clearing ditches, and building the second house. During the night he slept in another man's bed, making love to his wife. At first he worried, but every fear he raised was broken and scattered by her words. They didn't worry about Charles Xavier. His coming would always be heralded by the sounds of the motorbike.

Ted and Eliud rarely spoke. Eliud gave instructions and Ted followed. In their tasks Eliud had a confidence that Ted envied. A self-assurance of the way things ought to be. Ted knew little about carpentry, but Eliud was patient in his lessons, with the calm of a father teaching a son, only broken by a few times when Ted fucked up so badly that Eliud, rather than yelling or throwing a fit, would quietly order him to take some buckets to the reservoir to go get more water.

The carrying of water was a task that was now mostly being handled by the women. Ted refused to let the insult of breaking the assigned gender role get to him. If anything, he took pride in his refusal to accept a cultural norm, and in doing so, gave himself a secret point of dignity which in his mind put him, in at least one way, above his teacher. It helped him keep his head held high when the old men hooted at him.

"Going to go buy a dress missy?"

"No sway in that backside."

"Pretty hardworking girl like you should find a husband."

The women carried the buckets atop their heads, their hair tied up in scarves to provide cushion and support. They would glide down the path, hands rarely rising to re-balance the load. Ted tried it once, but was quickly soaked by his failure, his pride stung by the laughter of Mrs. Seraphin and some of the other women. Once he met Camilla alone upon the path, a full bucket on top of her head, and he reached out and glided his fingers down the curve of her hip. She slapped him and walked away, all without spilling a drop. That night their lovemaking was so vigorous that Ted feared everyone in the town would know.

Though they rarely spoke when working, Ted wasn't blind to the thoughts of Eliud. The gawky man continually tried to find things to do for Mrs. Seraphin. He tried to help her with her garden, but she sent him away with a few sharp words. The two Seraphin children were easier. He brought them down to where they were building the house and showed them how to measure, cut, and nail. However, their attention spans didn't allow for very lengthy lessons. Later he found a dog in the woods, a mangy mutt of the type that were often seen wandering the streets of Helston, though Ted had rarely seen any in Titou. After much coaxing he managed to get a string around its neck and brought it back as a gift for the stand-ins of the focus of his affection. The children greatly enjoyed the new source of entertainment until it ran away a few days later. Their mother had been less than pleased, which made Ted think she likely had something to do with the disappearance of the dog.

Eliud had better luck in helping Mr. Green with his garden. Though not optimal, Ted imagined it at least gave Eliud a vantage point with a good view. Mr. Green didn't really need the help. Though decidedly poor when it came to reading, Id was strong as a mule and could've done the work easily alone. However, Mr. Green didn't wish to use his nephew for such labors, seeing it as too close to the life he had lived with Malik. According to Mr. Green, Id was destined for better things, and so they sat day after day on the porch, Id struggling under the tutelage of his uncle, watched from afar by a businessman sitting at the entrance of his tent.

It had been raining most of the day when the man from the banana plantation arrived. People had returned early from their work, chased off by the collapsing heavens, and though the rain had stopped, most were more than willing to continue to use it as an excuse to lounge and enjoy the emerging sun. Ted was working with Eliud on the second house, his hammer blows energetic as they always were after spending the night in Camilla's bed. Charles Xavier had been gone three days. The plantation man came up the road in a Suzuki pickup, very similar to the government man, only his was red with no markings. The Suzuki pulled to a halt not far above the ruined mercantile. The plantation man got out of the passenger side, took off his sunglasses, and gazed around. The driver stayed where he was. The plantation man was wearing khaki pants, creased, and amazingly still clean except for a hint of red on the cuffs.

Eliud noticed them first. He rose up with a stifled curse.

"Fucking jackets."

Eliud dropped his hammer to the ground. Ted could feel the tension of the other man.

"Who is it?"

"Fucking plantation. Stay here."

Eliud marched forward, a crowd was beginning to form. Dead eyed figures with blank faces. The man from the plantation looked nervous. The people stared at him in silence. The same dangerous trill of every time the plantation was brought up shot up Ted's spine, but it was different this time. He didn't feel any fear, just the strange sense of detachment of the observer. Mentally he had to give the plantation owners credit, they at least had the smarts to send a local rather than a jake. The plantation man forced a smile onto his face and raised his hand in greeting.

"Hello everybody."

Nobody answered. The man swallowed a lump in his throat and pressed forward. A strange sense of pity filled Ted.

"Glad to see things up here are on the up and up."

A bird let loose a song in the distance. The man was sweating.

"I've been sent up here to tell you that we're going to get things up and running here again soon, and to let you know that of course everyone who had a job with us before, continues to do so."

Some of the crowd started murmuring, a few words making their way as far as Ted. They were hard to discern, but he got the gist. Various forms of "fucking jakes this" and dirty jackets that" floated softly on the breeze. The plantation man seemed uncertain. He nervously adjusted the tuck of shirt. Malik had emerged from his tent, but made no move to come closer. Eliud had managed to push his way to the front of the crowd. Ted looked around for Camilla. She was standing on her porch, watching from above.

"Uh…..we of course...uh….are very excited to get everybody back to work."

The driver side door of the Suzuki opened. The driver climbed out and began unloading four cardboard boxes from the back of the pickup and placing them next to the plantation man. The plantation man glanced at them, licked his lips, and forced himself to continue.

"On behalf of the owners, who will be celebrating the re-opening, they requested that I...uh….bring you this gift so you can celebrate as well."

The driver cut open the top of one of the boxes with a pocket a knife and handed the plantation man a bottle from within. The murmuring started again. It was a bottle of rum. Not the cheap swill that Malik sold, but expensive liquid gold. Ted recognized the label. He had tried some down in the capital when he had first arrived. An expensive drink to celebrate his coming to the island.

Mrs. Seraphin pushed her way to the front of the crowd.

"Rum. You send men to shoot at our children and you bring us rum."

People began shouting their ascent. The plantation man's smile faded from his face, replaced by a combination of confusion and fear.

"Um….standard protocol…."

The people shouted him down, their voices screaming derision and abuse. The driver reached for his hip. For the first time Ted noticed he had a holstered pistol on his belt. Ted felt his entire body began vibrating with anticipation and dismay. No. Please god no.

Eliud stepped forward out of the crowd. He walked casually, almost as if he was taking a pleasant stroll. The world quieted around him, the last bursts growing evanescent in the breeze. Eliud walked up to the plantation man, who along with his driver, had the air of an over twisted spring. Eliud smiled disarmingly. The plantation man and his driver visibly relaxed. Eliud took the bottle of rum out of the plantation man's hand and calmly examined the label. He leaned forward and whispered something in the plantation man's ear. The man smiled for a moment, but then his smile faded and his eyes grew wide. Eliud turned back toward the crowd, still examining the bottle, his finger running softly across the label. The plantation man and his driver scrambled for the Suzuki. They wrestled open the doors and slammed them shut. The engine cranked to life. Eliud spun and threw the bottle as hard as he could. It exploded against the side of the pickup, spraying its golden bounty over the red paint. People surged forward, grabbing for the boxes and bottles as they went.

The two men in the Suzuki looked panicked. The driver wrenched the wheel and swung it off the road into the mud. For a moment the tires refused to catch. The first of the second wave of bottles began to crash against the conveyance. Mud sprayed and the Suzuki got traction, yanking its way back up onto the road, spraying gravel as it lurched. It sped away down the road, glass smashing in its wake. Not a single bottle was spared. Eliud was laughing, a great booming laugh that echoed off the mountainside. People were laughing with him, others were hysterically screaming with glee, tears flowing down their cheeks. People were holding each other, some were even singing and dancing. Next to his tent, Malik started shaking his head. Above on the porch, Camilla went back inside. Ted remained at the house, unsure what to do or where to go. His heart was soaring, but the fear was there again. A deep primal warning of danger. He left the people of Titou to their celebrating, taking two buckets with him to the reservoir.

Charles Xavier arrived that evening looking bruised and haggard. Ted was sitting on the yellow house's porch, waiting for Camilla to bring him supper. The people of Titou packed around Charles Xavier, shouting greetings and yammering as one about the happenings of the day. Charles Xavier began to laugh, but his guffaws without warning turned into anger. He voiced boomed off the side of the mountain. With an angry wrench of his leg he kicked back on the motorbike and ascended the slope, scattering people and gravel in his wake. At the top Charles Xavier parked the motorbike and climbed off, his thin frame shaking with his wrath. Ted had never seen him so angry. Charles Xavier saw Ted watching him and gestured fiercely back down the hill.

"Idiots. Bloody idiots. Smashing rum bottles in the road. Don't they know what that could do to my motorbike tires?"

Charles Xavier strode past Ted and into his house, slamming the door behind him. Every muscle in Ted's body felt tight. He waited for a moment, listening, but no sound emanated out from behind the flowered sheets. He sat back down on the porch. Camilla came out a little while later with some food. She handed it to him before she went back inside. Her face was set in stone, unreadable. Ted ate alone and waited. When he got tired of waiting he thought about knocking on the door, thought better of it, and instead left his dirty dishes on the porch. Down below people were scouring the road, undoubtedly looking for even the smallest piece of glass.

Ted went back to his own house and prepared for bed. That night the sounds of Charles Xavier taking his marital right burst forth as they always did, but they seemed somehow lesser. They didn't bother Ted as they had before. He listened until they were done and then rolled over to sleep. Charles Xavier could have his pleasures. Ted knew it would be his turn again soon.

Chapter 24

"I know what you're doing Mr. Nelson."

Mr. Green was sitting on his porch, watching the sunrise and the stirring of people below. He caught Ted as he was coming from between Charles Xavier's house and his own. The old man didn't turn his head, but his voice was spiced with a heavy dollop of disapproval. Ted stopped in his tracks, unsure for a moment what to say, but his shoulders involuntarily rose at the challenge. Charles Xavier had left the day before and Ted was still riding high on the reconquest of his friend's bride. When he spoke, his voice was flat and measured.

"What am I doing?"

Mr. Green didn't rise to the challenge. Down below, men and women were finishing the last bits of hasty breakfasts and beginning to scatter down roads and paths, singing cheerily as they went.

"You should bury your nose in a book. Few troubles ever came from reading more."

Ted could hear Camilla humming somewhere behind him. She was going to do laundry, Ted's as well, though she had made it apparent that nothing was done for free. Ted hoped he would have the energy that evening to pay off his debts.

"I'll keep that under advisement."

"Good. Well, Avery will be stirring soon. I better visit my wife before he does."

Mr. Green rose and hobbled his way down the hill. He looked shrunk, less fierce than he once had been. A stooped echo of a former time. Ted headed down the slope at a different angle. Today he was helping Eliud again. His construction skills were getting better, at least to the point that Eliud rarely sent him to get water anymore. The second house was complete, a family already moved in. A third house was on its way, posts already buried, the start of the frame nailed in place. Eliud was guessing they would have just enough wood to finish the third house. Malik hadn't offered to bring anymore lumber and the pile was swiftly depleting.

When Ted arrived at the work site, Eliud, his shirt already off, was measuring a board for cutting. Though it was still morning it was already hot. It hadn't rained in a week, but a thick mugginess still clung to the mountainside. Ted knew that by the end of the day his t-shirt would be soaked through, but he refused to take it off, more out of habit than any other reason. His once pasty white flesh had been shifted a shade darker, bronzed slightly into a pale leather which shed flakes of dead skin at a constant rate. His hair curled around his ears and groped down his neck enough that he could feel it lift when he jumped. A beard clung to his cheeks and jaw, kept trimmed on the orders of the one who could make such demands. People passing the rising house smiled and waved in his and Eliud's direction, shouting greetings which Ted happily returned. Eliud kept to his work.

The two men labored mostly in silence, communicating through motions and nods, both knowing what needed to be done. Every now and again Ted would ask a question or for a clarification. Eliud always answered, but looked relieved when the auditory world collapsed back to the steady beat of hammers and saws. Ted didn't think Eliud found their time together unpleasant, he just seemed diminished without the fuel provided by the perpetual energy of Charles Xavier.

Charles Xavier was around less and less. He was always on the go, gone day and night, returning only long enough to sleep a few hours in his own bed and sit on his porch, drinking copious amounts of rum and making minor repairs to his motorbike. When he was home he looked overly drawn out, a man who hadn't achieved a full night's sleep in at least a month. Ted would join him from time to time and try to start conversations. Charles Xavier was always welcoming, but he was never able to give his full attention, the majority being focused on the mechanical marvel before him. He had purchased a small set of tools from Malik and with them he dismantled and put back together every piece of the machine, though as far as Ted could see, little if any of the work was needed or necessary. Charles Xavier was a little more vocal with Eliud, though even those moments were mostly limited to ribald jokes, suggesting heavily of his unending nocturnal conquests from while he was away.

The only thing that knocked Eliud from his mute stupor was the random kindness of a woman who seemed to have little to no interest in reciprocating whatever feelings he might have. Eliud would watch Mrs. Seraphin whenever she moved nearby. A hungering concentration which scattered the rhythm of his work, broken only by the sudden realization that Ted was watching him. These realizations were always followed by a casual look into the sky as though he had just been looking at birds not actually present in the sky, followed by a burst of energy as he threw himself back into his work with the focus of an automaton. One time the spell was broken by a mis-timed hammer blow which elicited loud curses from Eliud and stifled laughs from a group of passing women.

Ted's stomach rumbled. He looked up at the sun climbing higher up in the sky, hopeful that it would soon be time for dinner. The women of the town always brought him and Eliud dinner. They seemed to have some kind of system worked out, but how it was setup was beyond Ted. It seemed almost random. Ted was sure they were doing it for Eliud, the lone man of working age who had decided to stay and continue helping rebuild the town. The other men always made motions like they would help when they could, but the government work was hard, and the walks to the sites got longer as the work progressed. Some only returned every couple of days. Men and women both would collapse in their beds as soon as they arrived home, weary and difficult to rouse. No, the dinners were for Eliud. The inclusion of the man who worked alongside was just because they couldn't find a polite way not to serve him.

Ted brushed the sweat out of his eyes and shook his mane of hair. No, his conclusion wasn't entirely fair. The women who brought dinner almost always smiled warmly at Ted, with a few even giving him a polite word of greeting or two. Very little of the old hostility remained. The faces that passed by were open, emitting emotion for all to see. Perhaps it was nothing but the mutterings of an uncomfortable mind. People lingering more with Eliud was not a sign of disliking Ted. After all, the gawky man had been there long before him. It didn't matter either way, there was only one person whose attention Ted craved.

Mrs. Seraphin approached a plate of food in each hand. The long legged woman was wearing a bright yellow dress, stained at the hem, with a matching head scarf. It was rare for her to bring dinner. Increasingly she was leaving in the morning with those doing the government work. She nodded at the two men. Ted nodded back, though the gesture was largely ignored. Of all the people of Titou, Mrs. Seraphin seemed to be the last holdout. Though the outward hostility had cooled, she treated him little differently than the potato plants growing behind her house. One might water them, and be careful not to step on them, but they certainly weren't something you talked to. Eliud at least got the recognition of being a fellow human being, though it didn't go very far beyond that.

Mrs. Seraphin put the plates down on a cinderblock. Eliud watched her with a hungry look in his eye, fidgeting slightly, forcing the words from his nervous lips.

"Thank you."

Mrs. Seraphin gave just the hint of a smile at the corner of her mouth. She paused, waiting to see if there was more. Eliud was obviously struggling, desperately trying to push further words up his esophagus with all his might. The woman seemed to enjoy the antics of the young man. Ted could see it in her eyes. A flash of mirth and curiosity. Eliud spluttered, and finally ejected half formed words into the world.

"Thank you very much."

Mrs. Seraphin allowed herself to smile. A momentary breach that somehow seemed both warm and mocking at the same time. She waited a moment more, then growing bored, turned and walked away. Eliud watched every step, sucking air between his teeth. His eyes fell dejectedly to his thumbnail, turned black by the blow of his own hammer. Ted laughed to himself, but couldn't control the shaking of his body. Eliud gave him a dirty look. Ted gestured at the retreating straight backed form.

"Why don't you just say something to her?"

Eliud grimaced. His eyes filled with obstinate defiance. For a moment he bent to pick up more nails, but then he groaned and rose back up empty handed.

"What am I supposed to say to her?"

"I don't know. Talk about the weather. My grandfather used to always say that anyone could talk about the weather."

"That's chupid. Everyone already knows about the weather."

Eliud dropped his hammer and went over to eat his dinner. Ted joined him. The two men ate in silence, rinsing the dishes with a bit of water from the bucket they drank from. Both went back to their hammering. The afternoon eased its way forward. It took a moment for Ted to realize that the man next to him wasn't working anymore. He ceased his own rhythm and looked over. Eliud was staring at him, his eyes angry.

"I'm not chupid you know."

"I never said you were stupid."

"I went to university. Two years."

"Yeah, so did I. Four years. What did you study?"

"Engineering."

"Business management."

The two men lapsed back into silence. Eliud started hammering again, swinging the hammer harder than was needed. His mouth was a grim line. Ted went over to the water bucket, used a ladle to get himself a drink, and then brought a second ladleful over to Eliud. The other man stopped hammering, took in a deep breath, let it out, and accepted Ted's offering.

"Why didn't you finish?"

Eliud drank half the ladle and dumped the other half on his head. If flowed down his body, miniature rivers across his flesh.

"My father got sick, he had nobody else, so I had to come home. He was sick a long time. Close to three years before he died. Bad lungs. I got a job at the plantation, just the same as he used to have."

"Why didn't you ever go back?"

"Just didn't."

Eliud fell silent, but he didn't start hammering again. He licked his lips and tapped the hammer against his leg.

"I was doing pretty well in the plantation. I was already in charge of a crew. The money was all right. I don't know."

"It must have been difficult, not a lot up here."

Eliud sucked air in between in his teeth.

"I guess if I was from America I would think that too."

Clouds were making their way toward the mountain. Dark edifices that gave the promise of rain by evening, maybe sooner.

"I didn't mean it like that."

"No, you did."

Ted didn't know how to answer. Eliud took a few practiced swings with his hammer, driving in another nail.

"You're not wrong. You're not right, but you're not wrong either. There's plenty of things I miss. It's a different world up here, but you know, it's home."

Eliud looked up the hillside towards Mrs. Seraphin's house and then back down at his thumbnail.

"I had girl when I was in university. Thought I was going to marry her. It didn't last when I came back."

"What happened?"

"She had no interest in coming up here. She was originally from Savarin, over on the other side, a lot like Helston. I didn't think up here was much different, but she did. After living in the capital for a few years she didn't even want to go back to Savarin. Acted like she was too good for it. I don't know. I'm glad we're not together, but there's certainly some things I really miss."

Ted stared mostly at his feet while Eliud was talking. His mind was scrambling for the right thing to say. The best show of sympathy. When he looked up again the other man was smiling and raising his eyebrows in a suggestive way.

"Don't worry about me though. They can say what they want about Crispin's sister, but the woman had talent."

Eliud laughed and slapped Ted on the arm. Ted laughed too, a good hard unrestrained belly laugh that rolled and faded amongst the trees. It felt good to laugh. The two men started working again, lapsing back into silence. When the words came out of Ted's mouth, they surprised him just as much as Eliud.

"I was engaged once, or at last nearly engaged. She broke up with me right before I could ask her."

The words hung in the air for a moment before dropping to the ground. Ted's face fell with them, his eyes studying them as they writhed in the dirt, waiting for a response. He had never told anyone before. He had never said out loud how close he had gotten. Eliud stopped working, but seemed unfazed by the confession.

"What happened?"

Sandi sat at a table on the patio, a beer in her hand, mouth open with laughter, revealing the little gap between her top front teeth which always embarrassed her, sunlight streaming through her hair.

"I don't know."

Eliud's eyes were filled with sympathy. He gave Ted's shoulder a squeeze.

"Don't let the shit bury you."

The two men went back to working again, letting the ring of their hammer blows replace their voices.

Ted had saved for the ring for nearly a year. The man behind the counter had assured him it was a good buy. He had walked out of the store and opened the box, letting it twinkle in the sunlight. Making plans. It had to be perfect. Romantic. A rehearsal for a play that never saw the curtain rise. Cancelled in pre-production. Sandi had said the words. His eyes were full of tears. Arguing. The car outside the apartment. A stranger helping her load her clothes. She hadn't wanted much else, just her clothes and a few other random items. Things from her time before him. She had left him everything else. A fully furnished apartment and life. She had gotten into the car and it had driven away, taking her off to a new life, leaving it all behind. Leaving him behind.

It started raining as the afternoon turned to evening. Ted washed his arms and face with water from the bucket and wandered back up the slope. Eliud washed himself and went to eat supper at one of the houses. The women of Titou seemed to have a system worked out for that too. After supper he would go to sleep in a lean-to, his father's house a victim of Anji's wrath.

Fat raindrops were falling by the time Ted got to the cover of the yellow house's porch. Camilla made him supper, marking it down as she always did, and then they fucked in Charles Xavier's bed, Camilla biting her arm to stay quiet. Afterward they lay in darkness, both wandering through the world of their separate thoughts. Ted stared through the surrounding mosquito netting, out the glassless panes of the front window, listening for a familiar rumble. He rolled over to look at the woman next to him. She lay naked in the shadows, an outline in the darkness, staring upward at the wooden rafters and metal roofing that made up the ceiling. The rain was prattling away on the tin. He wanted to reach out and touch her, but he couldn't. Even the thought of it filled him with a strange fear. It seemed ludicrous, but still he remained unmoving, the chasm between them seeming to grow with every beat of his heart. She seemed so calm. So sedate. So sure. None of the things that he himself felt. Camilla coughed, giving Ted permission to release his own. She glanced over at him. Ted pulled the thin blanket over his naked form. The silence. Always there was silence. It felt maddening. Nothing but the thoughts ricocheting their way through his head.

"Do you think he'll be back tonight?"

Ted could feel Camilla shrug in the darkness. A slight vibration in the mattress.

"We'll hear the motorbike if he does."

Ted nodded, wondering if the communication was detectable through the springs. Camilla coughed again. Ted scratched his scalp.

"Eliud told me today that he went to university."

"He was always a bright boy."

Something winged by the window, a whooshing through the air. Maybe a bird, probably a bat. Ted hoped it didn't fling itself inside. He doubted it would, but one could never tell.

"What did his father die of?"

"Whose father?"

"Eliud's."

He could feel Camilla roll over onto her side. He could feel her gaze boring into him.

"He didn't tell you?"

"No."

"Then it's none of your business."

Camilla rolled onto her back. The world lapsed back into silence. Ted could feel his face burning with the rebuke. Ted's ears started straining again for the growl of a motor. The bat or bird winged past the window again, and then made a full circuit around the house before heading off into the night. Ted breathed in deep and let it out.

"I was engaged when I came here, or at least nearly engaged."

Camilla shifted herself on the mattress.

"Is that so."

"Her name was Sandi. She didn't want to get married. She wanted to leave. She wanted to go someplace else. She never asked me if I wanted to come."

Camilla rolled over to face away. Small streams of water were flowing off of the tin roof onto the ground. Ted could feel the moisture growing in his eyes, hidden from the world by the night. He could see himself sitting with Sandi when they had first moved into the apartment together. They sat on an old beaten up couch, her hand in his, her head on his shoulder, staring at a print of a Van Gogh landscape tacked to the wall. What a fool he had been. What a ridiculous fool.

"I still have the ring. It's in a box back home in Idaho. I didn't know what to do with it, you know, after she left."

Camilla grunted and yawned. In his mind Ted could see her features stretch like those of a lazy house cat lounging in the sun.

"Eliud was in charge of the spraying at the plantation, just like his father was before. Eliud's father never had any respect for what he was doing. Eliud was always a bright boy. He made sure people did things right. His father would've been better if he had done the same."

Ted was only half listening. He was gathering the courage to ask the next question. The query that had been floating through his brain each night of silence. He thrust it forth, desperate to get it out before his strength left him.

"Why did you marry Charles Xavier?"

Camilla shifted, the vibrations working their way over to him, running through the mattress with sudden dreadful fingers that made him wish he could suck the words back in. She rustled as though unable to get comfortable, then fell into a stillness so deep that Ted wondered if she had fallen asleep. He could see her high up on the mountain, above where even the trees grew, sitting amongst the flowers blooming in the sunlight, gazing across the world toward the endless distant seas. He could see Charles Xavier walking upward toward her, an infectious bounce in his step and a smile on lips. Camilla smiled back, and when he reached her he sat beside her, hand holding hers, promising the world while she sat listening and imagining what lay ahead. It had been that way with Sandi once, back when the world was nothing but a field of flowers filled with soon to blossom dreams. Camilla breathed in and let out another yawn.

"I'd throw the ring out. It does no good to focus on things that aren't in front of you."

Ted lay in the darkness, waiting, the feeling of his heartbeat the only way to mark the passage of time. Camilla's words were quiet, but they thrust themselves across the rift.

"He's always been a good man. He's always treated me well."

Ted chewed on the words. Examining them from every angle. Analyzing them for any sign of weakness or fault. Camilla was drifting, falling, her voice barely a whisper.

"He'd do almost anything for me."

The bat, Ted was pretty sure it was a bat, winged by the window again. Camilla's breath slowed, drawing her downward into the land of Nod. Ted stared at the window, alone, listening for the motorbike.

Chapter 25

It rained for an entire week and a little more. The people out
working returned and instead of going back out, huddled in their
houses and shelters, eyeing the passing clouds and their falling misery
with the soulful eyes of people who know that there's nothing to be
done, that they must wait. The only one who remained unfazed was
Malik, who stayed in his tent, emerging only to watch with mirthless
eyes that seemed to suggest a knowledge of the world beyond those
around him. Charles Xavier didn't return. The roar of the motorbike
didn't clash with the falling rain. Wherever he was, he either couldn't
return, or chose not to, preferring the warmth of whatever sanctuary he
had found.

Even Eliud was affected. The house stayed as it was, half built,
and Ted found himself with nothing to do day after day. Camilla
adamantly refused to allow him to lounge around her house. She was
a woman used to her time alone and the weather was no excuse. At
first Ted kept himself busy braving the rain and filling buckets from
the reservoir, but Eliud soon lessened the need to do so by a great deal
by placing them under the eaves of the houses to catch the water from
above. After that Ted spent most of his time reading. When he
finished his sodden copy of *Catch-22*, he braved the knowledge of Mr.
Green and knocked on the old man's door.

"What do you want?"

Ted had steeled himself for the encounter, but now in the moment
found his armor lacking. The old bastard eyed him up and down,
eroding Ted's defenses with a sullen glare.

"I...I was wondering if I could borrow a book."

Mr. Green's look softened for a moment, but quickly shifted itself
back into line with his exuded disposition. It was a weak spot. Ted

had suspected that it would be. The old man grunted and walked back into his house, coming back a few seconds later with a dog eared copy of *The Hobbit*. There were some requests he couldn't deny.

"Avery didn't enjoy it much when I read it to him. Maybe you can appreciate it."

Mr. Green shoved the book into Ted's hands and shut the door. Ted went back to his own house and read the book as slowly as he could, pouring over every word, making sure it would last.

After four days of downpour, screaming profanities erupted through the morning air. People rushed from their houses into the damp world, Ted amongst them, their curiosity overcoming all. Two men were rolling in the mud, grappling and trying to break free enough to throw the random punch. People started yelling. Children started screeching. Younger men waded in, grabbing what they could, pulling the two men apart. It was Buffalo Bill and Crispin, the latter's nose bent and bleeding. Eliud moved between the two struggling men.

"What the fuck is happening?"

Buffalo Bill spit blood onto the ground.

"This fucking jacket been stealing. I got Lizzies missing. I always see him sneaking about."

Crispin's voice was high and strained.

"Liar. Fucking liar."

"You're the fucking liar, just like you're fucking sketel sister."

Crispin threw himself against the arms holding him back, but to no effect. Eliud shouted to be heard.

"Enough."

He shifted toward Buffalo Bill.

"You have any proof?"

"He's always poking around."

"But do you have proof?"

Buffalo Bill's eyes emanated hate, but he shook his head no. The crowd murmured amongst itself. Eliud frowned, took in a breath, and let it out.

"Then that's that. Stay apart and quit fighting."

The two men were released, a slight smile playing its way across Crispin's lips. Eliud's next words were meant for the crowd, but his eyes stayed on Crispin the entire time.

"But if anyone is ever caught stealing, you better believe they're going to get a beating. We're all in this together."

Crispin turned and walked back toward his house. Buffalo Bill was still seething, so Eliud went over to talk to him. The crowd broke up, still murmuring. The bits and pieces Ted overheard weren't positive toward Crispin. It was obvious who was the more popular of the two men. People began to talk of other things that had gone missing through the years, stacking crimes atop suspicions. Ted climbed up the hill, shaking his head.

On and on fell the rain. The young grass with its shallow roots did the best that it could. Perhaps if it had been older, more mature, but no, the weaknesses had been laid from the moment the mud settled into place the day of Anji's wrath. On the sixth day the force of the rain intensified, pounding the ground with relentless wet fists that refused to let up. Ted was in his house, partially reading and partially thinking of the things he'd do to Camilla that evening, when the mountainside was filled with a sudden thunderous groan. He leaped to his feet and ran to the front window, just in time to see a section of the mudslide further down the slope slough off and crash into a cinderblock house on the edge of town. Somebody screamed. People rushed out into the rain. Camilla came out and swiftly moved down the hill. Ted pulled on his boots and quickly followed.

People were crowded around the affected home, jabbering at one another, the volume rising as each word vied to be heard above the rest. It wasn't a big landslide. The house was undamaged. The occupants were standing just outside their open front door, crying and holding on to anybody who felt the need to show how much they cared. Somebody was still screaming. Camilla pushed her way through the crowd, her arms full of shovels. She shouted something in Eliud's ear, but Ted was unable to hear above the crowd. She gestured sharply with a pointed finger. It was then that Ted saw it. The remains of a lean-to crushed between the mud of the slide and the house.

Eliud was already moving, Ted rushed forward to help, grabbing a shovel from Camilla who was swiftly handing them out. The shovels attacked the mud with a maddened frenzy, the stamina of the men boosted by the screams for help. Eliud was shouting commands. Mud was scattered back toward the crowd which shifted to avoid it. A dark fist appeared amongst the muck, scrabbling its way into the open air. Camilla rushed forward, shouting to be heard.

"Careful. Careful."

Eliud and another man dropped their shovels and fell to their knees, scooping the mud out of the way with their hands. The person on the other side did their best to help, shoving it forward. The hole grew and the eager hands reached in and pulled the woman free. She screamed in pain as they drew her out. Tears flowed freely down her face, intermingling with a coating of dirt and mud. The woman kept shouting and gesturing with whatever appendage she could back at the small hollow from which she came. Camilla climbed into the hole and emerged, dragging an unmoving child with her. The boy's foot was at an unnatural angle. His ankle was broken. Ted was overcome by a sudden onrush of queasiness at the sight of the backward facing foot. The woman screaming as loud as she could.

"Is he alive?! Is he alive?!"

Camilla pulled the boy into her lap. She pressed her head against his chest. For a moment her entire being was focused, but then her face erupted with relief.

"He's okay. Just unconscious."

The injured mother started crying, unashamedly blubbering as she shouted thanks upward toward the heavens. She crawled over, wincing in pain as she rolled onto her side, crawling over to be near her son, to put her hand on him. Camilla was wiping the mud from the boy's face. She gestured at the crowd, shouting commands.

"Water. Somebody get water."

Eliud and a few others ran to obey. They came back with water buckets in hand, half the water sloshed out in their rush to return. Camilla started washing the mud off the boy and others moved forward to do the same for the still crying mother. Camilla surrendered the boy into the arms of another. She rose and spoke a moment with Eliud. Together they began moving down the hill. Ted rushed to follow.

Malik was standing outside his tent, watching the commotion. As the small delegation approached he set his face into a hard mask, the display of a man who didn't want to be bothered. Camilla ignored it, launching her first salvo before she even stopped walking.

"Two people injured. One with a few broken ribs and one with a broken ankle."

Camilla halted her advance, her two followers stopping a few feet further back. She stood with hands on her hips, glaring upward at the hulking form of Malik as she spoke.

"We need you to take them down to Helston."

Malik glared back with a sullen tired glare.

"No doctors in Helston right now. Nearest ones would be in the capital."

Camilla's tone was no nonsense. The tone of a teacher pointing out the obvious to a reluctant child.

"Then take them to the capital."

Malik rolled his eyes.

"It's just a few broken bones. Just wrap them up and call it good."

"One's a child."

Malik sucked in air through his nose and let it out again. His face didn't crack, but his eyes gave him away. A sudden shift from defiance to concern. Camilla saw the breach too, she rushed forward to complete the route of Malik's will.

"His ankle is broken pretty bad. If we don't get him to a doctor it might heal wrong."

Malik's eyes broke away. He gazed at the crowd of people around the injured further up the hill and then down at his feet. When he looked back at Camilla it was obvious that she had won.

"Somebody would need to watch my shop. I can't afford anybody stealing."

Eliud stepped forward.

"I'll watch things while you're gone."

Malik eyed the gawky man for a moment, growling deep in his throat as he considered, then nodded his approval.

"Okay. Bring them down to the truck."

Camilla nodded her thanks. Eliud ran back up the slope to carry out the commands. The woman managed to come down on her own two feet, though with people on either side. Buffalo Bill carried down the boy. The woman was helped into the back of Malik's truck and the boy was handed up to her. Malik stood by his truck, watching the proceedings with a bored air. Crispin emerged from the crowd, carrying a bundle in a pillowcase. He moved to the back of the truck and started to climb up. Eliud stopped him.

"Where do you think you're going?"

Crispin half turned, one leg up on the bumper.

"Figured they might need help on the trip down."

People were watching, some commenting quietly, some purposefully loud enough to be heard. Buffalo Bill was standing nearby, his hands clenched into fists. Eliud gestured toward the pillowcase.

"What do you have there?"

"Nothing. Just some personal stuff. I'm going to stay down and look for my sister."

Buffalo Bill took a threatening step forward. Eliud gestured at the pillowcase again.

"Let's have a look."

Crispin scowled, though it was more of a pout.

"I'm not a thief."

"Then let us have a look."

Crispin hesitated then climbed down. Eliud took the pillowcase and rifled through it, Camilla standing next to him. The nearby people fell quiet. Camilla and Eliud whispered to each other, and then Eliud handed back the pillowcase.

"Have a good trip."

Crispin didn't answer. He turned and climbed onto the truck. Malik rolled his eyes and got in behind the wheel. The truck belched to life, black smoke bursting for a moment from the exhaust before turning to a more normal color. The truck lurched forward and began its descent, its large tires squelching in the mud. The crowd began to disperse. Buffalo Bill approached Eliud and Camilla.

"Did he have any money on him?"

Eliud nodded.

"Yeah, he had some."

Camilla laid a gentle hand on Buffalo Bill's shoulder.

"It's hard to tell one Lizzie from another. Either way, he's gone now."

Buffalo Bill's shoulders raised, and for a moment he seemed about to say more, but in the end he didn't. He let his shoulders fall and nodded. Camilla began walking up the hill. Eliud remained behind to talk with Buffalo Bill. Ted waited for a minute, letting Camilla get ahead, and then followed, the thought of Camilla shouting out commands filling his head. He was hard before he was even halfway to her door.

Chapter 26

The rain slowed, but didn't stop. Some of the men of Titou, Ted amongst them, worked to dig a new ditch to shunt the water flowing down the new red scar away from the town. Camilla directed them, giving instructions and moving on, expecting them to be carried out. The mud splattered workers listened. They did their tasks without complaint. Eliud wasn't amongst them. He sat in the tent below, carrying out his promise. When the ditch was completed, Camilla set them to digging out the half buried house.

After nine days the weather turned hot. The rain stopped, but only sporadically, continuing the occasional assault from time to time throughout the day. Steam rose from the ground and humidity hugged the inhabitants of Titou in its wet embrace.

Charles Xavier arrived home in the later afternoon, the roar of his motorbike signaling his return and the end of Ted's domestic revelry. Ted and the other workers, their arms and legs covered in mud, joined the throngs of people moving to welcome Charles Xavier home. The arrival of mail was always a highlight, but this time there was an added curiosity. There was a man riding the motorbike behind Charles Xavier. A man whose skin was a similar shade in color, but who otherwise stood out. The man wasn't a big man, but he was well built, though his middle was going a bit too fat. He wore hiking shorts and a blue raincoat over a fitted Nike polyester t-shirt. On his head was a tan boonie hat, nearly soaked through, the drawstring hanging to his sternum. On his back was a hiker's pack, a big one, the type used for long trips into the wilderness, stuffed full. The man's entire visage was splattered with mud, except for his front where he had been protected by the presence of the man in front of him. Ted knew who the man was as soon as he saw him. His stomach roiled with sudden apprehension and fear.

Charles Xavier stopped the motorbike next to the gathering crowd, smiling in his old way, gesturing toward the figure behind him.

"You wouldn't believe what they're sending through the mail these days."

Charles Xavier laughed and the crowd laughed with him. The man sitting behind climbed off the motorbike and looked around. When he saw Ted his eyes brightened and a smile broke his mouth, revealing very white teeth. The man walked toward Ted. When he spoke, his American accent sounded flat and out of place after so long of hearing nothing but the lyrical words of the locals.

"Ted, I'm glad to see you seem to be getting on okay. We've been worried."

Ted took the offered hand, doing his best to keep his face under control.

"Hello Mr. Douglas. Welcome to Titou."

Mr. Douglas nodded and gazed around again, his eyes settling for a moment on the red scar of the new landslide.

"It looks a little worse for wear, but a hell of a lot better than down on the coast."

People stood about them, some pretending to collect their mail, but the rest openly listening. Mr. Douglas's view tracked across the mass of curious humanity.

"Is there some place I can clean up, maybe where we can talk more privately?"

Ted chewed on the insides of his cheeks. He nodded.

"Yeah, sure."

Ted gestured upward toward the red house above. He headed up the hill, Mr. Douglas following, wheezing a bit as he came. A loud electronic beep split the air. Ted's head partially turned at the unfamiliar sound. Mr. Douglas looked at an expensive looking watch on his wrist and shrugged apologetically.

"Sorry, fancy thing counts steps, but I can't for the life of me figure out how to get it to quit beeping every hour."

Ted didn't answer. He just turned his head back forward and kept climbing.

At the house Mr. Douglas gave himself a sponge bath from a bucket of water. Ted sat out on the porch, looking over the town and the ruins of the banana plantation. People kept finding reasons to walk by, most a ways off, but the gutsy creeping closer, hoping to get within hearing range. Ted glared when they got too close, sending them scuttling back to their own business. Mr. Douglas's flat voice slivered through the window.

"I've been trying to get to you for weeks. The whole island's fucked. Airport's wrecked beyond belief, nothing but smaller prop jobs getting in or out, and pretty much all of those are military and Red Cross, you know what I mean. No way they were going to let a lowly Peace Corp drone fill a seat just to find a guy. Not a damn way in hell. Pretty much got told you'd either turn up or you wouldn't. Thank god you finally sent that letter. Your mother had been calling me every day. Good to hear her sound happy for a change. All the rest were screaming or crying. Christ. I don't want to say anything bad about her, you know, your mother, but good god. I thought it was bad when she thought you were dead, at least the crying broke up the screaming. Once she knew you were still alive it was nothing but when the hell we were going to get you back to the states. Should have let her loose on the bastards in charge of the relief effort, might have gotten here sooner."

Far below, the figure of Charles Xavier was talking to Eliud and Camilla next to Malik's tent, one hand on his wife and the other on his motorbike. It took Ted a moment to realize that Mr. Douglas had fallen silent. He knew it was his place to keep the conversation going.

"How did you get here?"

His voice didn't sound right in his ear, too strained, too forced.

"It was Jessica's idea. You remember Jessica, from Maine. Clever girl that one. Anyways, caught a flight to Barbados and paid off a fisherman to take me across. Took over a day. Cost a pretty penny, I tell you what. Never been so sick in my life. I still feel a little queasy."

Charles Xavier was pushing the motorbike up the hill, Camilla with him. Mr. Douglas came out onto the porch in a fresh shirt and pair of shorts. He arched his back, the vertebrae going off like firecrackers.

"Damn it feels good to be out of that pack. Fucking thing must weigh a ton."

Mr. Douglas's eyes followed Ted's, landing on the rising figures, before retreating back to his fellow American. He gazed at Ted for a moment, but Ted didn't turn to look at him. Mr. Douglas clicked his tongue, then arched his back again, squeezing out a few more pops.

"You going to get cleaned up too?"

"Yeah, sure."

Ted went into the house and undressed. He rinsed the sponge several times before using it on himself. Outside, Mr. Douglas exchanged a few words of introduction and welcome back and forth. Ted could hear Charles Xavier and Mr. Douglas laugh at one of Charles Xavier's jokes, the American's chuckle drowned out by the postman's guffaws. Camilla offered to bring them supper a little later, but Mr. Douglas politely refused. They were gone when Ted came back out on the porch, wearing his cleanest t-shirt, the one with the fewest holes, and a pair of gym shorts the same color as the house.

The red paint was peeling. Ted hadn't really noticed before. The broken windows. The loose sheets of tin on the roof creaking in the wind. The mud still piled up in the corners of the interior. The smell of mildew and rats. It had been a long time since Ted had noticed any of it. Mr. Douglas stared out at the world, watching the sun kiss the slope of the mountainside. Ted could still see the gaps where Anji had knocked over the trees. Mr. Douglas took it all in, sucked in a satisfied breath, and turned back to his host.

"You hungry?"

"I could eat."

"Well, then let's eat"

Mr. Douglas went back inside and Ted followed. From his pack, Mr. Douglas pulled out a propane stove, much fancier than the ones sold by Malik. He sent Ted for water. Ted took the bucket containing the water they had washed with and poured it on the ground outside. He then partially re-filled it from a larger bucket sitting on Charles Xavier's porch. He paused for a moment and listened. Charles Xavier and Camilla were talking softly inside, the words blended with the sounds of Camilla cooking. Charles Xavier laughed. Ted went back to his own house. Mr. Douglas insisted on dissolving some purification tablets in the water.

"Probably don't need it, but I didn't come all this way just to shit myself."

Ted didn't put up a fight. He sat on the cot and watched Mr. Douglas fill a collapsible pot from his bag with water and then add a box of Macaroni and Cheese. Ted ran a finger through his longish hair, it felt greasy, it probably needed a wash. Camilla preferred it when it was washed. Mr. Douglas's hair was cut short. A black skullcap. He hummed as he cooked, tunes with a steady regular cadence, popular Classic Rock songs from the radio. The tune broke off.

"Have you gotten any of the letters we sent?"

Ted glanced down at his feet next to the sticking out strap of his duffel bag beneath the cot. He raised his eyes to meet Mr. Douglas's.

"No. I haven't gotten any."

Mr. Douglas gave Ted a measuring look.

"We've probably sent five since the hurricane, at least three since you got word to your parents."

"I don't know, things have been pretty fucked up here."

"I can see that."

Mr. Douglas turned back to take the pot off of the propane stove. He strained the water with a fork into the sink without thinking and cursed when it didn't go down. He clicked his tongue and started stirring in the cheese powder. Ted glanced down at his feet again. Mr. Douglas chuckled and looked over his shoulder.

"Kind of funny. Here you live right next to the postman and you can't even get your damn mail."

Ted smiled.

"I don't think letters are what he's really interested in delivering."

Mr. Douglas laughed a bit and then went back to his stirring.

"Dinner's ready. It would be better if we had some milk to mix in, but I guess we'll just have to rough it."

They ate out of collapsible bowls, also from Mr. Douglas's pack. Ted still had some silverware. Ted didn't think it tasted all that good, but it did bring back some fleeting memories of college which he quickly quashed. Sandi sitting on the couch in her underwear and one of his shirts, eating Mac and Cheese right from the pot, watching *Smokey and the Bandit* on the TV, laughing where they dubbed out the apparently offensive bits. Ted stayed on the cot. Mr. Douglas sat cross legged on the floor. It was getting dark outside.

"Looks like things have been coming back together here."

"Yeah, it was a little hairy for awhile after Anji. It was a couple of weeks until any supplies got up here."

"It's always amazed me how well people pull together when they have to."

"Yeah."

"You been keeping yourself busy?"

"I've been helping where I can. A lot of people are working for the government clearing the roads, so I've been helping build a few houses. You know, trying to get everyone under better shelter."

"You look healthy enough."

"Yeah, Camilla's been taking care of me."

Mr. Douglas nodded, but didn't answer. They finished eating. Mr. Douglas washed the bowls and dried them with a bath towel from his bag. It had a faded cheetah on it. It was starting to get dark out. Ted waited until it looked like Mr. Douglas was finishing up.

"Are you here to bring me back home?"

Mr. Douglas ran a hand over the back of his neck. It was a big hand, with thick sausage fingers.

"Things are pretty bad on the island Ted. I know up here seems pretty fine, but overall Domenique is pretty fucked up."

"I'm doing a lot of good up here. Isn't that what I'm supposed to be doing? Helping these people?"

Mr. Douglas turned around and leaned back against the counter.

"This isn't exactly what we sent you up here for. There's protocols for this kind of thing."

"I've helped build houses and replant gardens. There's still a lot of work to be done."

Ted's voice was ragged. His fists were clenched and he was shaking a little. He could feel Mr. Douglas watching him. He bent his will to calming himself down, but to little effect. Mr. Douglas rubbed the back of his neck again. He took in a deep breath and let it out.

"Christ Ted, can you really tell me that these people need you? They've been getting along without you for a long damn time."

"Is that any reason not to help?"

"That's not how things work. We have protocols."

Ted drew in a breath and let it out. He could feel the vibration working its way down to his very being. Ted's eyes darted from Mr. Douglas to the blank cinderblock wall to his right, down at his feet, and then back to Mr. Douglas.

"Look Ted. It's not my decision. You'll get sent to DC for a bit, work in the main office, and then we'll find you a new posting to finish up your contract. These things happen."

A bird flew past the gaping hole that was once the front window, so close that Ted could hear the flapping of its wings. His gut was twisted into a knot.

"I don't want to leave."

"It's not my choice Ted."

The knot tightened.

"What if I quit?"

Mr. Douglas's eyebrows shot further up his forehead.

"What?"

"What if I quit? You can't make me leave."

The other man's face grew angry. His voice inadvertently rose in volume.

"Fuck Ted, do you even know what's going on here? This is a fucking paradise compared to further down. You don't have a damn clue."

Ted was quivering on the cot. His eyes darted to the cinderblock wall and back again. He licked his lips.

"I'm twenty-two years old. There's nothing you can do about it if I quit, is there?"

"Fuck Ted."

"Is there?"

"No."

"Then I'm staying."

Mr. Douglas stared down at the floor. He stayed silent for a moment, before pounding the counter with his hand.

"Jesus, I can't believe I came all this way for this horseshit."

"I'm staying."

Mr. Douglas threw up his hands.

"Fine, whatever. Where's the fucking bathroom?"

"Down behind what's left of the mercantile."

Mr. Douglas put on his boots, pulled a flashlight out of his bag, and stalked off. The people of Titou gazed out at the beam of light as it moved past. Ted started smiling the moment Mr. Douglas walked out the door. He was staying. There was nothing anyone could do about it. Not his parents, not Mr. Douglas, not anybody. Ted went out behind the house and relieved himself where the shower used to be. Grass was growing up around his bare feet. Ted raised his stream and let the golden liquid splatter across the rusted showerhead. The stars were twinkling overhead, beautiful to behold. His stomach gurgled. The Macaroni and Cheese wasn't sitting right. He stayed outside for a bit, happily looking upward at the stars overhead. When he finally went back inside, Mr. Douglas was there again, unfolding a sleep sack on the floor.

"I'm starting to get a bad back. Getting old sucks. Sleeping on a hard surface is supposed to help."

"Do I need to sign anything?"

Mr. Douglas didn't look up from his task.

"Look Ted, I'm going to have to stay up here until Malik gets back. Let's worry about this shit when I leave."

"I'm not leaving."

"So you've said. Let's go to bed."

Mr. Douglas stripped down to his skivvies, climbed into his sleep sack, and flipped off the flashlight. He was a whitey tighty man. Ted rubbed the dirt off of the bottom of his feet and climbed into his own sleep sack in the dark. The two men laid quiet, both staring up at the ceiling, the only noise coming from the air whistling through Mr. Douglas's nose. The bird flew by the window again, or maybe it was a bat. What would a bird be doing flying around in the dark? Ted couldn't stop smiling. He had won. There was nothing Mr. Douglas could do about it. He could try to convince Ted to change his mind, but there was nothing he could actually do. Next door, Charles Xavier and Camilla started in on the normal routine of their reunions. It started quiet, but rose in pitch as it moved towards fruition. Mr. Douglas let out a short bark of a laugh from the back of his throat.

"Shit, what are they doing over there, strangling cats?"

Ted didn't answer. He pretended to be asleep. The sounds rolled into his ears and ricocheted through his brain. It felt wrong to be hearing them now. Dirty. Voyeuristic. Ted was filled with inexplicable anger. He choked down a need to get up and stomp on Mr. Douglas's chest. The lust next door culminated and the sounds dropped away. Mr. Douglas snorted again and fell into a silence broken only by steady breathing. Ted lay awake in the darkness. Camilla had never been loud with him. She had always been stifled. Silent. Holding back. It didn't matter. He was staying. He still had time.

Chapter 27

Ted woke to the smell of frying dehydrated eggs. He could tell from the first moment that he'd be in a sour mood. He had dreamed of fucking Sandi. Prying open crusty eyes, he was greeted to the sight of Mr. Douglas in his tighty whities, cooking on the camp stove and dancing from foot to foot as he hummed to himself. A long line of ants marched from the open doorway to a spill from last night's supper. Ted pushed himself to a sitting position, still halfway inside his sleep sack. Mr. Douglas divided the eggs into the same two bowls they had used the night before and brought one over for Ted. His feet scattered the ants. Panicked they fled in all directions, abandoning the shattered remains of their kinsmen who had been unlucky enough to fall beneath the calloused soles. Ted took the bowl with a mumbled good morning and thanks, the pair mashed together into a single mostly incoherent phrase.

The line of ants began to reform. Mr. Douglas looked down, noticing them for the first time. His eyes followed them to their goal, a small pile of noodles near the edge of the cot. He bent over and with a casual flip of his hand sent the treasure flying out the door. The confused ants scattered again, desperately seeking what was no longer there. The two men ate in silence. The eggs tasted dry and crumbly in Ted's mouth. When he finished he put the bowl by the sink and went outside to pee. The outside world was covered in a thick layer of dew. A soft wind blew through the tree line. When he went back into the house Mr. Douglas was doing the dishes.

"I'm not going back."

Mr. Douglas didn't even bother to turn around.

"So you said last night."

"I just want you to know that."

Mr. Douglas grunted and turned his head.

"We can talk about it later."

Ted stood for a moment, feeling as though he needed to say more, but being unsure what else to say, surrendered the moment, got dressed, and went back outside.

Mr. Douglas stayed for eight excruciatingly long days. The excuse for his continued presence was that he needed to pay the rent for the dilapidated red house where Ted was staying, money that he apparently felt uncomfortable entrusting to anyone but Malik himself. However, Ted suspected it was nothing but a ruse to buy time to convince Ted to return with him to the states. If it was a ruse, it was a pretty good one, for the two men barely spoke except for during the morning and evening meals, and even then only polite pleasantries about the weather. They always ate from Mr. Douglas's pack. He refused to let Camilla cook for them.

Mr. Douglas spent most of his time sitting on the neighboring porch with Charles Xavier. The two men had quickly bonded over Mr. Douglas's knowledge of motorbikes. Charles Xavier's wasn't running as smoothly as it might, though it likely had more to do with his constant tinkering rather than any fault in the machine itself. Mr. Douglas's willingness to buy bottles of rum from Malik's tent probably didn't hurt the new friendship either. The fixing of the motorbike proceeded at a crawl.

Ted spent most of the day working on the third house by himself. As promised, Eliud remained at Malik's tent, watching over things until the proprietor's return. It was slow going. Ted was no carpenter and what little knowledge he had sponged off Eliud seemed to have melted away without the other man present. Doggedly he continued on, wandering down to Malik's tent every time he needed clarification or advice. The women still brought him dinner at midday, which raised his spirits, but none of them showed much interest in having a conversation. Ted often heard Mr. Douglas and Charles Xavier laughing, a noise he did his best to cover with rapid wild swings of his hammer. Sometimes, out of the corner of his eye, Ted would catch Charles Xavier gesturing down at him before the shared hilarity ensued. It was at these times that Ted most thought of Camilla. The feel of her in his arms. The feel of himself inside of her.

While the daytime was uncomfortable for Ted, the night time was pure torment. Each night he could hear Charles Xavier and Camilla go at each other like alley cats in heat. Each night Mr. Douglas made a snarky comment about it before rolling over and falling asleep. Each night Ted imagined smashing his head in with a rock. Mr. Douglas was the reason Charles Xavier was still in Titou, at least that's what Ted told himself. Normally Charles Xavier would've left for Helston, departing on his circuit of mail deliveries and infidelity, but he hadn't. It was cutting into Ted's time with Camilla.

Ted was not the only one unhappy with the situation. Camilla's displeasure was written across her face, growing darker each time her husband spent the day getting drunk on the porch. Charles Xavier and his guest would be sprawled out by late afternoon, Charles Xavier yelling for Camilla to bring him his supper. At times she would appear, but increasingly she refused to leave the house, letting her silence be the answer. In these moments Charles Xavier would laugh the loudest, long and hard, before rising to stumble inside to retrieve the food himself. By the fourth night, the sound of lovemaking stopped, replaced by hissed conversations and then an empty quiet.

Ted watched all as he worked on the house. He noted the rising tension with an appreciable air of anticipation which put a swagger in his step every time Charles Xavier was knocked down by his wife's hushed assertiveness. On the afternoon of the fifth day, when Charles Xavier and Mr. Douglas were well into their daily contest with the rum bottle, Ted in the throes of his madness returned to his house and went directly from the front door to the back. He found Camilla in her garden, weeding with her ass up in the air. Without a word he kneeled down in front of her, placing one hand on top of hers. She didn't look up. She simply pulled her hand away.

"What are you doing?"

Ted licked his lips, his eyes locked on the hanging neckline of her dress, following curves into the shadow.

"I need you."

"Not now."

"I need you now."

Camilla sat back on her haunches. She stared at Ted disapprovingly, her eyes tired.

"My husband is right in front of the house."

"I don't care. He's drunk."

At the word drunk a flash of anger shot across Camilla's face.

"Don't you just think yourself the little grindsman. If you're all pent up with oil than just go up in the trees and back fist yourself."

"Come up into the trees with me."

The corner of Camilla's mouth twitched. Ted leaned forward. She didn't lean back. He went in for a kiss. She slapped him hard across the face.

"I said no."

Camilla got up, went inside her house, and shut the door. Ted sat for awhile, rubbing his cheek. When that changed nothing he rose, walked into his own house, and did what Camilla suggested. It didn't help. If anything it made it worse. He tried to think of someone else, but all that flashed in his mind was either Camilla or Sandi, intertwining themselves into a naked yin and yang. When he walked back out of his house Charles Xavier and Mr. Douglas were laughing uproariously. The moment they saw Ted they fell silent, barely contained mirth playing across their faces. Ted could feel himself blushing. How could they know? Did they hear him talking to Camilla? There was no way they could've heard him. Mr. Douglas gestured with his hand, his voice slurred.

"Security breach at Los Pantalones."

Ted's anger was cut with confusion.

"What?"

Charles Xavier gestured at Ted as well, his voice just as slurred

"Your zippers down."

Both men erupted again. Ted zipped up his pants and retreated down the hill. That night as he and Mr. Douglas bedded down he heard Charles Xavier and Camilla fighting. Not just whispers, actual fighting with raised voices and dramatic flair. Ted couldn't make out what they said, but the sound brought a smile to his lips. Mr. Douglas stayed quiet.

Mr. Douglas didn't buy more rum the next day. He took a long walk in the morning, spent a good chunk of time talking to Eliud in Malik's tent, and then worked on the motorbike most of the afternoon. Charles Xavier didn't join him. The other man didn't appear from out of his house until after dinner, but Ted only saw him briefly from his vantage point at the site of construction.

Camilla didn't appear either, but she moved her way through Ted's mind, every step accompanied by a sultry swing of her hips. He banished her to the darkest recesses of his psyche, burying her beneath recitations of lists memorized in middle school. State capitals. Presidents. Kings of England. The Preamble of the Constitution. Nothing worked. She brushed them all out of the way with her callused hands, beckoning coyly with a finger. Not even the slip of a nail and the hammer crashing down upon his thumb did the trick. Through the pain she slipped her dress over her head and let it drop, revealing the round curves of her body beneath. By mid-afternoon, his entire being was buzzing as he climbed the hill. Mr. Douglas was sitting on Charles Xavier's porch, fiddling with the motorbike's carburetor. Ted grabbed the nearly empty bucket of water on the corner of the porch, dumped it out, and started moving toward the path to the reservoir. Mr. Douglas watched him quizzically.

Ted kept his pace measured until he got within the treeline. It was warmer within the confines of the forest. Sweat dripped out of his every pore. Two-thirds of the way up the trail he stopped and considered, but laughter up ahead spurred him back into movement. Two women came down the trail, water buckets on their heads. Ted nodded politely as they passed. Further up and further in. The reservoir sat before him. The marshy area behind the broken levy was alive with mosquitoes. Thousands in the air, fluttering en masse above a writhing carpet made up of millions of their fellows on the mud and shallow pools. Their high pitched buzzing filled the air, a constant thrum in the background.

Privacy. He needed privacy. He dropped the bucket by the trail, climbed on the broken edge of the dirt levy, and began working his way around. There were small footprints in the wet dirt. Children's footprints. His boot knocked a rock loose. It rolled down the embankment and splatted into the mud. A horde of mosquitoes rose and buzzed around him, humming in his ears. He swatted at them as he double timed his way across back into the relative safety of the thick foliage on the other side. Deeper he went, some of the more tenacious still hot on his heels. A noise to his right. A familiar sound.

Wet slapping. Guttural adulations. A trick of the wind, rising and falling with the breeze. Ted could feel the unconscious parts of his body react. The conscious mind told him to turn away, it was none of his business, but other parts called for a dramatically different decision. The breeze rose again, carrying the sounds with them. His feet turned to the right. His hand pushed away a branch. Deeper in he went.

The noises grew louder as Ted got closer, rising to a steady cadence. He was careful to be quiet. The ground eyed before every footstep. Every plant brushed past softly as a mother's kiss. He was maybe twenty feet away he finally saw them. They were laying on the ground. The man on top of the woman, both covered in a thick sheen of sweat. The man's pants were around his ankles, his blue shirt hanging unbuttoned. Though Ted could only see the top of his head he knew him instantly. The woman's legs were locked around Charles Xavier's middle, her yellow dress pulled up to her waist. Her fingernails clawed at his back, her face contorted with beautiful agony. She gasped with every thrust. Moaned with every withdrawal. Mrs. Seraphin's mouth was close to Charles Xavier's ear, desperately urging him on.

Charles Xavier raised himself, a smile splitting his face, his gaze tracing across the bounties of the woman beneath him. He looked upwards and his eyes locked onto Ted's. The smile fell away. The eyes in both heads widened. Charles Xavier threw himself back, leaving thin arms clutching at nothing. Ted turned and ran, crashing through the underbrush, fleeing from the sound of curses and stumbling steps. Fronds slapped him across the face. Twigs and small branches broke before his onslaught. The stumbles morphed into quick staccato steps, rapid footfalls that closed the distance. Ted redoubled his efforts, his chest heaving with exertion. The sounds of pursuit were getting closer, louder, shrinking the gap. The bony weight of Charles Xavier leaped onto his back. Ted took another stumbling step forward, shaking to remove the weight, another faltering stride, and then the two men fell into a gasping heap. Charles Xavier's voice was ragged, forcing the words out between desperate intakes of air.

"Please Theodore. Don't tell Eliud."

Hot anger boiled away Ted's fatigue. With a sudden lurch he removed the weight of the other man. He rolled and put his back against a tree. Charles Xavier, laying in the dirt, turned himself onto his side.

"Please."

"Eliud?! Fucking Eliud?!"

"Please. He respects me."

"You bastard."

The words rolled off of Ted's tongue, sweet as an elixir.

"You fucking bastard."

Ted could see the whites completely around Charles Xavier's wet eyes. They were desperate eyes. Guilty eyes. The eyes of a man whose entire world was about to collapse. Ted sucked back a load of snot and spit between his boots.

"What happened to too close to home?"

"Please."

"You bastard."

"I know about you and Camilla."

Charles Xavier's gaze was no longer desperate. It was steady. Ted's mouth was dry. Charles Xavier rose to a standing position, towering over the inert form of his rival.

"I know you've been fucking my wife."

Ted spit back, his words laced with venom.

"You're a piece of shit. You're a selfish piece of shit."

Charles Xavier shook his head, a sad look of disappointment across his face.

"Perhaps, but I'm not the only one."

The older man turned and began to walk away, down the mountainside toward Titou. Ted screamed after him.

"You fucking don't deserve her."

Charles Xavier didn't answer. The green foliage swallowed him up without another word.

Chapter 28

Charles Xavier left at the break of dawn. The repeated sound of the kickstarter mixed with a wide variety of curses gave way to a revving engine followed by a receding roar. Ted rose up on his cot, woken by the ferocity of the exit, covered in the sweat of a forgotten dreamscape. At best, Mr. Douglas rose to just below the level of consciousness. With a grunt and a wheeze he sank back below the waters, undisturbed by the world around him. The mountainside sank back into silence, broken only by a breeze through the trees and the soft hum of a few errant mosquitoes. Ted lay back down, but couldn't fall back asleep. He was gone. Charles Xavier was gone.

Charles Xavier had been the first to return to Titou the previous day. After their parting, Ted had sat in the forest for what seemed to be at least an hour before making his way to the reservoir to retrieve his bucket. By the time he had returned to Titou with it full of water, Camilla had already been sitting on her porch with her husband and Mr. Douglas had already been calling out that dinner was ready. Ted had left the water on his own porch, Charles Xavier watching his every move with the eyes of a puppy. Part of him had wanted to confront Charles Xavier again then and there. A public pronouncement for all the world to see, but he hadn't. Camilla had been smiling, at least until she saw Ted, at which point her face had turned to stone as she looked away. In the end Ted had retreated into the comforting shadows of his own domicile, retreating to another meal of boxed macaroni and cheese.

A medium sized brown spider was building a web in one of corner of the house, sticky threads connecting cinderblock, wood, and tin. It worked diligently, moving back and forth, constructing itself a place in the empty void. The sun made its climb from the night the same as it always did, transforming the world as it came. Ted lay in his sleep sack and waited for the morning sounds next door, his brain flitting with focused activity interspersed by random thoughts. Camilla smiling at him. Her face turning away in silence. Charles Xavier giving him a hearty slap on the back. The older man's desperate pleas in the forest. Sandi climbing into the car to leave. Camilla smiling at her husband, a secret smile given to nobody else. Charles Xavier on top of Mrs. Seraphin, humping away. His parents at home, his mother in the kitchen and his father sitting in front of the TV. Camilla on top of him as they made love, a finger of hush on his lips. A rum bottle passed back and forth, steadily draining pull by pull. Camilla frowning with disapproval.

Titou began to rise to meet the day. People climbed from their beds, heeded nature's call, and shouted greetings as they gathered to head off down the roads and trails. No sounds came from the house next door. No rustles. No squeaks. No scrapes. Just silence. Mr. Douglas rose with all the rest, forcing Ted to do likewise though no comment or order was ever traded between them. Mr. Douglas whistled as he made breakfast, something that was just barely identifiable as *Louie Louie*. He left the house soon after without a word. Ted waited for a bit, listening, but soon accepted his own need to do something with his day. It wouldn't do for Mr. Douglas to see him just sitting around.

When he went outside he paused to look at the yellow house next door. Camilla's door was shut, the house's interior dark, the broken window blocked by the flowered sheet. Ted could see his feet carrying him over. His arm rising up to knock. His voice saying the words, damning the only man on the island he could definitively call a friend. Tossing him aside like so much refuse. Taking his place beside the queen of the world. What did he owe Charles Xavier? What had he really been? It was simple. Walk over, knock on the door, say the words. Yell them if he must. He did none of these things. He stood where he was, gathering himself up for the lunge that never came. He turned away. Mr. Green was on his own porch, still trying to teach Id to read. Ted ignored them and walked down the hill.

The third house was almost complete. All that remained was the roof. Ted hammered away at it diligently. Bit by bit the last of the structure grew. Ted pulled the needed tin from the ruins of the mercantile. Mr. Douglas was talking to Eliud in the tent. Ted noticed them when he went to get the first few sheets of tin. They sat in the shadowy confines for over an hour before Mr. Douglas emerged, only to disappear up the path leading higher up the mountain.

At midday an older woman brought Ted his dinner, Spam and rice with some canned vegetables. Ted couldn't remember her name, but she smiled when she put the plate down so Ted smiled back. He ate alone, leaving the dirty plate on the cinderblock where the old woman had deposited it. She'd be back for it later. They always came back for the plates. Once upon a time the children would've picked up the plate, but with most of the adults gone they now ran through the town like wild animals. Screaming with feral delight, pushing and scratching, lost in a world of tribal games only understood by them. Where once they had hunted rats, now they went after anything that moved. Numerous chickens, at last coming home to search for the safety they had known before Anji's wrath, met their fate at the wrong end of a sharpened hoe. Those who provided fresh meat to their families were often rewarded with praise, an ugly cycle of incentive and escalation. The parents were busy. Only when there was blood did they step in to put the fear of wrath back in their progeny. Mr. Green often muttered that the children needed to be in school, but he was too busy with Id to do more than that.

Mr. Douglas came back down the mountain soon after dinner. He walked casually toward Ted who was working on the roof, nailing down sheets of tin. He looked up, hands in pockets, waiting for an opening between the deafening rattles of the hammer blows.

"Do you need any help?"

Ted paused long enough to consider before answering. He could recognize that the other man was looking for an opening to start a conversation.

"Hand me up a sheet of tin when I ask for it."

Mr. Douglas nodded. Ted went back to his hammering, the cacophony blocking any linguistic pursuits. Ted had a pretty good idea what it was Mr. Douglas wanted to talk about. Unfortunately, it was something he knew he couldn't avoid forever. The last nail was driven home. The piece of metal roofing was secure.

"Can you hand me up a piece please?"

Mr. Douglas did as he was told. Ted braced himself. Mr. Douglas began as soon as Ted's hands touched the hot metal.

"Is Eliud a good egg?"

It was not the question Ted expected. He did his best to hide his surprise as he moved the tin into position.

"Yeah, I'd say so. He's never done anything to make me think any less of him."

"I need to get back. It's been a nice vacation, but I can't wait around for Malik forever. I'm thinking of giving Eliud the rent money to pass on."

"That would probably be all right."

It wasn't until after Ted answered that he realized his opinion wasn't being asked for. Ted went back to hammering. Mr. Douglas waited patiently for the next opening. He wasted no time taking it once it arrived.

"I'm going to head out tomorrow."

Ted didn't answer. He just put the new piece of tin in place and started hammering again. Mr. Douglas picked up another sheet, but he didn't hand it up when Ted gestured for it.

"You going to give it up or what?"

"It's good to want to help people."

"Yep."

Ted stared down at the man from up high, waiting, feeling as though somehow Mr. Douglas still seemed to be looking down at him.

"Have you thought anymore about coming back with me?"

Ted couldn't hide the annoyance from spreading across his face.

"We've talked about this already."

"I know, but I don't think you fully realize what you're doing."

Mr. Douglas's face was trying to force itself to look empathetic, the type of face older people always tried to have when they were dispensing their own brand of wisdom. Ted thought about throwing his hammer at the other man. His retort was a little more of a bark than he meant it to be.

"I'm so glad you're an expert on what's best for me. Hand up the damn tin."

Mr. Douglas did as he was told. Even that small victory made Ted flush with pride. The older man shook his head.

"Look man, we've all been here before. This kind of shit happens, people get attached, but you have to remember that in the end it's just a job. You're getting too tight in with all this shit man. This isn't your place."

Ted's hand was clutching the hammer so tightly that his fingers were all white. He maneuvered the tin into place.

"What the hell are you trying to say?"

"Just that this is definitely not the place to get involved in other people's shit. I know…."

Ted didn't listen to the rest of it. He started hammering in nails. Mr. Douglas waited, not even picking up another sheet of tin this time, but once Ted had all the nails in he began hammering the already driven ones again. Finally growing tired of the game, the older man turned and started up the hill. Once he was gone, Ted climbed down to get another sheet himself. He watched the Peace Corps man go inside the red house above. The yellow house was still quiet. Ted stared at it, willing the door to open. When it didn't, he got back to work.

The last finishing touches were finished by late afternoon. Ted sat at the peak of the roof, gazing out across the town. Greenery was beginning to work its way over the ruins of the mercantile, the first invaders eating away at the former perimeter. A cool breeze blew across the mountainside. The house beneath him felt solid. It felt good. Women moved by with buckets on their heads, a few smiling and waving as they walked by. The house was ready for somebody to move in. Soon it would belong to someone, but it would always belong to Ted as well. It had a permanence that Ted had never felt before. An immutable stability which brought forth a sense of contentment. It was his. In its construction he was the lead actor, not just a supporting character.

The people began arriving home as the afternoon turned to evening. They came from road and path in knots of twos and threes, bent with fatigue from the day's work. Some moved toward their homes without noticing, others noted the addition immediately, but Buffalo Bill was the first to approach. He was muddy from the knees and elbows down. He walked to just below where Ted was sitting, his hand shading his eyes from the collapsing sun. He smiled when he spoke.

"So it's done then jake?"

Ted nodded, his face locked in a peaceful solemnity.

"Yep."

Buffalo Bill tapped the wooden wall with his knuckle.

"It's a good looking house. Big up, respect."

Ted smiled. He couldn't help himself.

"Thank you."

"Who's going to get it?"

"Whoever needs it I guess."

Buffalo Bill nodded, satisfied with the answer. More people approached, Buffalo Bill springing a leak in the dam that held them back. They came in ones and twos, and then all together. A great circle of people, laughing and jostling each other, the more technical amongst them examining every board and nail, nodding to themselves and throwing up the occasional declaration of a job well done. Some of the women began to clap and sing. Ted couldn't hear the words. It all collapsed down, filling the depths along with the complements and the beating of his own heart. He couldn't stop smiling. He looked out across the people of Titou. If he jumped from his perch he would not fall, he would fly higher and higher into the heavens. Lifted by the voices around him. Eliud was standing next to Malik's tent, his face split by a Cheshire grin. When Ted looked at him he nodded. Ted nodded back. Up the hillside figures stood on the porches of the red house and the yellow. Mr. Douglas and Camilla in their respective places, watching the commotion from afar. Ted's face was hot and flushed. His eyes were moist. It was too much. It was all too much.

Ted climbed down the ladder. Children began scrambling up it as soon as his feet touched the ground. The harsh voices of mothers joined the symphony. People packed around him, patting him on the back, shaking his hand, throwing sweetened words into his deafened ears. Ted was enmeshed in a sea of white teeth. His lips kept faltering, but he forced himself to smile at everyone. His humble replies became repetitive and automatic. The group of singing women shifted to a second tune. He was drowning. He could feel himself being sucked under. Tears were flowing freely across his cheeks, the sight of which elicited laughter and beaming gazes from those around him. Buffalo Bill gave him a hearty slap across the shoulder, yelled something at the crowd which made them laugh again, and then pulled Ted close to say something into his ear. Only a few words managed to successfully jump the narrow gap. Good job. Anji. Home. He pulled Ted into a tight embrace and then broke free.

Some of the women were inside the house, poking around, making plans. Clusters of people were already forming to discuss who was to be the beneficiary. Others began to move on, drawn away by the needs of the evening. The noose around Ted's neck loosened. Where once he was crushed now he was an island, just a last few people offering words and friendly taps and gestures. Ted gazed around him. Eliud was gone, disappeared back into the tent. The porches above were empty. Ted started making his way up the hill. A few light sprinkles fell from the sky. Mosquitoes buzzed around a few puddles.

Ted could see Mr. Douglas moving about inside the red house, preparing dinner and glancing down the hill from the corner of his eye. Mr. Green came out onto his porch. He stretched and gazed benevolently across the town. He was watching too. Ted could feel him watching. Ted paused for a moment. He hesitated. Fuck them. Fuck all of them. Ted moved onto the porch of the yellow house. His arm rose and his fist knocked on the door. Strong knocks. Determined knocks. Nothing but silence, just his own breathing loud in his ears. He raised his arm and knocked again. The door opened. Camilla stood on the threshold, gazing out at him, her face set in stone. They were all watching him. He didn't hesitate again.

"I'm sorry."

Camilla nodded.

"You should be."

Silence except for the buzz of the mosquitoes and a cough from Mr. Green. Camilla gestured with her chin back down the hill.

"The house is done then."

It wasn't a question, but Ted answered it all the same.

"Yes."

"It looks like a good house."

"Thank you."

Silence again. Camilla's dark eyes traced their way across his face, cutting into every detail.

"I'm guessing you're going to want to come inside."

Ted nodded.

"Only if you want me to."

Camilla took him by the hand and drew him inside. She sat him at the table and made him something to eat. Rice with spam. She didn't mark it down on the ledger. As he ate she let her dress fall to the floor. She moved about on her powerful legs. Preparing. When Ted finished his meal she drew him up and pulled the clothes from his body. He was pliable to her every whim. She left him there, naked amongst the scattered faded colors of his clothing. She climbed onto her bed, pushing her way through the mosquito nets. Ted stayed where he was. uncertain. Camilla motioned for him to follow. He did as he was told.

She wasn't quiet. She didn't try to hide anything. Her ecstasy drove him to heights never before achieved. He rose high into the night sky, Titou shrinking below him. The island of Domenique became a green dot surrounded by turquoise blue. He floated free above the entirety of the Caribbean, its surface scarred by clouds and storms. The stars shined brighter overhead, growing in brilliance the higher he went, reflecting their brilliance off of the Milky Way. Then he was falling. Plummeting downward. Faster and faster. Screaming as he fell into the warmth of Camilla's embrace.

Chapter 29

The sound of the motorbike woke them at some point in the middle of the night, a distant buzz growing louder as it approached. For a moment Ted lay still, halfway between worlds, listening to the expanding growl. Then it hit him all at once. He leaped from the bed, adrenaline pumping through his veins, fighting to make it past the folds of the mosquito netting. He fumbled through the darkness, desperately searching for his clothes. Out the window a light was climbing the hill. Ted pulled on his pants and shirt. The light flashed across the walls, momentarily chasing away some of the shadows. Camilla watched him from the bed, her face hidden in the gloom. There was no time to put on his boots or socks. He grabbed them and fled out the back door. Mud squished between his toes. With a quick glance between the houses he moved across the divide. Next to his door he almost slipped, but managed to catch himself, his hip knocking into the growing papaya stalks next to the window, rustling the leaves. With a last lunge down the muddy ramp he was through his backdoor.

The sound of the motorbike cutoff. Ted held his breath. Mr. Douglas was snoring softly on the floor. A quiet voice was singing to itself. The squeak of a spring as the kickstand was lowered. Footsteps on to the neighboring porch. A door opening and closing. Murmured voices dropping off into silence. Nothing. Ted put down his boots and inched over to his cot. His feet were muddy. He lay down on top of the sleep sack. Wind blew through the trees. The papaya plants rustled in the broken window frame. A night bird declared its loneliness. The world faded back away.

When Ted woke back up it was dawn. Mr. Douglas was dressed and rolling up his sleep sack. His backpack was open and half full.

He was humming to himself. Ted didn't know the tune. Ted cleared his throat.

"Heading out then?"

Mr. Douglas didn't look up from his work.

"Yeah, early bird catches the worm, or in this case, gets down the mountain. I gave your friend Eliud the money yesterday. Not much reason to stay."

Ted watched the other man pack, making no move to help. Mr. Douglas gestured toward the counter.

"I'm going to leave that camp stove here for the next volunteer. God knows when they're going to get shit together up here. I'm going to leave most of this box food too. I packed too much. Didn't know what I was going to find. Do me a favor and at least hide it somewhere so nobody steals it."

"Okay."

Mr. Douglas shoved the last of his stuff into his bag.

"God I haven't been looking forward to the hike back out of here. It's going to be a bitch getting off this damn island, but at least it ought to be a little easier than getting on."

Ted nodded, not really feeling like there was much to say. Mr. Douglas turned and looked at him.

"Last chance Ted."

"I've made my choice."

Mr. Douglas let out a long sigh.

"Are you sure?"

"You need to quit asking me that."

Mr. Douglas gestured towards the wall to his left.

"How do you think this is going to end Ted?"

"I don't know, but it doesn't seem like any of your business."

Mr. Douglas sighed again. He took a step forward, reached into his pocket, and held out a wad of colorful bills.

"Here's half the money I got on me. We still owe you for the past couple of months. When things get better or if you manage to get your ass back where things are still wired up, we'll see about getting you the rest."

Ted took the money. It was mostly fives, tens, and twenties, though he did see a hundred buried in the mix. Mr. Douglas lifted his pack onto his shoulders.

"You can stay here until the next volunteer shows up. Might be awhile. We're paying rent so might as well have somebody watching over the place. Just try to get it fixed up a bit and we'll call it square."

Ted was fingering the bills in his hands. Green, blue, red, and brown. He looked up at Mr. Douglas.

"Thank you."

"No problem."

Mr. Douglas opened the front door, but hesitated on the threshold. He looked back.

"Take care of yourself."

Ted nodded again. He could tell that Mr. Douglas wanted to say more, but he didn't. Ted was glad. He was tired of arguing with the man. Mr. Douglas turned and walked out the door. Ted rose and watched him from the window walk down through the town. The people of Titou were just rising. Men and women moving through the motions of starting their day. They all watched Mr. Douglas leave, no one looking directly, but everyone following him all the same. A few seemed to glance up at the house as well, though Ted was already moving away from the window. He took off his shirt and pants, reveling in his ability to stand alone and naked once again. The mud on his feet was dust. He wiped the worst of it away with a few swipes of his hand and climbed back into his sleep sack. The house was done. He had earned himself a day of rest.

When Ted woke again it was around midday. The leaves of the papaya plant growing through the back window swayed softly, greeting him back into the world of the living. He lay in his sleep sack awhile, reading the book that Mr. Green had lent him. After two chapters he grew restless and rose. He put on pants and peed out back in the old shower stall. He went back inside and ate some of the macaroni and cheese left behind by Mr. Douglas. It had drizzled while he slept. Ted could see the puddles on the ground and the steam rising upward into a sky smattered with lumbering clouds.

Each movement of his body felt refreshing. He was free. He was completely free. No, that was not entirely true. Ted walked over to his cot beneath the window, leaned down, and pulled the duffel bag out from underneath it. He pushed his way downward through the clothes, down to the bottom, grasping through cloth until he found paper. There were eleven all together. Eleven rectangles held together by a rubber band, all delivered by the hand of Charles Xavier. Four had the dove and American flag motif of the Peace Corps in the upper left corner. Seven had the swirling loops of his mother's hand. All remained unopened.

Ted felt no guilt for lying to Mr. Douglas. He owed him nothing. He owed the Peace Corps nothing. There was more for him in Titou than they had ever offered. Ted felt guiltier about the letters from his mother. It wasn't from a lack of caring, more a lack of not knowing what to say. He didn't need to open the letters to know what they said. Come home. Be safe. How could he do that? How could he explain what was going through his head? He knew what his mother would think of it. He knew what she'd say. It was his life, not hers. He had let them know he was alive. He'd write them again soon to let them know he was okay. Let them know that he was staying. Would she come to Domenique looking for him? Hard to say. Either way he needed time to figure things out. He didn't want to go back. He didn't want any part of his old life. He was content in Titou. Wasn't it enough for him to be content? He could see her crying in his father's arms. What kind of son could do such a thing to his mother? No, he mustn't think of such things. If he weakened now all was lost. He was winning. He could feel it. Every brick fallen from his friend's wall was another added to his own. Every moment was another step closer. Should he feel guilty? Why? He was not pushing his friend into the arms of other women. He was innocent. A bystander. Maybe they'd go back when it was all finished. Maybe they'd stay in Titou. The town was a nice place. Simpler. Better.

Ted dropped the bundle of letters into the empty bowl of the toilet. He picked up the box of matches left behind by Mr. Douglas. The flames didn't rise too high. They mostly sputtered in the damp air, chewing away slowly at the outside world until only ash remained. It was done. The decision had been made. Ted finished getting dressed. He was thirsty. He took a blue ten East Caribbean dollar bill from the wad left by Mr. Douglas and hid the rest in the empty back tank of the toilet. The smiling face of an eternally young Queen Elizabeth II smiled up at him next to a sea turtle. He shoved her in his pocket and started down the hill.

Few people were out and about. Most were gone, out working for government money. The few remaining kept to their own business, but Ted could feel them watching him as he walked by. When he turned his head to look back they would look away, their focus returned to their chores or whatever else it was they were doing. They seemed nervous and unsure. Ted waved at one old woman who had often brought him and Eliud food. She raised her arm in return, but it seemed more automatic then genuine. He waved at another woman in her garden. This one flashed a quick smile and waved back. That felt better. It was just in his head. It was just the weather. The humidity was rising, a thick soup covering the mountainside in which the mosquitoes didn't need to buzz their wings to float. There was never any energy in Titou under such conditions. Even the children were affected. Rather than their normal chaotic onslaught, they meandered in the tree line, hitting palms and branches with sticks. It was suffocating. Ted's own jauntiness didn't survive the walk down the hill.

The inside of Malik's tent was in a perpetual twilight, only lit by the light from the doorway and the sun filtering through the canvas. The tent was filled with tables, boxes, and cans, sorted into some semblance of organization, two narrow aisles running to the back. Eliud was sitting at the rear of the tent, the farthest from the sun. His body was slumped in a folding chair next to a cash box on a card table, his brow covered by a sheen of sweat, his shoulders sagging. At the sight of Ted, for a moment Eliud's eyes seemed to widen, but it may have just been a trick of the shadows. They looked normal by the time Ted managed to work his way back to him.

"Hello Eliud, how are things today?"

Eliud sucked in a breath and let it out. His voice sounded flat, muffled by the canvas.

"Fine."

"Any idea when Malik is coming back?"

Eliud shrugged. Even that slight movement seemed to weary him.

"No."

"Do you have any Coke?"

Eliud nodded and gestured toward a stack of red boxes under a table. Ted leaned down and pulled out a glass bottle. He didn't bother to ask the price. He handed Eliud the ten from his pocket and Eliud handed back his change. Ted placed the edge of the bottle's cap on the corner of the table and removed it with a solid whack of his hand. The Coke began to bubble over so he quickly raised it to his mouth. It was warm, but sweet. Oh so very sweet. Eliud was watching him.

"The Peace Corps man left today."

Ted quit drinking. Eliud stared up at him with tired eyes. Ted nodded.

"Yeah, left early this morning."

"You didn't go with him."

"Nope."

Eliud kept staring. It made Ted nervous so he took another drink. Eliud seemed out of sorts. Did Eliud know about Mrs. Seraphin? Did he know what Ted knew? Was that what this all was about? Ted gestured with the bottle.

"I was thinking we could get started on another house."

Eliud coughed and wiped the sweat from his brow.

"I've got to stay here until Malik gets back."

"Well maybe then I could get it started. I'd just need you to tell…"

Eliud's voice almost sounded harsh.

"There's no more building supplies."

"Maybe when Malik gets back."

"Malik doesn't give things away for free."

The two men fell silent in the shadows. Ted could feel rivulets of sweat tracing their way down his backbone. Ted finished the Coke and put the bottle on the table. He nodded at Eliud.

"I'll talk to you later then."

Eliud nodded back, but said nothing. Ted walked out of the tent. It was drizzling lightly again. It felt better to be back outside. Better to be back out in the open. He looked about. The house he had finished stood part way up the hill, fresh and new. It was still empty. Mr. Green was sitting on his porch with Id, undoubtedly hacking away

at the morning lesson. There was no movement in the yellow house
two doors down. Ted looked about, searching for something to do.
The mercantile was a hump of gray in the world of green and red.
Moss had begun to cover some of the cinderblocks and the two fallen
trees. The antenna tower stood defiantly like a middle finger. Ted
walked over to the ruin and got to work.

It drizzled all that afternoon, but Ted ignored it. He used a
crowbar to separate the blocks that still held together. A hammer to
shatter the remains of mortar. One by one he moved cinderblocks
from the chaotic remains of the mercantile to a growing orderly pile
next to it. From time to time a rat would scurry out, and if he was
lucky, and the rat unlucky, it would be crushed beneath his boot before
it could escape. He could feel people watching him. Not all the time,
just when it could be done non-intrusively. A glance when one raised
their head from working in their garden. A neutral stare when a person
came down to use the outhouses. They were all poker players. Their
faces showed nothing as they watched.

It started to rain harder. People began to make their way back
from the road crews. Some raised their eyebrows in surprise at the
growing pile of cinderblocks, but such things were quickly veiled
behind blank stares. Nobody said anything, nobody raised an arm in
greeting. They filed past in silence, seeking the shelter of their homes.
Only Mrs. Seraphin gave any sign of emotion. She came by in a knot
of women, their dresses stained red with the work of the day. The look
she gave Ted was pure loathing and hate. A focused concentration of
everything wrong in her world. When she passed, Ted kept his eyes
on his work, preferring the rough sides of the blocks to her gaze.

The rain began to fall in sheets. Ted's clothes were soaked
through. Miniature red rivers began flowing down the mountainside.
Titou seemed empty, everyone hidden away inside. Ted retreated up
the hill toward his red house up above. There was a man sitting on the
porch of the yellow house. Ted could feel Charles Xavier's eyes
following him as he made his way upward. Ted refused to look at
him, even a glance. He kept his eyes on his work boots squelching
through the mud, only raising his head from time to time to keep his
bearings. The lithe form of Charles Xavier was leaning back in a
chair, his blue postman's shirt half unbuttoned. As Ted drew close he

realized that the other man was not watching him, but rather staring at the motorbike parked in front of him in the rain. Charles Xavier's eyes were half closed and he didn't move as Ted approached. Ted ignored him. He climbed onto his own porch. His hand grabbed the knob of his door.

"What are you still doing here?"

The voice was quiet. So quiet that for a moment Ted was unsure if he had actually heard it. He turned toward Charles Xavier who was still staring at his motorbike.

"What was that?"

"I said you should've gone home."

The voice was flat, no emotion, but slightly slurred. Ted noticed the empty rum bottle next to the chair. Charles Xavier pushed on, his tone that of a man reciting a grocery list.

"This is our home. Not yours. This is not your place. You're nothing but a tourist, no matter how you pretend. We're here because this is the best we have. Why are you here Theodore? Why didn't you go when you had the chance?"

Ted could feel every muscle in his body tightening.

"I stayed to help."

Charles Xavier laughed. Not his usual mirth, but a deep dead laugh that worked its way up and out from his gut. A hint of contempt spiced the other man's words.

"You stayed for yourself. You're nothing but an emotional tourist, wallowing in the misery of others in hope of having some kind of epiphany. Do you think you're the first one? Do you think you'll be the last?

Ted turned to face the other man. He could feel his shoulders rising.

"You know nothing about me."

Charles Xavier emitted his mirthless laugh again.

"You can tell yourself whatever you want, but everyone here knows the truth. You're just another chupid jake. You get to choose Theodore. We don't. So don't pretend we're all the same."

Ted's hands were curled into fists. He took a step toward the other man, but still Charles Xavier didn't look at him. Ted could feel a vein pounding in the side of his head. His voice was louder than he meant it to be.

"You have no right to judge me."

Charles Xavier head seemed to loll loosely on his neck. His eyes rolled in his head.

"Rights. Listen to the pup go on about his rights. This isn't your place to talk about your rights. You're just a visitor here."

It was getting hard to think. Ted could see himself walking forward. He could feel his fist connecting to the side of Charles Xavier's head.

"Do you think I don't know what this is really about? Do you think I'm an idiot?"

Charles Xavier smiled, a split in an otherwise emotionless face.

"So what's it about then?"

"You're a hypocrite."

Charles Xavier began to laugh again, not the deep laughs of before, but high hysterical giggles that echoed around him. He barely managed to force out the words between the gales.

"You poor son of a bitch."

He was drunk. He knew he was losing. That was all it was. The foolish banter of a beaten man. The inebriated laughter rolled over Ted. He turned and walked into his own house, slamming the door behind him.

Chapter 30

Ted needed to see Camilla. He yearned for it. It rained hard for a week and a half. Red mud washed down the mountainside, streaking the spreading green and overcoming it in places. A small landslide occurred on the edge of town, but nothing was damaged and nobody was hurt. The people of Titou hid inside, leaving their refuges only to visit Malik's tent or the outhouses. Ted felt like a bear in a cage. Every time he came out to escape the stuffy confines of his house, Charles Xavier was waiting for him, drunk and ready to deliver more of the same. Ted would march past him without a word, down the hill with his eyes set forward. The other people he saw were little better, but at least they were silent. They watched him from their windows, porches, and doorways as he moved past. Some would look away when he looked at them, but increasingly they would just stare back, faces giving nothing away. Once a kid threw a rock at him. The boy's angry mother cuffed the back of his head and dragged him inside, but even then her eyes weren't friendly. The new house remained empty. Those with little stayed in their makeshift shelters or found friends and neighbors with generous souls.

Twice, Ted made his way down to Malik's tent to buy warm Coke. The soaked canvas was dripping anywhere water was allowed to pool. Eliud was hunched in his chair, slowly melting into his surroundings. The first time he at least halfheartedly returned Ted's greeting, though his eyes weren't warm and Ted's attempts to start a conversation proved futile. Beyond the initial hello, Eliud didn't speak until Ted was near the door.

"Why have you been moving the cinderblocks around?"

Ted paused. He chewed on the inside of his cheeks nervously.

"Just wanting to help."

"Is Malik paying you to do that?"

"No."

"Then cut it out. Malik has money. That's a job someone can do for money."

Ted didn't know how to answer. Eliud didn't seem inclined to add anything else. Ted escaped back into the rain.

The second time Eliud took Ted's money in silence, the change handed over with a look empty of any warmth. After that Ted quit going down for Coke. The bottles of sugar water weren't worth it.

Ted did jumping jacks and pushups to try and burn off energy. He tried sit ups, but the concrete was too hard on his back. The last few chapters of *The Hobbit* flew by. Ted tried to start reading it again, but it was no good. It did little to help alleviate his need to do something. He could march over to the porch next door. He could punch Charles Xavier in his grinning mouth. He could knock on the door and take Camilla in his arms. He could take her back inside. They could lock the door. They could make love, Charles Xavier just outside, having to hear everything. Such thoughts aroused him, a maddened frenzy which always ended with a sudden jolt of frustratingly deep depression. Tears would be in his eyes and he'd pound his fist into his pillow with horror and hope.

At the very least no such sounds emanated from the house next door. The infuriating melody of passion had given way to nights of silence. The darkness was only broken by the occasional raised drunken slur of Charles Xavier's voice released sullenly into the night. The words didn't carry, nor even the barest hint of the response, but respond she must, for the one sided conversation would continue. On those nights Ted would smile in the gloom, circling vulture like above the carnage of his former friend.

Ted rarely saw Camilla. At times he would see the back of her going down the hill to use the outhouses. He'd stand far back from the window, watching her climb down and back up, knowing that from the porch next door Charles Xavier was doing the same. Sometimes on the climb back she would look up and he knew she could see him. For a moment their eyes would meet and he'd feel weak in the knees, but then she'd look back down at her muddy feet. Her face was not blank, but rather a strange mixture of sadness and elation.

Charles Xavier would often make a similar journey, though for him it often included Malik's tent to buy a fresh bottle of rum. Ted was always filled with joy whenever he saw Charles Xavier returning with a new bottle. It meant that there would be an argument that night.

Sometimes when Charles Xavier made his way down the hill Ted imagined going over next door. He could sneak around the back. He could finally speak to her. Maybe even kiss her. He never did. The risk was too great. Charles Xavier was never slow about returning to his post. Once Ted actually went outside when he saw the other man rise and walk away. Ted opened his back door and climbed the slick chute of mud that had once been carved out stairs. He darted across the divide. He approached Camilla's back door. That was as far as he got. Mrs. Seraphin was outside of her house as well, squatting against it, her wet dress hiked to her waist, pissing on the ground. She didn't stop what she was doing when Ted saw her. She just gave him the evil eye until he retreated back into his own abode.

By the fifth day Ted couldn't take it anymore. He waited for Charles Xavier to head down the hill and then walked over to the porch next door, jumping the gap between the two to avoid the mud. He stopped in front of the door, took a breath in and let it out, and knocked. Footsteps sounded from the other side. The door opened. Mr. Green stared at him, waiting. Ted held out *The Hobbit*.

"I brought your book back."

Mr. Green's eyes traced down from Ted's face to the outstretched novel. He took the book in his own hands and carefully examined the spine and cover for any damage. Finding none he flipped quickly through the pages and nodded. He looked back up at Ted, his face blank. Ted didn't move. Mr. Green began to look impatient. Ted nervously licked his lips.

"I was wondering if I could borrow another?"

Mr. Green's face twitched for just a moment. A flash of pity before the mask returned. The old man turned and shuffled over to his bookshelf. Id was sitting in a chair, beating an uneven rhythm on the bottom of a pot with his hand, singing a partial and out of order version of the alphabet over and over, restarting every time he reached the letter Q. Mr. Green returned with two books, *Robinson Crusoe* and

Anna Karenina. Part of Ted wanted to laugh in the old man's face, but he didn't.

"Thank you."

Mr. Green nodded.

"Just be sure to get them back to me."

The door closed and once again Ted was alone. Charles Xavier was making his way back up the hill. Ted jumped the gap and escaped into his own house before the other man reached him.

On the seventh day, the parents of Titou could apparently no longer deal with their children being inside. First there were a few. Then more, the first escapees making it okay for the others to be released as well. They ran in a great herd about town, plastered in red mud from head to toe, the smallest struggling to keep up. Together they came up the hill. One got the idea first. A glob of mud came flying through the air to slap against Ted's front door. When nothing happened another glob followed, then another, then a rock. It all released with a sudden ferocity. Ted's house was under siege. Mud and rocks coming in from all sides, some making their way in through the empty window frames. One well thrown projectile nearly hit Ted in the head when he went to the window to see what was happening. After that, he hid in the corner by the refrigerator, wondering when it would end, his ears filled by the high pitched screams of children and the braying laughter of Charles Xavier.

A door opened. The sound of a callused hand slapping the back of somebody's head. The laughter stopping. A voice yelled over the childish war cries. Camilla's voice.

"Cut that out you little jackets. You want Mr. Malik to know what you're doing to his house?"

The children squealed with terror both mock and real and retreated down the hill, the youngest still trailing in the rear. Ted rose from his hiding place to look out the window, but Camilla was already gone, disappeared back into the shadows of the yellow house. Charles Xavier saw him looking and gave out a chuckle before tossing a small rock which bounced harmlessly off the cinderblock wall. Ted retreated back to the lonely vigil of *Robinson Crusoe*.

When the sun finally broke through, people left town again to return to work. It got hot. Very hot. Ted woke to the sound of the motorbike's engine kicking over. The growl of it coming to life, whipped into a frenzy with every twist of the throttle. With a roar, Charles Xavier left. Ted felt his entire being flood with elation. He was gone. The fucking bastard was finally gone. He didn't bother to eat breakfast. He was too excited. He got dressed and went outside to pee in the remains of the shower.

The entire world was thrumming. A droning that filled the air. There were millions of them. Countless buzzing monsters crowding the edges of every puddle and filling the air with their incessant high pitched thrums. They started assaulting him the moment they saw him. A mass of bloodsuckers eager to suck him dry.

Ted did his business as quickly as he could and retreated back into his house. Many followed him in, the glassless windows offering no protection. He looked out the hole that had once been the front window. People were gathering below by the shelter where the communal fire had once been. He left his house and walked down to see what was going on, ineffectually slapping at the mosquitoes as he went.

Camilla was at the center of the crowd, yelling out directions and handing out shovels. There weren't many people there, most having gone back to work. All that was left was a clutch of women, old men, and the children. Even Mr. Green and Id were in the knot. The only one missing was Eliud, who stood next to the entrance of Malik's tent, waiting.

As Ted approached the crowd began to disperse, shovels and hoes in hand. They spread across Titou and began to work, covering every bit of standing water they could find with red mud and dirt. None of them looked at Ted as he moved past. When he arrived at the shelter, Camilla was talking quietly to Mr. Green. Id was nearby, happily humming to himself as he filled in puddles, his congenial attitude broken only by the occasional angry grunt and wild wave of his hand to scare off the mosquitoes. Camilla looked tired. Even tired she looked beautiful. Mr. Green fell silent when Ted approached. Ted and Camilla looked at each other. He drank her in, every inch of her, his imaginary hands moving their way across her body. There was so much he wanted to say, but he couldn't. Silently and fervently he prayed for Mr. Green to move on, but the old man didn't budge an inch. The seconds ticked by. It was Camilla who broke the silence.

"Do you want to help?"

Ted nodded. She handed him a shovel.

"Fill in the puddles."

"Why…?"

Camilla didn't let him finish.

"Ask questions later. Get to work now."

The people of Titou worked all morning. Everyone worked. All, but the youngest of the children. Even Eliud, though he never strayed far from the tent. Those who didn't have shovels or hoes moved mud and dirt by hand. Some people talked while they worked, a few sang snatches of songs, but it was always silence when Ted was close by. Whenever Ted approached, people would grow quiet. They would work with heads down, no emotion on their faces. Some would move away to another place. Others would stubbornly stay, waiting for Ted to leave. Bastards. Fucking bastards. Ted wanted to throw mud at them, maybe even swing his shovel at a few, but he didn't. It was better to wait. It was better to prove himself. He resigned himself to working alone, but he never stopped working.

In contrast, Camilla was never alone. Wherever she went Ted watched her. She'd be working in one knot of people for awhile, and then would move off to order another group to hunt for puddles in a different part of town. She was tireless. A squat fireplug directing everything. Her words ricocheted in Ted's head. Later. Ask questions later. That evening. Charles Xavier was gone. He could ask questions that evening. He could say things. He could pull her close and kiss her. All it would take was time. With time things could be as they were once again. The feeling of her in his arms. The elation of standing atop the newly finished house. Mr. Douglas couldn't stop him. Charles Xavier wouldn't stop him. The world would not stop him. He knew where he was supposed to be.

They worked all day. By the late afternoon they were all covered in mud and mosquito bites. Every inch of exposed skin had been attacked. Some people had wrapped themselves with long sleeves, hoods, and gloves. Ted didn't, it was too hot as it was. His shirt was soaked through. His skin was covered by slickened salty grit that stung his eyes whenever he made the mistake of rubbing them. By late afternoon it began to rain. A sudden downpour that sent the people of Titou rushing back to their homes to find cover. It lasted only an hour. A sodden lash that erased the work of a day in a moment.

As the town looked out dejectedly at their failure, Ted gave himself a sponge bath in his house. He put on fresh clothes, trimmed his beard, and slicked back his hair in a failed attempt to tame the wild mop on his head. As he brushed his teeth he heard Camilla's door open and close, signaling her return. He felt himself stiffen at the thought of her. His hands began to shake. His body began to shiver. He forced himself to sit on his cot and wait. To give her time to get settled. She was undoubtedly soaked through, her dress clinging to her. A papaya branch from the window dipped and softly stroked the back of his head. How long should he wait? He didn't have a watch. Every minute felt like an hour. Ted counted in his head. He counted all the way to a thousand. He got up and brushed his teeth again. He paced. He thought about doing some jumping jacks, but he didn't want to start sweating again. He was already perspiring in the heat as it was. His palms were sweaty. He rubbed them on his pants. It had been long enough. Surely it would now be okay. He got up. What if she was giving herself a sponge bath when he knocked? What if she was already naked when she opened the door?

The throaty scream of the motorbike in high gear sounded in the distance. Ted froze. It was quiet at first, then grew, second by second, though it seemed minute by minute. Up the mountain it came. Higher and higher. Up past the gate to the banana plantation. Up past Malik's ruined mercantile. Up through Titou. Right to the house next door. The motorbike's engine stopped. Charles Xavier was singing to himself, but the words were impossible to hear through the roaring of blood in Ted's ears. The solid thumps of his heart. The door to the yellow house opened and closed again. Ted stood by his own door, his fists clenched, tears pouring down his cheeks, powerless.

It was the same the next day, and for nearly a week after that. Each morning Charles Xavier would ride off on his motorbike. Each day the people of Titou would be rallied to battle by Camilla. Each day they would be defeated. Each evening Charles Xavier would come home. Sometimes it rained in the morning. Sometimes it rained

in the afternoon. Sometimes it rained at night. It didn't matter. The
storms ranged from an hour to an entire day. Water pouring from the
heavens, finding new nooks and crannies to fill. Camilla was their
general. When people lost heart she lifted them up. Some she
encouraged, some she harangued, and with some she even pleaded.
The mosquitoes grew thicker in the air. Even Ted took to wearing
long sleeves and a hood. It didn't matter. They worked their way into
the houses, flying in through broken windows and whenever the doors
were opened. At night Ted slept crouched deep in his sleep sack, the
top folded over until things got too hot and he was forced to emerge
for air. There were fewer in the cool of night, but even then there were
too many. His arms and head itched terribly from countless lumpy
bites. He was glad he had no mirror, for he must look terrible, but
everybody in town looked terrible. It seemed impossible that so many
could exist in one place.

Camilla was never alone. There was not a single moment where
she wasn't with someone, either conversing or working alongside them
in silence. Sometimes Ted would try to work closer to her, but it did
no good. There was always somebody else around. Sometimes she'd
notice him watching her. She'd look up at him and their gazes would
meet, a sudden bridge across the distance. She'd give him a weak
smile and then go back to her work. Whenever she did his heart would
flutter as though a butterfly desperate to escape a jar, then crash down
deep into the bowels of his being. Her eyes were sad eyes. Some of
the saddest eyes he had ever seen. What was that monster doing to
her? What was that beast demanding? At night there was only
silence, blessed silence, but only two people knew what was being said
in quiet voices. Charles Xavier guarded her every night, and whenever
he was gone others watched in his place. Ted knew it to be true.
Charles Xavier had poisoned the well. The former friend turned foe.
The nemesis. Cunning and capable. A man who didn't understand
that the birds of his years of infidelity at last were coming to roost.
Ted only needed to say the word. The telling of the greatest sin would
be sweet upon Ted's lips.

Mrs. Seraphin was glaring at him from where she worked. Ted
ignored her. It was getting easier all the time to ignore her. All that he
saw was Camilla. Oh so beautiful Camilla. They could stay for

awhile. The Peace Corps owed him more money and he had savings at home. If needed he could work for Malik, or maybe find other work. They wouldn't need much. The world was rich and the world would provide. Maybe, if she wanted, he'd even take her to the States. Far from the small world of Titou. Far from the green speck in the blue known as Domenique. It didn't matter. All he needed and all he wanted was her. Charles Xavier could stay behind. He could be left with the things he craved most. He didn't deserve her. He didn't deserve such a woman made of dreams.

It began to rain again. A few drops, then more. The people of Titou, knowing what was to come, began moving toward their homes. Their backs were bent and their weary eyes didn't leave the ground. Only Ted stood up straight amongst them, his future lacking any uncertainty or fear. It was just a matter of time. He worked even as the others left to show them that he could, to show them that he was more than just some jake. A few watched him from their porches, blank faces showing nothing but weariness. It began to rain harder. He put his shovel on his shoulder and began to make his way up the hill. The mosquitoes buzzed around his head. He ignored them. He stared back at any person who dared look into his gaze, defiant. Already he could hear the drone of the motorbike. It didn't matter. It was all just a matter of time.

Chapter 31

Malik returned after a week of battle. He looked haggard. The big man had lost quite a bit of weight. His hard exterior looked softer. When he walked he shuffled, as though moving his bulk around took all of his energy. He offered no explanation of why he had been away for so long. Of the injured from the landslide, all he said was that they were recovering nicely. All of this Ted heard by creeping close enough to overhear conversations, but not so close that he was met with blank stares and people moving away. With Malik taking back his post in his tent, Eliud was set free. With a new vigor he set to work, filling the never ending puddles at twice the pace of the rest. Often Ted would see him working near Mrs. Seraphin, sometimes right next to her, but if she ever said a word to him Ted never saw it.

It was a few days after Malik returned that the first person got sick. One of the old women who had brought Eliud and Ted food when they had been building the houses. She was sweating with fever and quiet voices whispered to each other, though none would say the word. Camilla went down to look at the woman herself, then spent the better part of an hour talking with Malik. The conversation must not have gone well, for she left the confines of the tent with a face twitching with barely contained anger. Ted wanted to go to her then more than at any other time, but she went directly back to the home of the sick old woman, a place Ted knew he wouldn't be welcome.

Three more people fell ill the next day, all children. Two girls and the Seraphin boy. Camilla went down to Malik's tent again. This time there was shouting. Eliud went in to check on them, but beat a hasty retreat soon after. Unsure what else to do, he stood about ten feet from the tent, waiting. The people of Titou all found puddles nearby that needed filling. They listened. Ted stayed away. The yelling died down. People grew bored and wandered away.

That afternoon the old woman, the three sick children, their mothers, and any of their healthy children that couldn't be left behind, were loaded into the back of Malik's truck. Malik, his face gray, seemed barely able to lever himself up when he climbed into the cab. People waved their goodbyes, but nobody in the truck waved back. Eliud stood at the entrance of the tent, seeming unsure what to do, his eyes riveted to the truck. Mrs. Seraphin sat near the rear, her daughter pressed against her side, her back straight and her face rigid. Her mouth was a hard line. Her defiant eyes were staring up the mountainside. The truck started and lurched forward. Malik was hunched over the wheel, sweating, his eyes locked on the windshield in front of him. The truck missed a gear, started to bog down, caught it, and disappeared down the road. Eliud turned and walked into the tent, reclaiming his former post. People stood together in clumps, talking, wondering who would be next. That night Ted could hear Camilla and Charles Xavier arguing again.

They knocked on Ted's door the next morning. He was sitting on his cot, eating a breakfast of instant oatmeal, already dressed and ready to face the day. Charles Xavier was on the porch, flanked by Eliud and Buffalo Bill. All three men had crowbars in their hands. Close to a quarter of the town was behind them, arrayed in a loose half circle. Many others were watching from further down the hill. The crowd was quiet, no murmuring, their faces blank, waiting. Ted's entire body clenched with adrenaline. A vision passed through his head of three men beating him to a bloody pulp while the people of Titou looked on. Was this what it had come to?

Camilla stood just beyond the crowd, a solitary figure slightly divided from the mass, watching, her hands nervously playing with her fingers in front of her belly. For a moment their eyes met, and she did her best to smile at Ted reassuringly. Charles Xavier looked behind himself, then shifted so that he was between them.

"Theodore. We need the chemicals."

The voice was flat. No malice, but no jocularity either. An emotionless statement of fact. Ted took in a deep breath and let it out, giving him time to process.

"What chemicals?"

The crowd murmured and fell quiet. Eliud was shaking, an almost imperceptible vibration. Buffalo Bill shifted his crowbar from one hand to the other.

"The ones in the shed. The ones for killing bugs."

Ted's fingers involuntarily rose to the keys that hung around his neck. They weren't there. They hadn't been there for awhile. They were in his duffel bag, but he couldn't remember when he had put them there. Ted licked his lips.

"What do you need them for?"

"People are getting sick."

A mosquito buzzed by Ted's ear.

"That's not what those chemicals are for."

Ted wasn't sure if it was true, but he was pretty sure it was. Most of the jugs were for insects that affected crops. He didn't think any were for mosquitoes. Charles Xavier blinked, a slow movement, almost reptilian. It appeared that a part of the man was enjoying it, this show of power.

"It might not be what they're for, but Eliud says it should work. He knows a lot about such things."

Ted looked over at Eliud. The man's mask gave way momentarily and Ted could see the conflict. He looked back at Charles Xavier.

"What are you going to do?"

"Spray the puddles."

"I can't let you do that. It's not safe. It would be bad for people."

Charles Xavier gestured at the town behind him.

"Things are bad for people now."

"I'm sorry, but no."

Ted closed the door. The mass began moving between the houses. Ted could see them through the broken windows. He could hear their steps on the dirt outside. Ted opened his backdoor and pulled himself up the smoothed sides of the muddy chute. The crowd was smaller, mostly young and middle aged men. Those who had worked in the banana plantation. Some of the women were there as well, Camilla chief amongst them, standing in her vegetable garden, as though guarding it. The shed was still half buried. They'd have to dig down several feet to open the door. They didn't need to. The three men with crowbars began going at the roof.

"Get away from there!"

The shout echoed off the mountainside. Ted surged forward, a raging bull of sudden ferocity. The crazy bastards. The fucking crazy bastards. Couldn't they understand? Didn't they see the danger? The three men with crowbars looked up. Ted halted just a few feet away from them. The crowd watched.

"You stupid bastards. You can't be fucking around with stuff like this. The label doesn't say anything about…"

Charles Xavier's crowbar came down hard on the tin roof of the shed. His face was contorted with rage. Spittle flew from his mouth as he shouted back.

"You spoiled brat. People are sick and you yell at us about labels? No one cares about us here. You get that? We have to do what is needed. You don't like it, you don't have to stay here. We do. Fuck you and your labels."

The crowd was murmuring again. Some shouted encouragement, others stayed silent. Eliud moved forward and started pushing Ted back. Charles Xavier and Buffalo Bill went back to attacking the roof. Nails squealed and tin rattled. Ted set his feet, stopping his forced retreat. He felt flushed. His eyes were watering. Droplets of sweat fell from his brow. Stupid bastards. Stupid, stupid bastards. Ted grabbed Eliud's arm, the one holding the crowbar.

"Eliud. Please. You know they shouldn't do this."

Eliud's mask fell away for a moment again, a flicker of doubt quickly covered again by a resolute stubbornness to move forward. His voice was strained, choking down all emotion in its mimicry of Charles Xavier's declaration.

"We have to. People are getting sick."

With a final metallic squeal, the roof was ripped asunder. Charles Xavier gestured toward Eliud.

"Eliud, we need you to tell us which ones."

Eliud looked over his shoulder. Ted leaned in close, forcing words through ragged angry breaths.

"What about your father. Think about your father."

Eliud's fist connected solidly with the side of Ted's head. The crowd roared. Ted fell to the ground. He tried to rise, but Eliud gave him a solid kick in the gut, leaving him sprawled in the dirt. Eliud's face was contorted with rage. He was screaming.

"You don't talk about my father jake! You don't talk about my father!"

Eliud turned and marched back to the shed. The crowd was yelling. A mish mash of words blended together into a chaotic frenzy. Ted lay on the ground, shivering with anger and fright. Camilla pushed her way through the mass of people. Her eyes smoldered with the intensity of her will. She kneeled by Ted for a second, her words a quick whisper that barely made it past the ringing in Ted's ear.

"Stay down."

She stood above him. A fiery protective mother hen daring any to try and carry things forward further. At the shed, Eliud had climbed down into the interior. He lifted up the hand sprayers and then the jugs one by one into the waiting grasp of Charles Xavier and Buffalo Bill. The crowd cheered when he climbed back out. People rushed forward to help carry things. Back between the houses they went. Out of sight and out of mind. Camilla walked away as well, though she went a different direction. She paused to check on her vegetable garden, and then moved on, staying behind the houses. Ted remained on his side in the dirt for several minutes, trying to catch his breath. The ferocity. The hate. It had been terrifying. The fools. The fucking fools. Ted rose and followed Camilla's route.

At the road he looked back at the hubbub below. Men were standing around Eliud as he carefully measured chemical and water into a hand sprayer. Charles Xavier was shouting directions. Buffalo Bill was already moving about, spraying puddles. He turned and started climbing. The greenery closed in.

Camilla was sitting on a fallen tree a little ways up the path. A chunk had been cut out of the middle so that it was two halves on either side. It wasn't until Ted got close that he realized the tree was the same one that had claimed Eugene Hewitt's life. He shoved the realization down deep. Camilla looked up at him as he approached. Ted stopped a few feet away. Her eyes looked old, overfilling with the pains of the world.

"Why didn't you try to stop them?"

Camilla breathed in and out. She watched him, flooding him with the feeling that she was waiting for him to say more.

"It's not safe to be doing what they're doing. Every puddle in town. It's crazy. None of those pesticides are even meant for mosquitoes. It might not even work."

Her voice was soft, but firm.

"Maybe, it's possible it won't work, but there's definitely a problem. People want solutions to problems. They demand them, even if the solution seems crazy."

Her eyes were filled with defiance. Ted had to look away for a moment to recollect his resolve.

"You could've persuaded them. I know you could've. I know it's been you this entire time. I know that you're the one who got us through the hard times. Not him. Why live in his shadow? You don't need him to be happy."

Camilla's eyes grew hard. She stood up.

"I decide what makes me happy."

"There's so much you could do."

"Why do I have to live my life by your standards?"

Ted took a step forward, then another. The two of them were only a foot apart. Camilla was gripping her side with the opposite hand.

"You deserve so much better than him."

"He's a good man."

Ted steeled himself.

"No he's not. A good man wouldn't need to sleep with other women when he has one like you."

Camilla's eyes were moist. A few tears dribbled down her cheeks.

"You don't know him. He's my husband and I'm his wife. We get to decide what that means, not you."

Ted reached forward. His hands lightly gripped her upper arms. She didn't move away. She didn't move a muscle. The words were on the back of Ted's tongue. For a moment they stuck there. For a moment he held them back. For a moment there was only Charles Xavier's smiling face as he delivered a hearty slap on the back. Only for a moment. There was no turning back. There was only going forward.

"He's been fucking Mrs. Seraphin."

The slap was hard, a stinging fury across his face. She stepped back from him, tears streaming down her cheeks, her features twisted in anger. She slapped him again. Her voice boiling over with ferocity.

"Do you think I don't know? Do you think I'm a fool? He's my husband. Do you think I don't know my husband? Do you think I don't know what he is? What he does? You sad little jacket. You have no right. You have no right to tell me how to judge him."

She retreated, up the path, up into the trees. Ted thought about following. He thought about screaming her name. He did none of these things. All of the energy had gone out of him. He collapsed onto the ground, his back against the tree. He cried. He cried like a child. Great blubbering sobs that he wanted none in the world to see.

Chapter 32

Of the two graves, Eugene Hewitt's was the worse for wear. Mrs. Green's was well cared for. The original wooden cross, slapped together after Anji's wrath, had been replaced by a more robust marker of similar form. The grass around the marker was kept beaten down and fresh flowers often marked its presence. In comparison, Eugene Hewitt's grave was overgrown and forgotten. The horizontal piece of the cross was missing, leaving a single post, half covered in moss, standing defiantly in the tall grass. It was possible that nobody had visited it since old Mr. Hewitt, right before he disappeared. Ted wasn't sure why he was visiting it now. He had only come down to use the outhouse. The walk down through the middle of town had been too much. No more blank faces. No more sullen stares. They just ignored him. He was nothing. A wraith in their presence. He decided to return via a different route. Moving along the edge of town might take longer, but there were fewer people to ignore him.

It was hot. It had to be hot. He was sweating like a nun in a whorehouse. That was what his grandfather had always said. The fat cackling old bastard. On an especially hot day he was known to say it at least four or five times. A mosquito buzzed by Ted's ear. Ted ignored it. What else could one do but ignore it? He could swat at it, but there would just be others. They had sprayed the puddles three more times in the past week. They had even gone up and sprayed the area around the reservoir, but still the bastards persisted. Charles Xavier would claim that there were fewer of them, and he was probably right, though whether it was due to the spraying or the natural order of things was hard to say. Many puddles still remained, the pattern of rain and hot sun having persisted, teeming breeding grounds.

Nobody tried to bury the puddles anymore. The town had entirely thrown its hopes into the misused miracles of modern science.

The line of five houses stood before him. Mrs. Seraphin's house was still empty. None of the people who had gone down with Malik had come back, not even the big mercantile owner himself. Mr. Green sat on his porch with Id, valiantly moving forward in his efforts to get his nephew to the letter Z, or as they said on the island, Zed. His own house looked abandoned as well. A darkened hermit's cave. Camilla and Charles Xavier's house was in just as bad of shape, but it at least looked like a home. Charles Xavier was gone, off doing his routes, but he would be back that evening. He was always back that evening. Camilla was likely behind the house, working on her garden or doing her laundry. Aside from her own garden, she was also tending to Mrs. Seraphin's garden, and had, with permission, started planting behind Mr. Green's house as well. Ted often saw her walking past his back window to reach them, peering out through the papaya plants which endeavored to block his view.

She wouldn't talk to him. She wouldn't even look at him. He had tried to approach her while she worked in her garden. She had gotten up and without a word and gone back inside, shutting the door behind her. The first time she did it he returned to his own house, not knowing what to do. The second time, he had pounded on the door, tears spilling down his cheeks, yelling apologies until Mr. Green had come outside to glare at him. The third time he started weeding her garden. He spent the whole day at it, but never once did she come back out. There wasn't a fourth time. He stayed in his house the whole day, crying and feeling nauseous. His only solace was the fact that there were no sounds of lovemaking in the night time air. No sign of victory for his rival.

Ted kept walking past the houses. He couldn't do it anymore. Too many days of sitting alone with nothing to do but read and sleep. Too much time alone to think. His feet carried him to the path that led higher up the mountainside, past the fallen tree where Camilla had slapped him and Eugene Hewitt had died. She knew. Did she know the whole time? Did she care? Did it matter? So many questions left unanswered. Had she found out? Had Charles Xavier told her? When did she find out? What was his own place in all of it? Did she know that last time, when she was in his arms, their entwined bodies covered in sweat? Why wouldn't she talk to him? Why wouldn't she fucking talk to him? Why? Why? Why?

An image floated to the top. He'd come home early from work. He worked at the Albertson's. It was just a college job, a holdover until he could find a real job. They had just graduated. Sandi was carrying suitcases down to a car. Some kind of Toyota, or maybe it was a Honda. He was following her. Asking her questions. She wouldn't answer. The guy standing by the car had stuck out his hand.

"Hi, I'm John."

Ted had just stared at him. He didn't think he was looking at much. Just some generic guy in jeans and a t-shirt. Average looking. Average everything. No different from Ted himself. Why the hell had the guy thought Ted would want to know his name? Why the hell had he thought Ted would want to shake his hand? It was surreal, like watching someone else's nightmare. The asking turned to yelling. The yelling to crying. Silence. That's all he ever got was silence. She got in the car. The guy put the last suitcase in the trunk, gave Ted a half smile and a shrug, and then they were gone, on their way to Portland. Who had told him it was Portland? He couldn't remember. Some mutual friend who heard it through someone else who spilled the beans.

He had gone back upstairs to their apartment and sat down on the couch. Half the stuff in the place was hers. She had taken nothing but some clothes. Her paintings were still leaning up in the closet. The ones that weren't all that good, though sometimes Ted would catch her looking through them. Even her family pictures were still hanging on the wall. She didn't answer his calls or emails. Some of the messages he regretted, but not all. After a month a friend had helped him box up all her stuff. Two months later the same friend had helped him take it to Goodwill. Whatever Goodwill wouldn't take went in the dumpster. After six months he had tried going to Portland. There were people he knew in Missoula that he never saw. Portland was ten times the size. He came home to an apartment that was still nothing but her. He had known things had to change.

The paths above Titou weren't in as good of condition as the ones below. There were no government payments to fix them. Only a few people cared. Parts of the trails were washed out. Others were blocked by fallen trees, necessitating a scramble over. Fallen palms and leaves were rotting away in the undergrowth, slowly swallowed by the still living. Here and there some farmer had cut his way through or dug out a narrow shelf on a steep section, but mostly it was just the repeated treading of tired feet. The old farmers and their wives had returned from whence they came, back to the high mountainside to scrape their livings from rocky holdings that nobody wanted and waiting for death so that all could be reclaimed by the forest around them. Anji had just sped up the process.

Ted sat down on a rock to rest. He was tired. He felt exhausted. The bitter taste of bile was on the back of his throat. An old man walked by in bare feet, a straw hat on his head. For a moment Ted thought it was Mr. Hewitt, but no, just some other wrinkled hardened son of a bitch. The old man kept his face blank when he walked by, but at least he took notice that Ted was there. News always travelled slower the higher up on the mountain you went. Ted rested for about fifteen minutes. He took a watery shit in the bushes. He hurt. Everywhere hurt. His shirt was drenched in sweat. Up he rose and higher he went.

Camilla in his arms. Camilla's hand slapping his face. Her sad eyes looking back at him. Ted knew all of the paths. He had walked them for months when he had first arrived. Miles of hiking from farm to farm. Trying to give lessons to people who didn't seem to care. Why would they? Their own futures were close at hand. Nothing they learned would have benefits beyond their few remaining years. Here and there the trail divided. Right, left, right, right, left. It didn't matter. Each choice was random. Ted knew where he was, he just didn't care where he was going. On one part he found the path completely washed out. A steep slide of dirt down into a deep gully. He just turned back to the last intersection and took another route.

He came into a clearing with a rock where the path divided once again. He sat on the rock and rested. There was no buzzing of mosquitoes in his ears, just the call of birds and the rustling of the wind. A breeze blew across the clearing. Ted shivered though his brow was slick with sweat and gritty with salt. Camilla. She was there again. In his arms. Sandi was getting into the Toyota, or was it a

Honda? Ted got up and took the right hand path. It wasn't long before he arrived at another clearing.

Mr. Hewitt's farm was much the worse for wear. Almost all of the terraces were gone, washed away. The house of wood and corrugated metal was destroyed, torn apart by a landslide, its remains scattered and half buried from the top of the farm to the bottom. Grass and weeds grew everywhere. Here and there a few scattered remains of crops still fought on. Bananas, avocados, and papaya. Vegetables here and there. Everything scattered, the once discernible patterns of human thought almost completely gone. Halfway up the clearing a clump of corn sat on a terrace miraculously untouched. The corn was overgrown and drying out, its yellowing leaves covered in various hues of fungus.

The world began to swim around him. His head hurt. Stifling heat embraced his body. The bitter taste at the back of his mouth grew. He felt dizzy. He sat down to keep himself from falling. He retched and then started puking. A vile yellow mixture of water and macaroni noodles. His gut quit convulsing. His head still pounded. Ted sat in the dirt in silence. Waiting. A bird sounded its mating call. Another answered. The world steadied itself. He pulled himself up and started walking back down the mountain.

Chapter 33

They were walking through the park. It was springtime.
Everything was in bloom. Her hand was in his. His hands didn't
sweat anymore. She had mentioned it and then laughed as he turned
beet red. She was tucked in close. It was wonderful. It had all been
so wonderful. She kept laughing, breaking up her story.

"So I was so excited that I wrote Lost It on my calendar. I have
no clue why I thought it would be a good idea. I mean, c'mon, what
was I thinking? My mom figured it out right away. My step-dad
thought it was hilarious, but she was so pissed off. So fucking pissed.
I thought it was so funny that I started writing all sorts of crap on that
calendar, you know, just to fuck with her."

They laughed together. Despite the cool breeze, Ted was covered
in sweat. Sandi didn't ask him how he lost it. She knew that she was
his first. Stupid years of shame over nothing. Hell, she even seemed
to like it that way. It seemed to make her even happier that he had
asked her about her first time. Confidence. That's what she said. It
showed how confident he was.

It was their third date. She was house sitting out on the edge of
town. She did that kind of stuff all the time, a chance to escape the
squalor of the dorms. It was a big house. A nice house. It was just
him and her, and the owners' little pug dog. She was on top of him on
the couch, his back against a pillow. The taste of her lips. The feel of
her lithe body in his hands. She pulled her dress up and over her head
in one fluid motion. Camilla smiled down at him. No, it was Sandi.
She asked where the pug had went. The poor little bastard had been
underneath the pillow behind Ted's back. They had laughed as they
cooed and comforted him. The cot squeaked under them as they made
love. A frantic maddening sound that permeated the air and filled

every nook and cranny of the world. There was nothing. Nothing but her. Nothing in the whole wide world. They were both covered in sweat.

Ted started shivering uncontrollably. His bowels knotted and bile bit at the back of his throat. He swallowed it back down. Not yet. No, not yet, but soon. He fought off the dueling sensations. Demands from opposite ends.

"You know, technically we're all donuts."

Sandi had always used to say that. She found shit like that funny. He had said it to Camilla once. She had rolled her eyes, but at least gave a chuckle.

He didn't want to get up yet. He didn't want to get out of his sleep sack. He pulled it tight around him, waiting for the shift from cold to hot. It would come suddenly, forcing him to throw open the sweat drenched sleep sack. A back and forth seemingly without end. He needed to drink some water. Always more water. A bucket was by the front door. He'd do it when the cramps became too much. Everything might as well be done at once. It was better that way. Maybe he'd drift to sleep again. How many days had it been? When was the last time he had eaten? It took too much energy to cook. Sometimes he woke and it was light, sometimes dark. Strange things happened when he was asleep. The land of Nod was comforting, but horrifying. A world without focus, smeared by a great invisible hand. Voices outside, or maybe inside. Murmuring in whispers, punctuated by the occasional raised voice.

The door opened. Eugene Hewitt walked in. He was terrible to look at. Rotting skin hanging from a grinning skull. The toothy smile didn't match the eyes. The eyes looked worried, almost afraid. Eugene stood in the doorway. He kicked the water bucket lightly with a foot. He came no further. The eyes gleamed with anguish as they tracked across the house, taking it all in, judging everything. It was not the first time Eugene had appeared. Ted prayed it would be the last. During previous encounters he had yelled at the wraith. Screamed at it.

"I don't know you! Leave me alone! Just leave me alone!"

He no longer had the energy for such things. Ted groaned, but it was the best he could do. Eugene stared at him. Bright white eyes encased in the endless void of the skull's eye holes. Ted weakly thumped his fist against the cot. His head hurt. A throbbing dull ache across his brain. Everything hurt. Why did Eugene keep coming back? Why couldn't he leave him alone? Ted squeezed his eyes shut. The door closed. Ted opened his eyes again. Eugene was gone. The whole world faded away.

Mr. Douglas stood over Ted, whispering something. An endless mantra which grew louder with every cycle.

"You don't belong here. You don't belong here. You don't belong here."

Charles Xavier joined the Peace Corp man, a bottle of rum carefully cradled in his arms. He stared down at Ted, defiant, but sad. The two men's voices were in harmony. More people approached. More people added their voices. Mrs. Seraphin, her eyes filled with hate. Mr. Green, the white fringe of his hair frizzled around his head. Id, smiling with the enjoyment of being part of the group. Eliud. Buffalo Bill. Crispin and his sister. Bug Eyes. Young and old. Men and women. They packed into the house, pushing each other for a better position. People peered in through the broken windows and doorways. Ted's grandfather used his girth to push his way to the front. There was a flash of blonde hair somewhere near the back of the crowd, moving just at the edge of sight. No Camilla. Where the hell was Camilla? Where the hell could she be? They were gathering tightly around him. Too tightly. They were suffocating him. The press of bodies was cooking him alive.

Ted ripped open his sleep sack. Cool air washed across his sweat covered body. For a moment it felt wonderful, but then he started to shiver again. Terrible uncontrollable shivering. How many days? How many days has it been? A breeze blew in through the back window. The leaves of the papaya plants weaved and dipped, shadowed claws plunging down into his flesh. Carving and cutting. Slicing away at him. The breeze smelled like shit. He had been shitting in the old shower stall. Laying down now because he was too weak to even hold himself up. Cleaning himself with a sacrificed t-shirt. Sometimes he puked there too, when he made it. Everything smelled of puke. His bath towel, used for more than one cleanup, was crusted with it.

When was the last time he ate? He couldn't remember? How many days had it been? His throat felt dry. He needed to drink some water. He needed to keep hydrated. The house fell away. He was running. Sprinting as fast he could through the forest, bobbing and weaving to avoid branches and other obstacles. She was right ahead of him, naked as the day of her birth. Flashes of dark and light between the trees. Lithe then curvy. He screamed for her to stop. She didn't look back. She didn't answer. He broke into a clearing. Where did she go? Where did they go? Nothing. There was nothing there.

The front door opened again. He was back. The shade of Eugene stood before him again. The horrible eyes in the terrifying skull looked worried. Eugene took a step closer. Ted cowered in his sleep sack, but he couldn't look away. It was coming for him. Eugene took another step, and then another. Ted wanted to scream, but his throat was too dry. The boilers bubbled, but were unable to build up enough steam. The apparition approached. The time had come. The house collapsed into shadows. The skull fell away, leaving just two white eyes in the darkness. A skeletal hand reached forward to touch his brow. Cool fingers brushed back his hair. Eliud. It wasn't Eugene. Eliud walked back to the bucket, his form shifting back to that of Eugene as it receded. He returned with a cup of water. He held it carefully to Ted's mouth. Ted drank, though most dribbled out the sides and down his chin. Eliud said something, but Ted didn't answer. Eliud said something again, but it was lost. The papaya leaves danced overhead. Pixies performing for those wise enough to watch. Beautiful. So beautiful. Eliud was gone. There was nothing there.

A mosquito flew in the window and droned circles slowly in the air. Another followed, and then another. They danced in never ending twists and turns above his head. Ted pulled himself deeper into the confines of his sleep sack. The buzzing grew louder. More were coming in. Tens, hundreds, thousands. A great sweeping mass that plunged downward with sudden ferocity. Ted pulled the top of the sleep sack closed with his hands. Sweat was dripping from his brow. He could feel them on top of him. Battering themselves against him. Desperately trying to find a way in. A million high pitched voices screamed his name over and over. He was safe. They couldn't get through. They mustn't find their way inside. His entire body was

slick with sweat. His lungs screamed for cool refreshing air. He felt
one bite him, and then another. It was impossible. They couldn't get
through the sleep sack. Ted started thrashing, throwing himself this
way and that, crushing the bastards beneath the weight of his body.

Strong hands held him down, firm but gentle. The buzzing was
gone. The mosquitoes weren't there. A hand pressed a cool wet cloth
onto his forehead. It felt good, so amazingly good. He opened his
eyes. Her eyes were filled with concern. She was shushing quietly,
the way a mother might to her crying baby. Ted smiled up at her. His
hand raised to caress her face, but was held down by the confines of
his sleep sack.

"Sandi. Oh Sandi."

Camilla smiled kindly down on him. She re-wet the cloth in the
bucket next to her and pressed it back against his forehead. The
pounding in his head seemed to recede, though it didn't disappear.
The house was filled with shadows. It must be close to evening.
Camilla had a small kerosene lantern next to her, its wick flickering
happily. Ted tried and failed to raise his arm again.

"I'm so sorry. I'm so very very sorry."

Tears were flowing down his cheeks. She used the cloth to wipe
them away.

"It's okay child. It's okay."

"No it's not. You're a goddess. I love you."

She smiled again at him. That same kind smile. A calloused
hand gently brushed his cheek.

"I love you too. How could I not?"

She raised a glass to his lips and he drank. Cool wonderful water.
So sweet and pure. He finally got his arm freed from the sleep sack.
He raised up his hand and weakly grabbed hers.

"I want you to have everything you deserve. I want to give you
everything I can."

She took the hand off of hers. She gently laid it on her belly.

"You've done more than enough for me. You've given me more
than I ever thought I'd have."

The door opened. Charles Xavier stood at the edge of the light of
the lantern. He paused for a moment before walking in, carrying a
bowl and spoon. He handed them to Camilla and stood for a second,

looking down at Ted, his eyes taking it all in. There was fear in those eyes, with just a secret hint of hope. Ted stared back at his rival. Willing his body to rise. Wishing for his fist to close. Nothing happened. He was too weak. There was nothing he could do. Camilla nodded her thanks at her husband and he retreated back into the darkness, a shadow leaning against the counter, watching as his wife spooned oatmeal into Ted's mouth, cooing encouragement to get him to swallow. When the oatmeal was gone Camilla gave him another drink of water, rose, and walked over to her husband. Ted's free hand tried to clutch at her, but it couldn't hold on. The pair walked outside, closing the door behind them. Ted could them talking through the empty window frame, stray words making their way to his ears.

"........sick.........need..........something."

".......wait.......Malik........"

"God.......is.......he........needs.......now."

Silence. Breathing. The sound of assent, the words lost but the tone recognizable. Camilla came back inside. Charles Xavier did not. She sat down again on the edge of the cot. Her hand gently caressed his brow. The sound of his heart pounded in his ears. She was saying something, but he couldn't make out the words. Something about Malik, about being sick, something about the motorbike. Ted forced himself to focus, compelling the words into clarity.

"It's going to be a long trip. We need to get your clothes on."

Away. They were sending him away. They couldn't. She loved him. She had said she loved him.

"No."

The word croaked from between his dry lips. She was rooting around in his duffel bag. Pulling out clothes. She picked up a crusty sock and threw it into a corner. Jeans, t-shirt, sweatshirt, and socks. She unzipped the sleep sack. Ted saw a flash of white, red, and blue in the dim kerosene created light. The cold air felt good on his overheated body, but it set him to shivering all the same. She pulled off his shorts, ignoring the smell. Memories rose unbidden. Ted's mother dressing him when he was little. Pulling and tugging. Shifting him this way and that. Sweaters, his mother had always loved putting him in sweaters. Last to go on were his work boots. She tied them and stood. She towered over him. He rose up to a sitting position. He raised a hand, floundering for the neckline of her dress. His voice croaked again.

"No."

She pushed his hand back down. She enfolded him with her arms, pressing his head against the warm softness of her stomach. She hummed a soothing lullaby, rocking him back and forth. He lay there for a moment, fighting to not to give in the comforting warmth that promised peace and rest, then struggled to push himself away enough to look up at her.

"I belong here with you."

Her face turned stern.

"You have to go. You have to. You're very sick.

"I'll come back."

She smiled, a toothless tight lipped expression. There were tears in her eyes. Her hands cupped his face with a firm grip. Her entire being bored its way down into him.

"This is not your place, but don't worry, a part of you will always be here. A part of you will always be with me. It will be impossible for me to forget you."

She pulled his head against her midriff again.

"There's nothing more you can do here. You've done everything you can. Thank you."

The door opened again. Charles Xavier and Eliud came inside. Eliud was carrying a long piece of thin rope. Ted was too weak to fight. They hoisted him up between them. They carried him outside. It was dark. The sky was filled with stars. More people were waiting there. Mr. Green and Id watching from the porch next door. Random people were standing nearby. Buffalo Bill took Charles Xavier's place holding up Ted. Charles Xavier climbed onto the back of his motorbike. They lifted Ted onto the back behind him. His feet were placed on pegs and tied down with shoelaces, Buffalo Bill and Eliud arguing the best way to do it. They wound the long piece of rope around him and Charles Xavier, tying the two together. Ted was pressed tightly against the other man's back. Camilla double checked all the knots. Charles Xavier kick started the motorbike. Camilla leaned in and said something to him. Charles Xavier nodded and she moved away. He revved the engine, put it in gear, and down the mountain they went.

Chapter 34

Ted remembered very little of the ride down the mountain. He kept drifting in and out of consciousness, skipping between a world of vibrating growls and one of chaotic darkness. It was slow going. The headlight created only a small patch of illuminated world in front of them. Charles Xavier didn't dare go fast with the extra load. Ted's head lolled loosely on his shoulders. The road was mostly deeply rutted mud. Charles Xavier did his best to keep them on solid ground. The trees seemed to rustle and mumble as they went by. The power poles along the road like sentinels, some broken, the pointless wires hanging loosely where they still hung at all. At one point it started raining, soaking them both to the bone. It was still raining when they reached Helston. At least Ted assumed it was Helston. Ted woke up wet and shivering to the sound of Charles Xavier screaming outside a house. A light flicked on. A man came out, nearly invisible in the darkness.

"What the fuck is this?"

"I need to get him down to the hospital."

"Fucking road's half washed out. All this fucking rain. Probably have it clear by tomorrow."

"Can we use your pickup?"

"Fucking things broke. No spare parts."

"Fuck. You have any petrol?"

"You're fucking mad to be driving down this time of night."

"Do you have any fucking petrol?"

"You got any money?"

"Fuck you."

Charles Xavier's back was tight and hard as steel. A woman's voice sounded from the darkness.

"Is that Charles Xavier?"

The man turned and yelled back behind him.

"Never mind who it is."

"Just give him the petrol Thomas."

The man hesitated, grumbled to himself, then stalked off. When he returned he was carrying a jerry can. While he refilled the tank between Charles Xavier's legs, a woman came out with a glass of water. Ted could feel Charles Xavier sit up straighter. The woman flashed Charles Xavier a wonderful smile and handed over the glass.

"Who's the monkey on your back?"

"Peace Corps boy. Doing poorly."

"He looks pretty bad."

"See if he'll drink some water."

The woman took the glass and did her best to oblige the demand. Ted swallowed some, but most ended up on Charles Xavier's back. The man screwed the lid back onto the gas tank. Charles Xavier started the bike, put it in gear, and they were off again.

The road grew worse the farther down they went. At one point Ted woke to find Charles Xavier coaxing the motorbike around a slide, both feet sticking out to provide better stability as they crawled forward. The mud went up at a 45 degree angle to their right. A ravine fell off to their left. He woke again further down where another landslide had been cleared away, leaving a flattened rocky scar cut by ruts. It had stopped raining. Ted could barely think through the pain in his head. His legs and back were cramping terribly. At a flat space Charles Xavier got them up to speed. Ted started coughing and puked half digested oatmeal on Charles Xavier's shoulder. Both men pretended it never happened. Neither said a word to each other about anything. Charles Xavier might as well have been a mute. Ted's brain was too scrambled by his fever to coherently put together any thoughts. The motorbike hit a rock and Ted bit his tongue. Blood filled his mouth. Mr. Douglas filled his mind, ranting and raving as he never had before. Camilla held him close, his head pressed tightly against her stomach. Sandi laughed as some guy named Dave drove her away. No, that wasn't right, it was John, the mother fucker's name was John. Tears filled Ted's eyes and he began to sob. Charles Xavier ignored that too.

The world continued to blink in and out of focus. They were crossing a stream, maybe eight feet across, water pushing against the bottom of his boots. A long muddy stretch with trees on both sides, the motorbike spraying wet dirt into the air, coating Ted's back. The motorbike stopped, Charles Xavier standing with a leg on either side, his dick out, peeing on the ground, doing his best to miss the chassis and his leg. A steep section. Charles Xavier riding the brakes as he tried to keep them under control. Another town, indistinguishable from the one Ted thought must have been Helston. Ted couldn't feel his legs.

It was morning when they drove into the outskirts of the capital. Ted could remember it from when he had flown in. A brightly painted town of around fifteen thousand people right on the water, surrounded by tree covered hillsides. Small, but bustling. Cars, motorbikes, and people crowding its tight streets. It looked nothing like that now. The hillsides were mostly bare of trees. Numerous buildings of wood or cinderblock were collapsed. Concrete edifices still stood, though many were missing their roofs. Tents, blue tarp shelters, and lean-tos were everywhere. Cars and motorbikes were still on the streets, but only a few were moving. People milled about. Some carried tools. Some stood around fires in steel drums that stank of burning garbage. Some just seemed to be meandering. A few women had baskets or buckets balanced on their heads. Charles Xavier yelled at one group for directions.

"Hey, which way to the hospital?"

There was a strange nervous vibration in his man. Something Ted had never heard. One of the women approached, the basket on her head perfectly balanced.

"What kind of chupid jacket don't know where the hospital is."

Ted could feel Charles Xavier shaking, or maybe it was him.

"I'm not from here."

"Well that's pretty obvious hill boy."

"Please, I got a sick man here."

The woman gazed at Ted. She gave the directions, but for Ted her voice faded away, lost in the cacophony of waking city sounds. Charles Xavier put the motorbike back in gear and they were off again.

At the next intersection, a long line of people waited for their turn to be given a scoop of wheat from bags stacked high in the back of a truck. At another, men were scrambling up ladders, nailing a new roof on a building. Eyes watched them as they drove in deeper. One old man with no teeth pointed and laughed, long and hard. Most remained silent. Pressed up against him, it felt to Ted as though Charles Xavier was shivering violently, though perhaps it was just the vibration of the motorbike. Ted fell back into a feverish slumber.

When he woke again he was sure that it was Charles Xavier. The other man was visibly shaking, his back tense, his feet twitching. The hospital was a slab of concrete, all of the windows boarded up. Three big diesel generators chugged outside, painted a dark green and emblazoned with the American flag. A man in white was standing next to the entryway, taking a smoke break. The entryway was once glass, but now was just a yawning cavernous hole. Charles Xavier yelled at the man.

"I got a sick jake here. American."

The man walked over, said something to Charles Xavier, gave Ted a once over, and then ran inside. He came out a minute or two later with two others in identical uniforms, a stretcher between them. They untied the shoelaces attaching Ted's feet to the pegs and the knots that attached him to Charles Xavier. Ted couldn't hold himself up. His legs burned with pain when he moved them. The two men half carried and half drug him to the stretcher. They laid him down and hefted it between them. For Ted the world was slipping away once again. The last thing he saw was Charles Xavier on the motorbike, his head on a swivel, looking at the city around him, his eyes wide open, the eyes of a frightened child.

A sharp pain lanced Ted's arm. The plunge of a needle drawing blood. A second sharp pain was the IV sliding in. He was surrounded. Two doctors, one local and one American, he could tell by the accent, and three nurses. Thermometer, pressure cuff, heart rate monitors, and a barrage of questions. Ted did his best to answer them, but most responses were nothing but mumbled replies. He was in a bed in a long room, beds down either side. Every bed was filled. Men, women, and children. Some were just people laying there, a bare minimum of equipment. Others were surrounded by beeping machinery, breathing apparatuses pushing air in and out of their lungs. A few sported casts or other bandages. All had numbers written on their foreheads, one through five, written in red marker. All that were able were staring at him. Curiosity, bitterness, and a tired vacancy. They were all locals. One of the nurses grabbed a curtain and pulled it closed, surrounding Ted in a rustling world of white.

Camilla was holding his hand, the words he longed to hear still sweet on her lips. Charles Xavier was rushing home as fast as his motorbike would carry him. Ted was sitting on the couch, watching a football game with his father. He and Sandi were rafting on the Salmon River in Idaho. It was a gentle part, the raft moving forward at a medium pace, bobbing happily through the water. He was floating. Not in the river, but above the ground. Two local men were carrying him in a stretcher again. A third was moving alongside, holding the IV bag aloft as though it was his royal standard. They were moving down a hallway. Every other light above was dark. They passed through a doorway of glass, the door held open by a waiting nurse. Ted could see his reflection as they passed through. His eyes were sunk in a gaunt face covered in sweat. A bright red letter P graced his forehead.

"P?"

His voice barely registered, more spit than word, but one of the orderlies heard and gave a laugh.

"That's right. You be one lucky jake my friend. Priority. Straight back home for you. No dilly dallying with us savages."

The other two orderlies laughed. The one carrying the IV chirped in.

"Can't be wasting nothing on this one. No paperwork for him."

The three men laughed again. Snow was falling in Great Falls. He and Sandi were making a snowman in the parking lot of their apartment building. His mother was humming as she made Christmas cookies. Anji was washing over the world, screaming out her destruction. He was holding Camilla close, protecting her from the storm, protecting her from the world. Her hands were wrapped protectively around her stomach. There was no fear in her eyes, just grim determination.

He was in the back of a pickup truck. The sky overhead was blue, a few scattered fluffy white clouds lumbering their way forward high above. One of the orderlies was sitting in the back with him, still holding the IV. A truck rumbled past, a big green monster with the US flag emblazoned on the side, behind it was a squat concrete building with a brown tarp for a roof. Piles of rubble were on either side. The pickup kept hitting bumps or potholes. Ted groaned in pain.

Darkness. Two people were looking up at the stars above them, a man and a woman. The man pointed upward at the constellation Andromeda. He whispered something in the woman's ear. The woman didn't answer. They sat in silence. A man and a woman were lying in bed, the heat of recent lust receding. He was talking and she was listening. He asked her something, and it was only then that he realized that she was asleep.

The pickup was no longer moving, though the engine was still running. A harsh thrum loudly belching exhaust, almost buried beneath the sound of an airplane rotor. The two orderlies pulled the stretcher toward them. They tipped it toward the ground and caught Ted in their arms as he fell forward, supporting him between them. The orderly with the IV climbed to the ground and together they all started forward. It wasn't the same airport as when Ted had arrived. The buildings looked okay, but half the runway was buried beneath a massive landslide where once a high steep hillside stood. A clutch of large yellow construction vehicles were working along the edge of the slide. Caterpillars, front end loaders, and dump trucks. They looked like toys. They had barely made a dent.

The orderlies were moving him toward a plane. It wasn't a big plane. It had only seven seats counting the pilot's. The orderlies lifted him through the door and then dragged him to the bench seat in the back. They buckled him in as best they could and then hung his IV bag from a hook above his head. It was hot in the plane, but still he shivered. The pilot was in his seat up front, fiddling with switches. His jumpsuit looked military with an American flag on it. Another military man climbed into the front seat next to the pilot, an officer in camouflage. A man and a woman climbed into the two back seats just in front of Ted, both wearing white t-shirts and red vests with a big red cross across the back. They looked back at him curiously.

"So this is the one that bumped Lopez and Chuckles."

"I thought they already got all of our civvies out."

"Always one or two to come out of the woodwork. Every fucking time."

The man and woman turned forward again. The door closed. The engine went from idle to full power. Down the runway they went, up into the sky. Ted peered between his feet, out the window. Nothing but blue sky until the plane began to turn. Scattered colors. Azure ocean. Red dirt. Green grass and forest. Blocks of mostly grays and browns. Domenique fell away. The plane straightened out and all of it was gone.

Chapter 35

The boat rocked in the gentle swells, but nowhere near as badly as when they had left Barbados. The winds had made the sea rough, though the fisherman had laughed when Ted mentioned it. Ted hadn't puked, the Dramamine apparently worked. It wasn't a big boat, maybe twelve feet, all of it open to the world. It was the biggest boat he could afford, its daily possible catch low enough to make it affordable to abandon a day of fishing. The fisherman reached into a bag next to his legs and Ted tensed up. The fisherman laughed, pulled out a pack of gum, and offered Ted a piece to show there were no hard feelings. Ted took one, it was cinnamon gum. The man put the gum package back and concentrated on steering the boat, fingering a silver cross hanging around his neck as though its presence proved he was an honest man. The green smudge on the horizon that was Domenique moved steadily closer.

It had been four months since he had left. Half a month in the hospital, half a month resting, and three months working. The plane that had taken him away had landed in Puerto Rico, where a second plane had taken him to Miami, or at least that's what they told him. The first memory Ted had was waking in a brightly lit white hospital room, alone in a solitary bed, surrounded by medical machinery, half not being used. His parents had arrived a day later. His mother frantic and angry and his father perturbed looking, but calm. His mother's red hair was a frizzy mess of worry. The fluorescent lighting reflected off his father's bald head. When his parents first came in his mother couldn't seem to decide whether to gush over him or yell at him. In the end neither won out.

"You missed your grandfather's funeral."

Ted imagined the fat old man in his western shirt commenting on the heat. He tried to stir some kind of emotion within himself.

"When did he die?"

"A month ago."

"I'm sorry."

"What were you thinking?"

"I liked it there."

"You almost died Teddy. You almost died."

Ted's mother started crying. Big tears that ran down her cheeks. She rushed forward and wrapped her arms around him, sobbing into his shoulder. Ted put an arm around her, careful of his IVs. Guilt swept over him. Terrible deep stomach knotting guilt. His father looked out the window. Ted's mother released him and took a step back. Her face was red and puffy.

"Why Teddy? Why the hell would you do something so stupid?"

"I'm twenty-two Mom."

"Just because some slut broke up with you."

Ted's father shifted his attention back to the world inside the hospital room.

"Barb."

"Well it's the…"

"Barb, why don't you go downstairs and get a Diet Coke."

Ted's mother shot his father a dirty look, and for a moment she looked like she was going to say more. Ted's father just gazed at her, that neutral unblinking gaze he always used when he wanted you to know you needed to take a step back and calm down. A gaze gained by years of working as head of personnel. Ted's mother looked at her son, shivering and covered in sweat, acquiesced, and left the room. Ted's father sat down in a chair next to the bed. The two men sat quietly. As always it was Ted who broke the silence.

"Thanks Dad."

"She's not wrong."

Silence again. His father cleared his throat.

"They let Judy bring Jello shots to the company picnic this year. You ever seen two seventy year old women taking Jello shots?"

"No."

"Crazy shit."

His father left after a couple of days to go back to work. His mother stayed for over three weeks. At first she slept in one of the chairs in the room until a nurse convinced her it would be better for all involved if she got a hotel room. It took her a week to calm down, but Ted spent most of it sleeping so it wasn't too bad. She didn't even ask too many questions, though Ted's short answers to the ones she did ask might have had something do with that. It wasn't all bad. For a moment Ted was a minor celebrity. The local newspapers and TV channels, even the New York Times, all wanted to interview him. Ted's mother kept them at bay, claiming her son was too weak for such badgering. By the time he got out of the hospital the world had moved on. His mother also bought him a laptop, an unexpected gift when he mentioned how sick of watching TV he was.

Ted was feeling much better by the second week, though he still felt shaky and feeble. He spent most of his time perusing the internet and going through emails on an account he hadn't used since leaving for Domenique. Lots of friends from college, some whom he hadn't spoken to in years, sent him messages wishing him a speedy recovery. There was nothing from Sandi. Part of him wanted it, but part of him was glad as well. His mother filled the time with talking, just as she always had. It didn't seem to matter whether or not Ted listened.

"You were such a beautiful baby Teddy. Once, when you were a toddler, a random woman in the grocery store gave you twenty dollars just for looking so cute. You were such a happy boy. You used to run up to me and beg me to tickle you. Stubborn though, run right into a wall and get mad at it for being there."

Midway through the second week, Mr. Douglas called long distance from St. Lucia.

"Doing well?"

"Recovering."

"Good to hear. Look Ted, I don't know what your plans are, but if you're interested, I could pull some strings with some people I know with the Red Cross. Their stateside staging center for Domenique is right there in Miami. It wouldn't be anything too exciting, but it would still be helping out."

There wasn't even a hint of 'I told you so' in Mr. Douglas's tone. Ted appreciated that.

"That would be great. Thank you."

His mother had, of course, wanted him to go back to Idaho with her. She had been less than pleased to hear about his new plans. Several days of argument had of course followed, but in the end she gave in. There was little she could do to change Ted's mind. When they released him from the hospital he stayed with his mother in her hotel for a week while he looked for an apartment and she went clothes shopping for him. She bought only what he asked for. Plain t-shirts, blue jeans, socks, and a pair of shorts to sleep in. It was a battle he had won when he was in high school. She did insist that he allow her to give him some money so he could rent a furnished apartment in an all right neighborhood. In the end they settled on the gift being a loan and the neighborhood being a bit on the rough side. She left when Ted moved in. His mother was good at goodbyes. She pressed a new cellphone into his hand, made him promise he would call her every week, hugged him, said she loved him, and then was gone.

The job with the Red Cross turned out to be just as exciting as Mr. Douglas had promised. It was taking inventory. The staging center was a large rented warehouse where donations from across the country poured in via truck. There they were sorted, counted, and at times loaded into shipping containers to continue on their way. Piles filled the warehouse. Shovels, bulk packages of bottled water, jeans, canned goods, shirts, first aid kits, sweatshirts and sweaters, sporting goods, toiletries, shorts, and various other items ranging from useful to entirely unneeded. The largest pile was an ever growing mountain of stuffed toys. The sorters complained the most about the clothes and canned goods. Nearly half the clothes went straight into the dumpsters out back, too second hand and worn to be of any use. The canned food was better, with most of it still within its use by date, though as one volunteer pointed out, how many cans of green beans and creamed corn could anyone really eat. Ted's job was to count the stuff okayed by the sorters and then take it to the appropriate pile. He wasn't sure how much actually left the warehouse, that was somebody else's job, but many of the piles never seemed to stop growing, with the exception of basic foods, water, and toiletries. Tampons and batteries especially never stuck around for long.

Some of the workers went to happy hours at the end of the day. Ted joined them once or twice, but his heart wasn't in it. He didn't really try to remember any of their names. Some were nice and some were assholes. Ted just didn't really care. One woman in her mid-twenties named Leslie constantly found reasons to talk with him for a couple of weeks, often touching his arm or leg when they spoke. Ted didn't say much, but sometimes he'd give a little smile. After three weeks the seeking out turned into avoidance. Ted wasn't sad to have her attention go away.

Most evenings he walked through a park with trees grown in perfect rows, ride the bus back to his neighborhood, make dinner, and then read before going to bed. He got the books from a used bookstore down the street. *Les Miserables*, *The Odyssey*, *Wuthering Heights*, and *A Room With A View*. All fell to his voracious eyes. One time he didn't get on the bus, but instead sat on a bench and watched people walk by, looking closely at all their faces. For a moment he thought he saw Sandi in a group of women in evening dresses and heels, but it wasn't her, just some other blonde girl. When the world grew dark he laid out on the grass and stared at the stars in the sky, the few strong enough to breach the ever present light of the city around him. The next day he bought a bottle of rum, but it remained untouched, the seal of the cap never broken. At night he laid in bed, replaying things over and over in his head.

Aside from his coworkers, who he only spoke to as much as he had to, Ted's only real human contact was his mother who called every Sunday afternoon on the cell phone she had bought him. The only number saved on the phone was his parents'. She would tell him about everything happening back home and then ask him questions of how he was doing, which he answered with monosyllabic responses. When she handed the phone over to his father, it became just two men listening to each other breathe. Not much apparently had been happening at the plant.

He'd been working for two months when he rose to let a man sit next to his pregnant wife on the bus. The woman was at least seven months in. Her hands were protectively held over her swollen belly. The woman shifted in her seat and smiled. She took the man's hand and placed it on her belly. He stared down at it, then a smile stretched across his face. The pair gazed into each other's eyes, joy emanating between them. Ted looked away, feeling like a voyeur. It all snapped together the moment he stepped off the bus. A sudden flash of insight. That night he searched for airline tickets to Domenique, but there weren't any. The airport was still closed. He searched every night for two weeks. He read any article he could find, but they were few and far between. He went out and bought a hiking pack, sleep sack, and MREs. After three months he purchased a ticket to Barbados, shoved what little he owned in the pack, and left the cell phone and laptop on the bed.

There were lights in Domenique's capital, more lights than before. There were ships in the harbor, the holes in the jetty ripped by Anji filled with new stone. The fisherman didn't enter the calm waters on the other side of the jetties. He swept far around them toward a distant beach. He smiled in the growing darkness.

"Rather just avoid a lot of paperwork if it's alright with you."

Ted nodded. The accent was a little different, but it still sounded like music in his ears. About a mile up the beach there was a sheltered spot behind a spit of sand. The fisherman idled the motor. He rooted around in a small cabinet by his feet and pulled out a large black trash bag.

"Maybe waist deep or so here. Wrap your bag in this."

Ted took the garbage bag. He looked at the water. He handed the fisherman the other half of the agreed upon sum. He stripped off his clothes and boots and shoved them in the trash bag with his hiking pack. The fisherman laughed at the sight of Ted's pale naked body in the moonlight. The laugh dispelled any thoughts Ted had of shaking the man's hand. He waited for a wave to go by and then jumped over the side. The water was warm, but nipple deep. The fisherman handed Ted his bag.

"Thank you."

The fisherman nodded.

"Don't let a shark eat your nucka."

Ted started wading toward shore with his bag held over his head. The fisherman turned the boat and headed back out toward the open ocean. Ted stepped up onto the dry sand, images of Camilla filling his head. He had to know. He had to see for himself.

Chapter 36

Ted found the motorbike a little over a mile outside of Titou. It was on its side with grass growing up between the spokes of the wheels. The tires were flat and rotting. The chain hung loosely, no longer on its gears. The handlebars were bent. The engine had a crack in it. For a moment Ted allowed a vile thought to cross his mind, a bitter looking vision that swept through him with just the hint of sweetness. Ted banished it before it could take hold. It was primal and competitive. It had no place in his head. Ted wasn't very mechanically inclined, but he let himself imagine whatever went wrong was likely Charles Xavier's own fault. While not kind, it was a better alternative than the other. Charles Xavier had always been fucking with it. Ted stood over the motorbike for a moment, staring down at the wreck of Charles Xavier's dream, and then continued on his way. His stomach was in knots, tangles growing tighter with every step forward.

Ted had spent his first night just off the beach, and then headed out at first light. The walk up the mountain was much easier than the ride down had been. What had once been rutted mud had turned into a strip of fresh asphalt climbing alongside a line of power poles restrung with wires. The occasional pole was of a paler shade, revealing where former ones had cracked or fallen. The asphalt stream made its way through the treeless hills near the capital, roughened and yellowed by fallen former greenery, before disappearing into the ever thickening trees the higher went. The asphalt grew fresher as Ted climbed, until finally running out at a clutch of yellow machinery run by laughing men who watched Ted as he walked by. Ted could've sworn that he saw Bug Eyes amongst them, but he didn't stop to make sure. Above the pavers the power lines and road continued on, though the latter now made up of gravel. It was that way clear up to Titou.

Ted spent the second night a little bit off the road a few miles above Helston. The town had been a blaze of electric lights, twinkling in the descending darkness. When Ted had first reached the outskirts of the town he had thought about skirting around its outside. Charles Xavier had lots of friends in Helston. In the end, he decided he was being ridiculous and walked straight up the road. People watched him come through, their faces blank and unreadable as always. The next morning he started out again, reaching the motorbike around midday.

Titou looked different than it had before. The first thing Ted noticed was that the ruins of the mercantile and fallen gommier trees were gone, replaced by a half built edifice of cinderblock, rebar, and concrete. Next to the rising phoenix of the new mercantile was Malik's parked truck and a new bigger tent. The radio tower still stood defiantly, though a new antenna was perched on its top. Above the mercantile the ruined houses were gone, replaced by new houses of wood or cinderblock, and the damaged houses were all repaired. The lean-tos were gone and power lines hung from the poles. The world was mostly green again, as it had been when Ted first arrived, though straight lines of red dirt showed where digging had taken place. The path up to the reservoir was now a broad red scar, wide enough for a bulldozer to push its way through.

There were five men in the scaffolding around the walls of the rising mercantile. One near the top waved down when Ted walked by and Ted had to stop and shield his eyes from the sun to see who it was. Buffalo Bill smiled down at Ted, his signature jersey replaced by one for the Miami Dolphins.

"Look at this jake strutting proud as a cock on the walk."

Buffalo Bill laughed and the other men laughed with him. Ted recognized all but two of them. There was nothing but jovial friendliness in Buffalo Bill's tone. The laughter held no malice. Ted felt unsure, but he forced himself to smile and wave again. The men in the scaffolding hooted and clapped. Ted retreated into the tent.

The tent was at least twice as big as the original. Shelves filled the interior, forming straight aisles that ran lengthwise. Lights were strung up across the ceiling and round mirrors were hung up in each corner. Id was in one aisle near the door, down on his knees, restocking a shelf with Spam from a cardboard box at his feet, happily singing the alphabet to himself from A to S. Ted paused, unsure again. He approached slowly. Id stopped what was he was doing, rose and turned, his eyes level with Ted's. He smiled in his simple way, but his hands nervously fingered the can of Spam in his hand.

"Hello Id."

The simple man grimaced.

"My name's Avery."

Ted nodded.

"Hello Avery."

Id nodded and sank back to his knees to get back to work, returning to his shortened litany of the alphabet. Ted moved past him down the aisle, gazing at the labels. It wasn't the selection available before, but it was getting closer.

The back of the tent was separated from the rest by a bar made of plywood stacked on piles of cinderblocks. Behind the bar were a row of coolers filled with beer, soda, and milk. A small selection of fresh produce was on shelves next to the coolers and some boxes of rum sat next to them. The portrait of Malik's father was on the top shelf, leaning back against the wall of the tent, a few worn Teddy Bears around it. The flag of Domenique was pinned to the tent wall next to it. The only thing missing was the photo of Malik's wife. Two cots were behind the bar in a corner. On the bar, in the opposite corner stood the old cash register, chains bolted on either side wrapped through cinderblocks on the ground. A TV sat next to it, a soap opera flashing by on the screen.

Malik sat on a stool next to the cash register, a harlequin romance novel gripped in his big hands, artificial light gleaming off his bald head. The big body was not as it once had been. Fat and flesh sagged from tired bones. The bull neck was a turkey's wattle. The proud head sagged between soft shoulders. The tired old bullock raised his head when Ted approached. The only sign of surprise on the big man's face was a pair of raised eyebrows which quickly corrected themselves. The eyes were still fierce. The eyes still gave the hint that Malik was not a man to be fucked with. Malik carefully bent the top corner of his page, closed the book, and set it on the bar. He rose, straightening into a more imposing figure. He laid his fists down on either side of the book.

"Didn't expect to see you again."

Ted paused a few feet away.

"I'm just visiting."

The big man stared at him, let out a low chuckle, turned, and grabbed a bottle out of the cooler.

"Have a beer."

Malik popped the top off the beer and laid it on the bar. Ted walked forward, a nervous deer in the forest. He let his pack fall to the ground, took the cold bottle in his hand, and took a sip. It tasted good. Malik smiled.

"It's on the house."

Ted tried to get himself to relax. He took another drink and gestured at the outside world.

"Things have shifted pretty fast around here it looks like."

Malik nodded.

"We've been pretty lavished with attention the past few months."

Ted took another drink of his beer.

"What changed?"

Malik chuckled, a deep sound from his gut.

"Government folks never like to be embarrassed."

Ted finished his beer.

"What embarrassed them?"

Malik stared at Ted a moment, his head pointed at the plywood of the bar, his gaze cutting through his eyebrows. It made Ted feel awkward and uncomfortable. Malik chuckled again, more of a grunt than a sign of mirth. He turned and pulled another beer out of the cooler, popped off the top, and put it in front of Ted.

"Have another beer jake."

Ted hesitated, he didn't really want a second beer, but it seemed rude to refuse.

"Thank you, much appreciated."

Malik grunted and sat back down on his stool.

"If you'd like you can stay in the house while you're here. Got lights and water, but still no windows."

"Thank you, much appreciated."

Ted felt awkward again. He sat and fingered the label on his beer bottle.

"I don't want any charity."

Malik laughed, a real laugh this time.

"That chupid Peace Corps jacket keeps paying rent, but not sending anybody. Might as well have somebody in it for a few days."

Ted nodded, let his gaze fall to the plywood bar top, and finished his beer. He lifted his pack back onto his shoulders.

"Thank you again."

He turned and walked out of the tent. Malik watched him go, neither exchanging another word. The five brightly painted identical houses in a row sat at the top of town on the hillside. Ted's head was floating on a sloshing pail of suds. The five men in the scaffolding hooted at him from above. Ted raised his hand in greeting again, but otherwise ignored them. He started making his way upwards. The shelter where the communal fires had been was gone, replaced by a new shelter filled with children crowded around tables roughly according to age. A young man was standing next to a movable chalkboard, lecturing one group about long division, gesturing with his hands as he talked. Eliud noticed Ted as he walked past. The two men met eyes and Eliud smiled. Ted smiled back, but continued on his way.

There weren't many people in town. A few women of various ages working in their gardens and a few old men sitting in the shade on their porches. Some didn't even look up as he passed. Some noticed, but only stared with blank faces. Others noted him with a light of recognition in their eyes, a friendly smile on their faces, and their hands raised in greeting. Ted raised his own in kind. Some even called out to him, which Ted returned without stopping. It all felt genuine, but it made him feel uncomfortable. It didn't feel right.

Ted's eyes were on the yellow house, but his footsteps carried him toward the red one. Mr. Green was sitting on a chair on his porch next door, watching a small TV on a milkcrate, its rabbit ear antennas stretched to their maximum. As Ted drew closer he could see that the old man was watching a BBC documentary. Mr. Green ignored him as he approached, but his voice sounded the moment Ted stepped onto the red house's porch.

"You never returned my books Mr. Nelson."

The voice was flat and emotionless. Mr. Green never took his eyes off of his program. Ted bit his lip, trying to think of how to answer.

"Excuse me?"

"A man should always return what's not his."

Ted chewed on the inside of his cheeks. His hands closed into loose fists. What the fuck? A myriad of retorts and reactions slipped through Ted's mind, but he shuffled them all away. He didn't have time. Dealing with a cantankerous old man wasn't why he was there.

"I'm sorry."

"I got them back."

Ted waited, seeing if there was anything else. Mr. Green ignored him. Ted opened the door and walked inside.

The inside of the house didn't look much different than when Ted had left it. Dirty concrete floor and empty window frames, but the fridge hummed happily and there was water in the toilet. The mass of papaya plants completely filled the back window, blocking the view outside. One woody stalk had bent itself completely inside, the upper leaves brushing the underside of the metal roof, three small papayas clustered in the foliage, yellowing with growing ripeness. The cot was still in its place below the back window. The sleep sack was still on top of it, the zipper half undone showing the red white and blue of the interior. A few dead papaya leaves lay on top of it. The duffel bag was still under the cot, though it was empty except for a pair of crusty boxer shorts that apparently nobody wanted.

Ted let his pack drop to the ground. He went to the sink and turned it on. Clear water flowed out. Ted took a drink, bending his head down below the spigot. It was cool, not cold, but still refreshing. He sat down on the cot. The sleep sack smelled of mildew. There was rat shit in the corner of the room where the tables and chairs had once been. He took a few deep breaths and let them out. He removed his clothes. The same clothes he'd been wearing since leaving Barbados with the fisherman. He took a washcloth from his pack and scrubbed his body with water from the sink. He put on deodorant and slicked back his hair. He put on a clean pair of jeans and a button up shirt, leaving the top two buttons loose. He took his time lacing back up his boots. He sat back down on the cot. A familiar humming moved past the blocked back window, sounding a tune without a melody. Ted sat and listened, then stayed and sat some more once he could no longer hear the sound. A bird winged by, chirping its song. Time flowed past, thickening from water to syrup. Ted got up and drank more water from the sink. He slapped a little water on his bare cheeks. He took a deep breath, let it out, did it again, and opened the back door.

All traces of the steps hewed by Mr. Hewitt were gone, completely worn away into a steep ramp of dirt. Ted pulled himself up and surveyed the world. The chemical shed's roof had been put back on, but it was still half buried. A newly planted vegetable garden sat between it and the back door. Tanias, yams, potatoes, peas, onions, carrots, and garlic. Replicas in various stages of growth were behind all the houses. A single garden stretching from Camilla's to Mrs. Seraphin's, broken only by rows of apparel hanging from clotheslines, swaying gently in the breeze. The area behind Camilla's house had been dug down to its original level to about six feet back from the house, the border defended by a retaining wall broken only by a set of steps, all made of cinderblocks. The area behind Mr. Green's house was dug out as well, though the retaining wall was only half finished.

She was weeding in the garden behind Mrs. Seraphin's house. Her familiar form on hands and knees moving between the rows. She was wearing a blue dress with a matching handkerchief wrapped around her head. She didn't seem to notice him. He walked toward her. The sound of Mr. Green's TV program wafted through the air. He stopped by the corner of Mrs. Seraphin's house, watching her, waiting. Camilla looked up. For a moment there was shock in her eyes, but it faded quickly. She rose and stretched her back. Ted took her all in. The bump was there. Emotion flooded through Ted. Elation. Anger. Sadness. Worry. He had been right. He had been right to come. He didn't know what to say, so of course he blurted the wrong thing.

"Where's Charles Xavier?"

Camilla's hands closed protectively over the bump. She eyed him warily. Ted could see fear, just a trace, hidden away, but still there. It made him feel sick to see it. He wanted to rush over. He wanted to take her in his arms, but he didn't. He kept his distance. Camilla stayed where she was as well, neither moving forward nor retreating.

"He's doing his mail routes. He'll be back in the morning."

Ted nodded. His mouth kept throwing out words before his brain had a chance to process them.

"Same as always then."

"He's not perfect, but it's no business of yours."

Ted stood, more unsure than when he began. He couldn't take his eyes off of the bump. It was Camilla who broke the silence.

"What are you doing here?"

Ted licked his lips.

"I know Camilla. I know it's my baby."

One of Camilla's feet shifted, turning itself toward the yellow house down the row. Her arms wrapped around the protruding bump of her belly, shielding it from the outside world.

"No, it's my baby."

Ted could feel himself shaking.

"Why didn't you tell me?"

Camilla's gaze fell to her feet.

"I did, if you knew how to listen."

They lapsed into silence again. Camilla's voice sounded tired when she spoke.

"You need to go home. This isn't your place."

Ted took a tentative step forward.

"It doesn't have to be your place either."

"Please…"

"I want you to come back with me. You and the baby can have better life than this."

Camilla's dark eyes flashed with sudden anger. Her voice cracked the air like a whip.

"What's wrong with this life? What's wrong with what I have?"

Ted licked his lips again. They were dry and chapped.

"Charles Xavier…"

"Tried to be your friend."

"He…"

"Is what he is."

Ted gestured with his hand toward her.

"You don't have to put up with it."

Camilla's hands balled into fists. Tears streamed down her cheeks.

"What do you know of what I put up with? What do you know of what's important to me? Nothing. You don't know me. You know nothing about me."

Ted could feel tears in his own eyes.

"I know I love you."

"No you don't."

Ted could feel the rising beast within himself. He struggled to keep it under control.

"Yes I do."

"I'm not even a person to you, just a thing that fills a need."

The tears were running down Ted's cheeks.

"That's not true. I..."

The whip in Camilla's voice cracked again.

"Did you ever think to ask? Did you ever even wonder, or were you too distracted by the view through your own eyes to even notice?"

Camilla seemed to slump into herself, a collapsing volcano after an eruption.

"I'm tired now. The baby. Can we please discuss this more later? Please."

Ted's fists were closed. When had that happened? His breathing was rapid too, shallow and in quick succession. Those words. Those words she had said. They weren't true. None of them were true. It didn't matter. The sight of Camilla showing weakness rocked him to his core. He could see her eyes pleading with him, silent prayers crossing the divide. He had never seen her show any fragility before. The anger fell away, leaving behind only concern and frustration. The woman was with child, and here he was, arguing with her. What was he doing? Shame. He was filled with shame. He looked down at his feet, his voice stammering.

"Of course. Of course. The baby comes first."

Camilla nodded and began to move away.

"Thank you."

Ted stayed where he was. Camilla moved past him, far out of arm's length. Ted bit his lip as she passed.

"I'll check on you this evening. Let me know if you need anything."

Camilla didn't answer. She moved down the row of houses to the yellow one, climbed down the new steps, went inside, and shut the door behind her.

Chapter 37

Ted went back to his own house, ready to wait, but unsure how to do it. A father. He was going to be a father. Ted pulled the old sleep sack off of the cot, unzipped it completely, and used water from the sink to try and wipe away most of the mildew. He took it outside and hung it over an empty clothesline. The sack's interior, flapping lazily in the breeze, brought to mind the start of college football games and walking in front of the university administration building. It had been right there, just below the flagpole, that she had kissed him and first said the magic words. A sudden surprise. Her lips on his. Ted shook his head and turned away. Such things were long gone and best forgotten. He went back inside and used the toilet. It felt strange to sit on what had for so long been nothing but a porcelain decoration. The curtain was gone, but he didn't mind, let the world see him as he was. When he flushed he remembered the money. He opened the top tank, but it wasn't there. He wasn't that surprised. An image of Camilla keeping track of what she did for him in her little book filled his head, but he shook it away as well. It didn't really matter what had happened to it, the money was gone either way.

With nothing else to do, Ted went out onto the porch and sat down with his back against the wall and his legs splayed out in front of him. He looked at the world about him, willing himself to glance over at the house next door as little as possible. Fat happy clouds were meandering their way overhead. Titou spread its way down the mountainside. The old Titou was gone, replaced by a poorly done facsimile. In the plantation, the fallen trees had been cleared away, replaced by newly planted saplings which would grow into copies of what had been there before.

Ted left the comfort of the porch, braving the descent through the mixed smiles and respective nods of those going about their business. The shelter where Ted had seen Eliud teaching the children was empty now. The children were gathered at a flat spot below on the edge of the tree line, practicing soccer drills under Eliud's watchful eye. The grass was battered down all around them, in some places worn to bare red dirt. Ted worked his way around them, keeping to the long grass near the trees.

The graves were not hard to find. Mrs. Green's was covered in flowers, her cross new and freshly painted white. Eugene Hewitt's was nothing but a rotting post sticking up out of the ground, soon to disappear as though it had never been. Ted stared at it, trying to conjure up the young man's face, but it wouldn't form beyond indistinct shadows. He had been real once, undoubtedly with hopes and dreams, but Ted had no idea what any of them might have been. Ted felt nothing. The memory of Eugene wasn't fading, for Ted, it was as it always had been. Someone cleared their throat. Ted looked up to find Eliud standing a few feet away.

"We've been meaning to spruce things up a bit for him, but things have been rather busy."

Ted nodded.

"I'd like to think he'd like that, but I don't know. I really didn't know him that well."

Eliud walked forward to stand beside Ted, looking down at the dilapidated grave.

"He was a good man. We grew up together. He used to beat my ass because my father had more money, but to be fair, I used to call him quashie so I probably had some of it coming. He was better by the time I came back. Smiled a lot more."

Ted tried again to imagine the man described.

"What changed?"

"Who knows? None of my business."

The two men stood quietly. Some of the children were watching them. Eliud turned and yelled at them.

"Get back to your drills you nosey jackets."

The children did as they were told, but Ted could still feel the glances and corner of the eye stares. Ted gestured toward the children.

"So you're a teacher now."

Eliud smiled ruefully and shook his head.

"Yeah, Camilla told me to, about a month after you left. Said she was sick of the little ones just running around. Mr. Green didn't seem that interested in taking it back up."

Two of the larger boys started fighting in the middle of the field. They were rolling in the dirt, their peers circling and hollering. Eliud moved away in a jog to break it up. Ted watched him go and then climbed back up the hill. The yellow house almost seemed to be glowering at him as he ascended. Ted shook off the need to knock on the door and returned to his own porch instead. The fight below had been broken up. The children started scrimmaging, the larger children fighting for the ball, the younger scattered around the perimeter of the action, looking for an opportunity to come their way.

It was approaching evening when a loud whistle pierced the air and echoed off the mountainside. Men and women began flowing out of the banana plantation's gate, dispersing once they hit the road. Most walked toward their homes in Titou, some moved down the road, and some walked up. They filed by on their way to the paths that would take them higher up the mountainside, fewer than they had once been. Eliud came up the hill as well, whistling, his long arms swinging jauntily. He waved when he approached and Ted waved back. Eliud stopped at the end of the porch.

"Sorry about running away on you. Little jackets get into all sorts of trouble if you let them."

"No worries."

"How about you give me half an hour to clean up and then join me for supper."

Ted felt a slight shudder of anxiety, an old reaction to an old world. An uncomfortable sense of gratefulness swept through him.

"That would be nice, thank you."

Eliud smiled and gestured with his hand.

"Good, just two houses down."

Eliud moved on, whistling again. Ted watched him walk along the row of houses, past Mr. Green's and into Mrs. Seraphin's. The sun was getting low on the horizon. The world was silent, the singing of the birds and brush of the air through the trees broken only by the occasional distant cough. The yellow house sat quietly, waiting. Ted watched the darkening sky, his glances morphing into longing stares. He rose. His fists clenched and unclenched. Sweat dotted his brow. He took a step forward, then another. He turned. He walked away, following Eliud's footsteps. After dinner. He'd check on her after dinner.

They ate out on the porch. It was a simple meal of canned chicken, a few spices, and fresh vegetables mixed with rice. When Eliud went inside to bring out their plates, Ted tried to discern the interior world surreptitiously through the half open door. Eliud caught him when he came back out. He handed down the full plate and a glass of water with a halfhearted upward bend of his lips.

"She doesn't live here anymore. Malik told me to move in when I started teaching. He said no student is going to respect a teacher living in a lean-to."

Ted took the plate and glass.

"What happened to her?"

Eliud shrugged.

"Heard the boy got better, but she never came back up. Not sure after that."

Ted stared down at his plate.

"I'm sorry."

Eliud shrugged again.

"It was just a flight of fancy. She never was what I wanted her to be."

Eliud went back inside to get his own plate. Ted glanced through the door again, but could see nothing. He looked down at his plate again, wondering who it actually belonged to. They ate mostly in silence, the sound of chewing loud in Ted's ears. After dinner Eliud brought out a bottle of rum and put a splash in each of their empty water glasses. He raised his into the air.

"To Titou."

Ted raised his own glass and clinked it against the other. They both drank deep and Eliud refilled their glasses.

"I'm glad to see you're still alive. I wasn't so sure when we sent you down."

Ted set his glass down on the rough wood of the porch.

"Thank you for checking in on me. I don't know what would've happened to me if you hadn't."

Eliud shrugged.

"Camilla told me to. She was worried."

Ted looked over, but the other man was focused on the last bits of sunlight reflecting through the golden liquid in his glass. A thousand questions shot their way through Ted's head, but not one found its way to his mouth. Ted picked back up his glass and took another drink. Eliud let loose a yawn.

"I'm surprised you came back up here. Staying long?"

"For a bit. I can't believe how much things have changed around here."

Eliud laughed quietly.

"Yeah, the world works in mysterious ways."

Ted looked down the hill. He could see the children playing again, though they weren't actually there. He could see one child amongst them, a larger boy, big and bulky. The child was laughing with delight, a bull in a china shop, bowling the other children over in his efforts to get to the soccer ball. Camilla was watching too, a big smile splitting her face. They weren't in Titou anymore. They were in Idaho at his parents' house. The exterior was covered with colored lights. A decorated tree was visible through the window. The ground was covered in snow. They were all bundled up, throwing snowballs at each other. They were all laughing. Ted's parents were watching proudly from inside. The boy turned away to gather up more snow, and when he turned back he was a little girl with freckles across a pale nose and blonde hair escaping the confines of her knit cap. Her smile was a familiar one. She threw the snowball and hit Camilla in the face. The girl bent over to make another, but when she rose she was the boy again, dressed in cap and gown, making a speech before his senior class, ready to depart in three months for his father's alma mater. Ted sat in the audience, Sandi next to him, holding his arm, eyes brimming over with tears. The boy was sitting in an office, typing away at a computer, neighboring skyscrapers visible through the window. The boy stopped and looked out the window, his eyes searching for something not there. The cityscape wavered and disappeared, revealing Titou once again. People were filing out of the banana plantation's gate, a bulky young man amongst them. His back was bent and he looked tired, far too worn down for his age. His weary steps ascended the mountainside, up toward a yellow house where a white haired man in a blue postman's shirt waited for him with a glass of rum and a smile.

Ted shook his head to clear it.

"When did the plantation reopen?"

"About two months ago."

"It seems strange given all they did."

Ted glanced over at Eliud. The other man was staring down across the town. A faint smile graced his lips.

"We couldn't fix roads forever. Titou is the plantation. It would've been a shame to let it die after working so hard to save it."

The two men finished their drinks in silence. When the glasses were empty Eliud rose and took Ted's from him.

"I need to take care of some things before I head to bed."

Ted got to his feet.

"I've got some things I need to take care of myself. Thank you for dinner."

Eliud nodded and smiled. For a moment, the two men stared at each other, both unsure what to do next. It was Eliud that broke away.

"Have a good night my friend."

"You too."

Eliud took the glasses back into his house. Ted climbed down off the porch and started walking back. Mr. Green's house had a light on in the window. Ted could hear the TV playing inside. The red house was dark. The yellow house next to it was black as well. Ted mounted the porch. He stood before the door. The curtains were drawn, blocking any view inside. His fist rose and knocked against the door. Silence. Not a sound or hint of movement. He knocked again. He waited. He leaned in close. His voice sounded loud in his own ears.

"I'm sorry Camilla. I'm sorry for scaring you."

Ted swallowed. His mouth was dry, making the words hard to say.

"I just want the baby to have the best life possible."

Ted's heart pounded, pulsing blood cells throughout his body, the slide of which set his extremities to tingling. The house remained mute. No answering declaration. No argument. Nothing. Ted tried the knob. It turned with a metallic squeak. The door opened. Ted stepped over the threshold. His hand clumsily muddled its way through the gloom to find the switch. It clicked on with sudden brightness. The blanket covered mattress was on the floor, surrounded by mosquito netting tacked to the ceiling. The once broken apart cabinets had been replaced. A card table and two folding chairs were set up in a corner. Shelves made up of wooden boxes stacked on their sides held clothes. The house was empty. Camilla was gone.

Chapter 38

Ted and Sandi were lying in bed, her hand in his, both staring upward at the darkened popcorn ceiling. He was talking. A quiet drone that filled the room around them. Words circulating in the steady flow of air from the heating vents, floating upon invisible strands of his hopes and dreams about the future. Marriage. A house of their own. Kids. The steps forward taken by so many before. Her hand trembled in his and he gave it a reassuring squeeze. She says nothing, her silence assumed by him to be acquiescence.

The world shattered with a sudden blinding flash of light. Pain blossomed across the left side of Ted's jaw. Ringing filled his ears. A man was screaming in the distance, the voice growing closer much quicker than seemed natural.

"Where is she you son of a bitch?! Where is she?!"

Sharp pain burst on the right side of Ted's head, just in front of his ear. The voice retreated again into the distance and rushed back. There was a weight on top of him. Ted pushed at it with all his might. The mass went tumbling to the floor. Ted rose from the cot where he had been sleeping in his clothes, no sleep sack, desperately trying to claw the world back into focus. Charles Xavier was rising from the floor, screaming unintelligibly, his eyes wide with horrific madness. Morning light streamed through the broken frames of the windows, wrestling its way through the leaves of the papaya.

"What have you done fucker?! What have you done?!"

Charles Xavier charged forward. Ted twisted and pushed him into the back door. Charles Xavier caught himself and charged forward again. Ted's fist connected with Charles Xavier's face. He fell back against the door, blood running from his nose. He tried to push himself up again, but Ted's fist hit his abdomen, doubling him over into the fetal position on the floor. For the first time Ted noticed how thin and small the other man was in comparison. Ted towered over him, his bulk easily a third again Charles Xavier's. Ted was breathing hard. He pushed his hair back away from his face. His head hurt from the initial blows.

"I don't know where the fuck she went."

Tears flowed from Charles Xavier's eyes. Wracking sobs shook his sparse frame.

"She's gone. She's gone. I did my best to be the man she deserves, and still she's gone."

Ted's fists opened. His shoulders slumped. He reached down and pulled the crying man into a seated position before collapsing onto the cot. Charles Xavier sat with his back against the wall and his face buried in his hands and knees.

"I never deserved her. Never. I couldn't even give her the one thing she wanted. She'd give me anything. I just wanted to do the same for her. I don't care about the rest. I don't care. I can't live without her."

Ted could feel his eyes brimming over. Charles Xavier was shaking, a frightened deer sensing its coming end. Ted reached out a hand and grabbed the other man's shoulder. He gave it a reassuring squeeze.

"She probably just went up the mountain. You told me that she did that sometimes when she's upset. Remember."

Charles Xavier looked up at Ted, his face smeared with tears, snot, and blood. In his eyes Ted could see him scrambling for the offered lifeline, his psyche desperately trying to reach it before it was pulled back or lost. There was fear in his eyes. Horrible and helpless fear.

"She needs to be careful. She's pregnant. The baby. She said it was our baby. What if something happens to the baby?"

Charles Xavier buried his head in his hands and started crying again. Ted, unsure what to do, couldn't tear his eyes away. Our baby. She said it was our baby. Not her baby. Ted could see himself lying next to Camilla in the darkness. For a moment it was Sandi, then Camilla again. Him talking, her silent. Always silent. Speaking with her eyes. The smell of her. The feel of her. Charles Xavier on top of him in the forest. I know. I know about you and Camilla. A friendly smile. An offer of rum. Take the jake. Nobody is going to shoot a jake. A motorbike ride through the darkness. Listen. You never listen. Not your place. You don't belong here. He's my husband. My husband. A guy named John holding out his hand. Why had he thought it would be okay to shake hands? A single star in the night sky. One of many. Thousands. Millions. Our baby. Taste it my friend. It's sweet. So very sweet. Ted gave Charles Xavier's shoulder another squeeze. He knew what he had to do.

Ted reached behind him. The single small golden fruit looked so fragile. He carefully plucked it from its perch. He held it delicately in his hand. His other hand grabbed Charles Xavier's wrist. He forced it out from under the crying face. Charles Xavier looked up at him, fear filled eyes bleakly gazing at a world out of his control. Ted gingerly placed the papaya into Charles Xavier's hand. For a moment they held it together, and then Ted let go. Charles Xavier sat gazing down at the golden fruit. Ted rose, picked up his pack and boots, and walked out the door. On the porch he pulled on his boots and tied them. He hoisted the pack onto his back. He started down the hill.

It was early morning. The sun was laboring to lift itself above the horizon to begin another day. The people of Titou were just beginning to rise. They went about their business, oblivious of the stranger walking amongst them. Helston first. Then the capital. Then back home. Back where he belonged. Papaya plants were everywhere. Beside the houses, scattered along the tree line, and thick behind the rising phoenix of the resurrected mercantile. How was it that he had never noticed them before? How was it that they had managed to escape his gaze?

Id was by the entrance of Malik's tent, babbling to himself an unintelligible song. Id waved at Ted as he walked past. Ted waved back. An older man was opening the gate of the banana plantation. Ted turned and looked back up the hillside at the town of Titou. At the top of the clearing were five matching houses. On the porch of the red house stood a man holding a papaya in his hand, looking downward at a departing figure. Above the row of houses was the forest and growing bulk of the mountain. Camilla was somewhere up there, high above both of them. Ted turned his back on all of it and walked away.

321

Acknowledgements

Special thanks to Aaron Clutter, Kenton Erwin, Marcus Hart, Jane O'Keeffe, Jessi Lynch, and Liz Knowles Ryan for volunteering to be readers for this book. Writing is one hell of a process, and this book wouldn't have reached completion without their help.

Also thank you to Robo. Every story starts somewhere, and the kernel of this one began with a deliciously odd tale told next to a campfire. Never change you quirky son of a gun.

The Uncanny Valley

We all know a Paul. A person who seems to see stuff that isn't there.
The type the polite call quirky and the blunt call nuts. Conspiracies?
He's got a few. He's got his finger on how the world really works. He
knows what kind of shit is coming down the pipe. Flee across the
West Texas desert to Mexico? Makes sense to him. Feel like you're
being watched? You bet your ass someone is watching. Best turn off
your cell phone. Troubles? Of course, that's just part of life. Doubts?
No time for doubts. Shit is getting real. Get in, buckle up, crack open
a beer. The only real question is how far down the rabbit hole are you
willing to follow?

An Unsated Thirst

They say that an author's first stories are their most raw. Here is a
collection of S.W. Campbell's first short stories and writings.
Combining both published and unpublished work, An Unsated Thirst
explores victory and defeat, triumph and shame, and an unflinching
view of our naked selves. How ones views such stories is dependent
upon the mood of the reader. Whether we are at our highs or at our
lows. However, it is hard for any of us to claim that such stories are
ones that we cannot identify with. Contained within these pages are
parts of our lives which we try to forget, though they are an important
part of what makes us whole. Such stories should be embraced,
accepted within ourselves so we can better accept them within others.

Check out more at: **www.shawnwcampbell.com**

About the Author

Shawn Campbell was born in Eastern Oregon in 1983 after a harrowing drive through a fog. He currently resides in Portland, Oregon where he works as an economist and lives with a lovely house plant named Morton. *Papaya* is his second novel. His other works include the novel *The Uncanny Valley*, a short story collection *An Unsated Thirst*, and numerous short stories published in various literary reviews.

For more information and books go to:

www.shawnwcampbell.com